PRAISE
THE FIVE STA

The Five Star Republic is an absorbing adventure that provokes thoughts of what-might-have-been along with glimpses of a future that might still be achievable in our time. With their direct, lucid prose and painstaking research, Janeen Webb and Andrew Enstice have given us the beginning of what promises to be a major trilogy as well as an alternate history imbued with hope and promise rather than regret. – Pamela Sargent

Multigenerational, sweeping across three continents, a rich and multinational cast of characters compete for gold, love, independence, and a surprising scientific development that changes everything. Inventive and absorbing alternate history. – Nancy Kress

A visionary novel of a world that might have been...promises to be one of the major SF books of the year. – Lee Harding

Enthralling...a page turner...it builds a credible picture of how solar might have trumped oil. Scientifically accurate and full of political intrigue, *The Five Star Republic* is the compelling account of a lost opportunity that might have been. – Rob Gerrand

The authors have woven historical and fictional characters into the rich and glittering life of Nineteenth Century Melbourne, justifiably known at the time as the Paris of the South. The clothes, weapons, furniture, buildings, social conventions, manners and language have been researched meticulously. Imagine Anthony Trollope setting his Palliser novels in Victoria, and you have the idea... – Sean McMullen

The nineteenth century voice is pitch perfect. This alternate history is a triumph! – Dena Bain Taylor

An epic work in every possible way! This alternate history takes what we know, remember and imagine and sets us on a path toward the growth of what might have been: *The Five Star Republic*'s 19th century problems, opportunities, successes and reversals point to what could have been a very different technological future—powered by the sun—and one which could still be within our grasp. Literary historians Janeen Webb and Andrew Enstice have delivered a powerful fable that will resonate with readers all over the globe. – Venero Armanno

Janeen Webb is a multiple award-winning author, editor and critic who has written or edited a dozen books and over a hundred essays and stories. She is a recipient of the World Fantasy Award, the Peter MacNamara SF Achievement Award, the Australian Aurealis Award and four Ditmar Awards. Her most recent novel is *The Gold-Jade Dragon* (PS Publishing, UK, 2021).

She has taught at various universities, is internationally recognised for her critical work in speculative fiction, and has contributed to most of the standard reference texts in the field. She holds a PhD in literature from the University of Newcastle, NSW.

She has lived in numerous countries, and currently divides her time between Melbourne and a small farm overlooking the sea near Wilson's Promontory.

Andrew Enstice won the Bridport Prize for poetry at the age of nineteen. He was awarded a scholarship to Emmanuel College, Cambridge, graduating MA, and holds a PhD from Exeter University. His first book, *Landscapes of the Mind* (Macmillan, UK) remains the definitive study of Thomas Hardy's literary landscape in his Wessex books.

He swapped the academic world for life as a scriptwriter and producer with Granada Television in Manchester, UK. He lived for a while in the mountains of Northern Italy, hiked in Sumatra and northern Thailand, and travelled round Australia before settling in Melbourne, where he taught in various universities. He now lives in rural Victoria. He has written and directed for the theatre – his play about the nineteenth century gold rush, *Crossing the River*, premiered in Melbourne. He has published numerous works, quite a few with Janeen Webb.

THE FIVE STAR REPUBLIC

CITY OF THE SUN: BOOK ONE

by
Janeen Webb
and
Andrew Enstice

IFWG Publishing Australia
Gold Coast

www.ifwgaustralia.com

Acknowledgements

The Authors wish to thank the following people for their support, aid and inspiration:

Juliet Anderson, Louise Berry, James Cappio, Greg Chapman, Jack Dann, Helen Doherty, Janice Drewe, Ian Drury, Michael and Joanna and Katie Enstice, Liz Farrell, Rob Gerrand, Lee Harding, Gerry Huntman, Patrick LoBrutto, David Marsh, L.E. Modesitt Jnr., Christopher Mogan, Steven Paulsen, John Polglase for his tireless work in the Cornish archive Kresen Kernow, Amy Reytar at the US National Archives and Records Administration, Robert Sessions, Susanne Shaw, Mark Shirrefs, John Sinisgalli, Stephanie Smith, Kerry Spokes, Nick Stathopoulos, Jonathan Strahan, Dena Taylor, Dianne Walker, Phillip Webb, Philip Worboys.

The Authors also wish to acknowledge the traditional owners of the lands where this story is set, including the Arrernte people, traditional owners of the Mparntwe lands upon which the fictional city of Helios will be built.

This is a work of fiction. Where historical figures appear, their actions and opinions are fictitious. Their attitudes—both good and bad—are faithful to the times.

PART I

The Eureka Stockade

"Perhaps to the pompous obstinacy of Governor Hotham may be hereafter traced a declaration of Independence on the part of our Australian possessions, and their severance from the British Crown."

Editorial after the Eureka uprising, *The Mining Journal and Railway Gazette*. (London, 1855)

"By and by there was a result, and I think it may be called the finest thing in Australian history. It was a revolution—small in size; but great politically; it was a strike for liberty, a struggle for principle, a stand against injustice and oppression... It is another instance of a victory won by a lost battle. It adds an honourable page to history; the people know it and are proud of it. They keep green the memory of the men who fell at the Eureka stockade..."

Mark Twain, *Following the Equator*. (1897)

Prologue:
Bloody Sunday

Australia: The British Colony of Victoria

December 3rd, 1854

Hector was running, running as hard as he could towards the stockade. He dodged through flapping tents, barely managing to stay on his feet as he jumped over guy ropes and pegs, avoiding the mess of tools and holes and mullock heaps that dotted the ground, ducking under washing lines and behind lean-to sheds, trying to stay out of sight. His lungs were burning: dust from the diggings was mingling with acrid smoke from smouldering fires, making him cough; and with each breath came a harsher chemical smell that tore at the back of his throat—the reek of gun powder. The red-coats were firing on the miners.

His eyes were stinging now, his vision blurring with tears, and his nose was starting to drip. He scraped his ragged sleeve across his face, trying to clear his vision as he ran, too frightened to stop. The noise was deafening: above the clash of metal and shouts and screams and gunfire came a huge explosion that left his ears ringing. Someone was using blasting powder. Nothing looked right any more. He knew he had lost his way in the chaos. But he had to keep moving. He heard a high-pitched whine and jerked back as dirt kicked up near his feet. The musket shot had missed him—just. He burst through a tangle of rope and timber slabs that leaned crazily where a makeshift hut had collapsed, and he stumbled into open space. He was in a large clearing. And the clearing was full of mounted men, too many for him to count.

The men were all armed with pistols and knives.

One of them shouted above the din: "You, boy! You stop right there."

Hector stopped. He looked up, straight into the mouth of the shining long-barrelled Colt pistol that was aimed at his head. He froze in his tracks, scarcely daring to breathe.

The Captain of the riders considered for a moment, before he tilted his pistol skywards.

Hector breathed again. The morning sun felt hot on his face, and he had to shade his watering eyes against the glare to look up at the horsemen towering above him. The horses were dark with sweat, the riders dusty and travel-stained. Hector could see they'd been riding hard.

"What are you doing out here?" the first man said. "This is no place for a child."

"Looking for my father, sir."

"Then you just had a lucky escape, boy. The Captain never misses."

The Captain, a stocky well-muscled young man who sat easily in his saddle, spun his pistol back into its holster before he spoke. "What's your name, son?" he asked.

"Hector Munro, sir."

"The journalist's boy?"

"Yes, sir."

"And how old are you, Hector?"

Hector, scruffy and soot-stained and sweating from his run, took a deep breath and tried to look taller. "I'm nearly seven, sir."

"Nearly seven, eh?" The leader's stern face creased into a smile. "My name is Captain McGill," he said, "and these"—he gestured towards the horsemen—"are the famous California Rangers."

Hector just stood there, hot and flustered and speechless, staring up at this powerful man.

Captain McGill went on: "I have a kid brother your age, back home in America. And I wouldn't want any family of mine on a battlefield. You get yourself home this minute, do you hear? Go."

Hector braced himself. "I can't, sir," he said.

"Can't?" McGill hesitated. "Where's home?" he asked.

"Back that way," Hector said, pointing vaguely behind him. "I can't get back across."

"And where's your father?"

"Up at the miners' stockade, sir. Gathering material, Mother said."

"He would be." McGill thought for a moment. "Listen to me, Hector Munro," he said at last. "You can't stay out of doors. It's too dangerous. Things are about to get worse here. Do you know the main shops, up behind the stockade?"

"Yes, sir."

"And do you see that path over there?" He pointed with his whip.

"Yes, sir."

"Then follow it. It will take you around the perimeter, past the Chinese diggings. And when you see the shops, you run across and get yourself inside one of them. And stay there. The General Store would be best. Do you understand?"

Hector nodded, relieved to be on his way. "Yes, sir."

One of the men tossed him a sixpence. "Get Mr Cole to give you some lemonade," he said. "Running's thirsty work."

The others laughed.

"Thank you, sir," Hector said.

"Run," said McGill.

Hector ran.

When he reached the stockade, everything had changed. The blue-and-white rebel flag with its distinctive five stars still fluttered on its post, but the ramshackle jumble of overturned carts and bits of timber that had made up the barrier was now a scattered pile of debris. The din of conflict was still deafening. Hector couldn't see any miners fighting, but the red-coats were everywhere, shooting at anything that moved: he saw men lying on the ground like broken, blood-stained dolls, and under the throat-burning smell of gunshot he caught the hot, iron reek of blood. He felt sick, dizzy. He tripped, fell, cut his palms on sharp gravel, and stayed for a moment on hands and knees, his stomach heaving. All he wanted now was to find his father. Then he would be safe. So he crawled forward, angling towards the shops.

The last little bit seemed to take forever: Hector was sure he would be shot. He was almost crying when he finally emerged, torn and bleeding, at the start of the row of canvas and timber structures. He crept quickly from doorway to doorway, peering inside, looking for help, hoping against hope his father would be there. He was too scared to call out, too scared to do anything but keep moving, keep looking.

He wasn't alone. He glimpsed the back of a very tall man in a black robe ahead of him, just as the man ducked inside one of the shops. A priest. Hector felt a surge of hope, and followed.

When he reached the entrance to the General Store, Hector froze. A man was leaning against the counter, obviously injured, his face obscured by the approaching priest. Hector, standing behind them, saw the priest put his arm around the man, as if to support him. But then both priest and man jerked violently. The man cried out, then went limp. Hector watched the priest lower the body to the floor, saw him take something from inside the man's coat and tuck it swiftly under his robe. He bent to close the man's eyes, and Hector saw the man's face.

"Dad?" he cried out. He took an involuntary step forward. "Dad?"

The scarecrow-thin priest turned, a tall whirl of black robes. He loomed over Hector, leaning down until his face was close to the child's, so close it almost touched.

"You saw nothing," he hissed. "*Do you understand? Nothing.*"

Hector looked up into watery blue eyes that shone with malice. He saw a grimy face of unshaven bristles and sparse, sandy hair. He smelled sweat and stale beer and tobacco, and instinctively backed away from the threat.

The moment was broken by the arrival of the shop owner.

"What happened here?" he asked.

The priest straightened up, his face now a mask of professional sadness. "We lost him, Mr Diamond," he said. "A sudden collapse."

"It was only a graze. He should have been alright." Diamond shook his head, and put the jug he was holding carefully onto the counter. "I only went out for a minute to get him some water."

"These things can be deceptive," the priest replied. "I've given him the rites." He held out a large, bony hand for the shop owner to shake. "And I'm needed elsewhere. I must be off."

"Thank you, Father," Diamond said.

"See to the boy," the priest replied, already heading for the door.

Hector watched, dazed, as the long-legged priest strode away.

Diamond put his hand on Hector's shoulder. "You'd better sit down, son," he said.

Hector flinched away from the touch. He bent to look more closely at his father, but Diamond restrained him.

"Best not," he said kindly.

And suddenly Hector's throat was stinging and his head was pounding and he couldn't hold back the tears. Huge sobs wracked him, and Martin Diamond held him until the sobs subsided into hiccups. Then he poured a glass of water for Hector, the water he had fetched for the boy's father.

"Drink this," he said. "You'll feel better."

Hector gulped it down. "I don't understand," he said at last.

"Nor do I, lad," Diamond replied. "It makes no sense to me."

A sweat-stained miner suddenly appeared in the doorway. "The Traps!" he yelled. "The Police! They're coming. They're bayoneting anyone they find. Get out. Now."

He didn't wait for a reply.

Hector could hear him shouting his warning along the line of shops. He was aware, now, that the battle noises were coming closer again.

"Here!" Diamond pulled open a cupboard door under the counter. "In you go." He gave Hector a push. "Listen, son," he said, "I'll pull this shut behind you. You'll be safe under here. This door looks like a plain wall. I keep extra stock out of sight in here."

"But…"

"No buts, Hector. You've had a bad shock, and now you need to hide. There's no time to get you away. Things might get ugly here."

Hector crawled into the cupboard, curling himself around huge jars and bottles, too exhausted to argue.

Diamond handed him the water jug. "Now promise me you'll stay quiet," he said. "Stay quiet as a mouse. Don't make a sound. No matter what you hear, don't make a sound."

"I promise," Hector said.

"Good lad. I'll come and let you out when it's safe. Don't come out by yourself. I'll get you home to your mother when things calm down. Alright?"

Hector nodded.

"Good." Diamond pulled the door closed.

And everything went black.

Huddled in his tiny cave, Hector could scarcely breathe. He heard shouts and screams and curses as the Traps came closer. He thought he heard Mr Diamond cry out, but he couldn't be sure. He heard booted feet scraping on the boards, heard whoops and crashes and breaking glass as looters moved into the Store, and smelled the sweetness of spilled boiled candy and liquorice and sherbet as the contents of the shelves spilled onto the counter and leaked into his hiding place below. It was easy to keep his promise to stay quiet: he was scared stiff.

Alone in the dark, he couldn't stop thinking about his father, lying dead on the floor out there, lying a couple of feet away from him on the other side of the closet wall. He worried that his father might be cold, lying crumpled on the floor like that. He knew it wasn't right, leaving him there. None of it was right. He waited, too terrified for grief.

Finally the noises subsided, growing fainter and fainter. Hector strained his ears, listening for footfalls, frightened that the Traps or the looters or the priest would come back, come back and find him. He stayed quiet, quiet as a mouse, and listened hard. And still Mr Diamond did not come.

Hours later, Hector woke with a start. He did not remember falling asleep— only that he was staying silent in the darkness while chaos erupted on the other side of the thin partition that protected him. But now the silence was absolute in his stale, stuffy cupboard. He couldn't hear a single sound. He felt for the water jug and took a long drink. The water was tepid, but it helped. He tried to move: he was stiff and sore and his head ached horribly. He felt around him, touching glass bottles and rough timber shelves. He couldn't feel a door latch. Panic welled up suddenly in his chest and he fought to breathe. He was trapped. They had locked him in and left him in the dark to die. He had to get out. He ran his hands across the walls, pushing himself until his back was against the door. And then he felt it—the latch scraped against his back. Hector stifled a shout of relief. He had forgotten that the door was behind him. He wriggled around, turning carefully in the tiny space until his fingers found the latch where it dropped into its slot in the doorframe. He pushed it up, gently at first, then harder until he felt the door give. He opened it a crack, feeling colder air on his face. The shop was silent, and dark. But not as dark as his hiding place—there was still summer twilight outside.

Hector thought for a moment. He couldn't lock himself in again, he just couldn't. He would have to come out sooner or later. Slowly, he inched the door open, until it touched something hard, and stopped. He couldn't open it any wider, so he squeezed through the narrow gap and stood, stretching his aching body. As his eyes adjusted to the gloom, he could make out the broken wreckage of the looted shop. He bent to see what was blocking the cupboard door, and gasped in shock. The door was stuck hard against the body of Mr Diamond, lying on his back in a pool of blood. Beside him, the bloodstained body of Hector's father lay where the priest had left it.

Hector froze. He didn't know what to do. His mind filled with impossible thoughts: he couldn't leave them, but he knew he should get help. But where should he go? He didn't know who he could trust. His world had turned upside down. He couldn't go to the police—if they had done the killing, they might kill him too; he couldn't go to the church, not after that priest had threatened him. He wondered if he should try to go home—but what if home wasn't there any more? What if his mother wasn't there?

He was still standing helplessly between the two bodies when he heard someone speak his name.

"Hector Munro?" The voice was a soft American burr. "Is that you, boy?"

Hector turned, momentarily blinded by lantern light.

Captain McGill put his lantern down in the doorway and reached Hector in three paces. He swept him up in his arms, and carried him firmly out of the room.

Hector was too worn out to argue.

McGill called to one of his men. "Jeremy, can you take over here? I want to get this one somewhere safe, maybe find him something hot to drink. He's in shock, poor kid."

"Sure, Captain," Jeremy replied. "Any wounded in there?"

"Two dead," McGill replied grimly. "The boy's father and Diamond, the shopkeeper—he's still wearing his apron." He made a fist. "That miserable English captain, Thomas, had no control of his men—they were killing bystanders for the hell of it. It's a slaughterhouse in there." He took a deep breath. "Tell the others to keep looking for the wounded. They'll be hiding from the authorities—the word is out that Commissioner Rede's police are killing prisoners. It started when Captain Ross was shot dead after he had surrendered. The least we can do now is help where we can to protect the injured. I, for one, want no more deaths here today."

1854: The Aftermath
Chapter 1

The following afternoon Captain James McGill, washed and brushed, made his way along the main street of Ballarat. With him walked an older man, well dressed but tired-looking. The goldfields town was quiet today—most of the twenty thousand or so inhabitants were staying off the streets, mopping up after the terrors of yesterday's battle, staying out of trouble. The police were everywhere. Traps who had taken part in the attack on the miners' stockade swaggered like conquerors, but a small group of smartly dressed native troopers reined in their horses and nodded a courteous greeting. McGill tipped his hat in acknowledgement.

Despite the heat, the two men walked briskly, stepping carefully over the debris that lay scattered about. The hot summer air was sour, heavy with the smoke of still-smouldering fires: after the looting, Diamond's General Store had been torched, along with several other buildings where the rebels had taken shelter. The structures that were still standing were nearly all simple frames, covered either with canvas or palings split out of pine, six feet long, and nailed on like clapboards. The commercial buildings, especially the cheap hotels and gambling houses, had gaudy fronts painted with flashy signs. McGill saw that patrons were trickling back into the Star, the Eldorado, and the Magnolia.

A dishevelled man lifted the tent flap of The Lucky Strike and staggered out.

"Hey, McGill," he shouted. "What are you still doing here?"

McGill turned, instinctively reaching for his revolver.

"No!" his companion said. He put his hand on McGill's arm. "Take it easy. The man's drunk."

"You let us down, McGill," the drunk continued. "We won't forget that in a hurry! You're not wanted here any more."

McGill stopped in his tracks.

"Keep moving," his companion said. "Don't give the police an excuse to lock you up. We both know you wouldn't survive a night in their custody."

McGill swallowed hard, but nodded. "Point taken," he said. "Let's go."

The two men quickened their pace, striding along the dirty, gritty street. As they turned a corner, they startled a flock of pink-and-grey galahs squabbling over a torn sack of grain spilled during the looting. The birds flew up, squawking.

"At least the parrots are getting something out of this," McGill said ruefully. He mopped his sweating brow with his handkerchief. "This is my second summer here," he added, "but I'm still not used to this December heat."

His companion nodded. "I doubt we'll ever be used to it," he said. "It's not natural."

The men turned into a narrower, dusty lane lined with slab huts and tents. A few spindly gum trees, too thin and twisted to be cut down for mineshaft props, had been left standing: now they provided a little, sparse shade.

McGill wiped his brow again. "That's better," he said.

At last they found the right address, and presented themselves at the modest timber home of Mrs Morag Munro.

McGill stepped forward and knocked.

Morag opened the door immediately.

"Captain McGill, do come in," she said, her voice soft with the lilt of the Scottish islands. She looked questioningly at McGill's companion.

"Allow me to introduce Mr Tarleton, the American Consul," McGill said quickly. "Mr Tarleton has been here in Ballarat these past few days on official business, and I am escorting him at present."

Morag held out her hand to the newcomer. "You're very welcome, sir," she said. "Do come in."

She ushered her guests into her tiny parlour, where a circular-topped tripod table had been draped with a delicately embroidered linen cloth and set for tea. McGill noted with anticipation that beside the elaborate floral-patterned tea service and Sheffield cutlery there was a plate of fresh-baked scones, a dish of preserves, and a seed cake on a decorative stand.

"Allow me to introduce Mrs Clara Seekamp," Morag said.

Mrs Seekamp seemed agitated. She fidgeted constantly with the buttons on the simple blue-grey dress that complemented her black curls and startling cornflower-blue eyes. She looked up warily from her perch on the only armchair and inclined her head. "Captain McGill."

"It's a pleasure, ma'am," the captain said, bowing slightly. "And may I present Mr Tarleton, the American Consul."

"Mr Tarleton. This is a most unexpected meeting." Clara looked hard at the man.

"Ma'am." The consul bowed.

"And Hector, of course," Morag said. She put her hand on her son's shoulder. "Hector has something to say to you, Captain McGill."

McGill's heart went out to the grieving boy. He wanted to hug him, tell him everything would be all right. But he could not. Constrained by the hopelessly inadequate conventions of the social situation, he said only: "Of course."

"I have to thank you, sir," Hector said, his voice high and quavery.

"You're welcome," McGill replied around the lump in his throat. "And how are you today, Hector?"

"Well, sir," Hector replied.

Morag patted her son approvingly. "You can stay for tea," she said, "then maybe run along to join Mrs Seekamp's children over at her house."

Hector nodded and moved to sit silently near the window, as far as possible from the adults. He stared out, pretending interest in a kookaburra that had alighted on a post to watch for unwary lizards.

"Do sit down," Morag said to her guests. "I'll pour."

The men settled themselves on upright wooden chairs, and Morag occupied herself with the business of handing around cups and plates, offering embroidered serviettes, sugar for tea, jam for scones.

James McGill accepted a scone and looked around at the oilcloth-covered floor, painted walls and lace curtains of the simple diggings home. The room smelled faintly of furniture polish and wood smoke, and it was cool after the heat outside. Everything seemed much too ordinary after yesterday's calamitous events. He thought that Morag Munro looked rather fetching in her hastily assembled widow's black, which set off her pale skin and copper-red hair to perfection. He suppressed the thought, reminded himself that her lovely grey eyes were red-rimmed from weeping, and concentrated on balancing his fragile teacup and plate.

"It was kind of you to invite me, ma'am," he said. "I don't want to intrude on your grief at such a difficult time, but I did want to check that Hector is all right. And you too, of course."

Morag smiled across at him. "And I have yet to thank you properly myself for rescuing my son," she said. "Twice, I believe."

"Any man would have done the same, ma'am."

"Perhaps, but you were the one who did. And I thank you."

"My pleasure, ma'am." McGill smiled back at her. "The second time was easy," he added. "I recognised the red hair instantly."

Morag instinctively smoothed her own coppery curls. "It runs in the family, I'm afraid," she said. "I always tell Hector that he has to behave when he's out in public because people will remember the red hair."

"True enough," Clara said. "It's hard to mistake it." She turned to McGill. "But you were not, I understand, in time to rescue Hector's father."

"Alas, no, ma'am."

"And you have your liberty."

"Clara," Morag began. "I don't think this is the time…"

"It's exactly the time, and the place," Clara replied, her Irish accent becoming more strident as she spoke. "And I want to know what really happened." She rounded on McGill. "And where *exactly* were you when we needed you?" she said bitterly. "After all your fine words at the meeting at the Adelphi Theatre, the men trusted you. Those miners would never have taken on the British troops if they hadn't thought they had your cavalry at their backs. My husband never stopped talking about you, about how well trained you are, about how you won with small numbers in the Mexican War. He reckoned that mounted Rangers with Colt pistols and those wicked-looking Bowie knives were worth any number of British troops with outdated single-shot muskets and bayonets. So where *were* the famous California Rangers when our men were attacked?"

Captain McGill looked down and shifted uncomfortably in his seat, trying unsuccessfully to stop the bright red blush that spread across his neck and face and right up to the roots of his curly brown hair.

Clara pressed the point. "Our men were dying under the Southern Cross flag," she said. "Where were you?"

"We were on a wild goose chase, ma'am," McGill said at last. He lifted his gaze to meet hers. "We were told there were fresh British troops bringing up cannon, and we rode out to intercept them. In a closed stockade, cannon fire would have been catastrophic. So we went."

"Well, the result *was* catastrophic, wasn't it?"

McGill had no defence. "We were tricked, ma'am," he said simply. "I fell for the oldest trick in the book. I thought the information was reliable. We all did. Lalor's best men marched out too, led by Nelson."

"Why?" Clara asked. "Everyone knew the whole camp was full of spies. Why on earth would you believe an informant at a time like that?"

"Because the information came from a man we all trusted, ma'am," McGill replied. "Dr Yates Carr: he had never been involved on either side. He said he was only telling us what he had heard to save lives — as a doctor, he believed it his duty to save lives." He hesitated: "He may have been duped too, of course. The British would rely upon a man of conscience to try to prevent bloodshed."

"But my husband said you were a West Point man," Clara said. "Surely there must have been a better strategy than that? You left the place undefended!"

"We rode back hard, ma'am, as hard as we could, as soon as we realised we'd been deceived. But we were too late. The Eureka Stockade had been lost." McGill stared at his boots again.

The Consul spoke: "If I may make an observation, Mrs Seekamp," he said, "I would suggest that this whole business has been about military strategy, and that the British strategy was *very* well planned indeed."

"Oh?"

"Look at the facts, my dear: the British knew that the Rangers had pledged to defend the miners, but would not attack. So they devised a ruse to draw them off. Then the British forces attacked at dawn on a Sunday, when nobody expected it and there were very few men about; and the British already had further reinforcements on the way. Looks like a well-planned operation to me."

"But how could they know that Captain McGill would ride out?"

"With respect, ma'am," Tarleton said, "your husband was right about the military training. And it is precisely Captain McGill's background that allowed the British strategists to predict his response. He did what any trained officer would do in that circumstance."

Clara was not appeased. "Well at least not all of the Rangers fell for it," she said. "Your deputy stayed, with some of the men. Lieutenant Charles Ferguson fought like a hero, by all accounts." She paused. "He's in prison now, for his pains. I saw him this morning. He's chained to my husband."

"Ah, Mr Ferguson: yes," said the vice-consul.

"You know him?"

"That's mainly why I'm still here, ma'am. He's an American citizen." He hesitated.

"And?" Clara prompted.

"And a very well-connected young man," Tarleton conceded. "I'm staying here to oversee his release. You may rely upon it, he's being well taken care of."

"Which is more than can be said for my poor Henry," said Clara. "They wouldn't even let me bring him food."

"Mr Seekamp is the editor of *The Ballarat Times*," Captain McGill explained.

"And he was arrested early this morning for seditious libel," Clara chimed in. "Arrested for reporting the truth of the Independence meeting at Bakery Hill, and for publishing articles by Morag's husband, Duncan Munro—whose murder your California Rangers entirely failed to prevent."

She turned away, close to tears.

Morag leaned forward. "Can you help Mr Seekamp?" she asked. "You must have some influence."

"I'll put in a word, of course," Tarleton replied. "But I have no jurisdiction here. Your friend should engage a lawyer for her husband's defence."

"Do you think it will come to a trial?" Clara asked.

"No way of telling, ma'am," Tarleton replied. "All that's clear to me at present is that Governor Hotham wants to avoid an international scandal. The

French Consul, Comte de Chabrillan, will arrive tomorrow. I am advised that he will negotiate for the French and other European prisoners, as will I for the Americans."

"That will leave mostly Irish miners," Clara said thoughtfully.

"Indeed, ma'am," said Consul Tarleton.

"How convenient," Clara said. "A rabble of disaffected poor Irish is just what the British press will offer up to their readers, just what the conservative squatters would like to believe." She squared her shoulders. "Well, Mr Tarleton, you've helped me make up my mind. I can't let them get away with that. I'm Irish too. There are principles at stake here. *I* will edit *The Ballarat Times* until Henry is released. The troops ransacked Henry's office and confiscated most of the copies of today's paper, but they can't stop *me* from getting out a new edition. And I'll print what Henry would have. Let's see how they like that!"

Tarleton looked sceptical, but before he could voice his objections Morag deftly turned the conversation.

"But you'll finish your tea first," she said.

The tension was broken. Clara smiled at her friend. "Naturally. And I won't forget that you also have important arrangements to make," she said. "And I'll be here to help you."

"How remiss of me not to enquire about the funeral," said McGill, glad that the conversation had changed direction. "I'd like to attend, of course. When is it to be?"

"There are no arrangements yet, I'm afraid," Morag replied. She dabbed at her eyes with a handkerchief.

Clara took up the story. "All the casualties are laid out in the barracks, waiting for the doctor to perform his *post mortem* examinations," she said. "The guards wouldn't even let Morag in to see her husband. It's a disgrace."

"I daresay they have protocols to follow," the Consul said drily.

"And they don't want the families getting a close look at how their men folk were butchered," Clara added tartly. "Poor Morag will never really know how Duncan met his death."

"The priest was there," Hector said, from his forgotten place by the window.

"What did you say?" said Morag.

"What?" said McGill.

"Which priest?" said Clara. "Father Smith?"

Hector couldn't go on. He shook his head.

Morag rose and went to him. "It's all right," she said, taking his hand. "You can tell me. It's all right."

Hector clung to her, trying not to cry.

"When I found him," McGill said softly, "he was in the General Store, standing between two bodies: his father, and Martin Diamond."

"And the red-coats burned the Store to the ground late last night," Clara added. "So we can't go back there."

"I know," McGill said. "It's fortunate that Hector wasn't still hiding in there. He'd have been trapped."

Morag shuddered at the thought. "Can you tell us what happened, Hector?" she asked gently. "This is really important."

Hector shook his head. He tried again: "The priest—not Father Smith, another one—was there when Dad died," he managed at last. He took a ragged breath. "Then Mr Diamond put me in the cupboard. He told me to stay quiet as a mouse." Hector knew he couldn't hold back the tears much longer. "It was dark, and I could hear things, terrible things, but I didn't move," he blurted out. "And when I came out later, Mr Diamond was dead too. I don't know what really happened. I didn't see." He was sobbing now, and his mother held him tight.

"You poor child," she said, stroking his hair.

"You were very brave," said McGill. "I'm proud of you."

Hector straightened a little at this, but did not see the look of concern that passed between his mother and Captain McGill.

"Best we keep this between ourselves," McGill said softly.

Morag nodded her assent.

"Agreed," Clara said. "Witnesses aren't popular with the authorities just now."

"And Hector has been through more than enough," Morag added, her arms still wrapped protectively around her son.

Tarleton looked thoughtful, but said nothing. He rose deliberately, and put his cup, saucer and plate carefully back onto the table.

McGill took his cue, and stood. "Thank you for a delicious afternoon tea, Mrs Munro," he said. "I enjoyed it very much. Such fine fresh baking is a delight rarely found in my part of the diggings."

"Then you must come again, Captain McGill," Morag replied. "On a more auspicious occasion, I hope."

"Indeed," said McGill. "I'll look forward to it."

"And I also thank you for your hospitality, ma'am," said Tarleton. "But we must not trespass upon your time any longer. I have, unfortunately, more business to attend to."

"And I," said Clara, "have a newspaper to run."

Left alone, Morag was thoughtful as she cleared the tea things. She understood, all too clearly, that the circumstances of her husband's death were far from resolved. She looked at Hector, tear-stained but recovering and tucking into another piece of cake. "*It's too late for Duncan,*" she said to herself. "*But I will protect my son. No matter what it takes, I will protect him.*" But from whom, or what, she had no idea.

Chapter 2

Across the Ballarat diggings at Bakery Hill, Alec Buchanan sat dealing with his correspondence at a small writing desk in the private sitting room of the Prince Albert Hotel. The room had every appearance of luxury: a rich red-and-blue Turkey rug was spread over the oilcloth-covered floor, the walls were painted a pale green, and the windows were draped in lace-trimmed white net and curtained with heavy dark-green velvet. The room was furnished with horsehair stuffed armchairs and side tables that held oil lamps whose ruby cut-glass bases supported velvet-trimmed shades. A carved cedar table held pride of place in the centre of the room, its matching high-backed chairs placed carefully around the walls, and, this being summer, the ornate fireplace was hidden behind an embroidered screen.

Buchanan was carefully dressed, his dark tailored clothes and fresh white linen shirt reinforcing his air of understated wealth. A leather-bound accounts ledger lay open on the desk, and he wrote swiftly, frowning slightly as he consulted the ledger and prepared the remaining business of the day. A discreet tap at the door interrupted his concentration.

"Enter," he said.

The door was opened just wide enough to admit Mrs Parsons, the landlady, firmly corseted and dressed in respectable black with just a touch of lace at her throat to remind patrons of her position. "Excuse me, sir," she said. "There's a gentleman of the clergy here to see you. He hasn't got an appointment, sir. But he says it's urgent."

Buchanan made a show of consulting his fob watch. "Well, Mrs Parsons," he said, "I have a little time before Mr Train arrives. You'd best show the gentleman in."

She opened the door wider and barely had time to say, "This way, if you please sir," when a priest pushed past her into the room.

"Mr Buchanan," he said.

Buchanan, a tall, well-built man who carried his thirty-six years easily, stood to meet this graceless interloper. The priest was taller, thinner, slightly older—a scarecrow of a man in his long black robes. He had brushed his thinning hair, but he still appeared rumpled, dishevelled, as if he had not slept. He needed a shave, and he smelled stale.

Buchanan stepped back. "And you are…?" he began.

"Father O'Hanlon," the priest replied, his accent a thick Irish brogue that grated on the Scotsman's sensibilities. "It's a pleasure to meet you, sir."

"Well, Father O'Hanlon," said Buchanan. "I only have a little time before my next appointment, but a man of the cloth is always welcome. Please do take a seat. Can I offer you some refreshment? May I offer you tea, perhaps?"

O'Hanlon shook his head. "Thank you, no," he said.

Buchanan caught the priest's quick glance at the drinks tray on the sideboard. "Sherry, then?" he asked.

"Ah, yes, I do believe I will. Thank you."

Buchanan, always a gracious host, crossed the room and poured two small glasses of amber-brown sherry from the decanter. He handed one to O'Hanlon, then raised his own in salute. "Your very good health, sir," he said.

"And yours," the priest replied, draining his glass at a gulp.

Buchanan put his own barely tasted glass down on a side table, sat down in one of the armchairs and deliberately crossed his legs. Despite the obvious hint, he did not offer a second glass to his guest.

"And now, Father," he said, "perhaps you will be good enough to tell me what brings you here this afternoon."

O'Hanlon sat forward awkwardly on the edge of his chair. He glanced down at his hands for a moment, his fingers still nervously twisting the stem of the empty sherry glass. He put the glass aside deliberately and appeared to make a decision. He faced Buchanan squarely. "I'll come straight to the point," he said.

"That would be best," said Buchanan, "though I think it only fair to warn you that I have already given Father Smith a generous donation for the miners' funerals."

O'Hanlon waved the idea aside. "I've been helping the poor bereaved souls, of course," he said. "But this is not about the funeral, at least not directly."

"What, then?"

"I understand you are a man of commerce, Mr Buchanan," he said. "I understand, if I may be blunt, that you are here because you may be interested in certain properties and leases that might become available after the law, shall we say, takes it course here."

Buchanan was puzzled. "I assure you, Father, that I am no threat to your flock," he said. "My visit here has been long planned: I always come at this time of year to check the accounts of the lands that I manage for a parent company."

"Jardine Matheson, yes," the priest said promptly.

"Indeed," said Buchanan. "You seem to know a great deal about my business arrangements."

"Enough to know that you manage more than just land," said O'Hanlon. "To know, in fact, that you manage some very interesting—shall we say 'Chinese'—imports; to know, in fact, that you are associated with a certain Mr Ah Zow Chan."

"Now look here, Father," said Buchanan. "My business is my own affair, and none of yours. And I don't like your tone. Perhaps you'd better leave."

O'Hanlon held up both long, bony hands. "Please," he said. "I have a business proposition, of a rather delicate nature. I need to be sure I'm talking to the right man."

"Go on," said Buchanan. "I'll allow that I have a number of business ventures, not all of them in land."

"Well," said O'Hanlon, "the thing is, sir, I've come into possession of a very valuable mining lease. And I want to do a deal."

Buchanan was intrigued. "What kind of deal?" he said. "And how does a priest come to own a gold mining lease?"

"Not gold, Mr Buchanan. Copper. It's a very rich find. The owner had barely begun to develop it when gold was discovered and all his workers decamped to the diggings. He came to the goldfields too, hoping to make enough to fund the copper lease."

"Go on," said Buchanan.

"He died in my arms, Mr Buchanan, during the riot. And the lease passed to me."

"I see."

"And I am looking for a well-connected businessman to take it over for me, sir. I am looking for a powerful man with connections enough to see me right in return for the copper."

"But why not just give it to the Church?" Buchanan asked. "Wouldn't the Church reward you?"

O'Hanlon shook his head. "The Lord helps those who help themselves," he said. "Politics is as cut-throat inside the Church as anywhere else, and my Bishop would take the credit, thank you very much, and I'd be left out in the cold."

Buchanan still did not want to let the issue drop. "But isn't it your duty to hand it over?" he asked. "You have your vow of poverty, after all."

O'Hanlon could not conceal the anger that flashed in his pale blue eyes. "I grew up in poverty, Mr Buchanan," he said. "I grew up in a village of grinding, dirt-poor Irish poverty. People died of cold, died of starvation, died of despair. I can assure you poverty has nothing to recommend it."

"And you obviously have no intention of returning to it," said Buchanan.

"Ah," said O'Hanlon, "none at all. I see we begin to understand each other at last."

"I think we do, Father," said Buchanan. "Do you have the lease?"

O'Hanlon reached inside his cassock and withdrew a crumpled packet tied with red string. Wordlessly, he passed it to Buchanan.

Buchanan rose and crossed to his desk, slid the package open and smoothed the parchment he found inside. He read swiftly. "It seems to be in order," he said at last. "But the name on the lease is that of Mr Duncan Munro. The journalist?"

"The same," O'Hanlon agreed.

"Then his widow has a claim on it," said Buchanan. "She'll claim it for her son."

"That depends on her circumstances," O'Hanlon replied. "There are a lot of claims about. She would know about the lease, of course, but her husband did not take her with him to inspect the site. She would have to have the documents to establish exactly which one belonged to Munro. And the official records can be vague, open to challenge."

"Perhaps," Buchanan said thoughtfully.

"And then there's the question of Munro's part in the uprising," O'Hanlon continued. "His editor has been arrested for sedition, but it was Munro who wrote those articles. One of the ringleaders, he was."

"Even so," said Buchanan. "The man's dead."

"And in no position to argue," O'Hanlon replied.

"Let me think on it, Father," Buchanan said. He slid the package out of sight beneath his own papers. "Let me make a few enquiries. There may be something that can be done to help you."

O'Hanlon stood. He held out his hand. "I'd like to keep the lease with me, if it's all the same to you," he said.

"What lease?" Buchanan replied.

O'Hanlon paled visibly. His hand shook.

"Calm down, Father," Buchanan said equably. "Your secret is safe with me. I'll need the paperwork to verify the claim, as I'm sure you'll understand." He smiled thinly. "You have your deal, Father. I think we can do business after all. And you'll find me a not ungenerous patron."

O'Hanlon's look was murderous. "That remains to be seen," he said.

"Indeed it does," Buchanan replied, "but as I said, leave it with me. You have my word I will return it to you if there's nothing I can do with it to our mutual advantage."

"Trust the word of an opium trader?"

"*Opium* isn't illegal." Buchanan let the implication hang between them.

O'Hanlon took one threatening step towards Buchanan, but hesitated at the sound of a knock at the door.

"That will be Mr Train," Buchanan said, consulting his watch again. "I have a meeting with him now." His voice was steady, but his dark eyes dared O'Hanlon to act against him. "Allow me to show you out, Father."

"I'll be back," O'Hanlon grated.

"I have no doubt you will," said Buchanan, moving to open the door. He stood aside. "Good day, Father."

"Good day to you, then," O'Hanlon said. He turned and strode from the room, brushing uncivilly against George Train.

"Who was that?" Train asked, his American accent loud in the silence that followed O'Hanlon's hasty departure.

Train was young, fresh-faced, and brimming with enthusiasm. He was shorter than Buchanan, and fussily dressed: his dark hair was stylishly combed, and he wore a red brocade waistcoat under his sober business suit. "The man has no manners, no breeding at all," he added.

"He's just one of the local priests," Buchanan replied. "He was looking for financial help, as usual."

"What else?" Train shrugged. "But I'd be cautious around that one, Buchanan," he said. "He has that lean and hungry look."

"My thoughts exactly," Buchanan replied, "and anyone can see he has a temper on him." He crossed back to the drinks tray. "May I offer you something?"

"Whisky, I think," Train replied, smiling. "The sun is well and truly over the yard-arm."

"Excellent. I'll join you." Buchanan poured measures into cut glass tumblers. The two men clinked glasses, comfortable in each other's company.

"Ah," said Train. "That's a very good malt."

"Indeed. I import it myself," said Buchanan, sipping his scotch. "Shall we take a look at the paperwork?"

Train smiled. "I think you'll find everything in order for our transaction."

"And everything here will soon be back to normal as well," Buchanan added. "Governor Hotham has sent enough men to control the rabble. Riots tend to be bad for business—and there's been trouble here ever since poor Bentley's hotel burned to the ground."

"So there has," Train said, smiling broadly. "But riots don't tend to bother the sheep. My men tell me they are expecting a good clip this year."

"That's encouraging, George," said Buchanan. "But there will inevitably be commercial issues to be dealt with after the upheaval. We'll need to keep an eye on Hotham—he has only the best interests of the landowners at heart. His proposal to auction off the goldfields lands to the squatters is making our investors nervous."

"True," said Train. "It's always a mistake to imagine that landed gentry are best placed to run a business."

Buchanan chuckled. "Nicely put, my friend. We can only hope that the Colonial office will veto any such proposal."

"I wouldn't rely on common sense from that quarter," said Train. "As you say, we'll need to watch out for any further developments in that direction."

"Well," said Buchanan, "I'm dining with one of the magistrates this evening. I shall certainly have one or two interesting implications to discuss." He raised his glass. "Shall we get down to business, then?"

Train returned the salute. "To business," he said.

Chapter 3

Next morning the banner headline of the hastily re-named *Ballarat and Southern Cross Times* read: *MINERS BETRAYED*. Clara Seekamp was as good as her word: she had taken over as editor, and the articles she published were every bit as inflammatory as those for which her husband now languished in jail.

On the front page, Clara wrote:

> It has come to the attention of this writer from highly reliable sources that the Independent California Rangers, who had pledged to defend the Eureka miners, were falsely tricked into riding out to intercept British troops and cannon. While the defenders' backs were thus turn'd, the British troops attacked with stealth at dawn on Sunday morning. There were only a small number of men about, and these were soon forced to surrender after a bloody battle.
>
> Of the thirty or so killed, The Ballarat Times can report that only eleven miners came from Ireland. Others were from Canada, Wurtemburg, England, Nova Scotia, Petersburg, Wales, Scotland, Eberfeldt, Prussia, Rome, and one man from Goulburn NSW: a truly international roll call of the dead. One hundred and thirty prisoners were taken by the victors, who then committed all the brutalities of darker ages; and further innocent persons fell victim to their blood thirstyness.
>
> Finding few miners to fight, the cowardly troopers then set about murdering unarmed bystanders: Mr Duncan Munro and Mr Martin Diamond were found dead in the General Store. The Store has since been burned to the ground. It seems to this writer that Mr Diamond's General Store was made a target of the soldiers' rage owing to its having served as a meeting place for the miners' Committee of Defence.

It is now incumbent upon His Excellency Governor Hotham to investigate these murders and address the whole disgraceful situation. Sir Charles Hotham has accepted a warm welcome to our shores and has been feted like a king: he must now do his duty to prove himself a competent Governor. He must govern for all, not just a landholding minority. For what is a diplomatist? He is a compound of caution and speciousness, as far as one can tell. Let us all hope that His Excellency now proves capable of more than empty promises and looks to reforming the dire situation in which we residents of Ballarat find ourselves.

"I'm quite proud of it," she told Morag.

"And I'm proud of you," said Morag. "Henry will be pleased. And Duncan would have applauded you too." She hesitated. "It's a brave thing to do. But is it safe?"

Clara's smile was defiant. "What can they do about it?" she said.

Chapter 4

At midday in the Star Hotel, Captain James McGill was sitting down to lunch with George Train.

"I've taken the liberty of ordering the mutton pie," Train said, pouring wine for both of them. "Supplies are short. I thought it best to order ahead today." He beckoned to a serving girl, who hurried off to the kitchen. "I was worried there'd be nothing to be had but kangaroo." He grinned.

McGill did not smile back. "Kangaroo is good eating," he said. "But mutton pie will be just fine, I'm sure. Thank you."

"I've never tried kangaroo—I'll take your word it's edible." Train shrugged. "In any case, I wanted to meet with you before I return to Melbourne tomorrow," he said. "We have things to discuss."

"I can't imagine what there is left to discuss," McGill replied. "It's over."

"For the present, yes," said Train.

"Well, then?"

The maid reappeared, carrying a heavy tray. Conversation ceased while she placed hot plates before the men, dished up the steaming pie and offered greens and potatoes and gravy.

"This smells good," McGill remarked.

"It certainly does," Train agreed, tucking his napkin under his chin. "We may have our differences, McGill, but at least we can share a good hot meal."

McGill merely nodded, giving his attention to the food.

Train tried again. "I know you're disappointed," he said.

"Disappointed?" McGill put down his fork. "A lot of good men died out there! You could have helped us. You *should* have helped us."

Train shrugged. "Please, don't blame me overmuch. I never thought that an armed uprising was the right way to go about securing independence for this colony."

"And your actions made that abundantly clear," McGill replied. "So why are you giving me lunch today?"

"I've spoken to Consul Tarleton. We think it would be best if you go back home to the States for a while, at least until things quiet down here. I'll arrange for your passage on one of my ships."

"I'm in no real danger," McGill said bitterly. "The uprising failed. The authorities are only interested in the miners who actually fought at the stockade. Accommodations are already being made. Ferguson has been released. I don't think anyone will be paying much attention to me now."

"You were the military leader," Train replied. "I can assure you that Commissioner Rede will not let the matter rest. He as much as accused Tarleton to his face of orchestrating an American plot against the Victorian government." He shrugged. "There's no evidence, of course—Tarleton has been very careful. But Rede isn't known for his finesse: he's a brutal man, and he has been embarrassed by events. The goldfields are under martial law now, and Major General Nickle is in control. Rede won't forgive that. You're not safe here."

"I'll take my chances," McGill replied.

"Then I beg you will be careful," Train said. "The fact that Nickle has come here himself means that Britain is taking the situation very seriously indeed. The man has been used at every uprising against the Empire: he got his knighthood for putting down the Canadian rebellion. He's here to enforce obedience, make no mistake about that."

"I'll be careful," McGill replied. "But I'm not ready to cut and run for home just yet."

"As you wish," said Train. "I won't press you. But remember: the offer stands. If matters change for the worse, come to me. I'll get you out."

"I appreciate that," McGill said. "I'm sure it won't be necessary, but you have my thanks for your courtesy."

"Courtesy be damned," said Train. "You're a valuable asset, McGill—and I'm a man of business."

McGill finally smiled. "I'll bear that in mind," he said.

Chapter 5

Later that afternoon, Major General Nickle—elderly, uniformed, tired and short-tempered after a very long, very hot march from Melbourne—rapped loudly at the front door of *The Ballarat and Southern Cross Times*. He was not alone: a small group of armed guards waited behind him as he knocked. He did not wait for an answer. He strode inside.

Clara was seated at a simple table, writing. She stood instinctively to meet her adversary. "Who are you? And what exactly is the meaning of this incivility?" she said.

"Allow me to present myself," he replied. "I am Major General Nickle, here to assume military control of the Ballarat area. And I'm sure you know why I'm here, Mrs Seekamp." He looked around the cluttered room with interest. "Martial law is in place now, and *I* am that law. I've done you the courtesy of coming myself, lest my men are provoked into unnecessary unpleasantness."

"Come to do what, exactly?" Clara asked, trying to keep her voice from trembling. She was all too aware that her situation was perilous: a woman alone with an armed and powerful man had little defence.

"To inform you that your newspaper is hereby prohibited from further publication," he said. "You are to cease operations immediately."

"But…" Clara opened her mouth to protest.

"There will be no negotiation, Mrs Seekamp," said Nickle. "My men will confiscate all copies of today's printing, and you will publish nothing further until the order is lifted. Do I make myself clear, madam?"

"Abundantly," said Clara. She crossed her arms protectively and retreated behind the table.

Nickle barked an order: "Men! In here." He picked up a copy of the morning's paper from the desk and shook it. "Take every copy of this rag that you can find. Take them away and burn them."

The guards filed in through the open door, knocking over a side table as they jostled in the small space.

"And be careful how you go about it," Nickle added. "This is to be done by the book. We aren't here to destroy the lady's property—not today, at least."

Clara yielded. "That stack by the door," she said, pointing. "All the unsold copies are there."

"Thank you, Mrs Seekamp," said Nickle. He ran his fingers through his greying hair. "We'll not trouble you any further."

As his guards collected the papers and filed out, Nickle wagged an admonitory finger at Clara. "Now, madam, you'll admit, I trust, that I've treated you fairly."

Clara just nodded.

"Good. Then you won't do anything stupid, like printing an illegal edition, will you?"

"No," she replied. "I wouldn't dream of it." She didn't pretend to offer a smile.

"Then we understand each other," he replied. "And don't think to try my patience, Mrs Seekamp. I've allowed you to keep your press and your premises, for now, but you must understand that my response to any infringement of your paper's suspension will be swift and decisive. I've controlled more situations like this than you've had hot dinners: I fought in the American and the Napoleonic wars, and I put down the rebellions in Ireland, then Canada. I assure you nothing you do here will surprise me."

"A man of experience, then," Clara said, recovering her composure and ignoring the threat.

"Indeed," he said wearily. "I have a great deal of experience in these situations. And I have further work to do. So I'll take my leave, madam."

He turned on his heel and strode to the door.

"And I'll bid you good day, sir," Clara said to his stiffly retreating back. Behind her own back, she had her fingers crossed.

Chapter 6

The next day, the day of the funeral, dawned fiery red as the sun rose into a clear sky of cloudless cerulean blue. By mid-morning the temperature had soared above the century, and by midday the police sergeant had recorded 104 degrees Fahrenheit in his logbook. It was a bad day to be out in the sun, a bad day to be burying the dead of the Eureka Stockade.

Major General Nickle had decreed a mass funeral. The decomposing bodies of all the dead were loaded onto horse-drawn drays to be carted to the Ballarat Cemetery, where burials were to be offered officially by Father Smith for the Catholics and Theophilus Taylor for the Protestants.

The mourners—the women clad in various forms of black, the men wearing black armbands—were constrained to follow the drays on foot: the long, sweltering, straggling procession wound its way through the baking hot town and out to the burying grounds. There was no shade anywhere, no relief from the scorching sun on a route that the officials had kept carefully away from the barracks, fearing reprisals. In the event, the weather was too hot for violence.

Morag Munro walked quietly, conscious of the murmur of a dozen different languages around her, her head bowed under her parasol. Beside her walked Hector and Clara: the three of them made a small knot in the mass of bereaved widows and children trailing along in the oppressive heat.

"I'm melting," said Clara, plying her fan vigorously to cool her cheeks.

Morag patted her own perspiring face with a handkerchief. "I can't think of a worse day to be burying poor Duncan," she said.

"And the smell," said Clara, wrinkling her nose. "It's awful."

"I know," Morag said. "All those bodies, in all this heat—it's bound to be awful."

Clara sighed. "We'll just have to do our best," she said. "We're almost at the burying ground. It won't take much longer."

Their conversation was interrupted by a soft American voice: "May I join you, ladies?"

31

"Captain McGill," said Morag. "How very kind of you to come. Do please walk with us."

"It will be my pleasure, ma'am. I want to pay my respects—to all the fallen, and particularly to Mr Munro and Mr Diamond."

As McGill fell into step with Morag and Clara, Hector dropped back a pace or two.

"How is he?" McGill asked gently. "This has to be a very hard day for such a young boy, to be walking to his father's funeral like this."

"He's bearing up," Morag responded. "He's a brave boy." She dropped her voice to a whisper. "But he's having nightmares," she added. "Terrible nightmares: he screams in the night. But he won't talk about them, or his father. He just keeps it all bottled up inside."

"Give him time, Morag," said Clara.

"I agree," said McGill. "He'll talk when he's ready."

He dropped back to walk beside Hector, offering him a dry bandanna. "Here, take this," he said. "Put it on the back of your neck, inside your collar. It'll soak up the sweat, and stop your collar from chafing."

"Thank you, sir," Hector said.

McGill helped him to arrange the cloth, then stepped forward again to keep up with the ladies.

Clara paced moodily, staring at the armed troops lining the route of the funeral procession. "It seems I owe you an apology, Captain McGill," she said at last.

"I doubt it, ma'am," McGill replied.

"There are two-and-a-half thousand troops here now, Captain, under Nickle. He's a major general. And he has field guns. And we are under martial law."

"I'm well aware of all of that, ma'am," McGill said ruefully.

"Which means your information was right after all," Clara said. "But the timing was wrong. You thought they were close enough to strike. So you did the right thing, riding out."

"But with the wrong result," he replied. "I was still tricked."

"Oh, I agree it was cleverly done," Clara conceded. "And I think that Nickle may have been the strategist who devised that trick."

McGill was all attention now. "And what makes you think that?"

"When he came to close down my newspaper he told me he'd had a lot of experience in putting down rebellions. He said he'd suppressed the Irish and the Canadians. He was trying to scare me."

"I doubt he succeeded in that," said McGill. "I'll warrant you're not so easily frightened."

"True," Clara replied. "But he did make me think back over our conversation with Consul Tarleton at tea. Nickle has been in command all along, and he has enough experience to have planned the whole thing."

McGill shrugged. "You may be right," he said. "But there's nothing to be done about it at present."

"I agree," said Clara. "But I thought I should speak my piece, to clear the air between us at least."

"I appreciate it, ma'am," McGill said. "There's not many here have taken the trouble to think it through."

"Are we friends, then?" Clara asked.

"Friends," said McGill.

"Good," said Clara. "There's something I want to ask you."

"Ask away."

"It's about Charles Ferguson."

"Oh?" said McGill. "What about Lieutenant Ferguson? He's safely out of prison, now."

"I know," said Clara. "I heard that he was given a change of clothes so the witnesses could not positively identify him, and he was released." She frowned. "The guards still won't let me take fresh clothes to Henry, so someone pulled some strings. It was probably your Consul."

"Probably," McGill agreed. "So what was your question?"

"What I want to know is, why did Mr Tarleton say Lieutenant Ferguson was well connected?"

McGill smiled, despite the solemn situation. "He's about as well connected as it gets, ma'am," he said. "He comes from old money, at least in American terms. His father was originally married to the sister of the US Secretary of the Treasury, then to Charles' mother, the sister of the Senator for Connecticut."

"So politically too hot to handle," said Clara.

"That's about the strength of it, ma'am," said McGill. "Putting him on trial here would create an international fuss of the first order, which your Governor most certainly does not want. But don't underestimate Ferguson as a man," he added. "He more or less ran away from home, and survived a lot of Indian attacks, including being shot in the back with an arrow when he was only seventeen. He's seen a lot of action. He's a very handy fighter."

"And how old is he now, may I ask?"

"Twenty-one," McGill replied. "He's a veteran."

"And what about you, Captain McGill?" Clara asked. "Are you a veteran too?"

"Indeed I am, ma'am. I fought in the Mexican War. But I'm four years older than Ferguson."

"I see." Clara fell silent for a moment, assembling the pieces of the political jigsaw in her mind. "Ferguson's release means the authorities will still be looking for a scapegoat," she said at last. "And that scapegoat could well be my poor husband."

McGill looked thoughtful. "I fear you may be right," he said at last. "But we'll talk later: the service is getting underway." He doffed his hat, despite the blazing sun, and stood beside Morag, Hector and Clara, to listen to Father Smith intone the age-old ceremony for the Catholic dead. High above them, a thin cry pierced the air: a pair of wedge-tailed eagles soared, riding the thermals of the rising heat, indifferent to the human tragedy playing out below.

When it was Duncan Munro's turn to be lowered into the earth, Father Smith stepped forward to administer the burial rites. Behind him, assisting, was the tall, black-robed scarecrow figure of O'Hanlon.

Hector ducked instinctively behind Captain McGill, shaking with fear.

"What's wrong, Hector?" his mother whispered.

Hector was too scared to speak. He reached up and clutched McGill's hand.

"Leave him to me," McGill said gently. "You do what you need to do now."

Morag was distraught. "Thank you," she said.

She turned and moved forward, trying not to look at the dark ooze staining the new Californian pine coffin, trying not to breathe. She claimed the widow's right to scatter the first earth into her husband's grave. The handful of pebbles, as they fell, sounded cold and final on the coffin lid at the bottom of the hot, dusty hole.

Morag wept.

Blowflies buzzed guiltily in the background. Clara stepped up and put her arm around her friend's shoulders, offering comfort. "Hush," she said softly. "Don't give the bastards the satisfaction of seeing you cry."

Morag let Clara lead her away from the open grave as more victims were being lowered to their final resting place and soldiers on burial detail moved in behind the priests to fill the gravesite quickly with earth. She straightened her shoulders. "I'm fine," she said. "Where's Hector?"

"McGill took him on ahead," Clara said. "It was too much for him at the last."

"He seemed afraid of the priests," Morag said.

"Who wouldn't be?" Clara replied. "They were putting his father in a hole in the ground. It was suddenly too real for him, that's all."

"I hope so," Morag said quietly, as the two women turned for home. "I do hope that's all it is."

As McGill steered Hector through the crowd one of the miners stepped across to block the way.

"You've got a nerve, McGill, showing your face here," he muttered.

"I'm here to pay my respects," McGill replied equably.

"There's many a man as blames you for this," the miner said. "It should've been you in that coffin. Maybe it soon will be." He spat. "I'd watch my back, if I was you."

He turned away, blending easily into the crowd.

McGill leaned down close to Hector. "Don't let it bother you," he said. "It's only gossip. Everyone's upset on a day like this. Everyone's looking for someone to blame."

Hector nodded, unable to speak. He still held tightly to McGill's hand, his only security in a dangerous world.

Chapter 7

Next morning, the sun was bright in a hot summer sky. The air already tasted of dust, and Morag was up early, keeping busy about her household chores before the heat should become intolerable. A sharp rapping at her door surprised her. She peeked around the curtain and gasped in shock.

"Hector," she said, "run and fetch Captain McGill. Tell him it's urgent. Go!"

Hector didn't need to be told twice. He slipped through the back door and ran like a hare, dodging tent pegs and washing lines.

The insistent knocking came again. "Open up," a rough voice shouted. "We know you're in there."

Morag, her heart in her mouth, opened her front door to the three blue-uniformed policemen standing there. Before she could speak, a tall red-faced sergeant with thinning hair and a day's dark stubble on his chin brandished a sheet of paper at her.

"An order for your eviction," he said.

Morag just stood there for a moment, speechless with shock.

The sergeant barked an unnecessary order: "This way, men!"

"There must be some mistake," Morag managed at last.

"You are Mrs Duncan Munro?"

"Yes."

"Then there's no mistake." He thrust the paper at her. "Here, see for yourself. It's signed by a magistrate, fair and square."

Morag's hand shook as she took the paper. She read. "I don't understand," she said at last. "My husband paid for this place. There's no money owing."

"Not my problem," the sergeant replied. "I'm not paid to understand. I'm just following orders." He pushed past her into the sitting room.

Morag smelled his acrid sweat, smelled the stale beer on his breath.

"And my orders are to evict you."

"It says here you have to give me notice," Morag said desperately.

"I just did," the sergeant replied. "What's in here?"

Morag said nothing.

He shoved her aside. "Bedroom," he said, leering. "And here we have a lonely widow. Doesn't that give you an idea, lads?"

Morag backed away, only to find her arms grabbed and pinioned by the two younger men.

"Bring her in here," the sergeant said, reaching to unbutton the flap of his trousers. "We might as well have some fun."

Morag screamed.

One of the men clamped his hand over her mouth.

She bit him, hard, and screamed again when his grip loosened.

He slapped her, gave her a rough push in the direction of the horsehair mattress. "You'll regret that," he snarled.

"Hold her," said the sergeant.

Morag twisted and fought to free herself, but the men were too strong. She found herself being dragged towards the waiting sergeant.

"Stop right there!" McGill stood in the doorway, breathing hard. He had been running. "Take your hands off that lady!"

The sergeant glanced contemptuously at McGill. "This is police business, mister," he said. "Better leave us to it if you don't want to get hurt."

"I said," McGill repeated, "take your hands off that lady." His voice was calm, but there was murder in his eyes.

"And I suppose you're going to make me? There are three of us. Do you think you can take all of us?"

McGill reached inside his shirt. There was an audible click as he cocked the hammer of his Colt revolver and pointed the long barrel squarely at the sergeant. "Five bullets," he said, "for three rapists. That's pretty good odds. I never miss."

The two cadets released Morag's arms and backed away. "No harm meant," one of them muttered.

The sergeant spun and grabbed Morag, holding her in front of him as a shield.

"Coward," said McGill.

"You won't shoot," the sergeant said.

McGill raised the Colt higher to aim at the man's head. He sighted along the barrel. "Try me."

"You'll hang for it," the sergeant grated.

"You won't be alive to see it," McGill replied.

"Sir," said one of the men from beside the window.

"What?"

"There's more miners coming, sir."

"Looks like trouble," his partner added.

"My middle name!" Charles Ferguson's voice chimed in lightly from the sitting room. "Need any help in there?"

"I've got it covered," McGill replied. "The sergeant here was just leaving."

The sergeant considered his position. "I could have you charged with hindering police business," he said.

"I could have you charged with assaulting this lady," McGill replied.

"Put the gun down and I'll let her go, then."

McGill lowered his weapon.

The sergeant slowly released his grip on Morag. He took a pace towards McGill and the doorway. A knife gleamed as he slipped it from his shirtsleeve into his hand.

McGill was too quick for him. He twisted the knife out of the man's hand and pressed the barrel of the Colt to his neck. "Now you will apologise to the lady," he said softly.

The sergeant had no choice. "Sorry," he muttered through clenched teeth.

McGill stepped aside.

The sergeant made for the door. "We'll be back," he said, hastily buttoning the flap of his trousers. "Don't think you've heard the last of this. That eviction order still stands. We'll have her out of here by sundown." He glared at McGill. "And you'd better watch your step. Dangerous places, these goldfields: anything could happen."

Ferguson stood back to let the sergeant and his men through Morag's sitting room. "And we'll all be watching you," he said, drawing the words out into a challenge.

The sergeant did not reply.

Ferguson and the miners cheered as the Traps left the house, red-faced and empty-handed.

Morag ran to McGill, and clung to him, shaking. "Thank you," she said. "Thank you so much."

"It's all right," he said, putting a protective arm around her shoulders and leading her gently to a chair in the sitting room. "Have they hurt you?"

Morag rubbed her arm. "A few bruises, probably," she said. "But thanks to you nothing worse than that." She shuddered, barely managing not to cry.

"Hector found me," McGill said. "It was a lucky thing I was close by."

"And I was with him," Ferguson said. "Lieutenant Charles Ferguson at your service, ma'am," he added.

Morag looked up to see a lean, wiry man with a mop of unruly blond hair. "Lieutenant Ferguson, thank you," she said, still shaking.

"Not at all, ma'am." Ferguson grinned. He pushed his hair out of his eyes. "I brought along a few of the men, just in case. They've no reason to like the Traps."

"And I have every reason to fear them," Morag said, "especially after this morning." She turned back to McGill. "Do you know where Hector is now?" she asked.

"I sent him to Mrs Seekamp's house," McGill replied. "I thought it best to keep him out of harm's way."

"That was well done," Morag replied. "Thank you."

McGill smiled at her. "Do you know why the sergeant was here in the first place?" he asked.

Morag bent to pick up the eviction order that she had dropped in the scuffle. "They brought this," she said, handing it to him.

McGill read it slowly. "It says there is an irregularity about your husband's purchase," he said.

"I don't know what that means," said Morag. "He paid for the house. I have the receipt. There is no debt."

"It means," said Ferguson, "that you are being punished for your late husband's political writings." He paused. "You can challenge it, of course," he added. "There is a firm of solicitors here already handling claims for damages during the riots. You could speak to them."

"But they won't be able do anything before sundown," said McGill. "Those ugly police will be back, with reinforcements."

"True," said Ferguson.

"So we'll have to move you out today," said McGill. "Can you go to Mrs Seekamp's house, at least for now?"

"I'm sure I can," said Morag. "It's a big house."

"That's settled then," McGill replied.

"Do you need my help?" Ferguson asked.

"I'll take it from here," McGill replied. "I know you have business to attend to this morning."

"Right you are, then," said Ferguson. "I'll be on my way."

"Thank you again, Lieutenant Ferguson," Morag said.

"My pleasure ma'am." Ferguson turned back to McGill. "Be careful," he said softly. "That sergeant is out to make trouble."

Chapter 8

An hour later, a small procession of dusty miners arrived at Clara's front door with a dray carrying all of Morag's worldly goods.

Hector ran to his mother, careless of the men watching.

Morag hugged him fiercely. "My hero," she whispered. "You found Captain McGill, and he arrived in the nick of time." She smiled across at McGill. "Thank you."

McGill stood silent while Hector's words tumbled out. "Captain McGill sent me here," he said. "And then a man came to say you were on your way, and to wait."

"Quite right," Morag said. "We'll be staying here for a while until things are resolved with the paperwork."

Hector's face fell. "They don't like me," he whispered to his mother. "The older boys, I mean. They make fun of me."

"It's just for a little while," Morag said. "We'll both have to be brave, Hector. We've nowhere else to go."

"And I'll look out for you," McGill added. "You just tell me if there's any trouble."

"Really?" Hector asked.

"Really," McGill answered.

Hector managed a smile.

Clara ushered the miners towards a small room at the back of the house. "Just pile everything in here," she said brightly. "We'll sort it out later." She smiled. "I've made fresh scones," she added. "The least I can do is to offer you tea. Just come along to the front room when you're done here."

"Our pleasure," one of the men replied.

"And I want to hear all about it," Clara said. "I want to know everything that happened."

While Clara was busy handing around scones and tea, Morag entered the room with McGill and Hector at her side. "I must thank you all for coming to my rescue," she said simply. "I really appreciate all you've done for me today."

"Don't mention it, Mrs Munro," one of the miners replied. "We protect our own."

"And you just send for us if they come back," another of the men added.

There were nods of agreement around the room.

"Those bastards need a lesson in manners, especially that Sergeant Dunn." The digger smiled. "We'd welcome the chance."

"You know him?" McGill asked.

"Let's just say our paths have crossed," the man replied. "He's a nasty piece of work."

The miners headed back to the diggings once they had drunk their tea and reassured themselves that the women were safe, at least for the present.

McGill helped Clara to carry the dishes to the scullery, seizing a private moment to talk with her.

"You'll need to look after your friend," he said. "She's had a bad shock."

"Well, yes, of course," Clara said. "But Morag will be fine. She's pulled through worse than this."

"I want you to promise me you will send for me if the police turn up here," McGill said earnestly.

"Here?"

"They might. That sergeant, Dunn, won't want to let it go. He was humiliated in front of his cadets. It won't be hard for him to find out where Mrs Munro has taken refuge."

"Then I will send one of the boys if we need you."

"Good."

"But I must say it's outrageous that we should have to take such precautions," Clara added, "in our own homes."

"Nevertheless," said McGill, "these are dangerous times. I'll be here if you need me."

"It's still a scandal," Clara said. "Those police think they can do whatever they like and get away with it."

"They *can* do whatever they like," McGill replied. "They're the only law here at present."

"Well, I can write about it in *The Times*. I'll be back in business soon. I can cause a public stink. They can't stop me."

McGill was suddenly very serious. "Be careful, Mrs Seekamp," he said. "Think about it: the Commissioner's blue-coats are the bottom of the barrel, retired scum dredged back up by Rede to do his dirty work. Those are the same thugs who went on a killing spree after the stockade. I know. I was there. Those police got away with murder, Mrs Seekamp, but it's the miners who are in jail. Do you really think those same police have anything to fear from the law?"

Clara sighed. "I suppose you are right," she said. "I promise I'll be careful."

Chapter 9

Alec Buchanan was still finishing morning tea in the dining room of the Prince Albert Hotel when Father O'Hanlon, his black robes flapping, strode in unannounced and dropped unceremoniously into the chair opposite.

"Well?" he asked, without preamble.

Other hotel guests turned to stare.

Unfazed, Buchanan signalled to the landlady to bring another cup.

"Tea, Father?" he said.

Mrs Parsons, the very picture of outraged black-clad Protestant propriety, put the china down so hard in front of O'Hanlon that the cup rattled in its saucer. Before the priest could pour, she seized the teapot and stalked off in the direction of the kitchen.

"I'll just freshen the pot, Mr Buchanan," she said over her shoulder, "for your *guest*." She almost spat the last word.

Buchanan smiled. "We really will have to do something about your manners, Father," he said. "If you are hoping to advance in the world, such rude behaviour simply will not do."

O'Hanlon scowled.

"You have a certain unenviable reputation," Buchanan went on. "I've done some checking. And I have to tell you here and now that although you may be accustomed to bullying the hapless members of your flock, such heavy-handed tactics will not work in the world of business. Some subtlety is required. And," he added meaningfully, "some patience."

"Patience be damned," said O'Hanlon. "I get things done."

"Language, Father," Buchanan admonished, just as Mrs Parsons bustled back into the room with a fresh pot of tea.

"Will there be anything else, Mr Buchanan?" she asked, pointedly placing the teapot just beyond O'Hanlon's reach.

"No, thank you, Mrs Parsons," Buchanan replied. "We have everything we need."

"Very good, sir," she said. "I'll leave you, then."

Buchanan waited until she was out of earshot to say: "Events are in progress, Father, but, like it or not, you must be patient."

"Meaning?"

"Meaning that I had a useful conversation with a magistrate."

"And he didn't waste much time, did he?" O'Hanlon said. "The Munro widow has just been evicted. The whole of the diggings is buzzing with the news. It was a nasty affair, by all accounts."

"It was a necessary first step," Buchanan replied, tight lipped.

"Well, I'm glad to find you think as I do on matters of business," O'Hanlon said.

Buchanan bridled. "I doubt it, Father," he said. "*I* stay well within the law."

O'Hanlon shrugged. "So?"

"As I was saying," Buchanan continued, "I met with a magistrate who has agreed that there may be, shall we say, certain irregularities about Mr Munro's affairs that may require further investigation."

"And how long will that take?"

"It will take as long as it takes, Father. The wheels of official power grind slow, as I'm sure you know. We cannot proceed with undue haste in a matter such as this. But it does, at first glance, appear that we can proceed."

"And the lease?"

"Is safe, Father." Buchanan allowed himself a small smile at the priest's discomfiture. "You'll have to trust me."

O'Hanlon's face darkened. "I'd sooner trust the devil himself," he said.

Buchanan lost patience. "You came to me, Father," he said, "with what is, after all, purely a business proposition. You have your deal. And now you must live with the consequences. It is fortunate for you that I, at least, am a man of honour." He placed his serviette onto the table, and pushed back his chair. "And now I have an appointment to attend, Father. So I'll bid you good morning." He rose.

O'Hanlon stood too. "You'll not be rid of me so easily," he grated.

The two men faced each other across the table, Buchanan's well-groomed elegance a stark contrast to the priest's untidy hair and rusty black robes.

Buchanan sighed. "Your aggression does you no credit, Father, no credit at all. You will hear from me when I have news. And until then, I'll thank you not to intrude upon my affairs." He straightened his well-cut coat. "I'm sure you can see yourself out."

Buchanan turned and crossed to the door of the dining room with an easy grace, then mounted the private staircase to the guest rooms.

O'Hanlon was left to stalk through the public area, past the enquiring gazes of the curious patrons of Mrs Parsons' hotel.

O'Hanlon made for the front door, head down, muttering under his breath. He did not see the man waiting there for him until it was too late.

"A word, Father," McGill said.

"Not now," O'Hanlon replied. "I'm busy." He did not stop, but kept walking.

"As are we all, Father," said McGill, matching his pace to the priest's long-legged stride. "This will only take a minute. I'll walk with you."

"I said," O'Hanlon grated, "I'm busy."

"Then I'll get straight to the point," said McGill. "Allow me to introduce myself…"

"I know who you are, Captain," said O'Hanlon. "What do you want?"

"I need to find the priest who was in Mr Diamond's store when Duncan Munro died," McGill said. "It's important."

O'Hanlon caught his breath.

McGill heard.

"Nothing to do with me," O'Hanlon said brusquely.

"A priest was seen thereabouts," McGill said. "Father Smith thought it might have been you. Were you in the vicinity at all?"

"I was everywhere that day, Captain," O'Hanlon said, breathing again, realising on the instant that McGill could not suspect the truth. "It's my job. I gave what help I could to the wounded; I dealt with the dead and dying."

"Yes, yes, Father," McGill said. "But…"

"I can't help you," O'Hanlon said. "Try one of the others."

"I'll do that, Father," said McGill.

"Then I'll bid you good day," O'Hanlon said, turning abruptly towards a ramshackle row of tents. "I have an urgent visit to make."

McGill watched him go, knowing in his bones that this man was hiding something. He shrugged—there was no reason he could think of that a priest would lie about attending a death. He made a mental note to keep an eye on O'Hanlon anyway. He didn't trust the man an inch.

Chapter 10

Morag and Clara spent an hour or so re-organising Clara's house to accommodate their new situation. Morag's furniture was added to the household. Clara's children were moved out of the second bedroom and, much to their delight, allowed to set up their beds in the back section of the house, away from parental control. Morag's bed was installed, along with her tripod table, a chair, a wooden closet for her clothes and linen, and a camp bed for Hector.

"He'll be better in my room, at least for a few days," Morag confided to her friend. "His nightmares are still bad."

"It will take time," Clara said. "Don't worry, Morag. Hector is a sensible lad. He'll come to terms with his father's death in his own way."

"I hope so," said Morag. "I do worry about him."

Clara hesitated. "Will you mind terribly if I leave you for a while?" she asked. "I have an appointment at the Courthouse."

"Not at all," Morag said. "I'm fine now, really I am."

"Thanks," said Clara. "I won't be long."

A little later, Morag was still sorting out her belongings when Clara bustled back into the house, breathless with excitement.

"You'll never guess who I've invited to dinner tomorrow evening," she said. "You must join us, Morag. Please do say you will."

"Of course I shall," Morag said. "What's all this about?"

"I've sent my eldest across to the camp to invite Captain McGill," Clara continued eagerly. "And I've asked McGill to bring Lieutenant Ferguson along too. He's such a hero. I think it's time we met him socially, don't you?"

Morag smiled. "If you say so," she said. "We were introduced this morning when he came to my aid with Captain McGill, but it was hardly a social occasion. I should certainly like to thank him again for his help."

"Do you think he's good-looking?" Clara asked.

"I hardly noticed," Morag replied. "Things were so very difficult at the time."

"Of course," said Clara. "Sorry."

"Don't be. I'm fine. But didn't you meet Lieutenant Ferguson when you went to see Henry in prison?"

"I saw him, yes, but we were hardly introduced. He struck me as a handsome man."

"I see," said Morag. "And that's why we are having dinner?"

"No," said Clara. "That's not it at all."

"Why, then? You haven't told me the occasion for all this fuss yet."

Clara grinned at her friend. "The Comte de Chabrillan and his wife, the Countess Celeste, have accepted my invitation," she said triumphantly.

"My goodness," said Morag. "However did you manage that?"

"Well," said Clara, "Mr Tarleton did say that the Count was coming here to negotiate for the European prisoners, so I was keeping an eye out for him. I thought I might interview him for *The Times*, for when the suppression is lifted, to get a different perspective as it were."

Morag suppressed a chuckle. "Of course you did," she said. "What happened?"

"I managed to arrange an introduction at the Courthouse," she said. "I arranged to speak to him after his men were released."

"And did they release them?"

"Oh, yes—of course they did. But that's not really important."

"Isn't it?"

"Well, yes, I suppose it is. But while I was waiting I contrived to overhear the most amazing gossip."

"I'll admit I'm intrigued," said Morag. "You must tell me."

Clara linked her arm through her friend's, and lowered her voice conspiratorially. "Well," she said, "it transpired that that pompous old man Nickle has refused to receive the Countess, fearing for his own reputation with what passes for society in Melbourne!"

"Goodness gracious," said Morag. "What possible reason could a General have to snub a Count?"

"The reason of the lady's past," Clara replied.

"Oh?"

"Rumour has it," Clara said softly, "that Celeste de Chabrillan was an actress, a circus rider, and a famous courtesan. It seems that the Count was her favourite lover, and when he married her he was sent out here to the Australian colony as French Consul to escape the scandal at home. Intriguing, isn't it?"

"You're enjoying every minute of this, aren't you?" said Morag.

"Of course I am," said Clara. "Certain people around here have been very rude about my own background with the Circus."

"But you were never a courtesan," said Morag.

"No," Clara replied. "But I was an actress. And for some I could name, it amounts to the same thing."

"So you feel a certain sympathy for our visitor," said Morag.

"I feel a certain curiosity," Clara replied. "Whatever else transpires, it should be a lively evening." She smiled again at her friend. "I've reserved the private dining room at the Prince Albert."

"Is that quite proper?" Morag asked.

"For a woman alone, probably not," Clara replied. "But for the editor of *The Ballarat and Southern Cross Times*, it is certainly acceptable. Besides, this house is nowhere grand enough to entertain aristocracy."

"But Clara," Morag said, "I'm in mourning. I could attend a meal here at your house, but I can't go to an hotel."

"Of course you can," Clara retorted. "No one here would expect you to keep strict etiquette after all the upheaval. These are extraordinary times. We're under martial law, after all. And besides," she added, "I'm sure Duncan wouldn't mind."

"But I don't have anything to wear," Morag said. "Not to an hotel dinner."

"Stop being difficult," Clara replied. "Your evening dress is lovely, if I recall."

"But it's green, Clara," Morag said. "Green velvet. I must, at the least, wear black. I couldn't possibly have my dress dyed black in time to wear it tomorrow evening."

Clara thought for a moment. "I have something I can lend you," she said at last. "I have a black dress that will come up nicely for evening wear." She smiled at her friend again. "Now will you come?"

Morag yielded. "Very well," she said. "If you can dress me, I can make an effort to be sociable."

"Good," said Clara. "That's settled. And now my dear, you must help me plan a menu. I've never entertained a Count before."

"I'm afraid your menu will depend entirely on what Mrs Parsons can procure," Morag replied. "Everything is in such short supply after the riots."

"True," said Clara, her enthusiasm undiminished. "But we can at least give her a shopping list."

Chapter 11

The next evening, the evening of Clara's dinner party, the two women dressed early and walked the short distance from the Seekamp house to the Prince Albert, determined to be well ahead of the guests.

"I just want to supervise Mrs Parsons' final arrangements," said Clara.

"I'm sure everything will be fine," Morag replied. "But I don't suppose it will hurt to check that all is in order."

Clara felt more than ready for the occasion in her low-cut formal gown of midnight-blue velvet with full skirts and high-puffed long sleeves. Her black curls had been smoothed and coaxed into ringlets, and around her neck she wore her mother's diamante brooch pinned to a blue velvet ribbon that matched her dress.

"How do I look?" she said as they walked. "Will I do?"

"Clara, you know you look wonderful," Morag replied. "I wish I could feel as confident as you." She smoothed her skirts nervously. She was wearing Clara's plain black linen dress, converted into evening wear by the addition of a deep-fringed Indian shawl exquisitely embroidered in red and blue and gold silks, draped low on her shoulders and pinned at her bosom. Over her shining auburn ringlets she wore a black lace mantilla, as befitted a widow, and on her feet she had, perforce, to wear her black walking boots.

"I'm not at all sure about this," she said to Clara as they entered the hotel.

"You look lovely," Clara replied. "Stop worrying."

There was no time for further doubts. Mrs Parsons stepped forward to greet Clara. "Ah, Mrs Seekamp, do come through," she said, ushering the women quickly towards the private dining room.

"She must have been waiting by the door," Clara whispered.

Morag nodded, suppressing a smile.

"I'm sure you'll find everything in order," Mrs Parsons was saying.

The table had been covered with a heavy white linen cloth, and a central Sheffield silver candle stand dominated the setting. Six places had been properly laid out with matching linen napkins and the hotel's best china, silverware, and sparkling glassware. The green velvet drapes had been drawn and the side lamps already lit so that their ruby bases glowed in the evening light. A silver drinks tray had been furnished with a cut-glass decanter of sherry and matching glasses, and set on a side table ready for the arrival of the invited guests. The room had a cosy elegance that suited Clara's purpose very well.

"It looks very fine," Clara said. "Thank you, Mrs Parsons."

"It's all as you asked, Mrs Seekamp." Mrs Parsons moved around the table, lighting the six tall candles. "Will there be anything else?"

"What's all this?" Clara said, gesturing to the sideboard where, she had just noticed, two bottles of red wine had already been decanted, and several bottles of various shapes stood ready. "I don't recall ordering such quantities of wine."

Mrs Parsons permitted herself a tight smile. "Indeed not, Mrs Seekamp, nor of such high quality," she said. "The wine is a gift from the Count. He asked me to say that he hopes you will not object to his offering this small addition to your dinner arrangements."

For once, Clara was speechless.

"That's very kind, I'm sure," Morag supplied.

"Indeed it is," Mrs Parsons sniffed. "And very generous."

"And the final menu?" Clara asked, regaining her composure.

"Roast lamb, Yorkshire pudding, boiled greens," Mrs Parsons said promptly. "It's all that was to be had in the market, after the riots and so much spoilage with the heat. And there's boiled pudding with syrup for dessert."

Clara did her best to hide her disappointment. "I'm sure it will all be most delicious," she said.

A soft tap at the door alerted the landlady. "That will be your guests arriving," she said. "I'll just show them in."

"She did it to spite me," Clara whispered to Morag behind Mrs Parsons' retreating back.

"I don't think so," Morag whispered back. "I did try to warn you that supplies are terribly short."

"No help for it now," said Clara.

A maid opened the door, and Captain McGill stepped smiling into the room. His appearance had been transformed by a visit to the barber and the bathhouse: smooth-shaven, washed and brushed, McGill looked handsome in his formal black evening suit, starched high-collared shirt, black silk tie and soft polished boots.

But Clara only had eyes for his companion.

"Good evening, ladies," McGill said, offering a tight, formal bow from the waist. "Mrs Seekamp, allow me to present Lieutenant Charles Ferguson."

"Delighted to make your acquaintance," Ferguson responded, his midwest American drawl a little more pronounced than McGill's. He bowed in his turn. "And allow me to thank you for inviting me, Mrs Seekamp."

"It is entirely my pleasure, Lieutenant Ferguson." Clara extended her hand.

Ferguson kissed it, holding her fingers for just a beat longer than propriety would dictate.

Clara took a deep breath. "And you've met Mrs Munro, of course," she said.

"It's a pleasure to see you again, Mrs Munro," said Ferguson. "I trust you are recovered from yesterday's excitement?"

"Thank you, yes," Morag replied. "I must thank you again for your kindness."

"Not at all," Ferguson replied. He glanced back at Clara as he added: "I'm always happy to be of service to a lady."

Suddenly, Clara remembered her manners. "May I offer you sherry?" she asked.

"Thank you," both men replied.

The business of pouring and handing around drinks allowed Clara a moment in which to observe the new arrival. Ferguson was taller and slighter than McGill, lean, muscular, and clearly fit. Despite the best efforts of the barber his sandy blond hair still appeared tousled, and although his evening dress matched McGill's he wore it with an easy grace that spoke of his breeding. His blue-green eyes sparkled with mischief, and the smile he offered Clara was boyish.

"I'm so glad that you could join us this evening," she said.

"I am truly delighted to be here," Ferguson replied.

Clara smiled back at him. "And you are, by all accounts, the hero of the stockade," she said brightly.

McGill looked down at his boots.

"I don't know about that, ma'am," Ferguson replied. "I did what I could."

Morag, aware of McGill's sudden discomfort, spoke quickly. "I still don't understand how so many California Rangers came to be here at all," she said. "Perhaps you can tell me, Lieutenant Ferguson?"

"I've wondered about that too," Clara said, reclaiming Ferguson's attention. "Most of the Americans here are forty-niners: they simply took ship from the Californian gold rush to the Australian one, so there's no mystery there. But the Rangers are different."

"Not that different, ma'am," said Ferguson. "The tale is quick to tell. The Rangers were being paid out, and the men decided to try their luck at the

Australian diggings. Some of them pooled their money, bought a ship, and hired a crew to sail from San Francisco."

"And re-sold the ship when it arrived in Melbourne," McGill added. "So every man recouped enough money to finance his equipment for the Ballarat gold fields."

"That was clever," Morag said.

"What a wonderful scheme," Clara added. "Were you with them on the voyage?"

"No," Ferguson said. "I joined with them here when the situation warranted it."

"As did I," said McGill.

"And what of your own story, Mrs Seekamp?" Ferguson said, smoothly changing the subject. "I understand you are now the editor of *The Times*."

"Indeed I am," she replied. "And I'm just waiting for martial law to be lifted so I can publish my next edition."

"I applaud you," Ferguson said. "I admire your spirit. We need independent writers. Someone should expose that man, that..." he hesitated, choosing a milder expression for the ladies, "that pompous fool of a Commissioner, Rede," he said at last.

"What do you mean?" said Clara.

"I mean," Ferguson replied, "that if Rede hadn't been so full of his own importance, so determined to enforce the letter of the law, the whole military involvement need never have happened here."

"Before my husband Duncan was killed," said Morag, "he was writing an article about Commissioner Rede's recruits. I remember that he said much the same thing."

"Rede couldn't get enough volunteers here," Ferguson said. "So he brought in retired prison guards from Tasmania—from Port Arthur. Those men already had the worst reputation for brutality and corruption." He paused. "And you, Mrs Munro, had the misfortune to experience their brutality at first hand."

"And the very good fortune to be rescued by Captain McGill and yourself," Morag replied, smiling.

Ferguson bowed slightly, accepting the compliment. "You had a lucky escape," he said. "I recognised that sergeant: I saw him bayoneting unarmed prisoners after the stockade. He's a dangerous man."

"Those bayonets have caused no end of trouble," McGill added. "Rede gave them to his recruits. The miners hated him for that."

"Why?" Clara asked.

"Because bayonets are military weapons," Ferguson replied. "Police don't usually have them. Rede gave those thugs too much control, made them feel too powerful. They started really throwing their weight around, treating free miners like prisoners, like convicts. It was sheer stupidity. It made the whole situation so much more explosive."

"And then it did explode," said Clara. "And I shall certainly write about Rede's culpability."

"Bravo," said Ferguson. "That will make for controversial reading. I'm sure your husband will be pleased that you will be keeping *The Times* in circulation with such interesting articles." He smiled at her. "Your husband and I were acquainted, as you know, at the Commissioner's pleasure." He rubbed his wrists at the recollection of handcuffs. "I am sorry to hear that Seekamp has not yet been released."

"Nor is he likely to be," said Clara, "as far as I can tell."

"Then you must call on me if you need anything," Ferguson said, smiling. "Anything at all."

Ferguson was interrupted by the arrival of Clara's other guests.

The door was opened and the Comte de Chabrillan entered the room. On his arm was the most beautiful woman Morag had ever seen.

Clara stared with the rest.

"Madame Seekamp," said the Count. "Allow me to present my wife, Celeste, Comtesse de Chabrillan."

As Clara stepped forward in her role as hostess, she felt suddenly dowdy and provincial in the presence of such a fashionable Parisian beauty. Celeste de Chabrillan swept into the room, tall, blonde and graceful. She was wearing a very low-cut off-the-shoulder evening dress of claret-red velvet, styled in the most recent Paris design, the bodice slashed and ruched to reveal a panel of gold brocade beneath. Her full skirts swept the floor above matching red satin shoes and her long kid-leather gloves had been dyed red to match. Her corn-gold hair had been piled high, braided and curled so that a single ringlet fell to brush the left side of her neck, about which she wore a gorgeous teardrop diamond necklace that sparkled in the candlelight. The perfume she had chosen was a heady blend of rose and exotic spice that seemed to fill the room.

"Delighted, Madame Seekamp," said Celeste, her heavy French accent making her seem all the more glamorous in this plain goldfields hotel.

Beside her, her husband was ugly. Despite his cutaway black evening jacket over black trousers and shiny pumps, despite his white shirt with its high collar and loosely-tied black silk cravat, he looked somehow predatory. A powerfully-built man, Lionel de Chabrillan was shorter than his wife. His facial features seemed overpowered by a large nose and dark red fleshy lips that were not disguised by the full black side-whiskers that he wore. He carried himself confidently, and exuded an air of sensuality that worried Clara as he kissed her hand.

"You are both very welcome," Clara managed to say. "Allow me to present Captain McGill, Lieutenant Ferguson, and Mrs Munro."

The introductions made, Clara was relieved to find that her guests soon relaxed and were disposed to be sociable.

The Comte accepted a sherry glass that looked fragile in his large hand.

"It was thoughtful of you to provide wine for us," Clara ventured.

"My pleasure," de Chabrillan responded. "A number of cases of French wine were brought up from Melbourne with us, in the expectation, shall we say, of more formal engagements in my capacity as Consul." He shrugged. "And since martial law has intervened, and I find that I am no longer required in my official role, your kind invitation this evening allows me to put the wine to far better use." He raised his sherry glass in salute. "I trust it will prove acceptable."

"I have no doubt it will be far better than the hotel dinner," Clara said, surprising herself. She blushed. "What I mean, your Excellency, is that fresh food is exceedingly scarce after the riots. I'm sure Mrs Parsons has done her best."

The Comte gallantly waved her concerns aside. "Do not trouble yourself on that account, Mrs Seekamp. We shall have civilized company, good wine and a hot meal: what better evening's entertainment could we ask?"

"My husband is right," Celeste said, touching him lightly on the arm. "This is all very civilized. I must admit, I didn't know what to expect, coming here after such upheaval."

"Did you think to find us unshaven savages?" Ferguson teased.

"Of course not," Celeste replied. "But after Monsieur Bentley's splendid hotel was burned down, I did wonder what the accommodations might be."

"But here we all are, safe, sound, and sophisticated." Ferguson's drawl was all easy charm. "And permit me to say that you look splendid in scarlet, Countess," he added, smiling mischievously.

Celeste fluttered her red fan and smiled back at him. "You should not believe all you hear, Lieutenant Ferguson," she said.

"Indeed not," Ferguson replied. He looked straight across at McGill as he added: "Unlike some, I make it a rule to believe none of what I hear."

McGill's face darkened. The allusion to his own credulity in the matter of Dr Carr's deception at the stockade was clear to everyone. But before McGill could say anything in reply, Ferguson, his point made, lightly returned the conversation to more social matters.

"And I believe only half of what I see," he added. "Particularly here on the goldfields."

Celeste laughed. "Is there false gold about, then?" she asked.

"There's false everything," said Clara. "We have every kind of rogue here. And a lot of them are disguised as our protectors: it's often hard to tell which ones are the greater scoundrels."

"But you must admit that there are a lot of honest people here as well," Morag said.

"Of course there are," said McGill. "Beginning, I believe, with our present company."

As if on cue, Mrs Parsons knocked and entered the room carrying a silver-domed serving tray. Behind her, the hotel serving-maids followed with covered dishes, which they set down on the sideboard.

Clara, self-conscious in her role as unescorted hostess, directed her guests to their seats. She was delighted and more than a little relieved when Ferguson moved to hold her chair for her.

"Will there be anything else, Mrs Seekamp?" Mrs Parsons asked. "Millie here will dish up for you." She lowered her voice. "I've taken the liberty of carving the roast in the kitchen," she said. "It's all sliced ready."

"Thank you, Mrs Parsons," Clara replied, warming to the landlady for so neatly sidestepping the formal etiquette of carving the meat in the absence of a male host. "We have all that we need."

Despite Mrs Parsons' exceedingly plain cooking, the party was convivial— helped, no doubt, by the generous flow of the Comte's fine French burgundy. The conversation soon turned to matters of fashion, and Lionel de Chabrillan regaled the company with anecdotes of the foibles of the French court. Even Morag relaxed, laughing with the rest.

Chapter 12

Across the diggings, in the sparsely furnished barracks house of Commissioner Rede, another dinner was taking place. The earlier function hosted by General Nickle in his role as controller of martial law had ended, and the guests had departed to their own arrangements. Four men—Commissioner Robert Rede, Major General Robert Nickle, Chief Magistrate Charles Hackett, and the youngest of the group, businessman Alec Buchanan—now sat down in spartan surroundings to a dinner remarkably similar to the one provided by Mrs Parsons for Clara and her guests at the Prince Albert Hotel.

An orderly poured claret for the men. Commissioner Rede, whose thin features, receding hairline and bushy sideburns served only to emphasise his fifty years, rose to carve the roast. "It will be plain fare this evening, gentlemen," he said. "Supplies are short in the town."

Nickle smiled. "It smells good to me, Rede," he said. "I'm an old campaigner."

"I'm sure we'll manage very nicely," Hackett offered, swirling the rather thin wine in his glass. He rubbed his temples. His face was drawn, lined with weariness. "These are difficult times."

"Indeed," said Buchanan. "But at least the lamb in this district is said to be excellent. Mr Train, a business associate, told me recently that this has been a very good season for his properties here."

"And he is not affected by the uprising?" Nickle asked.

"Not so far," Buchanan replied.

"It's all about control," said Rede, helping himself generously from the dish of boiled greens held for him by the orderly. "The miners are a greedy, unruly rabble. Everyone wants something for nothing."

"There was much more to it than that," said Nickle.

Rede bridled. "Oh? What makes you think that?"

"Many things," said Nickle. "I notice that *The Ballarat Times* has published a long list of grievances, citing the high cost of mining licences and the like."

"That rabble-rousing rag," said Rede, "has caused nothing but trouble."

"And its editor is in jail now," Hackett added.

"Where he belongs!" said Rede.

"And yet," said Hackett, "it is true to say that the cost of licences has been a very vexed issue."

"And it has been my thankless job to enforce it," Rede added. "I've had to increase the police presence significantly."

"I understand you brought in men from Tasmania," Nickle said. "Old prison guards, brutal men."

"Some of them, yes," Rede replied. "I had to get the job done."

"Was that wise?" Nickle asked.

"They were all I could get," said Rede. "A lot of my men resigned to dig for gold themselves. And I judged that my small company of native troopers were too sympathetic towards the miners to exercise the required force."

"Even so…" Nickle began.

Rede bridled. "The trouble isn't *just* about my men and their enforcement of mining licences, is it, Hackett?"

Hackett shrugged. "I'll concede that Governor Hotham's proposal to auction off the goldfields lands to the squatters has sparked a great deal of outrage."

"And it hasn't helped matters that he refused to meet with a deputation of miners to discuss the situation," Rede added.

"No," said Hackett. "I'll grant that added fuel to the fire."

"It would," said Nickle. He shook his head. "But I fail to see why the Governor would wish to convert the goldfields into private property."

"His purpose is to relieve the government of the trouble and expense of collecting the licence duties," Rede answered shortly.

Buchanan turned to Hackett. "Can Governor Hotham really convert the entire goldfields to private property?"

"I imagine he feels that the recent English Enclosure Acts provide a legal model," Hackett said.

"A model for revolution, in my view," said Nickle. "Such a step would effectively convert hard-working free men into serfs — at a stroke their enemies would become their taskmasters."

"When you put it like that," said Buchanan, "I take your point."

"And may I ask how the business community is reacting, Mr Buchanan?"

"We are watching the situation carefully," Buchanan replied. "Businessmen from around the globe have invested heavily in developing the amenities that support these goldfields. My associate, Mr Train, for example, imports prefabricated building supplies from San Francisco." He glanced around. "I'd wager this barracks house is one of his constructions. Total privatisation would mean significant losses for commercial investors." He hesitated, then added: "There would, of course, be a requirement for adequate compensation."

Rede just shook his head.

"But surely the opportunity to purchase additional land would be of particular interest to you and your associates?" Hackett said.

"Naturally," said Buchanan. "As you know, I oversee some exceedingly large landholdings here for Jardine Matheson, and others. But it is my understanding that the Governor intends to restrict his proposed acquisitions to established squatters."

Hackett looked thoughtful. "If the scope were to be widened," he said, "the wealthier miners would certainly agitate for the right to buy gold-bearing land."

"Indeed," said Buchanan. "All the more reason for businessmen such as myself to keep an eye on any likely changes to the status quo."

"Which there will not be," Rede said. "Not while I'm Commissioner here."

"Nevertheless," said Nickle, "it will be prudent to make some changes, to keep the peace." He shrugged. "I was summoned here because the Victorian goldfields are the richest on earth—the Empire cannot afford to jeopardize such a prize for the sake of a few minor concessions. I can't reasonably impose martial law here for more than a few days. Something must be done."

"Understood," said Rede. "But I assure you that I intend that law and order *will* be strictly kept."

Nickle sighed. "These things follow a pattern," he said. "Ever since the Americans won their independence, the Empire has been determined to keep control of its remaining colonies and their resources. As you say, Rede, it's all about control. Your recent experience isn't unique, gentlemen: I was sent to take charge of the Australian forces earlier this year when the first signs of serious unrest began to show. In my experience, now is the time to make some small concessions. If we give a little, we will avert further conflict. If we give nothing, the rebels will fight on. They always do."

"I don't like the sound of that," Rede said, his mouth set in a stubborn line. "I don't think we should give an inch."

"You may not have a choice," Nickle replied.

Rede scowled. "You don't have to remind me that you have taken control. But I warn you, if you give them something, anything, they'll just want more!"

Hackett spoke up quickly, attempting to calm the growing tension between the Commissioner and the General. "Well," he said, "at least it is fair to say that the miners started the battle by firing that volley of shots at Captain Thomas' men."

"True," said Rede. "On that much we are agreed."

Buchanan was fascinated. "Does it make a difference to know who fired the first shot?"

"From a legal point of view, yes, I believe it does," said Hackett.

"But it doesn't change the basics of the conflict," said Nickle.

"Perhaps not," said Hackett. "As a magistrate, I'm bound to say that such things are always complex. In this instance, the Reform League's push for the right to vote is most interesting. It's basically Chartist, of course, but the idea certainly appears to be close to the hearts of the Americans—we have so very many of them here on the goldfields, and they are loud advocates for democracy."

"Mark my words, the Americans are playing a deep game," Commissioner Rede said darkly. "I attended a dinner they gave for their Consul, Tarleton, at which the assembled company offered a toast to the Queen, but not to her officers. It was a deliberate slight! And then that hothead McGill gave a rousing speech, and there could be no doubt about his intentions."

"Would that be Captain James McGill—the military leader of the California Rangers?" Nickle asked.

"The very same," Rede replied. He shrugged. "Tarleton responded with a speech that exhorted his countrymen to obey our laws. But I now believe that that was just for show. I have it on good authority that the Californians have been urging on the mob with a view to Americanizing this Colony. They are up to their necks in this uprising—they are aiming for revolution."

"Revolution?" said Hackett. "That's a strong word."

"Independence is the word being bandied about," Nickle said. "Governor Hotham certainly fears the worst. There's no doubting that the Americans were advocating revolution when the miners held their meeting. The men were flying the Stars and Stripes as well as the Union Jack up on Bakery Hill that day."

He reached inside his coat and withdrew a folded sheet of paper. "Here," he said, holding up the paper. "I have been reading the local reports, trying to understand exactly what happened here. I confiscated the newspapers when I closed down *The Ballarat Times*. Let me read you a little of what Henry Seekamp had to say:

> *Bakery Hill is obtaining a creditable notoriety as the rallying ground for Australian freedom. It must never be forgotten in the future history of this great country that on Saturday, Nov. 11th, 1854, on Bakery Hill, and in the presence of about ten thousand men, was first proposed, and unanimously adopted, the draft prospectus of Australian Independence. We refer to that of the "Ballarat Reform League."*

Nickle paused, checking the paper. "Here," he said. "I was right. Seekamp says that: *the union jack and the American ensign were hoisted as signals for the people to assemble…*"

"I told you those Americans were the ringleaders," Rede said.

Nickle ignored the interruption. "And here, Commissioner Rede," he said, "is the crux of the problems with *your* heavy-handed police force that we were discussing earlier." He resumed his reading: "It says here that the first resolution was a demand for the instant dismissal of one Sergeant-Major Milne. It was unanimously carried."

"Did you dismiss him, Commissioner?" Buchanan asked, interrupting.

"Governor Hotham did," Rede grated. "He was wrong to do it: one does not give in to such demands."

"In any case," said Nickle, "the miners had the wit to see Milne was a symptom, not the cause of their problems. They went on the record to say he was but a tool in the hands of the Government that employed him. Their second resolution censured the insolent language of the Colonial Secretary, the Surveyor General, and the Chief Commissioner of the Gold Fields—that's you, Rede—for what they called *sneering contempt at the miners' appeal for investigations into the practices to which the men are subjected.*" He paused, sipping his wine.

"It's all rubbish!" Rede said, his face mottling red with anger. "Who do they think they are?"

"Aggrieved men, obviously," Hackett said. "Is there more, Nickle?"

"Much more," Nickle replied. "I'm sure you know that the miners passed a vote of 'No Confidence' in the Legislative Council. You can read the text of it later for yourself, if you are interested. I'll let you have a copy. I kept several."

"Much obliged," Hackett replied.

"The interesting thing," Nickle went on, "is just how American the language of the miners' declaration sounds." He consulted his newspaper cutting again. "*Taxation without representation is tyranny,*" he read out. "That sounds very like the American Declaration to me."

"I keep telling you," Rede said, banging his fork on the table for emphasis, "the Americans are behind it all!"

"Steady on," said Hackett.

"I think," said Nickle, deliberately refolding his paper and returning it to his jacket pocket, "that it all comes down to a question of how different nationalities view the world."

"What do you mean?" Buchanan asked.

"I mean," said Nickle, his voice grown thoughtful, "that the miners have come here, freely, from the four corners of the earth. They are all seeking their fortunes, but they carry with them different expectations, different ideas of what is possible. The English Chartists ask only for reform, but for the Americans and the French, revolution is part of their personal history. For them, it's perfectly possible to imagine such a thing happening here."

"Well," said Buchanan, "if revolution was the objective here, I would venture to say that it has failed."

"For the moment, yes," said Rede. "But I don't believe in coincidences, and I tell you it was no accident that the American Consul happened to be visiting the goldfields at the time of the uprising."

"Well," said Hackett, "I, for one, would have liked to hear what Tarleton himself had to say about it. I was disappointed that he was not at your reception, Nickle."

"That was not possible, alas," the General replied. "A delicate matter: I could not invite the American Consul without inviting the French Consul as well."

Buchanan looked puzzled.

"And that would also have meant inviting the wife," Rede sniffed.

"My little reception was held to reassure the worthies of Ballarat that everything is under control," Nickle said. "Many of the ladies would have felt obliged to decline had the Countess been in attendance."

"Perhaps," said Hackett. "But this is not Melbourne. Governor Hotham's wife is the daughter of a Lord, and couldn't possibly be expected to receive the French woman who invented a dance as scandalous as the can-can. But here on the goldfields people are inclined to stand less on ceremony. I think there are many who might have been pleased to meet the Count, and his Countess. He is a man of great influence, after all."

"For my own part," said Buchanan, "I admit that I know nothing of the politics of this matter. But I suspect that the ladies of Melbourne would be more forgiving if the Countess were less beautiful." He smiled. "She is an exquisite creature."

"She's trouble," said Rede. "And I propose to avoid anything that will give the slightest excuse for social unease. I intend to keep a very firm grip on everything that transpires here. This situation is far from settled. It will never be resolved while Captain James McGill remains at large." He turned to Nickle. "I think you're wrong to offer concessions, General. But if you do, I'd still advise you to keep a sharp eye on McGill."

"Understood," said Nickle. "I've no doubt that the man is worth watching."

Buchanan thought it advisable to change the subject. "And I, of course, am most interested in whatever additional business opportunities may arise," he said lightly. "I'd like to hear your thoughts, Commissioner."

Buchanan kept to himself the realisation that George Train, the colony's leading American entrepreneur, had been here on the goldfields together with the American Consul at the time of the uprising. Buchanan didn't believe in coincidences either.

Chapter 13

At the Prince Albert Hotel, Clara's dinner was reaching its end. The dessert dishes had been cleared, and although the conversation was still animated, Morag nudged Clara's foot under the table.

"It's time," she said softly.

Clara considered for a moment, but rose to the occasion. "Ladies," she said, "I propose that we withdraw to the sitting room and leave the gentlemen to their port and cigars."

As they all stood, the Count bowed to his hostess. "I hope that you have no objection if a business associate of mine who is staying in the hotel joins us for a cigar," he said.

"Of course not," Clara replied. "A friend of yours will be most welcome."

"Thank you," said the Count. "I will just have the maid leave a message for Mr Buchanan that he may join us when he returns from his dinner engagement, if he so wishes." He smiled. "Ladies?"

The women repaired to the sitting room and settled themselves comfortably while Mrs Parsons brought tea.

Celeste surprised her hostess by slipping off her satin evening shoes. "I find that my shoes are always too tight in hot weather," she said. "I hope you do not object if I relieve my poor feet a little while we women are alone."

"Certainly not," Clara replied, smiling as she rose to pour the tea.

Morag could only nod in agreement, tucking her own booted feet further out of sight under her too-long dress she accepted a teacup from her friend.

"And now that we can talk more freely," said Celeste, "I want to say how much I appreciate your invitation this evening. I'm sure you are aware that your dinner party here has saved me no little embarrassment." She shrugged. "These things do not bother my Lionel in the slightest, but I do not like to be an encumbrance to him. It was good to be able to say to Mr Buchanan when we met earlier this evening that we were unable to attend the function hosted by General Nickle because of a prior dinner engagement."

Clara could not suppress her delighted grin. "It has been an absolute pleasure," she replied. "I'm happy to have offered an alternative to that horrible old man. I don't like him one little bit."

"Clara!" said Morag.

"Sorry," said Clara. "I should be more circumspect in my comments. I may have had rather more wine than usual this evening." She giggled.

Celeste laughed too. "No harm done," she said. "I don't like him either."

"And besides," said Clara, "I did so want to meet you."

Celeste raised a delicate blonde eyebrow. "Why would you want to meet me?" she asked.

"My friend was once an actress," said Morag. "She felt that she might have some reminiscences to share with you."

Clara turned to Celeste. "Forgive me if I am impertinent, Countess," she said. "The truth of it is that I had heard that you were once associated with the Circus, as I was myself, and so I thought we might become friends." She sighed. "Even here on the very frontier of civilization, people can be so censorious."

"Indeed they can," said Celeste, relaxing once more.

"You are not offended, then?" asked Clara.

"Not in the least. When I was just sixteen I was indeed a circus rider, and then an actress and a dancer in Paris."

"I was doing the same in Dublin," said Clara, "at the same age."

"Remarkable," said Celeste. "And what brought you to the goldfields?"

"The usual thing," Clara replied. "A husband. It was the same for Morag." The women all laughed, sharing the truth of their situation.

"Well, I'm glad we can be friends," Celeste said. "And there is another lady, a dear friend of mine, who I think you will enjoy meeting. She is Countess Marie von Landsfeld, otherwise known as Lola Montez, and she too is an actress who was born in Ireland. She writes that she is soon coming to Melbourne and the goldfields."

"I shall look forward to meeting her," Clara said, then added: "But I must say that Montez doesn't sound very Irish."

Celeste smiled confidentially. "Her parents are Irish-Spanish, and she was actually christened 'Maria Dolores Oliver Gilbert', which is Irish enough— but when she found herself in altered circumstances she changed to a more Spanish name. She undoubtedly has the looks to carry it off: she has the most beautiful dark hair and eyes. She is in America, at present, on a world acting and dancing tour. She is bringing her whole theatre group to Australia. I must arrange for us all to meet when she arrives."

"How exciting," said Clara. "That will certainly give me something to look forward to."

"And you must come as well, Morag," said Celeste.

"I'm afraid my own background is much more conventional," Morag said ruefully.

"No matter," said Clara, waving the objection aside. She paused, listening to the sound of heavy footsteps in the hallway.

"That will be Mr Buchanan arriving," said Celeste.

The Count rose to greet his guest. "Ah, Buchanan, do come and join us," he said. "Allow me to introduce Captain McGill and Lieutenant Ferguson, both of the Independent California Rangers."

"Delighted to meet you," Buchanan responded. He accepted a glass of port and sipped judiciously. "Excellent," he said.

The Count smiled. "It is from my personal store," he said.

"I'm honoured to share it," said Buchanan. He turned to McGill and Ferguson. "And I am very pleased to make the acquaintance of the leaders of the California Rangers," he said. "I have been dining this evening with Commissioner Rede. I must say that I was most interested to hear the official version of the battle."

"I would quite like to hear that myself," said McGill. "So much is still unclear to me."

"Well at least it seems clear that the miners fired the volley of shots that precipitated the action," said Buchanan.

"I had understood that the police fired first," said the Count.

"That's closer to the truth," said Ferguson. "It was a single shot from a trooper that started it: the shot that wounded Captain Ross, the Canadian. I should know. I was standing right next to him at the time. I barely escaped with my own life."

Buchanan looked surprised.

The Count shrugged. "Ah well," he said, "as my countryman Voltaire has it, *history is a fable upon which we have agreed to agree*. I don't doubt the official version will prevail."

"I haven't agreed to anything," Ferguson said sharply.

"I don't think you have to," said McGill. "These things just happen."

"Perhaps," said Ferguson. A slow smile lit up his face. "But it now occurs to me that I may allow the delightful Mrs Seekamp to interview me after all. Perhaps my eye-witness account will set the record straight."

"Perhaps," said Buchanan. "But I confess it's the question of how the authorities will react next that interests me most. I should warn you, Captain

McGill, that Commissioner Rede blames you for the uprising. He told me that he intends to keep a very close watch on you."

McGill laughed. "In that case," he said, "I'm afraid the Commissioner will be sadly disappointed."

Buchanan smiled. "As for myself," he went on, "I have commerce to think about. And I understand that you, Lieutenant Ferguson, are also a man of business."

"You are very well informed," Ferguson said guardedly.

"Not at all," Buchanan replied. "I have merely had a recent conversation with a mutual acquaintance, the American importer Mr George Train, who remarked that a Lieutenant Ferguson of the Ballarat goldfields had bought a Californian pine frame and a large tarpaulin cover, suitable for a theatre."

"The Adelphi Theatre, yes," Ferguson said. "We opened with the Empire Minstrels."

"Successfully?" asked Buchanan.

"Very successfully," Ferguson replied. "I've sold the theatre on, of course."

"I'm sure that was a sensible decision," Buchanan replied. "Such ventures can be highly volatile."

"True," the Count said abruptly. "And I believe you said that you also have a business proposition that might be of interest, Mr Buchanan?"

Buchanan put down his glass. "Indeed I have, your Excellency," he said, suddenly serious. "Gentlemen, the location of a very rich copper deposit has come to my attention, and I propose to establish a consortium to develop a new copper mine. I am, at present, merely investigating the possibility that like-minded gentlemen might find such a venture of interest."

McGill shook his head, but Ferguson smiled. "It would, at the least, make an attractive change from gold," he said.

"Perhaps," the Count replied. "But then, perhaps not." He shrugged. "But at the very least I should like to discuss it further with you at a later date, Mr Buchanan, when you are in Melbourne."

"It would be my pleasure," Buchanan replied.

The Count checked his fob watch and rose to his feet, signalling the end of the conversation.

"My carriage will arrive soon," he said. "I propose that we should join the ladies for the last of the evening."

"Excellent idea," said Buchanan, as the men all rose to follow the smiling Count into the sitting room.

At the sound of masculine footsteps approaching, Celeste hastily donned her shoes. All three ladies were seated and properly attentive when the gentlemen joined them.

The Count moved smoothly to his wife's side. "Ladies," he said. "Allow me to introduce a business associate, Mr Alec Buchanan."

Buchanan bowed to kiss Celeste's hand. "We met earlier, Comtesse," he said. "It is a pleasure to see you again."

"And this lady is our hostess, Mrs Seekamp, current editor of *The Ballarat Times*," the Count continued, enjoying the effect of this introduction.

"Delighted to meet you, Mrs Seekamp," said Buchanan, clearly startled.

"And her friend, Mrs Munro," said the Count.

"Charmed," said Buchanan, bowing again to hide his surprise. "Allow me to offer my condolences, Mrs Munro," he added.

"Thank you, sir," Morag said simply. "I appreciate that."

Buchanan hesitated. Caught off guard, he scarcely knew what to say at being introduced without warning to Duncan Munro's young and attractive widow, a woman he had never expected to meet, a woman he had so recently dispossessed. He felt a sudden, uncharacteristic need to make amends. "I understand you have a son," he said at last to cover his embarrassment.

"Yes, Mr Buchanan. My son Hector is not quite seven years old."

"It's a terrible thing for a boy so young to lose his father," Buchanan continued. "If there is ever anything I can do to help him, please do not hesitate to ask."

"That's kindly said," McGill remarked.

"It's kindly meant," Buchanan replied. "I am serious, Mrs Munro. Please do call on me if I can be of assistance to the boy."

Morag was overwhelmed. "Thank you," she managed to say. "That is very generous, sir."

"Not at all," said Buchanan, clearly relieved. "One helps where one can."

Mrs Parsons knocked lightly. "Excuse me," she said. "The carriage is here."

"Then we shall take our leave," said the Count. "Thank you, Mrs Seekamp, for a most delightful evening."

Celeste kissed Clara on both cheeks. "We will meet again," she said. "And I hope soon."

"As do I," said Clara.

Celeste kissed Morag too, before she turned and took her husband's arm.

"My dear," the Count said. "Shall we?"

As they walked from the room, Buchanan quickly moved to follow. "And I, too, will take my leave," he said. "It has been a pleasure to meet you all." He bowed, and let himself out of the sitting room by the guests' private door.

Clara relaxed. "Well, that was a most enjoyable evening," she said. "I'm glad you were all able to be here."

"And I trust," said McGill, "that you ladies will allow me to escort you home?"

"We'd be grateful for your company," Morag answered, comforted at the confirmation that McGill was to be her escort. "Crossing the diggings is so dangerous at night," she said. "And I will own that yesterday's events have made me more than a little nervous."

"Perfectly understandable," McGill said. "Don't worry—I'll see to it that you are safe."

Morag smiled. "Thank you," she said. "And you must know that Hector will be very pleased to see you too."

"And I him," McGill replied. "I confess I'm fond of the boy."

"If you've no objection, I'll walk with you," Ferguson said, grinning. "After such a dinner, the exercise will be most welcome."

"It will be a pleasure," Clara said happily, knowing that the smile she returned was not entirely innocent.

The evening air was still very warm, and the night sky was clear. McGill offered his arm to Morag, and Clara took Ferguson's as they set off in the direction of Clara's home. Above them, the myriad stars of the southern hemisphere were spread out in a blaze of glory: the Southern Cross burned clear and bright, and the radiant glow of the Milky Way was enough to light up the pathway. The new friends walked in companionable silence until Ferguson took up the thread of his earlier conversation.

"Are you still thinking of interviewing me, Mrs Seekamp?" he asked.

"Certainly I am," Clara replied.

"In that case, would tomorrow afternoon be convenient?"

"Most convenient. Perhaps you would care to join me for tea?"

"It will be my very great pleasure," Ferguson said. "I'll be sure to tell you all my secrets."

Clara laughed. "Not all, I hope, Lieutenant Ferguson," she said. "But I would be interested to hear about your adventures with the Indians. Captain McGill said you were wounded by an arrow."

"Indeed I was, Mrs Seekamp. I still have the scars. Perhaps you would like to verify the truth of them for *The Times*?"

"Now that is wicked, Lieutenant Ferguson," Clara said, grateful that the darkness hid the blush that now stained her cheeks.

"I'll bear that in mind," he replied, "when I show them to you."

It's been a long evening," Morag said. She leaned more closely as she walked beside McGill. "Thank you for being so solicitous, Captain McGill. I really appreciated it."

McGill smiled in the darkness, feeling protective towards her.

"The pleasure was all mine," McGill replied. "Truth be told, I was very glad you were there."

"And what did you make of Mr Buchanan?" Morag ventured.

"He's a sharp one," McGill replied. "But his offer to help Hector seemed genuine."

"I do hope so," Morag said. "But I should scarcely know how to go about asking for his help."

"I would be glad to speak to him on your behalf," McGill said, "if the occasion should arise, and if you feel I could be of assistance."

"Thank you," Morag replied. "That's kind of you."

"I know this is hard for Hector," McGill said. "I thought it would help him if I could find the priest who was there when his father died, but I've had no luck. The man seems to have disappeared."

"Thank you for trying," Morag said. "I really am grateful for your concern for us both. It means a great deal to me."

"I'll do whatever I can to help you," McGill said softly. "You must know that."

It was Hector who opened Clara's door the moment the adults arrived. His anxious face lit up with a smile when he saw that McGill was there.

"Were you waiting for me?" Morag asked.

"Not really," Hector said. "I just thought that you would be along soon."

"Hello, Hector," said McGill. He reached down to ruffle the boy's hair.

Hector shyly slipped his hand into McGill's. "Hello, sir," he said.

"It's good to see you, Hector," McGill replied. He squeezed the boy's hand, wishing he had more to offer the grieving child.

Clara interrupted the conversation. "Well, here we are," she said, a little too loudly. "I'll say goodnight."

"And I'll take my leave," said Ferguson. He glanced quickly at Clara, caught her almost imperceptible nod. "Good night, Mrs Munro, McGill."

"Good night, then," said McGill. "And thank you again, Mrs Seekamp, for a delightful evening."

"My pleasure, Captain McGill," Clara said. "I'll just go in ahead and check on the children. I'll leave you to say your goodnights."

As Clara went in, Morag turned back to McGill. "That wasn't very tactful," she said.

McGill smiled. "I daresay she only meant to give us a moment together. I'll say good night, and leave you to your son," he said. "Good night, Hector."

"Good night, sir."

"Good night, Captain McGill," Morag said. "Thank you again for everything: you've been a tower of strength through all of this ghastly business."

"Thank you ma'am," he replied. "And please, do call me James. As I said, I hope I may continue to be useful. May I call on you again, Mrs Munro?"

"I'd like that. And please do call me Morag."

"Morag, then." McGill smiled in the darkness, savouring her name. "Good night, Morag."

"Good night, James."

Chapter 14

Next morning, Morag found Clara sorting through her wardrobe. "Are you planning new clothes?" Morag asked.

"I don't know," Clara replied. "It's just that I felt so"—she hesitated, searching for the right word—"so *outdated* last night."

"I can't imagine that Melbourne has anything that might begin to compare with the fabric or the designs at Celeste de Chabrillan's disposal," said Morag.

"Perhaps not," Clara replied, "but I thought I might at least refurbish some of these in a more recent style."

"Are you planning more social occasions?" Morag asked.

"I don't know," Clara said again.

"You are simply restless," said Morag. "Nothing is yet settled about Henry, or *The Times*."

"You think I am just seeking a diversion?"

"Would that be so terrible?"

"No," said Clara. "I suppose not." She grinned at her friend. "In any case, Lieutenant Ferguson is willing to let me interview him. He's coming to tea today."

"That will be an interesting diversion, then, won't it?"

"I imagine so," said Clara.

"I'll make myself scarce, then," Morag said. "You'll hardly want Hector present."

"Thanks," said Clara. "He's been through enough, poor child." She smiled. "Did you really enjoy my little dinner?"

"Very much," said Morag. "I'll admit I was nervous, but everything went off very smoothly. It was a great success."

"Thank you," said Clara. "And now, you must tell me what you think of the Count and Countess."

"Celeste is lovely," said Morag. "And Lionel de Chabrillan is charming." She giggled. "But I can't help thinking that he looks like a short, ugly vampire."

75

"You've been reading Mrs Radcliffe's stories again," Clara replied, feigning severity, "or worse, Mr Le Fanu's tales."

Morag smiled. "You read them too," she said. "Everyone does."

Clara shrugged. "I may have glanced at them."

"In any case," said Morag, "I'll own that I've been reading that new book, *Feast of Blood*. The vampire is really quite sympathetic—he loathes his condition, poor thing—but he still preys on women." She put her hand defensively to her own throat.

"Morag, you constantly amaze me," Clara declared. "But yes, one has the impression that the Count's appetites are voracious." She thought for a moment. "I like him, though. He really doesn't care what anyone thinks of him. He has the woman of his dreams, and he can afford to be generous. I think the Comte and Celeste are very well matched."

"Indeed," said Morag. "They are very attentive to each other." She regarded her friend for a long moment before adding quietly: "And what about you, Clara? Is there a new man in your dreams?"

"I don't know what you're talking about," Clara replied.

"Do you not?" Morag said softly.

"If that's the case, I'm not the only one," Clara retorted. "Captain McGill was very considerate to you, and you didn't seem to object to his attentions."

"He's a kind, thoughtful man," Morag said. "But Clara, I've just buried Duncan. I'm grieving. It's far too soon for me to be thinking that way."

"It's never too soon," Clara replied. "We women have to be practical. You must consider your position. You have your boy to think about."

"Hector is all I *do* think about," said Morag. "But I don't have to be hasty: the house is paid for, and I'm sure the misunderstanding about the title will be cleared up. I have a little money put by to see me through until then."

"Well don't leave it too long," Clara said. "And if you like McGill, don't push him away."

"I know you're right," Morag said wearily. "I'm just not ready for another man—at least not yet."

Chapter 15

The sun had set and Morag had joined Clara in the sitting room when Oliver, Clara's eldest, rushed in. The boy was panting from exertion.

"Fire!" he gasped. "Mrs Munro's house is on fire."

Morag jumped to her feet.

"Are you sure?" said Clara.

"I ran all the way to tell you," Oliver replied. "The police are already there. They won't let anyone close. There were men with buckets of water, but the police said it couldn't be saved. They kept them away."

Clara exchanged a meaningful glance with Morag, who was already making for the door.

"Come on Hector," Morag said. "We must see for ourselves."

"It's not safe, Morag," Clara said.

"I know," Morag replied. "But I must go."

"Then I'll come with you," Clara said. She took her little pepperbox pistol from the sideboard and stuffed it into her skirt pocket. "There," she said, "I'm ready. And Oliver, you go and find Lieutenant Ferguson and Captain McGill. Tell them what's happening. We may need their help."

"Yes, Mum." Oliver was already on his way, his eyes shining with excitement.

Morag, Hector and Clara found themselves coughing from the acrid smoke as soon as they stepped out of doors. They could see the flames long before they reached what was left of Morag's house. It was just as Oliver had said: armed police ringed the burning building, threatening anyone who came close, deliberately letting the tinder-dry dwelling burn to the ground. It came as no surprise to Morag that the sergeant who had assaulted her was in charge.

He recognised her as she drew near, holding her son by the hand. "It seems you won't be moving back here after all," Sergeant Dunn said, his face a triumphant smirk. "These wood and canvas buildings burn so easily in this hot weather."

His meaning was clear, but Morag said nothing.

"And it seems your American friends aren't so much use after all," he added as McGill and Ferguson arrived, out of breath in the smoky air. "It seems the famous California Rangers are never there when you need them. They can't even put out a fire."

McGill stiffened at the insult.

Morag put a hand on his arm. "Don't react," she said. "He's looking for an excuse to shoot you down. Anyone can see he's been drinking."

"She's right," said Ferguson. "We should walk away. There's nothing we can do here."

"He as good as said he lit the fire himself," Clara whispered. "He knows there's nothing we can do."

"Not right here, not right now, perhaps," McGill said slowly.

"Leave it," said Ferguson. "Give him nothing." He took Clara's arm, and began to move away, shepherding her through the crowd.

"I need a minute more," Morag said.

McGill put a hand on her shoulder. "I'm right here," he said. "Take your time."

Morag nodded. She moved a step closer to the flames, feeling the heat on her face. Hand in hand with her son, she stood for a long moment, watching her future burn.

A little later, her face streaked with soot and tears, Morag walked slowly back to Clara's house with McGill. Hector was by her side, still trembling.

"I'm ruined, James," she said wearily. "I was relying on selling the house to keep myself afloat, financially that is."

"It's too soon to think like that," McGill replied. "The situation can still be made good. Once the business with the title is resolved, you can sell the land. The land is the greater part of the value of titles on these goldfields, and its price is going up all the time."

"But what if I can't get the title back?" said Morag.

"We'll cross that bridge when we come to it," McGill said firmly. "You should start with meeting the solicitors Ferguson was talking about: Curwin, Walker & Co, I believe he said."

"You're right, of course," Morag said. She straightened her shoulders. "I do have some small savings to tide me over."

"Forgive my asking," McGill said, "but is that all?"

Morag shook her head. "My husband had the deeds to a copper lease. He thought it would be valuable, but I couldn't find the papers when I looked through his things this morning. They weren't in his cash box with the receipt for the house. I thought he might have hidden them somewhere—he sometimes tucked things away under the floorboards. I was waiting until it was safe to go back to search…" She trailed off, dabbing at her tears with her handkerchief. "Everything happened so quickly."

"I know," McGill said. "And I'm sorry to say it, but if the papers burned with the house there's no way for you to claim your husband's lease for your son. Without the deeds to prove the claim, your case would be impossible."

"I feared as much," Morag said. She sighed heavily. "I suppose I'm just tired. Everything looks so hopeless right now."

McGill touched her hand. "If you'll forgive the American expression, my dear," he said, "you've had one hell of a week."

Morag smiled weakly.

"And you've been there to save me at every turn, James," she said. "You don't know how much I appreciate that."

"It's my pleasure, Morag," McGill replied. "I hope you know that."

In answer, Morag smiled up at him.

"Would you feel safer if I stay the night?" McGill asked.

He felt her hand tighten on his arm.

"I could sleep in the sitting room," he added hastily. "Any intruder would have to get past me."

"That's very kind, James," she answered. "But I've imposed on you enough for one day." She sighed. "That disgusting sergeant has had his revenge on me. I'm sure Hector and I can sleep safe in our beds tonight."

"If you're sure," said McGill. He did not voice his thought that Dunn's revenge had not yet extended to himself. He knew, in his heart, that the man had marked him out for some future unpleasantness. He was not particularly concerned. He could fend for himself. Right now it was Morag and her son that he wanted to protect.

"I'm sure," Morag replied. "When we get back to Clara's house I just want to clean up and go to bed."

"We're almost there," said McGill. "I'll just walk you to the door, and take my leave."

"Thank you, James. Shall I see you tomorrow?"

"I'll look in on you in the morning," said McGill. "Just to be sure everything is under control." He bent down and patted the boy on the shoulder. "You did well today, Hector," he said. "Look after your mother."

"I will, sir," Hector replied.

As they reached Clara's door they met Ferguson, who was just leaving.

"I'll say goodnight, then," said Morag.

"Good night," both men responded.

"I was planning to take a stroll around the area," Ferguson said. "Care to join me, McGill?"

"Excellent idea," McGill responded. "I was thinking the exact same thing."

The two men set off in silence, walking slowly along narrow paths where lamplight spilled through open windows or threw up shadows in thin canvas tents. Smoke from the house fire hung so heavily in the night air that the murmur of domestic conversation was punctuated by coughs and sneezes.

"No sign of Dunn's men," Ferguson said at last. "We've walked a full circle. I figure it's safe enough for the women and children now. I guess I'll bid you good night."

"Good night, Charles," said McGill. "I'll no doubt see you tomorrow." As he turned for home, McGill smiled to see that despite the drifting smoke the low hills of the district still showed as a black outline in the pale moonlight, as if to mark the border of this fragile human settlement, so tiny in the vastness of the untamed Australian landscape.

Morag was soon asleep, exhausted by the events of the day. But Hector lay wakeful on his camp bed, afraid to go to sleep, afraid of the nightmares he knew would come. He lay quite still as the hours passed, careful not to wake his mother. And so it was that he saw Ferguson, silhouetted by moonlight, slip silently into Clara's room.

Chapter 16

Christmas that year was a subdued affair. Morag and Clara had done their best to create a festive meal, despite the food shortages and high temperatures, but nothing seemed quite right.

"This is when you notice the difference most, isn't it?" Clara said, perspiring as she lifted a boiled pudding in its calico cloth from its pot of steaming water. "The mercury was showing one hundred and five degrees, last time I looked—I made a note of it for my paper." She patted her face with a damp handkerchief. "A heat wave at Christmas reminds me like nothing else that I'm a long way from home."

"I've been thinking of home too," Morag replied, dishing mushy greens into a serving bowl. "But then, Scotland can be so very bleak at this time of year. I can't say I miss those winter winds."

"At least there you can sit around a fire and get warm," Clara said. "It's so hard to find a way to cool down."

"True," Morag replied. She straightened her tired back, and mopped her brow. "I must admit I'm glad the cooking is done."

"And I'm glad we had the good sense to go to the midnight mass," said Clara. "The church will be stifling today."

"I'm afraid the service was a struggle for poor Hector," Morag said. "He still won't go anywhere near the priests."

"He'll come around," Clara said. "Give him time."

The meal was ready, and the women had changed from caps and aprons into lighter clothing when McGill arrived in company with Ferguson.

"Whew!" said Ferguson, by way of greeting. "I haven't been this hot since I crossed the desert at the Humboldt Sink, on my way to the Californian diggings." He collapsed dramatically into the nearest chair, and sat fanning his face with his hat.

Clara laughed. "In that case, let me give you a cool drink. I doubt they had lemonade out in the Californian desert."

"Indeed they did not!" Ferguson accepted the proffered glass and saluted his hostess. "Merry Christmas, everyone!"

Morag poured a glass of lemonade for McGill, who was still standing, holding an armload of packages.

"These are for all of you," McGill said, handing a large paper bag to Oliver. "You're the eldest: you can share them out."

The children clustered around, immediately disappointed to discover that the boiled sweets had turned into sticky, sugary lumps in the heat.

"Sorry," said McGill, watching with amusement as Clara's youngest son attempted to prise red and white striped bulls-eyes apart with a spoon.

"Never mind, William" said Clara. "They'll taste just the same."

William seemed unconvinced, but kept trying anyway.

Hector's eyes widened as he unwrapped his own gift. "A riding crop," he said. "Thank you."

"My pleasure," said McGill. "Since I'm teaching you to ride, you should have a crop of your own."

Morag smiled at McGill. "It's very kind of you."

"He'll be a good rider," McGill replied. "He's a natural in the saddle."

"I'm sure he will," Clara said distractedly.

"Is something wrong?" Ferguson asked.

"She's had some bad news, I'm afraid," said Morag.

"It's Henry," said Clara. "They've moved him to the Melbourne Gaol. The authorities really are planning to try him for sedition. They've set a trial date in the New Year: the twenty-third of January." She shrugged. "I always thought he'd be home for Christmas."

"Is there nothing to be done?" McGill asked.

"Other than engaging a decent Melbourne lawyer, I'd say no," Ferguson replied.

"He didn't actually write the anti-government articles himself, did he?" McGill asked.

"No, but he published them," Clara replied. "And besides, all the posters for the miners' meeting were printed at *The Times*."

"And is that everything?"

"Not entirely," Clara said. "*The Times'* other journalist, John Manning, was arrested at the stockade as well. He will stand trial later with the miners." She shrugged. "So when it comes to Henry's own trial, we'll just have to wait and see how things turn out."

"Well," said Ferguson, "at least McGill and I can look in on him for you. We are planning to ride to Melbourne early in the New Year to conduct some business with the redoubtable Mr Train, so we can certainly visit Mr Seekamp."

"And we can arrange for whatever he needs," McGill added.

"Oh, thank you," Clara said, smiling at last. "It will be a relief to know how he is coping. I've heard terrible stories about the Melbourne Gaol."

Chapter 17

It was the end of the first week of the New Year when McGill and Ferguson set off on the long ride to Melbourne, leading two pack-horses behind their own high-stepping mounts. They had planned to take the trip in easy stages, riding out early in the hope of reaching wooded country before the heat of the summer's day became unbearable.

On the outskirts of the town they passed a makeshift Aboriginal camp—a few rough shelters made of curved bark. In the centre of the clearing was a smoking fire. The few people who were about were wary: they watched, but did not speak to the horsemen. A pile of freshly scraped fur and animal remains lay nearby, where the night before a kangaroo had obviously been laid to roast on the hot coals.

"It's as good a cooking method as any," Ferguson said, gesturing at the heap of leftovers where a skinny cur was circling, trying to sneak a bite. A bare-breasted woman, almost as thin herself as the starveling dog, shooed it away. Ferguson affected not to notice her. "It saves a lot of fuss if you clean the skin off after the meat is done," he added.

"If you say so," McGill replied. "I prefer my meat properly butchered first." He paused to wave at a little group of pot-bellied children who had now appeared, wide-eyed and naked as the day they were born, to peep from behind a scrubby wattle tree at the passing strangers. "Kids are the same the world over," he said. "But I hate to see them living like this."

"I daresay they're happy enough, poor little beggars," Ferguson said. "The best thing we can do for them is to leave them alone. They're much better at surviving in this land than we are."

"True enough," McGill replied. "But I can't imagine why they'd want to hang around the goldfields. There's nothing for them here."

Ferguson shrugged. "Maybe it's their land in the first place," he said. "But as to why they stay, your guess is as good as mine."

"The native troopers seem contented enough, though," McGill said.

"They're good men," Ferguson replied. "Better men than any of the rabble that Rede dredged up to do his dirty work. Not that he appreciates them—I hear they're paid less than the others."

"Why does that not surprise me?" McGill said.

Ferguson's grin was wry. "We've all just had a hard lesson in colonial politics, James," he said. "Come on: best we pick up our pace. We need to make the spring in good time."

For answer, McGill urged his horse to a faster trot, and the men rode on in comfortable silence until, at mid-morning, they arrived at the edge of the goldfields. They dismounted to lead their horses through the treacherous maze of abandoned diggings. There was no shade here, but the men were heading for a well-known waterhole, a clear-water spring surrounded by high rocks.

"There," said Ferguson, shading his eyes against the glare. "I caught the glint of sun on water. This way, I think."

"Good," McGill replied, leading his horses in single file behind Ferguson as they threaded their way between boulders. "I could use a drink myself."

Minutes later they found the spring. As they rounded the jagged rocks a flock of startled white cockatoos flew up, shrieking their alarm to the skies. And then a mob of wallabies scattered, bounding away easily over the rocky terrain.

McGill laughed. "It's late in the day for wallabies to be grazing," he said. He poked with his boot at the scant grass that grew around the waterhole.

"They were probably just lying in the shade of the overhang," Ferguson replied. "They like to stay close to water in this heat."

"I know how they feel," said McGill. "But I guess we'd best get on with it." He started towards the water.

"Hold on a minute," Ferguson said. He began methodically stamping his feet, and kept stomping heavily until a darkly banded snake slithered away from the water's edge to disappear among the rocks.

McGill saw the flash of sunlight on its cream underbelly as it slid into a crevice. "Thanks," he said. "I didn't see it."

"I just caught the shine of it," Ferguson said. "Tiger snakes are bad news. I always check for them near waterholes."

"Their venom must be horribly powerful," said McGill. "One of the diggers told me they are more deadly than cobras."

"That wouldn't surprise me," Ferguson said. "I never heard of anyone who survived a bite from a tiger snake."

McGill shuddered. "Sometimes I think that everything in this country is dangerous," he said.

"Not everything," Ferguson replied. "Just most things."

The men drank and refilled their water bottles before letting the horses drink, muddying the edges of the waterhole. Everything was still and quiet except for the drone of summer cicadas and the contented sounds of drinking horses. Ferguson stood, loosely holding the reins of all four mounts while McGill walked a little way apart into the rocks, intending to relieve himself.

A pistol cracked behind the two men, and McGill felt the sharp wind of the shot that barely missed his shoulder. In one smooth motion he turned, drew his Colt, and fired.

Sergeant Dunn toppled forward onto the hot ground, stone dead: he had been shot cleanly through the heart.

Ferguson lowered his own pistol. "That's torn it," he said.

"What the hell was he doing here?" said McGill. "I thought it was a bushranger ambush. I thought it was a robbery."

"It was an ambush all right," Ferguson replied. "But it wasn't for robbery. Dunn has been stalking us, ever since that incident with Mrs Munro. He wanted us both dead."

"I know," said McGill. "But I never expected he'd try something like this."

Ferguson tucked his pistol away and walked towards the body. "Look," he said, pointing. "The man had a second single-shot pistol, and a bayonet. He must have thought he could shoot one of us in the back and pick off the other from the cover of those rocks." He smiled grimly. "He reckoned without your reflexes."

"Too good, I'm afraid," said McGill. "It would have been better if I had just wounded him."

"Maybe, maybe not," said Ferguson. "Who knows what lie he would have told to have us locked up? We Americans are not exactly favourites with the British command. We'd have been easy prey in custody, unarmed and chained." He spat on the ground. "Dunn has killed that way before. I warned Clara that I saw him bayoneting prisoners at the stockade."

"But how did he come to be here, just waiting for us?"

"We made no real secret of our plans to ride out today," Ferguson said slowly. "We bought our supplies at the general store yesterday morning. It wouldn't have been hard to guess which way we would take. Every rider heads for this spring. It's the last reliable water for miles."

"He must have camped here overnight, then," said McGill.

"Probably," Ferguson agreed. "That's the most likely explanation."

"I guess we'll never know," said McGill. He turned the body over with his boot. "Faugh!" he said. "The man reeks of strong drink."

"Probably helped him to mess up his shot," said Ferguson.

"He wouldn't have needed any help to miss me with *that* pistol," McGill replied. "You couldn't hit a barn door at close range with that thing."

"Whatever the reason," Ferguson said, "he's left us with a problem. The hunt will be up when his superiors find he's missing."

"Dead," McGill corrected.

"Just missing, I think," Ferguson said. "The man's a drunkard. Nobody will be surprised that he's wandered off into the diggings. Men fall down mineshafts all the time."

"The bullet hole will suggest it wasn't an accident," McGill said morosely.

"True, but he might never be found," Ferguson replied. "Look around, McGill. Dunn chose this place because it's isolated. He knew we would stop here to water the horses, and he knew this particular water hole is surrounded by piles of rocks and mullock heaps for him to hide behind."

"Obviously," said McGill.

"Yes. But it gives *us* the advantage now. This part of the diggings has been thoroughly worked out: there are derelict shafts everywhere. It's treacherous ground."

"What are you saying?"

"I propose that we strip off the sergeant's uniform—it's the only thing that identifies him—then drop him deep into a disused mineshaft. If he isn't found quickly he might never be discovered. In this heat, he won't last long. If the body is found later, it won't be recognised."

McGill was sceptical. "But surely his men will search around the diggings."

"Yes, but I don't think they will come this far. There's no reason to suppose that anyone would look for Dunn out here. They'll be searching closer to the barracks and the hotels." He paused, considering, then added: "Dunn was not a popular man. He bullied his men. My guess is that his underlings will be relieved when he doesn't come back. They won't search too hard."

"And how do we get rid of the clothes?"

"We burn them," Ferguson said decisively. "We search for his campsite, and we burn his gear, we get rid of everything. We'll throw his weapons down another shaft. It will be as if he was never here."

"I don't know that I'm comfortable with all this," McGill said. "I could always just go back and tell the truth: that I shot in self-defence, that I didn't know the attacker was Sergeant Dunn."

"It's a noble thought," Ferguson replied, "but it would be suicide. You'd hang, even if you lived long enough in prison to make it to trial."

"You're probably right," McGill conceded. "So what do you suggest? Everyone knows we are on our way to Melbourne. Should we deal with Dunn and just head on as planned?"

"I think so, yes."

"Well," McGill said, grimacing, "let's at least get on with this part."

The two men bent to the task, removing Dunn's uniform as they talked.

"He's a heavy lump of a man," Ferguson said. "Even dead he's a nuisance."

"Heavy work," McGill agreed. "But, as you say, necessary." As he pulled off the sergeant's trousers, his face twisted with distaste. "Even the thought of this dirty, flabby old body touching that beautiful young woman makes my skin crawl," he said. "It's disgusting."

"Everything about the man is repulsive," Ferguson agreed. "He stinks." He tugged at the jacket. "What's this?" He plucked a folded paper from the breast pocket. "Let's see." He smoothed the paper and read:

Camp Ballarat
Jan 5th 1855

To Sergeant Dunn,

In view of your deposition sworn this day before him, to the effect that you recognised James McGill as the man who fired upon Private Boyle of the 40th Regiment at Eureka on Dec 3rd, with fatal effect, Stipendiary Magistrate Mr. Hackett has this day issued a warrant for the apprehension of said James McGill. You will advise your men accordingly, and take such steps as are necessary to bring McGill before Mr. Hackett to answer the charge.

(signed) C.J. Carter
Sub-Inspector of Police

Ferguson handed the note to McGill. "That lying son-of-a-bitch," he said. "Here's your answer, McGill. This is Dunn's ticket to take a free shot at you, at both of us. It's dated yesterday. He must have gone straight to Carter when he learned of our plans."

McGill read. "But Carter would know this isn't true," he said, handing back the letter. "It's common knowledge that I was away from the stockade with the Rangers when the action occurred," he added bitterly.

"Yes," Ferguson agreed, "but even if Carter was sure the man was lying, he couldn't ignore a deposition: he would still have the magistrate issue the warrant so that the matter could be officially dismissed."

"Meanwhile," said McGill, "we both get killed resisting arrest. That's neat. Dunn gets his revenge, and he's home clear."

"As you say," said Ferguson, "this evil brute planned to get away with two more murders. It's a good job you shot him first."

"I should have killed him more slowly," McGill replied through gritted teeth.

The grisly task was finally completed. All traces of Dunn had been erad-
icated: red-and-black bull ants were already busily reclaiming the tumbled
spoil from the mineshaft for their nest. McGill and Ferguson sat resting by the
waterhole, still discussing McGill's escape.

"We'll have to get you out of the country now. You'll be the prime suspect,"
Ferguson was saying. Absently, he brushed dirt from the knees of his trousers.
"And don't forget that Commissioner Rede is looking for a way to strike back
at you. This would give him the perfect excuse."

"I know," McGill said. "Should we still ride straight for Melbourne?"

"Too risky," Ferguson replied. "If Dunn is declared missing, the authorities
will want to question you. We'll be stopped on the way."

"But Melbourne is my only real hope," said McGill. "Consul Tarleton had
an escape plan in place for me after the uprising. But it involves leaving from
Melbourne."

"Will the plan still hold?" Ferguson asked.

"If I can get to George Train, yes," said McGill. "He is authorized to arrange
passage for me on a ship sailing from Port Melbourne. It will look like just
another one of his many business dealings with the American government."

"Then the best way for you to reach Melbourne undetected would be to
travel by ship from Geelong," said Ferguson. "That way you would arrive at
the port, where you need to be."

"It sounds like you have it all worked out."

"Not really: we still have to figure out how to get you to Geelong."
Ferguson suddenly grinned mischievously. "I've got it," he said. "You'll need
a disguise. And I know just the thing."

"I'm not going to like this, am I?" said McGill.

"Maybe not," Ferguson replied. "But I guarantee it will work."

"Go on."

"We'll slip back into town tonight, borrow some clothes from Clara and
Morag, and dress you as a woman," Ferguson said, trying not to laugh. "Then
you can simply take the early morning coach to Geelong and board a ship
from there to Melbourne—as any lady would."

"No," said McGill.

Chapter 18

Late that night the two men approached the outskirts of the Bakery Hill settlement. They tethered their horses in a copse of tall gum trees near the outer path. The night air was heavy with the smell of eucalyptus. Above them, a koala grunted loudly, announcing his presence, claiming territory.

Ferguson laughed. "Best you wait here, McGill," he said. "Stay under cover. I'll walk the rest of the way to Clara's house, and I'll be back with a change of clothes for you as quick as I can."

"I have to come with you," said McGill.

"Why? It's really not safe."

"I must at least bid farewell to Morag," McGill replied softly. "We have an understanding. I can't just disappear."

"Oh," said Ferguson. He thought for a moment. "In that case," he said, "there's nothing else for it. At least let me go on ahead. I can alert you if there's any sign of trouble."

"Thanks," McGill said. "Let's do it."

McGill and Ferguson reached Clara's house without incident. The children were in bed, and, except for Hector, were all sound asleep. Clara and Morag were sitting companionably in the parlour, Clara sewing and Morag reading another of her favourite gothic stories by lamplight when Ferguson arrived unannounced.

Clara sprang to her feet. "Is something wrong?" she asked.

"Is James alright?" said Morag.

Ferguson put a finger to his lips. "Yes," he said very quietly. "He is—at least for now. But he needs your help."

Morag dropped her voice to an urgent whisper: "What is it?" she asked.

"Best he should tell you that himself," Ferguson replied as McGill slipped

91

into the room to stand beside his friend.

Morag ran to him, searching his face for an explanation.

McGill took both of her hands in his. "I have to go away for a while, my dear," he said simply. "I need to return to America. It's urgent."

"But…"

"He's been falsely accused of a shooting," Ferguson said softly. "And after the stockade, it's not safe for him to stay here to try to clear his name."

"It's more than that," McGill said slowly. "I've been thinking it over, and I believe I can trust you three. Telling you this will mean that I entrust you with my life. I beg you will not betray me."

Clara could not contain her curiosity. "What is it?" she asked.

"I think that Ferguson has guessed already," McGill replied. "So I might as well own that I have been acting for the American authorities to take care of our citizens on the diggings."

"Which explains why the Consul spent so much time with you," said Ferguson.

"So why is that dangerous?" Morag wanted to know. "It seems a perfectly reasonable thing to do."

"In itself, yes," McGill replied. "But it was also in my brief to steer the miners towards democracy," he said, "should the opportunity arise. I helped the Reform League to draft its Declaration."

"Ah," said Ferguson. "That part of the resolution that says *that it is the inalienable right of every citizen to have a voice in making the laws he is called on to obey, that taxation without representation is tyranny,*" he said, quoting verbatim. "I thought that sounded familiar."

"And the meeting's resolution to secede from the Empire if the situation did not improve?" Morag asked.

"That too," said McGill.

"Then it's clear that you cannot risk being brought before a magistrate," said Clara. "You would certainly be tried for sedition if this came to light. If Henry is to be tried just for printing the Declaration, you definitely would not be safe."

"Nor would he be safe in prison," Ferguson added. "He's not a British citizen: he has fewer rights here than your husband. And besides, we've been warned that Commissioner Rede is looking for any excuse to be rid of McGill—that Scottish businessman, Buchanan, said as much when he joined us after Clara's dinner."

"So how can we help?" Clara asked, as usual getting straight to the point.

McGill looked uncomfortable.

"I plan to disguise him as a woman," Ferguson said. "We need to borrow some clothes."

Clara put her hand to her mouth, stifling her giggles.

Morag looked firmly at the floor. "Do you think it can work?" she asked at last. "He's big for a woman."

"He'll be fine as long as no one looks too closely," Ferguson said. "The plan has the virtue of being unexpected."

"It certainly has that," McGill said ruefully.

"Come on, then, Mr Ferguson," Clara said. "You can help me find some suitable clothes." She gave Morag a very straight look. "We'll leave you two in private to say your farewells."

Ferguson took the hint and ushered Clara out of the room.

They had scarcely left when Hector emerged from the bedroom, wide-eyed in the lamplight. He smiled to see McGill.

Morag spoke softly. "Captain McGill has to go away for a while, Hector. He came to say goodbye."

Hector's lower lip trembled. "You can't," he said.

"I must," McGill replied.

Hector ran to McGill, who hugged him fiercely.

"I'll miss you," McGill said. "You must know I would never willingly abandon you. But these things are not always in our power to control." He straightened up. "You will look after your mother, won't you?"

"Yes, sir."

"And will you do one more thing for me?"

Hector nodded.

"Will you take care of my horse?" McGill said. "Make sure he is properly curry-combed and exercised?"

Hector nodded again. "Yes," he managed to say.

"Good," said McGill. "Sunny is yours, then. I'm sure Lieutenant Ferguson will continue with your riding lessons."

"It's too much," Morag said. "That's too valuable an animal to give to a child."

"Nonsense," McGill replied. "The boy needs a horse, and Sunny is a fine mount. I wouldn't want him sold off. He'll serve Hector well."

"If you're sure then," Morag said. "Hector, say thank you."

"Thank you, sir."

"And now you must run along to bed, Hector," McGill said kindly. "I need to speak to your mother."

Hector did not want to go, but he could not refuse. "Good night, sir," he said, trying hard not to cry, at least not before he reached the safety of his own bed.

"Good night, Hector. You'll see me again, I promise."

McGill drew Morag aside. "We don't have much time," he said. "This is for you." He pressed a small calico drawstring bag into her hand.

"What is it?"

"Gold," said McGill. "The largest of the nuggets is enough to be melted down and made into a ring for you," he added. "I had hoped to have it done myself as a surprise for you. The rest should keep you afloat until your affairs are settled. And please, do take all of the things left in my lodgings. Ferguson will fetch them for you. They may be of some use."

Morag looked up at him, her eyes shining with unshed tears.

He bent to kiss her.

She hesitated.

"I know this may be too soon," McGill said. "But Morag, you must know how I feel about you."

She nodded. "I feel the same way," she whispered. "Perhaps I shouldn't—but I do."

McGill took her in his arms, and this time she did not resist his kiss.

When at last they drew apart she said: "You will be careful, won't you James?"

"I'll be very careful." He smiled sadly. "After all, I have you to come back for."

"Of course you have," she replied. "Always."

"And Morag," he said seriously, "I want you to promise me that if you need financial help you'll go to Buchanan. He will honour his pledge to help Hector, if you ask him."

Morag looked doubtful. "Are you sure?" she said.

"I'm certain. He won't go back on his word, freely given before the Comte de Chabrillan and all the company that evening."

"Then I'll keep it in mind," Morag said.

"One last thing," McGill said softly, "before the others come back." From inside his shirt he withdrew a small, leather-bound volume, warm from contact with his skin. "I know you like to read," he said. "This is my favourite. I had it in my saddle bag for the journey to Melbourne."

Morag read the title: "*Lyrical Ballads*," she said.

"Romantic poetry for a beautiful lady," McGill replied gallantly. "Read it and think of me."

"I'll always think of you," Morag said. "Thank you, James: it means a lot to me to have something that you hold dear as a keepsake."

"Ahem," said Ferguson, coughing theatrically in the doorway. "It's time you were dressed, McGill."

Chapter 19

"**T**hese are the best I could find," Clara said. She held out a black skirt, a bonnet, a brightly coloured shawl and a parasol. "I thought you should wear your own shirt, McGill: your shoulders are too broad for anything Morag or I own."

"Or I could unpick the stitching on something," Morag said. "James could cover it with the shawl."

"Better his own shirt," said Ferguson, "in case the shawl should slip."

McGill scowled at him. "Don't enjoy this too much," he said.

"I wouldn't dream of it," Ferguson replied, grinning from ear to ear.

McGill climbed into the skirt, pulling it on over his trousers and boots and tucking in his shirt.

"That looks a bit bulky," Clara said sceptically.

"Then I'll be a fat lady," McGill replied. "I'm not going without trousers. I might have to run for it."

"True," said Ferguson. "Here, let's try the bonnet and shawl."

Morag adjusted the shawl for him. "Not bad," she said at last. "You could just about pass, but you'd better stay out of bright light."

"What about the pistol?" Clara asked. "That's not ladylike."

McGill hitched up the skirt and tucked the Colt firmly into the waistband of his trousers. "I'm not going anywhere unarmed," he said. "And before you ask, my knife is in my boot."

"Any man who makes advances is in for a surprise, then," Ferguson said.

McGill was aghast. "That's not to be thought of," he said.

"No, I suppose not." Ferguson was suddenly all business. "And we have stayed too long. We must be on our way."

"Farewell, then," said McGill. He kissed Clara's hand: "Thank you for all your help," he said. He turned to embrace Morag. "One last time," he said, kissing her lightly. "Never doubt I'll return for you as soon as I may."

"Goodbye, James," said Morag. "Go well, and come back safe."

95

As the two men reached the door, Ferguson turned back. "Remember, we were never here tonight," he said.

"Of course you weren't," Clara replied.

"And if anyone should ask, all you know is that McGill set off for Melbourne. You haven't heard from him since."

"Which will be true," said Morag.

"But how will you account for your being back here so soon?" Clara asked.

"I doubt anybody will notice. But if someone should happen to enquire, I'll just say that circumstances changed and McGill has gone on ahead," Ferguson said. "I'll set out again tomorrow, to conduct my business as planned. Nothing should look amiss. Good night, ladies."

The men disappeared into the darkness outside, leaving Morag and Clara alone in the house once more.

"Well, that's upsetting news and no mistake," Clara said at last. "I'll never be able to go straight to sleep. Shall I make us a pot of tea?"

"I think you should," said Morag. She sank back into her chair. "I feel as though my whole world has just turned upside down again."

"That's because it has," Clara replied, heading for the kitchen.

McGill's journey to Melbourne was uneventful. He kept to the corner of the coach as it jolted its way along the rutted track that passed for a main road, shading his face with Clara's bonnet. The road was busy, though most of the traffic was heading the other way: there were always new recruits travelling towards the goldfields, eager to try their luck. McGill saw that many of them were on foot, some heavily laden, one or two pushing wheelbarrows bristling with picks and shovels. The luckier ones travelled on horseback, or rode in the supply drays.

A woman sitting on the bench beside McGill looked about nervously when a flock of black cockatoos flew up, screeching, disturbed by the coach as it passed through a dense patch of tall eucalypts. "I've heard there are bushrangers active in these parts," she said, to nobody in particular.

The fat man sitting opposite fished in his trouser pocket and came up with a small pepperbox pistol. "Don't worry, ladies: I'll protect you all!" he said. He smelled strongly of sweat and beer, and he waved the pistol about, smiling amiably and including McGill in his offer.

"Most kind, sir," the woman said.

McGill said nothing. The man was clearly more of a threat to himself and his fellow passengers than to any highwayman.

One or two of the other coach travellers made sporadic attempts at conversation, but when McGill did not respond with anything more than a nod or a smile they assumed he did not speak English—a common enough situation on the polyglot goldfields. He was soon left to himself.

At Geelong, McGill paid for his steamer ticket and boarded the ship unnoticed. He remained solitary as it made its way to Port Melbourne.

George Train was as good as his word: by next morning McGill was aboard the sailing ship *Arabia*, waiting for the tide and San Francisco-bound. He stood at the rail, watching the dolphins that sported in the bay, watching the fledgling city of Melbourne slip into the salt-hazed distance: the ships at the makeshift pier, the tent-city at Emerald Hill, the campfires and wood-and-canvas huts of Sandridge. His heart was heavy. He'd become fond of this strange, alien place. He longed to stay, to protect Morag and Hector, but knew he could not. He was determined that he would return, but had no idea when or how that might be.

Chapter 20

Some ten days later, the long spell of hot weather broke. Heavy black clouds rolled in, thunder boomed, and a sudden downpour turned the dusty diggings to mud. The baked clay of Ballarat's streets ran rivulets of dirty water that pooled in cracks and crevices, and everywhere people scrambled to shore up sagging canvas roofs that filled, bellied, then overflowed, bucketing rainwater down upon the hapless inhabitants.

Morag was busy setting out pots and buckets and basins to catch the drips from Clara's leaking tin roof when Clara came in, shaking out her hair.

"It's miserable out there," she said. "I've had to leave my coat and umbrella in the scullery. They're dripping. But at least the rain has laid the dust."

"I count that a blessing," Morag replied. "Hector has been coughing horribly this last week. And besides, the rain won't last long—it never does. Did you really need to go out in it?"

"I had to collect the post," Clara replied. "I'm hoping for something from Henry." She paused. "There's a letter for you," she added, looking inquisitively at the slightly damp envelope she now held out to Morag. "I wonder what it can be—this is the stationery of The Prince Albert Hotel."

"There's only one way to find out," said Morag. She broke the seal and read quickly.

"Good heavens," she said. "It's from Mr Buchanan."

"What does he want?"

"He is here, in Ballarat. You are right about the notepaper: he is staying at Mrs Parson's hotel. He asks if he might call upon me."

"Then invite him here to tea tomorrow afternoon," Clara said promptly. "The weather will have cleared by then. One of the boys can take your note across to the hotel." She paused, considering. "I wonder if this is about Hector," she added.

"We'll know soon enough," Morag replied.

99

By the following afternoon the sun was shining once more, and the air was warm and steamy. The tea things were laid out in Clara's parlour, which had been quickly set to rights once the deluge stopped. There had been a minor upset when Clara's eldest son swooped upon an enormous huntsman spider sheltering under the table: Oliver had knocked over a chair in his effort to catch it. The hairy spider had scuttled away, but it had eventually been seized and evicted. The furniture had now been restored to its proper place, and the aroma of fresh-baked scones wafted from beneath the delicately embroidered cloth that covered them.

Morag sat nervously twisting her handkerchief as the two women awaited their guest.

Buchanan was punctual: he knocked at Clara's door at precisely three o'clock, and stood carefully wiping his muddy boots on the mat.

"Good afternoon, Mr Buchanan," Clara said, ushering him into the front room.

Morag rose to meet him.

"Mrs Munro," he said, bowing very slightly. "It's good of you to receive me."

"Not at all, Mr Buchanan. Do sit down."

Clara busied herself pouring tea, scarcely able to contain her curiosity.

Buchanan accepted a scone, spreading it thickly with plum jam. He bit into it and smiled appreciatively at his hostess. "You've a lighter touch than the redoubtable Mrs Parsons," he said.

"That's Mrs Munro's baking," Clara replied. "I can't take the credit for it."

"Excellent," Buchanan said. "And now, if you will forgive me, Mrs Munro, I'll come straight to the point of my visit."

"I'd appreciate that, Mr Buchanan," Morag said.

"Well," said Buchanan, "you will recall that I offered my services in the matter of your son when you and I were introduced at The Prince Albert Hotel."

"Indeed I do, sir," Morag replied. "It was most kindly done."

"And as I am a man of honour, Mrs Munro, I am here to discuss the furtherance of that matter. I should perhaps explain that I chanced to meet Lieutenant Ferguson last week, at the establishment of Mr George Train, the American importer. And in the course of the conversation I enquired after your health, and subsequently learned that you have experienced further difficulties: the fire that destroyed your home, and the legal complications that surround that property."

"You are very well informed, sir," Morag said warily.

"I'm a man of business, Mrs Munro," Buchanan replied. "Information is my stock in trade." He cleared his throat. "I had, in any case, to return to the diggings this week to negotiate a different matter, so I took the opportunity to enquire into the availability of schools for your son."

"Oh," Morag gasped.

"I intend that I should provide for his education," said Buchanan, "at least for the present, until your prospects are more settled."

"That's more than generous, sir."

"To that end, I have had my agents investigate the schools in Melbourne, and I have to say that although you and I are both of the Catholic faith, I have little trust in the schooling provided by Irish priests: their own educational standard is so poor. But we are both also Scottish, and it transpires that the Presbyterian community has brought from Scotland an accomplished teacher to take charge of their Academy. The Scotch College, as it is known, is flourishing under its headmaster, a Mr Robert Lawson. It is there that I intend, with your permission, to enrol your son."

Morag had not expected this. "I don't know what to say," she offered at last.

"You have time to think about it," Buchanan replied. "Your son can be enrolled at any time."

"It's not that, Mr Buchanan," Morag replied. "I just can't think of any way that Hector could live in Melbourne."

"My apologies, Mrs Munro," Buchanan said. "I had meant to say that there is a boarding house near to the College, run by a Mrs Macbeth. I shall be happy to pay for Hector to be housed there during term time."

Still Morag hesitated, but said nothing. The silence became uncomfortable.

"Is there something wrong?" Buchanan asked at last.

Clara spoke up. "I know it isn't my place to interfere," she said, "but Mrs Munro has recently been taking stock of her own position."

"Thank you, Clara," Morag said, giving her friend a stern look. She braced herself, deciding that her only path at this juncture was to reveal her actual situation. "I'm sorry, Mr Buchanan," she said, "but the truth is that I fear will not be able to stay here in Ballarat beyond Mr Seekamp's return. I expect that I shall have to seek a suitable position in Melbourne, perhaps as a governess or housekeeper." She looked down at her hands. "And I find it difficult to arrange my son's future when I am so very uncertain as to my own."

"Bravely said," Buchanan replied. "I applaud your honesty." He thought for a moment. "In that case," he said, "allow me to offer you a different proposition."

"And what would that be?" said Clara, interfering yet again.

"I myself will soon be in need of a new housekeeper," he said, "when Mrs Mosley leaves my employ to join her daughter on a sheep station in New South

Wales. We have yet to settle on a date for her departure. And so, Mrs Munro, if you would care to consider taking up that position, we could solve all of your difficulties at once. I shall offer you a small stipend, together with your room and board. I can assure you that you will find it a well-run household."

"May I ask what the accommodations are?" Morag said.

"Certainly you may. My new Melbourne house is quite spacious. Mrs Mosley has a comfortable bedroom and a sitting room on the ground floor, and there is a box room opposite that could be fitted with a bed for your son. I think, Mrs Munro, that you would be happier to have him close to you."

"Yes, indeed," Morag replied. "He has yet to recover from the death of his father." She hesitated, then added: "There's one more thing, Mr Buchanan."

"Yes?"

"There's the matter of Hector's horse."

"Your son has his own horse?"

"Not exactly: it's just that Captain McGill was recently obliged to return to America, on urgent family business, and he gave his white stallion, Sunny, to Hector to take care of. Lieutenant Ferguson is teaching my son to ride."

"I see," said Buchanan. He smiled. "And would you have any objection to stabling McGill's horse with my own? I'm sure my groom would oblige by continuing your son's riding lessons. Would that be acceptable?"

"Oh, that would be wonderful," Morag replied. She stopped, and put her hand to mouth, fearing she had been too effusive.

"Then I'll consider it all settled," Buchanan said. "I shall write to you setting out the terms of our agreement, and if you find everything satisfactory, we shall proceed in due course." He turned to Clara. "Do you know when your husband is likely to return, Mrs Seekamp?"

"Well," said Clara, "his trial is set for the twenty-third of January. I have not heard from him recently, but I have every hope that he will be acquitted."

"You are confident of an acquittal?" Buchanan asked.

"I don't see how my husband could be convicted," Clara replied. "Just after the attack on the Eureka Stockade the Melbourne *Age* published a draft of a Declaration of Independence. That article went further than anything my poor Henry ever wrote in *The Ballarat Times*, and *The Age*'s editor hasn't been arrested. So yes, I am quite confident. I plan to travel to Melbourne next week to attend the proceedings."

"Then you must allow me to escort you," Buchanan replied. "I shall be returning on the twenty-first. Will that be convenient for you?"

"Of course," Clara replied. "And your company would be greatly appreciated. The roads are so dangerous these days."

"It will be my pleasure." Buchanan rose to his feet. "And now, ladies, I must take my leave. Thank you, again, Mrs Seekamp, for your hospitality."

He nodded to Morag. "And you and I, Mrs Munro, will meet again as events unfold."

As he stood to take his leave, Morag suspected that she had been thoroughly manoeuvred into accepting his offer, but she was at a loss to see an alternative.

"Goodbye, Mr Buchanan, and thank you," was all she said.

Just as Buchanan reached the front door, Hector arrived, flushed from running. He stopped short when he saw that his mother had a guest.

"Hector," Morag said, "this is Mr Buchanan."

"Pleased to meet you, sir," Hector responded dutifully.

"And we are to meet again soon, young man," said Buchanan. "But for now I really must be on my way: I have business to attend to."

"Well, that was more than either of us bargained for," Clara said as she closed the door. "I think I could do with another cup of tea."

"I'll join you," Morag responded. "I have to say I'm not entirely easy about this. I don't imagine Mr Buchanan gives something for nothing."

"Perhaps not," Clara replied. "But then again, he's a very rich man and he can afford to be charitable. I think he feels sorry for Hector, which is all to the good."

"Perhaps you're right," said Morag, brightening a little. "I'm so relieved he at least didn't want to send my boy to a Catholic school. I could not have agreed to that. Hector's still terrified of the priests. He has nightmares about them."

"Poor child," Clara said.

"And besides," said Morag, deciding to make the best of it, "Captain McGill may return soon. I can look upon my new station as Buchanan's housekeeper as a temporary accommodation."

"And a very comfortable one at that," said Clara. "I have heard that Buchanan's new house is one of the finest in Melbourne. I can think of worse fates than managing it for him."

Chapter 21

When Clara returned from Melbourne, tired and out of sorts from the long trip, the news she carried with her was not good. "Henry's been gaoled for six months," she told Morag. "The judge was that horrible pompous little man, Redmond Barry. There he was, strutting about all dressed up in his scarlet robes and his ermine trimmings and his full curly wig, lecturing the jury and insisting that my poor Henry was a serious danger to civilized society. The whole thing was a setup. Henry didn't get anything remotely like a fair hearing. He didn't deny publishing the newspaper, of course, but since *The Age* and *The Argus* and who knows how many other papers had all published the same Miners' Declaration, it was hard to see why Henry should be on trial at all. But Judge Barry pushed the jury very hard, and in the end they found Henry guilty of seditious libel, as charged. I could scarcely believe it."

"That's terrible," Morag replied. "Though I must admit I've been hearing rumours that the government is out to quash any dissent."

"So Barry made an example of Henry," said Clara. "It was clear from the start that he planned to do it. It's not fair."

"No," Morag said. "None of it is fair, my dear."

"It'll be the miners' turn next," Clara said gloomily.

"Is there a trial date?"

"February the twenty-second," Clara said promptly.

"The men will have a lot of support," Morag said. "The trial will be very closely watched."

"It will indeed. And I have every intention of supporting the miners' cause in *The Times*," Clara said defiantly. "They're hardly likely to get a fair trial with Barry and his cronies on the bench."

"That's more like your usual self," said Morag. "You looked so down when you came in."

Clara lowered her voice. "It's not just the conviction," she said. "Henry has been drinking heavily. He looks awful. Heaven knows what he finds to drink in prison."

"Anything can be bought," said Morag. "It's probably the gaolers selling their rum rations."

"Well, whatever it is," said Clara, "it's doing him no good at all. I really do fear for him."

"I'm sorry to hear that," said Morag. "Try not to worry too much. Henry will pull through this. And in the meantime, you and I will manage somehow." She smiled at her friend. "After all, you do have a newspaper to run," she added.

Chapter 22

A few weeks later, in the discreetly panelled dining room of their Collins Street Gentlemen's Club, Alec Buchanan and George Train sat discussing the outcome of the trial of the Eureka miners. The two businessmen were partaking of a substantial lunch, consisting of excellent steak pie washed down by equally excellent claret. Buchanan, immaculately turned out as always, felt like an elder statesman in the company of Train, who at twenty-five affected a brash, enthusiastic American style that belied the fact that he was only ten years or so younger than Buchanan himself.

"Well," said Buchanan, "it appears that everything is settling down nicely. The miners have had their day in court. No jury would convict them—they are all free."

"I was there, in the gallery," Train said. "It was very dramatic. In the end, Judge Redmond Barry outright *directed* the jury to find the miners guilty. And when the jury refused to do it, Barry was so red in the face I feared he'd have a fit. He was in a towering rage, but he had no choice. He had to acquit the men."

"He certainly made no secret of his position," Buchanan said. "He'd have hanged the miners if he could."

"Which is probably why the jury refused to convict them," Train said. "One has to admire Mrs Seekamp for publishing that newspaper piece detailing the penalties open to Judge Barry if the charge was proved: treason isn't just a hanging offence—the judge could have condemned those men to be hanged, drawn and quartered."

Buchanan shuddered. "And we think we live in a civilized society," he said. "No decent man would condemn another to such a barbarous fate."

"Civilization is only ever a thin veneer," Train said cheerfully. "And in the end, things turned out better than they might have done for the miners. I understand that even Henry Seekamp is to be released early, to return to his newspaper."

"It appears that everything is now back to business as usual," Buchanan said. "After such a clear rebuff from the citizenry, Governor Hotham will think twice before he proceeds with his plan to auction the goldfields to the squatters."

"Indeed," said Train. "It's clear that such a course would be most ill-advised."

"So no real harm has been done," said Buchanan. "We've even made a tidy profit along the way."

"And you're happy with that?" said Train.

"Certainly," said Buchanan. "Aren't you?"

"I must admit I am a little disappointed."

"How so?"

"It could have been so much more," Train replied. "Look at the news-papers." He gestured to a side table, where a stack of Melbourne papers jubilantly proclaimed victory: *Miners Vindicated*, the headlines trumpeted. *Goldfields Commission Report Recommends Reforms*. "They don't see the truth of it, do they?"

"What truth?"

"That this just strengthens British rule: the miners have lost. The old men who run the government have made a few small concessions to popular sentiment and tightened the reins. These people," said Train, warming to his theme and waving his fork for emphasis, "the miners and their supporters, are so accustomed to subservience that they are celebrating a few crumbs when they could have had the whole pie."

Buchanan was thoughtful. "Independence?" he asked.

"I do mean Independence, yes, indeed. It was so close."

"Commissioner Rede was convinced that the uprising was a plot to Americanize this colony," Buchanan said, choosing his words carefully. "He told me he thought that Consul Tarleton was involved. Tarleton was certainly there at the time."

"Rede doesn't know the half of it," Train said.

"It did not escape my attention that you were there as well," Buchanan added.

Train lowered his voice conspiratorially. "Captain McGill offered me the Presidency, you know."

"Did he indeed?" Buchanan said, not bothering to hide his scepticism. "And was it his to offer?"

"Well, yes, in a manner of speaking. He wanted me to open my warehouse and let him requisition my store of Colt pistols and ammunition, so the miners could be properly armed." He shrugged. "You of all people will understand why I refused. Those guns are worth a fortune: I can get two hundred and fifty

American dollars apiece for them here. No sensible businessman would give away such valuable stock."

"Perhaps not," Buchanan replied. "But if you had?"

"If the miners had won the stockade and declared an intention to establish a democracy in Victoria, then the American government would have been in a position to help them withstand any British reprisals."

Buchanan paused, thinking this through. "But surely," he said, "Governor Hotham would simply have called in all the troops from the other colonies to restore control."

"There are more free miners than soldiers. Properly armed, they could have prevailed. Superior technology almost always prevails."

"And if they had prevailed, as you put it, surely Britain would have sent its fleet from India to retake the colony," Buchanan said.

Train waved this objection aside. "British attention is all on the war with Russia right now. And America has its Pacific Squadron—a large part of their fleet," he replied. "The way I see it, Buchanan, if Britain can try to annexe California—and it most certainly did try to do just that—why should America not help to liberate Victoria? There's more gold here than there is in California. It's a rich prize."

"You would do all this for trade?"

"Of course. America has already opened up Japan and China. A free port here in Victoria would be most advantageous."

"I see," said Buchanan.

"You trade with China yourself," Train continued. "A free port would surely be of interest to you."

"Perhaps," Buchanan replied. "But George, should you be telling me all of this?" he added quietly.

"I don't see why not," Train replied. "We're both men of business. And it's no secret that President Pierce has declared it his foreign policy to encourage the spread of democracy around the world."

"But this time it was not to be?"

"Alas, no," Train replied. "I judged that McGill's armed rebellion would not achieve the right result. In my view, the transition to Independence should be an economic one. But mark my words, Buchanan, the opportunity will come."

"Well," said Buchanan, "that remains to be seen." He paused. "Have you heard from Captain McGill? Mrs Munro said that he had returned home on family business."

"McGill is in Boston, for the present," Train replied. "Consul Tarleton and I thought it best that he should go."

"It's probably just as well he's safely at home in the States," said Buchanan.

"The Commissioner seemed disinclined to let the matter rest."

"My thought exactly," said Train. "And I doubt the Commissioner will be happy about even the smallest reforms that are happening here."

Buchanan laughed. "But you, George, will at least be pleased that the new Miners' Right to vote will virtually give manhood suffrage to Victorian citizens. That's close to American democracy."

"And I'm not saying that isn't a good thing," Train replied. "It's a step forward." He shrugged. "But it's a consolation prize. The men will be voting for representatives who are themselves ruled from afar: overseers. It's only one step up from a slave camp."

Buchanan bridled at this. "Now hold on there, Train," he said. "Don't you think that's going a bit far? Look around you. We're citizens, not slaves."

"I don't mean to give offence, Buchanan," Train responded. "Truly I don't. A man in your position can do well enough out of the British system, I acknowledge that. You've become a rich man by manipulating your business interests to suit the Empire. But times have changed, between your generation and mine. The gold rushes have changed everything, for America and Australia both. Surely even you must allow that the real wealth here goes to your political masters."

"But it's the same in California. Your Government takes its taxes."

"You know I don't mean the taxes, Buchanan. Anyone can see that Britain is draining the wealth out of this country for its own ends. Almost all of the gold gets shipped to England. How much stays in the colony? I estimate it at ten per cent at best. Imagine what Victoria could be if it kept its wealth for its own development, as California has done."

"It's hard to see how Melbourne could develop much faster," Buchanan said. "But I'll own that our terms of trade would be greatly improved if the colony had more gold at its disposal."

Train pressed his argument. "And think about this new copper consortium of yours that I've invested so much money in," he said.

"All set up and ready to start as soon as we can get enough labour," Buchanan replied quickly.

"Yes," said Train. "I know. And we all expect to profit handsomely. But we also know that the Empire will demand that the ore be shipped to England for processing. And after that, every length of copper pipe and wire, every brass tap, every copper sheet and nail and screw that we need here will have to be bought back at hugely inflated prices."

"True enough," said Buchanan. "Do you think we should develop our own copper smelter then?"

"I most certainly do. It would be an easy thing to recruit skilled workers from Cornwall. My sources tell me that things are bad in the Cornish mines.

Work here in Victoria would have to be an attractive alternative to the slow starvation that awaits them there."

"Then the consortium should most certainly consider it if the mine proves rich enough."

"And I'll wager that your government here will prevent it," Train replied.

"Twenty pounds?" said Buchanan.

"Twenty it is," Train said, smiling.

Buchanan held out his hand. "Done," he said. "You have your wager."

"Done," Train replied. "I'll look forward to collecting my winnings."

The men shook hands on it.

Chapter 23

When Henry Seekamp returned in April to his house on the diggings, things were not at all to his liking.

"Just look at you," Clara said when he arrived at her door, dusty and dirty from travel and much the worse for the rum he carried in his hip flask. His blond hair was darkened with grime and sticky with sweat, his brown eyes bloodshot and watery. "How much have you had to drink today?"

"That's no concern of yours," said Seekamp. He stumbled into the front parlour and stood facing his wife.

"Not my concern?" Clara echoed. "I don't want the children to see you like this."

"They're your children, not mine," Seekamp replied.

"Henry!" said Clara. "You know they look upon you as their father—you adopted them when we married."

"Then I can un-adopt them now."

"No," said Clara. "You can't. Let me help you down to the bathhouse. You'll feel much better for a bath and a shave."

"I don't need a bath."

"Oh yes you do," said Clara, "and a shave. If you plan to sleep here tonight, that is. You reek!"

"I'll sleep where I want," Henry said, lunging for her. "And I'll smell how I want. You're my wife, and I want my rights."

Clara was aghast. "If you won't let me help you clean up," she said, "I'll go back to the paper and leave you to sober up here. I have tomorrow's edition to prepare. I'll be back later. There's food in the larder if you're hungry."

Seekamp grabbed her by the arm. "You don't have to go," he said. "I'm back. I'll run the paper."

"No need to worry," said Clara. "It's been doing very well. And you're clearly in no fit state to run anything right now. Let go of my arm."

113

Seekamp tightened his grip. "It's my newspaper," he said. "I'll run it as I see fit. I don't want your help."

"Have you forgotten you used my savings to set up the paper, Henry? It's my investment. You can't expect me to give up all the work I've put into it, just because you walk through the door." She twisted away from him. "And you can keep your hands off me."

Seekamp grabbed for her again.

Clara dodged out of reach.

"I've been in prison for that paper," Seekamp said. "It's mine to do with as I please." He began to slur his words. "And so are you. I've been a long time without a woman. Come here."

Clara sidestepped so that the armchair was between them.

"And don't think I don't know what you've been up to," Seekamp continued. "You've been undermining me at every turn, you and your fancy friends."

"Henry!" Clara tried again. "You know that's not fair. I've been doing everything I can to keep the business sound, for both of us."

"I don't want to hear it," Seekamp muttered. "You're my wife, and you'll do as I say. You'll obey me if you know what's good for you."

He began to sway slightly, and Clara had the presence of mind to steer him towards the couch before he fell onto it.

As Seekamp lapsed into a drunken stupor, Clara fled the house.

When she arrived at Ferguson's lodgings, he was immediately concerned. "You're shaking," he said. "Has Seekamp hurt you?"

"No, he just grabbed my arm," said Clara. "I knew he was drinking in prison, Charles," she said, "but I never expected this. Truly I didn't. He tried to force me."

"You're safe with me," Ferguson replied. "He won't want to fight me."

"He's too drunk to fight anyone," Clara said.

"What will you do?" said Ferguson.

"I can't go back there," Clara said.

"And you can't stay here with me," said Ferguson. "Tongues would wag. Is there someone you could go to?"

"Not now that Morag has taken up her post with Buchanan," Clara said. "And it's not just me: I'll have to take my children. I can't leave them to Henry's tender mercies."

"What about Mrs Parsons?"

"I can't afford to stay at the hotel."

Ferguson grinned. "I've had a good week," he said. "I'll give you enough to stay overnight. And if you confide in Mrs Parsons, she will be discreet. She has no time for drunkards, so she can be relied upon not to tell your husband that you are staying with her."

"But after that, what can I do?"

"Tomorrow, you should go to the Countess de Chabrillan. She likes you. She will help. I'll escort you, if you like. I have business in Melbourne in any case."

Clara hugged Ferguson tight. "Charles, that's brilliant," she said. "That's a perfect solution. I'm sure Celeste will help work something out."

"That's settled, then," said Ferguson. "I'll buy the coach tickets for early tomorrow morning, so you won't have to be seen until we leave for Geelong. Our passage on the Melbourne boat can be bought on the docks."

"But I'll need my things, clothes and so on."

"I'll fetch them," Ferguson said. "I'm in the mood to give that man a lesson in manners."

"Don't," said Clara. "He's horribly changed, but legally he's in the right of it. I am his wife."

"Damn the law," said Ferguson. "In my book he has no right to abuse you, or any other woman, married or not."

Chapter 24

By the time Ferguson delivered Clara to the French Consulate, she had completely regained her composure.

"Lieutenant Ferguson, you are most welcome," the Count said. "And Mrs Seekamp too, of course."

"I'm afraid we bring something of a problem," said Ferguson.

"Nothing that can't be solved, I'm sure," the Count replied. "Do come into the sitting room."

"My poor dears!" Celeste fussed as Clara explained her dilemma. "How perfectly horrible for you. Of course you must stay here with us until things are settled."

"I can't thank you enough," said Clara.

"Not at all," the Count replied. "We have plenty of room. My secretary will find some refreshment and accommodation for the children, and then we shall all take tea. There's someone I would like you both to meet."

Clara's children, subdued by their sudden flight from the diggings and more than a little overawed by the Count's grand house, were led away to be given milk and biscuits in the kitchen, leaving Celeste to ring for tea for her guests.

The maid was just setting down the tray when the sitting room door was dramatically flung open. The woman who entered so theatrically was a dark-eyed, raven-haired beauty wearing a crimson dress, heavy gold jewellery, and an overpowering perfume blended of musk and roses.

Clara stared at the newcomer.

Ferguson immediately rose to his feet.

"Oh, I beg your pardon, Lionel and Celeste," the woman said. "I had no idea you had guests."

The Count smiled indulgently at her. "Allow me to present Lieutenant Charles Ferguson, and Mrs Clara Seekamp," he said, not a whit disturbed by the woman's grand entrance. "This lady is Madame Lola Montez, the Countess Landsfeld."

"Delighted," Lola said, her voice a husky contralto.

"The pleasure is all mine, I assure you," Ferguson replied, gallantly kissing the perfumed hand that she held out to him. "Your fame goes before you, Madame Montez."

"And I too am pleased to meet you," Clara said, finding her voice and her manners. "The Countess has told me so much about you."

"Ah," said Lola. "You are the Irish actress. I also have been hearing about you. I had not expected to meet you so soon. I myself am about to visit your goldfields to perform at the Adelphi Theatre. I'm quite looking forward to it." She slid gracefully into the chair beside Clara, accepting a cup of tea from the maid. "I know already that we will be such good friends."

"That's settled then," said the Count. "I'm sure you ladies have a lot to talk about." He rose. "So if you will excuse us, I would just like a word with Lieutenant Ferguson in my study."

Ferguson hurriedly put down his tea, untasted, and regretfully followed his host from the room.

"**I**t's about this copper venture of Buchanan's," the Count said without preamble as he closed the study door. "What do you know about it?"

"Not a great deal, I admit," Ferguson replied. "But it does sound promising."

"And will you invest?"

"I think so, yes. I know that George Train is putting money into the project, and he's as sharp a businessman as any."

"Then I should like to meet your Mr Train."

"Certainly," said Ferguson. "I have business with him tomorrow afternoon, as it transpires. Shall I ask him to call on you?"

"Excellent notion," said the Count. "I would be most interested to hear his views."

"Delighted," said Ferguson. "I'm glad to be of assistance."

"There's one more little thing you might help me with," the Count said. "It concerns Madame Montez."

Ferguson grinned. "I'm always ready to help a lady," he said.

Chapter 25

By the beginning of June, Melbourne society was buzzing with the news that the Americans were to hold a lavish Independence Day ball and supper. The dance hall on Russell Street had been hired, together with the adjacent supper rooms. It had been decided that the event would do double social duty, serving also as the French celebration for Bastille Day. The American and French Consuls would co-host the occasion: red, white and blue were *de rigueur*. The Fourth of July Ball, 1855, was to be an extravagant gala event, and invitations were eagerly sought after. Governor Hotham and his immediate circle would not, of course, be present at a function hosted by the Comte de Chabrillan—everyone else, it seemed, was vying for the opportunity to attend. Every tailor and dressmaker in Melbourne Town was busily stitching evening clothes, each gown seemingly more lavish than the last: competition in the fashion stakes was fierce.

In the sunny morning room of the French Consulate, Celeste was taking tea with Clara and Morag. "You must come to the ball, my dears," she said, "both of you. We shall be hosting a small private dinner beforehand. I'm sure you will enjoy it."

Before Morag could respond, Clara answered for both of them: "We'd be honoured to attend," she said promptly.

"But Clara," Morag said, "whatever shall we do about clothes?"

"I have already taken thought about that," Celeste replied. "With your permission, I have instructed my seamstress that she is to alter one or two of my own dresses for you."

"How wonderful," said Clara, remembering Celeste's fashionable Parisian wardrobe.

Celeste reached across and patted Morag's hand. "For you, my dear, I have chosen a black velvet gown. We will need to take it in a little, and we can add some discreet red and blue trimming for the occasion. It will be quite proper."

Morag fought back the tears that suddenly threatened to overwhelm her. "You are very kind," she managed to say. "But I should also remind you that I am now Mr Buchanan's housekeeper: it is hardly my place to attend a ball."

"Nonsense," Celeste replied. "You are my personal guest. And I refuse to choose my friends according to somebody else's rules."

"In that case, and if my presence will not cause you embarrassment, I shall be delighted to attend," said Morag.

Clara looked at her friend appraisingly, thinking how far she had come in such as short space of time.

Celeste permitted herself a small chuckle. "Besides," she said, "since my friend Lola Montez will be very much in attendance, I can't imagine that anyone will blink to see you there with me." She turned to Clara: "And I should ask you how you will feel about dining with Lola," she said. "I know you two got on famously when you met, but that was before her tour of the goldfields. She did, after all, take a horsewhip to your husband after that unfortunate review he published in his newspaper."

"I applaud her," Clara responded, with some venom. "If I'd had a whip handy when he set upon me drunk, I'd have done it myself!"

"Bravo!" Celeste replied. "I should like to think I would do the same." She shrugged. "And as for your ball gown, I have laid out two that seem to me to be suitable. When the seamstress comes, you may decide between them."

"Thank you, from the bottom of my heart," Clara said. "I find that I am beginning to feel a little better about life after all."

"Then you must stay here with us for as long as you need," Celeste replied. "I know what it is to be abused by a man."

"You are so generous," Clara said, grown very serious of a sudden. "I can never hope to repay you."

"There is no need," said Celeste. "I have not forgotten your own generosity in hosting that most opportune dinner for Lionel and myself at the diggings. It was a thoroughly enjoyable evening." She paused. "And that reminds me," she said. "I must tell you that my husband has asked the charming Lieutenant Ferguson to escort Lola to the ball. Lionel felt it would be appropriate for her to be introduced by one of the leading Americans, and the Consul, of course, will escort his lady wife."

Clara's face darkened, but she said nothing. There was nothing she could say.

"And between ourselves," Celeste went on, oblivious to Clara's expression, "I think Ferguson is rather smitten. Lola told me that he has agreed to pay for a new evening gown for the occasion—she is attending his tailor in Flinders Lane to have it made."

"Most fortunate," said Clara, suddenly feeling, quite irrationally, less pleased to have one of Celeste's elegant hand-me-downs for the occasion.

"In any case," said Celeste, "I'm glad we have it all settled. I shall tell my husband that you will both attend. He will be so delighted."

Chapter 26

O n the evening of the ball, Charles Ferguson was angry, very angry indeed. In full evening dress, he strode purposefully to the hotel where Madame Lola Montez had her lodgings, intending to have it out with her. When he knocked at her rooms, she opened the door herself and stood back to let him admire her. She was wearing a daringly low-cut red velvet evening gown, its bodice trimmed with blue-black lace, its wide skirts flowing gracefully to the floor. Her dark hair was coiled about her head and bunched into a fall of ringlets held by a Spanish comb, and to complement the dress she wore a single blue sapphire on a gold chain, with matching sapphire drop earrings.

"Charles," she said. "Do come in." She smiled at him mischievously. "How do I look?"

"Expensive," Ferguson replied. He reached inside his jacket and took out a flimsy piece of paper. "I've just had the bill from my tailor."

She turned about, showing off the dress. "Don't you like it?"

"That really isn't the point," Ferguson replied.

"Isn't it?"

"You know it isn't." Ferguson sighed, exasperated. "When I agreed to escort you this evening, you asked me to buy you a suitable dress."

"And you have," said Lola.

"I didn't agree to buy you a whole new wardrobe."

"But you have," said Lola. "And I thank you."

"Your new clothes cost me more than most would earn in a year."

Lola tried a different tack. "But Charles," she said, wheedling, "I thought you'd be pleased. I thought you were to be my new patron. I need a new man in my life."

"You need a banker. And I don't need to be played for a fool."

"I assure you that that was not my intention."

"But it is the result," Ferguson said. "No matter how famous you are, no matter how beautiful you look—and you know you are beautiful—I do

123

not appreciate being used in such a way. It makes you no better than any confidence trickster."

"You insult me."

"This"—Ferguson brandished the tailor's bill—"is the insult. I had to tip the tailor an extra five pounds so he would promise not to spread the story about the town. I'd be a laughing stock."

Lola put her hand to her mouth, not quite covering her amusement. A tiny giggle escaped her full red lips.

Ferguson tried, unsuccessfully, to maintain his outrage. He laughed, ruefully. "It wasn't my finest moment," he said.

"Poor man," said Lola. "In that case, let me be direct: you feel entitled to expect some return on your investment, do you not?"

"I'm intrigued," Ferguson said warily. "What did you have in mind?"

"You know what I have in mind," Lola replied. "Come here."

Ferguson grinned broadly and made to take off his jacket. "In that case, let me help you out of that very expensive dress," he said.

"No need," said Lola.

Ferguson flushed. "More of your games," he said.

"No, not at all," said Lola. "I mean now to give you a little something on account. After this evening's events are done, you may escort me home again." She smiled her famous, sultry smile, confident of its effect. "And then, if you wish, you may help me to take off all these very valuable clothes."

Ferguson relented a little. "Very well," he said. "If that's our bargain, I can wait until later. I can be patient."

"You misunderstand," said Lola. She locked the door. "You are far too tense, Charles," she said, taking his hand and leading him to the couch. "We shall be miserable all evening if you are still angry with me. Come here. Let me show you a little trick to help you relax. I learned to do this for King Ludwig. It was his favourite thing."

Ferguson smiled as she unbuttoned his trousers and took his sex in her soft, manicured hand, kneading him quickly to erection. She kissed him, hard on the mouth, her fingers moving deftly, rapidly all the while until he was rock hard, until she was sure of his need.

She pulled away, but he held her tight. "Don't stop kissing me," he said fiercely. "I want to feel your tongue in my mouth."

Lola laughed. "You still misunderstand me," she said. "Right now I have better uses for my tongue." She surprised him by kneeling before him, running her tongue along the length of his penis before slipping it into her mouth.

Ferguson groaned in ecstasy as Lola took him deep into her mouth, sliding him into her throat, expertly increasing his pleasure with her tongue and teeth. He found himself holding her head as she worked, her warm hands now massaging his testicles as he thrust into her. His climax, when it came, was explosive.

He was still stroking her curls when his speech returned. "Well, that was a surprise," he said. "I've never done that before."

Lola rose. "If you will excuse me for a moment," she said. "I'll just clean my teeth." She slipped quietly into the next room, leaving an astonished Ferguson to re-button his trousers and set his clothes to rights.

When Lola returned, he was leaning back on the couch, grinning roguishly. "I must say I'm looking forward to the rest of this evening," he said. "I can see you have a lot to teach me."

"Perhaps you will teach me," Lola replied, smiling back at him. "Perhaps you will show me what pleases you best. And now that we understand each other at last," she said, "I will own that I also am looking forward to it. But Charlie," she hesitated.

"What?"

"You messed up my hair!"

"Then allow me to help you repair the damage."

"I don't think so. But you can watch if you like."

Ferguson reached out, drew her to him and kissed her full on the mouth.

By the time they set off, arm in arm and very late for the private Independence Day dinner that was to precede the ball, they were laughing together like old friends.

Chapter 27

The dinner guests in the private supper room hired for the occasion were being served the second course by the time Ferguson and Lola arrived. The Count rose to his feet to welcome them.

"Ah, my dear," he said, kissing Lola on both cheeks. "There you are. I feared something was amiss."

"My apologies, Count. There was a delay about my dress," Lola replied airily. "I'm afraid poor Lieutenant Ferguson has been sorely inconvenienced."

"I have nothing to complain about," said Ferguson.

The American Consul also rose to greet the latecomers. "Welcome," he said. "I'm glad you have arrived safely. Madame Montez, your musicians are already in place in the ballroom, and now that you are here our preparations are complete. Everything is in order. But I do fear you have missed the oysters."

Lola smiled radiantly at the Consul, leaving Ferguson to answer his host.

"No matter," said Ferguson. "It has been my very great pleasure to escort Madame Montez."

The dinner proceeded smoothly, and when the dessert dishes had finally been cleared away, Consul Tarleton rose to his feet, tapping his wine glass for attention.

"Ladies and Gentlemen," he said, "I now propose that we join the rest of our guests in the ballroom. We have a small surprise in store."

Lola nudged Ferguson, and as the party prepared to move, she took the opportunity to slip away quietly through a side door.

Consul Tarleton and his wife joined the Count and Countess de Chabrillan, ready to lead their small procession as the double doors were opened wide to admit the group to the glittering main ballroom. Mrs Tarleton's evening gown was designed in the current American style: fashioned of a striking red, white and blue tartan silk, it had a low neckline and very wide skirts that emphasized the lady's tiny waist and set off her dark hair and glittering diamond jewellery. But Celeste de Chabrillan was undoubtedly the belle of the ball in her off-the-shoulder dress of deep blue velvet with a bodice of dark red and silver-white brocade that accentuated her pale skin and blonde curls. Around her neck she wore a circle of blood-red garnets, a reminder of the red velvet neck-ribbons worn by ladies of the French aristocracy in the time of the Terror, a grim reminder of the Bastille, and the guillotine.

As they joined the throng, Clara and Morag saw that American and French flags hung from the barrel-vaulted ceiling, and that the ballroom had been decked out in swathes of red, white and blue fabric tied with golden cords. The whole room glowed with the glamour of candlelight, the orchestra was playing, and the room was a swirling mass of elegantly-gowned ladies and their black-clad partners.

"It's beautiful," Morag whispered.

"Yes it is, very beautiful," Clara replied.

Lionel de Chabrillan bowed to his wife. "Shall we, my dear?" he said gallantly.

Celeste smiled as he took her in his arms and whirled her effortlessly into the press of dancers.

Ferguson moved to join Clara at the doorway. "Would you care to dance, Mrs Seekamp?" he said.

"I thought you were too busy with Madame Montez to be bothered with me," she replied tartly.

"Surely you're not jealous?" he asked.

"Of course not," she lied.

"Then dance with me, Clara," he said. "You must know that the Count asked me to escort Madame Montez. I could hardly refuse."

"I know," she sighed. "But you didn't have to buy her such a stunning dress."

"I'm afraid I did," he said ruefully, taking her arm and leading her towards the dance floor. "I really wasn't given any choice in the matter. The Count and Madame Montez had decided it between them."

"Was that fair?"

"Of course not. But the Comte de Chabrillan knows I'm flush at the moment, so no real harm has been done."

Clara smiled at last. "In that case," she said, "I suppose I'll have to forgive you, just this once."

"I'm glad about that," Ferguson said lightly. "Shall we?"

When the musicians stopped playing, the dancers were intrigued to notice that the hotel staff moved swiftly to re-set the chairs, creating a circular space in the centre of the ballroom. The American Consul rose to his feet to address the assembled guests.

"We have a surprise for you this evening, ladies and gentlemen," Tarleton said, smiling broadly. "I hope you have all now had the opportunity to take some refreshment. Please do take your seats. Before the dancing recommences, and in response to a special request from my American compatriots, the famously beautiful Madame Lola Montez, recently arrived on these shores after her successful American tour, has generously agreed to give a private performance of her famous Spider Dance for us. You will all be privileged to see Madame Montez dance before her show officially opens at the Theatre Royal."

The response was electric. Everyone started speaking at once. The Spider Dance was currently the talk of the town.

"*The Argus* said this dance is totally subversive and an affront to public morality," Mrs John Thomas Smith, wife of the Mayor, observed to her neighbour, Councillor Wells. "And a priest—O'Hanlon, I think his name is—wrote a letter to the paper that said that no respectable family should attend the Lola Montez show. He said it should be banned for indecency."

"Shall I escort you outside to the Supper Room, dear?" her husband asked—a trifle over-solicitously. "I could return to fetch you when it is all over."

"No, dear," she replied firmly. "I should like to see this notorious dance for myself, if only to know what all the fuss is about."

"I read that she had a rapturous response in Castlemaine," another of the city Councillors volunteered. "I heard the audience there called for endless encores, and that the diggers showered her with gold nuggets."

"But what about the scandal she caused in Ballarat?" his wife asked. "She took a horsewhip to the editor, Mr Seekamp, after he gave her a bad review."

"Good for her," said Mrs Smith. "The woman has spirit." She paused. "I wonder what his wife made of it?" She nudged her husband in the ribs. "That's his wife, Clara Seekamp, sitting over there with a woman in black velvet whom I can't quite place, and the Countess Celeste de Chabrillan."

"Then she's in dubious company," said Smith. "But I think the show is about to begin. Ladies: we are about to see this famous ballet for ourselves."

The excitement grew and the guests craned their necks for the best vantage points as the music began and Lola, clad in a gold-embroidered black Spanish jacket, flimsy red skirts, black stockings and low-heeled black shoes, moved gracefully into the centre of the ring and slowly began her erotic dance. She commenced her performance in the Spanish manner, her arms raised high above her head as she stamped her feet and twirled her skirts. As the tempo increased, she whirled faster, shaking her skirts higher and higher as she mimed her distress at having a spider caught among her petticoats. Soon she was spinning about the room, a whirlwind of gauzy red and black.

Her audience was transfixed.

Mrs Smith gasped. "I can see the tops of her stockings," she whispered to her husband.

"And I can see everything else: she's not wearing anything at all under that skirt," he replied, not missing a minute of the spectacle.

As Lola, the metaphorical spider disposed of, slowed her dance and sank elegantly to her knees, most of the dinner guests applauded enthusiastically. The dancer rose and took her bow, before slipping quickly out of the room to change back into her evening clothes.

The Comte de Chabrillan applauded loudly with the rest, as Celeste leaned across to whisper in his ear. "Really, Lionel," she said, "I don't see what all the fuss in the papers is about. It's a perfectly acceptable dance such as one would expect to see on any Parisian stage."

"Perhaps it is a question of sensibilities," her husband replied. "The English, I find, are not at all relaxed in the presence of the performing arts." He nodded at Consul Tarleton, who was smiling happily at the effect of Lola's startling performance. "But the Americans seem happy enough," he added cheerfully.

"**W**ell," said Clara, "that was exciting." She took a sip of her punch.

"A bit too exciting for my taste," Morag replied.

"Perhaps." Clara stood hurriedly. "You'll have to excuse me," she said. She put her hand to her mouth and dashed from the room. She returned to the table some fifteen minutes later, white-faced and shaken.

"Are you alright?" Morag asked.

"A little nauseous," Clara replied, reaching for her water glass. "It must have been the oysters."

"Possibly," said Morag. She gave her friend a very direct look. "You're not...?" she asked.

"I hope not," Clara said. She lowered her voice to a whisper. "But I'm worried I might be. I'm late: I've been counting days."

Morag put her hand to her mouth. "But it couldn't be Henry," she said.

"Of course not," Clara snapped. "I wouldn't let that drunkard near me. Not now. Not ever again."

"Then...?" Morag caught Clara's expression as she glanced across the room to where Ferguson was flirting outrageously with Lola Montez, who had changed once more into her ball gown, and now sat twisting her champagne glass as she laughed at Ferguson's jokes, pointedly ignoring the more censorious glances directed at her by some of the other guests—notably the Mayor and his circle.

"You don't mean...?" Morag said.

"Of course it's Charles," Clara said. "Who else would it be?"

"But...?"

"I know, I know," Clara said wearily. "You don't have to tell me where I stand with that one." She smiled weakly. "And I don't suppose I can entirely blame Lola for his behaviour here this evening, can I?"

"No," Morag agreed. "Ferguson is quite the ladies' man."

Clara changed the subject. "What about you?" she asked. "Have you heard from McGill?"

"I've had a letter," Morag said. "It seems that all is not well: he writes that he has major problems to contend with at home." She sighed. "I do not think he will be able to return anytime soon."

"Never mind," Clara said. "At least you are comfortably situated at Buchanan's house. Things could be a lot worse, for both of us."

"Indeed they could," said Morag. "And," she added, brightening up, "tonight we are free to enjoy ourselves." She beckoned to a waiter. "I think we should both have a little more of that delicious French champagne: I believe it is a great restorative."

"I believe you are right," Clara replied, accepting a glass from the silver tray.

The two women clinked glasses, and sat sipping their champagne, watching the ebb and flow of the guests at the Independence Day ball, watching the currents of their future swirling around them.

Chapter 28

Later that evening in the Supper Room, George Train, a little the worse for the Count's excellent wine and tactless as always, unwisely decided to engage Buchanan in conversation with his bitterest business opponent, the Mayor of Melbourne—a man whose opium imports rivalled Buchanan's own.

"Alec Buchanan," Train said formally, "allow me to introduce John Thomas Smith."

"We've met," Smith said shortly.

"Indeed we have," Buchanan replied. "If you'll excuse me, George, I must attend to the ladies."

"Surely they can spare you for a few minutes," said Train. "I have a business proposal for both of you, since you both have dealings with China. Something rather interesting has come my way from that direction."

"Later, perhaps," Buchanan said diplomatically. "I had just promised to get fresh punch for the Countess de Chabrillan and her friend Madame Montez."

"Who could scarcely be called a lady," Smith muttered. "Not after that performance."

"I beg your pardon?" The Comte de Chabrillan interrupted. "I could not help but overhear. Am I correct? Did I just hear you insult the Countess?"

"Your pardon, Count," the Mayor said hastily. "I meant no offence."

"How could you not mean to offend me by impugning the honour of my wife?"

"Ah," said Smith. "We have a slight misunderstanding, then. I spoke of Madame Montez, not your lady wife."

"And Madame Montez, the Countess of Landsfeld," the Count said, with heavy emphasis on the title, "is a particular friend of my wife." The Count set down his champagne glass deliberately onto the nearest table, and began to remove his jacket. "You will oblige me, sir," he said, "by defending yourself, as I shall defend the lady's reputation."

The colour drained from Smith's face, and he appeared suddenly sober.

"Could we not come to an understanding?" he said. "I have no wish to fight."

"But I do," the Count replied, raising his fists dramatically and assuming a boxer's stance. "I am your host, and you have insulted me."

Smith began, reluctantly, to remove his own black evening jacket, all the while expostulating that he had meant no harm. A small, animated circle of onlookers formed around the two men as they squared off and circled each other in the centre of the room. George Train began unobtrusively moving through the room, taking bets. It seemed that despite the Mayor's superior height and bulk, the smart money was on the Count, whose training was obvious to the experienced eye.

The American Consul appealed for calm. "Gentlemen, please," Tarleton said. "I beg you will desist. This is a celebration of liberty after all. Surely we can agree to allow a little free speech."

"Hear, hear," said Ferguson. Without another word he leaned back in his chair and slowly drew his Colt from inside his jacket. He laid the weapon casually on the table and placed his hands on either side of it. "Enough, gentlemen," he said softly. "The American Consul would prefer that no blood be shed on such an auspicious occasion." He grinned mischievously. "Sorry, George: all bets are off."

The Count was immediately contrite. "Of course," he said, bowing gallantly in Tarleton's direction. "I am forgetting my wider duties as your co-host. Our little dispute can be postponed to another date." He snapped his fingers. "Waiter! Champagne for everyone: I, Comte de Chabrillan, choose to make amends."

A round of applause greeted this theatrical performance. The onlookers drifted back to the ballroom and the festivities resumed, almost without missing a beat. Ferguson slipped the pistol back under his jacket.

The Mayor, however, was not amused. He snatched his own cutaway evening jacket from the waiter who still stood holding it, and stormed towards the door. "You'll regret this," he said under his breath as he passed the Count.

"Alas," de Chabrillan responded, "I regret many things. But never do I regret defending a lady from infamy. Good night, Mr Mayor."

Buchanan, smiling broadly at the discomfiture of his enemy, turned to find Train at his side. "I will have another glass," Buchanan said, deftly removing champagne from the tray held by a nearby waiter. "And perhaps, George, you and I can do business with your interesting Chinese connection after all."

The two businessmen were deep in discussion when they were interrupted by the Count de Chabrillan and Consul Tarleton, who were deliberately circulating among their guests, smoothing any remaining ruffled feathers after the Count's outburst of chivalry.

"Ah, Mr Train," said the Count. "And Mr Buchanan too: how fortuitous. I was just telling the Consul here about Buchanan's new venture into copper."

"It sounds an excellent proposition, I must say," said Tarleton. "Copper is an increasingly useful commodity. I applaud your enterprise."

"It's an exciting new development—we trust it will prosper," said Train.

"And there is every possibility that it will," Buchanan added quickly. "But, if I may be so bold as to take this opportunity to talk politics, perhaps you gentlemen both would be kind enough to tell me your views on the recent Eureka uprising." He smiled smugly at his fellow businessman, trapping Train into the debate. "While I saw it as little more than a local riot, Mr Train here imagines that Captain McGill was leading a bid for American-style Independence."

"For my own part," the Consul said warily, "I do not really know enough to comment on the particulars of that incident." He shrugged. "But here among friends, I will say that independence from Britain has been so very successful for America that I cannot see any reason that another young and wealthy country such as this one would not benefit from gaining a similar independence in the same manner. You have only to look around you: Melbourne has developed so quickly in the last year that one no longer recognises it. Think how much more it could be if it were free of the Empire that siphons off most of its wealth."

"Well said," the Count interjected. "My own countrymen fought long and hard to win their liberation from tyranny. My view is that it behooves a young, emerging country to do the same."

"That's two votes for future independence," Train said happily. "And if you'll forgive me this observation, I will say that I see it as a generational problem. Here in Australia we have old men, appointed from England, getting rich and fat on the labours of the young men who work the goldfields. I think those young men should be able to have their say. I think the time will come when they will demand it."

"You would think that," Buchanan laughed. "You are by far the youngest here."

"Ferguson is younger than I," Train retorted. "And he commands respect among his men."

"Nevertheless," said Buchanan, "it is still my view that the current Empire does serve our needs, at least for the present."

"Perhaps," said Tarleton, "for the moment." He checked his fob watch. "But I fear that I shall now have to leave this discussion, fascinating though it is." He turned to the Count. "It is time for the final toast," he said. "Will you accompany me?"

"It will be my very great pleasure," de Chabrillan responded.

The American and French Consuls walked side by side to the dais at the head of the ballroom. At a signal from Tarleton the orchestra stopped playing, and waiters began circulating among the crowd offering fresh flutes of French champagne. The guests waited expectantly.

Tarleton raised his glass. "Ladies and Gentlemen," he said, "I have no wish to interrupt your enjoyment of the evening with long speeches. But now that our glasses are all charged with the Comte de Chabrillan's fine French champagne, I give you a toast."

The seated guests rose to their feet, joining those already standing.

"To Independence," said the Consul.

"To Independence," echoed the Count, raising his glass in acknowledgement.

"Independence," the guests responded.

Alec Buchanan raised his glass in salute, and drank with the rest.

PART II

1872: The Telegraph

"...the country and colony will start ahead afresh, stimulated by the new blood which slowly and surely is uprooting the prejudices of the old settlers, who looked upon reform or enterprise as a crime of which only Americans were guilty."

George Train, *An American Merchant in Europe, Asia and Australia.* (1857)

Chapter 29

Hector Munro was hurrying. At twenty-four, he had become a striking man, with his mother's copper-red hair and grey eyes and his father's tall, athletic physique. As Alec Buchanan's private secretary, Hector was organising tonight's dinner to mark the final connection of the Telegraph. But first he had a personal matter to attend to: today James McGill would at last return on a ship from San Francisco, and Hector wanted to be at the Port Melbourne docks to greet him. He had brought Buchanan's carriage, having decided that McGill, in his new role as American Consul, should be conveyed to his new residence in style.

Today Hector had dressed with more than usual care: his well-tailored dark morning suit fitted him perfectly, and his crisp white shirt and pale grey cravat marked him as a gentleman as he made his way along the docks. He wove his way between sweating men hauling crates and boxes, past traders haggling over the early morning's catch, past stacks of fresh oysters. He avoided the ragged children begging for pennies as he strode along, looking for the pier where the *Nevada* would dock. The October morning was fine: pale sunlight lit the water, and a sharp breeze carried the clean smells of salt air above the heavier reek of fish and rotting seaweed. Hector caught the stink of hot tar and boiling pitch as he passed a slip where repairs were underway, and came at last to the space where brawny workers with heavy ropes awaited the ship now sliding towards its berth.

Hector had earlier informed McGill's American staff that they would meet their new Consul later: Hector wanted this first moment to himself. As the ship docked, he recognised McGill where he stood at the rail. The intervening seventeen years had done little to change the man: he had kept his athletic, muscular build, and the hair blown back by the breeze was still brown and curly. But he was not alone. The woman beside him was strikingly handsome, even at this distance.

Hector was suddenly apprehensive. This was clearly not to be the private

139

reunion he had planned. He was also uneasy for his mother's sake: she was so looking forward to McGill's arrival, and clearly did not expect him to be accompanied. Who, he wondered, was this new woman with McGill? Certainly his correspondence had not mentioned her.

He had not long to wait. McGill strode down the gangplank, straight to where Hector stood, surprising the young man by hugging him tightly, American-style.

"It's been a long time," he said. "But I'd have known you anywhere, Hector, with your red hair."

Hector laughed, embarrassed. "Welcome back, sir," he said, feeling suddenly uncomfortable in the presence of the beautiful woman who had joined them and now held tightly to McGill's arm.

The woman fluttered her long, dark eyelashes and smiled at Hector. "I hope, James, that you will you introduce me to your handsome young friend," she said.

McGill didn't miss a beat. "Mr Hector Munro," he said, "allow me to introduce Madame Lola Montez," he said.

"Delighted," Lola said huskily, extending her perfumed hand for Hector to kiss. "I just know we shall be such good friends."

Hector, taken aback by her familiarity, retreated into formality. "It's a pleasure to make your acquaintance, Mrs Montez," he replied stiffly.

"Madame," said Lola. "I prefer Madame, or Countess, if you like." She moved a little closer to McGill, smiling as she added: "I am not married—at least not at present."

Hector coloured. "My apologies, Madame Montez," he said. "And may I enquire how you came to be travelling in company with Consul McGill?"

McGill smiled. "As chance would have it," he said, "Madame Montez was on the same voyage. We had met before, in Boston, and when we renewed our acquaintance on the ship we discovered that we have friends here in common."

"And Consul McGill has been a most entertaining companion," Lola added, patting his arm possessively. "With his company, the days just flew by."

"I see," said Hector, wondering how to extricate himself from the situation without offending McGill and his lady friend.

As if on cue, Clara Seekamp arrived at the dock, waving breathlessly. She was stouter, more matronly than McGill recalled, but he recognised her immediately, her dark curls and blue eyes unchanged.

"Lola," she said, bustling up to the group. "You look wonderful—you've hardly changed a bit. I was afraid I would be late to meet you. I was just putting the finishing touches to my guest room for you." She stopped short, seeing her friend's companions. "And can that really be Captain McGill with you, Hector?"

"Indeed it can, Mrs Seekamp," said McGill. "What a delightful surprise."

"Have you come back to incite another uprising, Captain?" Clara asked, smiling archly.

McGill smiled back. "Perhaps," he said. "We shall have to wait and see."

Hector gallantly gave up his hopes for a private conversation with McGill. "I have Mr Buchanan's carriage," he said. "May I offer you its services, Mrs Seekamp?"

"Thank you, Hector, that would be lovely," Clara replied. "But I have already engaged a Hansom cab for this morning."

Hector hoped his relief didn't show. "In that case, Madame Montez, I trust that we shall meet again, in more convenient circumstances."

"And I also will call upon you, ma'am, when you are settled," said McGill, "if Mrs Seekamp has no objection, that is."

"None at all," Clara replied. "I shall be delighted to refresh our friendship."

"As shall I," McGill replied. He turned to Lola. "Is there anything I can do for you before I allow Hector here to whisk me away to my duties?" he asked.

"All taken care of," Clara said airily. "I have arranged porters for the luggage."

"Which is rather extensive, I'm afraid," said Lola. "But I'm sure they can send the larger trunks along later."

"Before you ask, Hector, I have no problems in that department," McGill said, grinning. "I'm sure your carriage will be sufficient for my sea chest. I always travel light."

"In that case," said Hector, "if the ladies will excuse us, we should be about our business. There are a lot of people waiting for you in Melbourne, sir."

"Then I'll bid you good morning, ladies," said McGill.

"Goodbye, for the moment," Lola said, her voice low and throaty. She kissed McGill on both cheeks. "Thank you for *everything*, James: it's been wonderful."

"The pleasure has been all mine, ma'am," McGill said, returning her smile.

Chapter 30

Once the luggage had been collected and the men were seated in the carriage, McGill relaxed, stretching out his legs.

"It was kind of you to meet me, Hector," he said.

"I wanted to talk to you before you arrive at the house," Hector replied, his face grown serious.

"Are you checking to see if my intentions towards your mother are still honourable?" asked McGill.

Hector blushed, for the second time that morning. "Not exactly," he said. "But I do want you to understand that Mother never gave up waiting for you."

"I know," McGill said softly. "And you want to protect her?"

"Something like that. She deserves to be treated gently."

"Certainly she does," said McGill.

"And I want to ask, privately, what really happened. When you left us on the diggings, we all thought you would come back. We thought it might take a year or two, but we believed you would come back."

"I wanted to," said McGill. "But I was overwhelmed by family matters." He sighed. "I returned to find my father dying. I am the oldest son: it was my duty to take over the family business, to take care of my mother and my younger siblings. And I did. I shouldered the responsibilities, and the responsibilities took over my life."

"I see," said Hector, thinking of his own situation, of his own unending duty to his mother. "Family is the most important thing, of course, but it does constrain us."

"I did what any honourable man would do," said McGill. "And just when I had the family situation under control, the Civil War began—and I was obliged to remain, to perform other duties."

"Oh, of course," said Hector. "I should have realised."

"It was not a happy time," McGill said softly. "But believe me, Hector, I have never stopped wanting to come back."

"And you never married?" Hector asked.

"Well, yes, I did, once," McGill said quietly. "It was during the Civil War. The war was dragging on. I had to rebuild the family business, and the family was pressuring me to make an advantageous marriage. It seemed impossible that I could ever be free enough to return here. I married then, to please my mother—and hers. It wasn't a love match, on either side. But we got on well enough, I suppose, Rose and I, for the little time we had together."

"What happened?"

"She died, Hector. She died giving birth to my daughter. She's also called Rose—Rose Marie—after her mother, and mine." McGill reached inside his jacket and extracted a creased sepia photograph of a solemn little girl dressed in a white frock, her fair hair bunched into ringlets. "That's Rosie," he said, passing the picture to Hector. "She's nine years old. She lives with my mother, who spoils her completely."

"Oh," said Hector. "Mother never said."

"She wouldn't have, I suppose," McGill replied. "I wrote to her, of course. But my marriage was so very short."

"And now you are back."

"Yes. I have finally managed to arrange a good commercial reason to be here, and here I am. My family business has prospered, and one of my brothers is taking care of the American operation while I am away—we are now heavily invested in the railroads, courtesy of my old friend George Train. Railroads are the coming thing, here in Australia, and I am here to broker a suitable deal to build them. I accepted the appointment as Consul when my government offered it because it combines official matters of trade with my own business interests, and with my own particular desire to return to Melbourne." McGill smiled. "But mostly I am here to see you, and your mother. I have missed you, and this country, very much: my friends still joke that I have never shaken the gold dust off my feet."

"And we are pleased to have you back, at last," said Hector, relieved to have managed to get through this talk about his mother without mishap. He laughed, briefly. "Mother has had Buchanan's house spring-cleaned, top to bottom, in case you should be offended by dust," he added.

"Then I'll be sure to notice," McGill replied.

"That would be prudent. It's our first port of call," said Hector. "I trust you are ready to take tea. She's had the cook baking special cakes in your honour."

"After five weeks at sea, you may believe me when I say I shall be delighted," said McGill.

"And that reminds me," said Hector, "I have to inform you that Sir Alec Buchanan requests the pleasure of your company at a private dinner this evening, at The Melbourne Club."

"*Sir* Alec?" McGill said.

"Recently knighted for his services to the colony," Hector replied solemnly.

"Well that's a turn-up for the books," McGill said. "He always was close to the government."

"And even closer now," said Hector. "He has such a lot of government contracts these days. This dinner is for his business associates, to celebrate the completion of the undersea cable, the last stage of our telegraph link to London. Tonight we will receive the first message. It's very exciting: this country will no longer be isolated."

"Fascinating," said McGill. "I shall be delighted to join you. And I shall be very interested to catch up on all the local news. Is Buchanan much involved with the Telegraph?"

"Heavens, yes," said Hector. "His consortium has financed the line construction—it's his fastest growing business venture. He practically owns the telegraph stations at Alice Springs, right in the centre of the Australian continent, and Port Darwin at the northern extreme. The telegraph link could not operate without those stations. It's a huge investment."

"Then it will be a most interesting evening," said McGill.

"And I'm sure you have news to tell of events in America," Hector replied, "given all that's happened since you were last here. We hear so little of what transpires there."

"That's one of the things I'm here to redress," McGill said. "I hope to promote closer ties between our two nations."

"But Victoria is just a Colony," Hector said. "We are ruled from England."

"At present, yes," McGill replied. "But in any case, Victoria's gold reserves make it a most desirable trading partner for the United States. I'm here to facilitate that trade."

"Is Mrs Seekamp right, then? Are you here to provoke another uprising?"

McGill laughed. "Not in the way she means," he said.

"But you still think our political situation needs changing?"

"Let's just say that I believe there are always opportunities for improvement. I have it on good authority that although a few concessions were made after the events of Eureka stockade, the same people are still in power. Does that seem right to you?"

"I can hardly tell, sir," Hector said. "This is the system I've grown up in. It's all I know."

"Well said." McGill sighed. "I tried once to change things through force of arms, and I failed. Now I have learnt that diplomacy is a much better instrument."

"Better for business, you mean?"

"If you like," said McGill. "Mrs Seekamp's jibe notwithstanding, my mission here is to facilitate trade."

"Sir Alec will be pleased to hear it," Hector replied. "He has great hopes for extending his American enterprises."

The two men lapsed into silence for a moment, until McGill turned to Hector. "There's something else, isn't there?" he said.

"Yes," said Hector. "How did you know?"

"I know you put a lot of effort into meeting me at the dock. Your face tells me something is still troubling you. What is it?"

Hector hesitated for a moment. "I want to ask you about my father," he said awkwardly, "while we have this little time to talk privately. I understand you might not want to speak of it, but I have to ask."

McGill was suddenly wary. "What is it that you want to know?" he said. "I didn't know your father well."

Hector turned to face McGill, deciding to take the plunge. He felt like a child again, tongue-tied and clumsy, as he finally blurted out his question. "You were there," he said. "Do you know who killed him?"

"No," McGill said cautiously. "I don't. It was a long time ago, Hector."

"Is there anything you can tell me? Anything at all?"

"All I can say to you is that when I arrived you were standing in the General Store, between the bodies of your father and Mr Diamond, the storekeeper. The official belief is that both men were bayoneted by the soldiers."

"I don't doubt that Mr Diamond died that way," Hector said, "but my father was alive when I reached the shop. Mr Diamond told me that Dad had only been grazed, nothing dangerous." He shook his head, as if to clear his thoughts before he rushed on with his story. "I keep going over and over and over it in my mind, but nothing fits the facts. Mr Diamond said he had only left Dad for a minute to get a jug of water. I saw a priest go into the shop ahead of me. When I got to the doorway, Dad died in the priest's arms, and he laid him on the floor. I heard the priest tell Mr Diamond it was sudden, and Mr Diamond said it didn't make sense." He sighed. "I try and I try, but that's all I can remember before Mr Diamond pushed me into the cupboard."

"And saved your life," said McGill.

"Yes," said Hector. "And then you found me."

"Have you checked the records?" McGill asked.

"Of course," said Hector. "The autopsy report says Dad died of stab wounds."

"Then he must have been stabbed," said McGill. "The doctor couldn't mistake that."

"Yes," said Hector. "But the question is: who stabbed him, and when?"

"Maybe he was stabbed later, when the Commissioner's police went on their rampage through the shops. You say he was lying on the floor. If those brutes thought he was just injured, they'd have bayoneted him. They were killing the wounded." McGill shuddered at the memory. "It was a savage attack."

"But," said Hector, "Dad wouldn't have bled if he was already dead, would he?"

"No," said McGill, "but there was a lot of blood on the floor where your father was found. And there were a lot of dead that day, Hector. It was a battlefield. I doubt the doctor examined any of them too closely: if he saw a stab wound, that would have been enough for the death certificate."

"Oh," said Hector.

"What about the priest?" McGill said quietly. "You say he held your father as he died. Did you ever find out which priest it was? Have you asked him what happened?"

"No, and no," said Hector. "All I remember is that he seemed very tall, and very thin, and he scared me." He sighed. "Mother tried asking Father Smith, who was our family priest at the time, but all he could tell her was that the only really tall priest who was at the stockade that day had already left the goldfields. So she never did get to speak to him."

"I tried too," McGill said. "But none of the priests I spoke to had anything useful to say."

"Thank you," Hector said. "I never knew that."

"There was nothing to tell you."

Hector shifted uncomfortably in his seat. "I still need to know what happened," he said. "I still want justice for my father."

"Listen, Hector," said McGill. "I know it's hard, but it would be better for you, for everybody, if you can let this matter rest. There's no way of telling what really occurred back there. Bad things happen on battlefields, Hector: not all deaths are caused by the enemy—old scores are settled, men are robbed, men are murdered. It's harsh, but all who survive come to understand that it is the way of the world."

"That's more or less what Lieutenant Ferguson tells me," Hector said. "But somehow my father's death still haunts me. I will always hope to find out the truth, someday." He smiled wearily. "Thank you for talking about it, in any case."

"And how is Ferguson?" said McGill, glad to change the subject.

"Much as he always is," Hector replied. "I ride with him, when I can. He taught me to shoot, when I was younger. We hunt, sometimes."

"Are you a good shot?" McGill asked.

"I never miss," Hector replied.

McGill shivered, hearing the echo of his own words, his own past. "Whatever happened to my horse?" he said, masking the moment. "He was barely four years old when I had to leave."

Hector grinned. "Sunny has lived to a ripe old age," he said. "You can visit him in Sir Alec's stables, if you like."

"Really?" McGill was amazed. "You've looked after him all this time?"

"Of course I have," said Hector. "He's my best friend."

Chapter 31

Clara's Hansom cab, loaded so heavily that it creaked ominously on its springs, finally rolled away from the docks and wound its way slowly through Melbourne and turned eastward towards her house on Richmond Hill. The two women relaxed, settling in to exchange their news.

"It's so good to see you again," said Clara. "It's been too long since you were here."

"And I am so pleased to be visiting at last," Lola replied. "Although I confess I'm sorry that Celeste has returned to Paris. It would have been delightful for us all to be together again."

"I know," said Clara. "But poor Celeste simply couldn't bear to remain here after the Count's death. Melbourne society was always suspicious of her, and the Mayor was especially nasty once she had lost her protector."

"I remember that Mayor," Lola said. "Lionel showed him up for the coward that he was."

"And he never forgave it," said Clara. "He took every little opportunity to embarrass Celeste. And he urged on the women who were so very cruel to her. Not that they needed much encouragement."

"Alas, yes," said Lola. "They were not entirely pleased with my performance either, as I recall."

Clara suppressed a smile. "No indeed," she said. "But your visit was short, and you carried it off bravely before you returned to America." She sighed. "But Celeste was here for a very long time. She did not much mind for herself, but she cared very deeply that she should not be an impediment to Lionel's career. It was hard for her."

"True," said Lola. "Her letters were very sorrowful."

"And what of you?" Clara asked. "What have you been doing all this time?"

"Well," said Lola, "I took my company back to America, as you know, and we toured California once more. Then the Civil War came: it was horrible, of course, but it provided such good opportunities for performers—we were very popular, and much in demand to entertain the troops." She giggled. "I don't care what anyone says—I thought that Robert E. Lee was such a nice man," she said. "And I got on terribly well with Ulysses Grant—he's President now, you know. The generals were all most accommodating. I expanded my troupe, and we were very successful. So successful, in fact, that I was able to stop performing for some years. I re-married, of course—but I'm afraid I was widowed once again. I seem to have no luck at all with men."

"*Or too much*," thought Clara, remembering Ferguson, wondering just how close Lola had become to McGill on that long sea voyage. She worried for Morag, knowing that her friend had pinned all her hopes on her reunion with this man. It would be too bad if Lola interfered. "What happened next?" she asked aloud.

"I got bored," said Lola. "I went back to the stage. I own the entire company now—I no longer dance myself. I just manage the company. And finally we had an invitation to return to Melbourne, so here we are. But that's enough about me, at least for now." She settled herself more comfortably on the cushions, gazing out of the cab at the bustling traffic where carriages and drays and overloaded wagons jostled for space and pedestrians avoided collision with them by trudging along on the very edge of the muddy road, stepping carefully around the piles of steaming dung left in the wake of the horse-drawn transport. "I can see for myself that things have certainly changed here," she said. "I scarcely recognise the city."

"It's the fastest growing city in the world," Clara said. "It's hard to keep up with the changes."

"And I hear it has grown large enough to support this publication of yours," said Lola. "You must tell me about it. Celeste writes that it has proved to be a most interesting venture."

The carriage lurched, avoiding a dray. Clara clutched at the seat, righting herself before she answered. "It's called *The New Day*," she said. "It's a women's journal: I print items of interest to women—stories and poems, gossip, household tips, fashion, recipes, horoscopes, theatre reviews and the like. I shall certainly write an article about your dance company. Celeste sends a fashion column from Paris, from time to time—that's always well received."

"Is that all?" Lola asked.

"Not entirely." Clara grinned mischievously. "I use *The New Day* to publish political articles of particular interest to women."

"Such as?"

"Such as the need to reform the laws relating to property, particularly the property of married women," Clara replied.

"Ah," said Lola. "I imagine that might be close to your own heart."

"Yes," Clara said. "When I left Henry, he got everything I owned. I paid for the *The Ballarat Times*, Lola. It was my money that built it, and my money that ran it. And because I daren't stay with a drunken husband, the law awarded him all my property. I was left with my children and nothing to support them."

"That's hard," said Lola. She lowered her voice. "I've lost several husbands, you know. Fortunately for me, they all died. You'd have been much better off as a widow."

"I know," said Clara. "It's a shame Henry wouldn't oblige."

"Indeed," Lola said, straight-faced. "It was most ungenerous of him."

"I don't know what I would have done without Celeste," Clara went on. "She and the Count took us in, and eventually found a comfortable house for us. The Count very generously put up the money for me to start the journal, and, thank goodness, it's been successful enough to support me."

"And you publish your political works unimpeded," said Lola. "I like that."

Clara grinned at her friend. "Indeed. Right now I'm supporting the women agitating for the right to vote," said Clara. "Did you know that here in Victoria women were accidentally given the vote in 1863? And when we dared to use it the next year, the men in Parliament took it away again? It's outrageous."

"Did you say *we*?"

"Yes. I voted in 1864, of course I did. I'm over twenty-one and I own property, so I was a person eligible to vote. And I did."

"Did it make any difference?"

"No, it didn't change the outcome," Clara said. "But the sky didn't fall either."

"What happened, then?" Lola said. "I'm intrigued."

"There were lots of cartoons about us in *Punch*," Clara said, with some venom. "Then those fools in Parliament changed the legislation back on the grounds that it was never their intention to include women in the Electoral Act—obviously they think that women aren't people, or at least persons!"

"So you can't vote again?"

"Not at the moment: women are subject to the laws, but we can't make them. We pay our taxes but we can't vote to say how our money is spent. *No taxation without representation*, as the Americans have it. The men won that right after the Eureka uprising—and my husband was the only one who went to prison for it. It wrecked his health, and our marriage. Anyway, that's all in the past. It's my turn now. We women want our rights too." Clara paused, out of breath.

Lola clapped her hands. "Bravo," she said. "Is there any hope you will succeed?"

"We must believe that there is," Clara replied, suddenly serious. "In the long run, we must achieve a change if this society is not to falter." She shrugged. "But we have a long way to go. The men in power fight us tooth and nail: they cling to their establishment, pretending that women are too weak and emotional to make simple decisions. It's nonsense, of course. In truth, it suits them very well to keep women powerless. Take this evening, for instance: Sir Alec Buchanan is hosting a dinner at The Melbourne Club for the shareholders in his copper mining consortium. I am a shareholder, but I am barred from attending."

"Why is that?" Lola asked.

"Because The Melbourne Club is for men only," Clara replied. "They take our money happily enough, but they won't invite us to share their dinner. It's too bad!"

Lola laughed. "Nothing much has changed, then," she said.

"Not yet," Clara replied. "But I swear it will. If not for my generation, then for my daughter's."

"Your daughter?" said Lola, looking puzzled for a moment. She shook her head. "I had almost forgotten: Celeste wrote to me when your daughter was born. How silly of me. How old is she now?"

"Charlotte is sweet seventeen, and very much looking forward to meeting you," said Clara. "And she's a handful of mischief, if ever there was one. She's quite the tomboy—she's learnt to ride, and to shoot."

"She takes after her mother, then," said Lola.

Clara left her thought unspoken: "*And her father.*" In this instance, she had no intention of telling Lola the whole truth, or even part of it. Why should she, when only Morag knew?

"And what has become of your sons?" Lola asked.

"The eldest, Oliver, has gone to America to work on the railways," Clara replied. "And William, the youngest, is working at the new copper mine in South Australia: Sir Alec found work for him there."

"And are you happy about that?"

"I'd prefer to see them more often," Clara admitted, "but they are grown men. They have their own lives to lead." She shrugged. "They don't need me anymore."

"Perhaps one of them will visit while I am here," Lola said.

"Perhaps," Clara replied, knowing how very unlikely that would be. They had not parted on the best of terms. "So tell me, Lola," she said, deftly changing the subject, "how did you come to arrive in company with Captain McGill?"

"It's Consul McGill now," Lola replied.

"Of course," said Clara. "I knew that. It will take some getting used to."

"Do you know him well, then?" Lola asked.

"We were acquainted at Ballarat. He was the leader of the California

Rangers, then. He was wonderful when Morag was in trouble after her husband's death." She lowered her voice conspiratorially: "The two of them have corresponded all this time, you know. I believe they still have an understanding."

"Have they indeed?" Lola said thoughtfully. "Well, all I can say is that I knew *James*"—she emphasized the first name—"from my American tour. And when I met up with him on the *Nevada*, he was a most delightful travelling companion—most amusing."

Clara looked directly at her companion. "You didn't...?" she asked.

Lola looked smug. "Maybe I did," she said. "And maybe I didn't." She shrugged. "There's not a lot to do on a five-week voyage."

"Then best we don't tell Morag," Clara said, reading between the lines.

"Tell her what, exactly?" Lola replied. "I haven't told you anything."

"Maybe not exactly," said Clara. "But I can guess."

"You shouldn't guess," said Lola. "You might guess wrong." She sighed. "And if you don't want to know, you shouldn't ask."

"I always ask," Clara said ruefully. "It's what I do. I can't seem to help myself."

"Then it makes you a good journalist," Lola replied. "But it also makes you, perhaps, a dangerous friend."

Clara shrugged. "I take my friends as I find them," she said. "And I trust that they will do the same for me."

Chapter 32

In his city offices, Sir Alec Buchanan was meeting with Mr Edward Cole—prominent businessman, bookseller and publisher, and self-made millionaire.

"I trust you are keeping my investments safe, Edward," Buchanan said, gesturing towards the armchair beside his desk.

"As safe as you are keeping mine," Cole responded, with his usual good humour. He sat down heavily. A man of middle height and middle years, his pink complexion, blond curls and wide smile masked one of the shrewdest business minds in the colonies. He had made and lost one fortune providing goods and services on the goldfields, and was well on his way to consolidating his second one. "I'm expanding my printing business, you know."

"I know," Buchanan responded. "I hear that my Chinese business associates at the Commercial Bank are financing that expansion."

Cole grinned. "It's a small business loan for a new press, nothing more," he said. "Although I will admit that I'm planning to expand my book emporium into larger premises on Bourke Street—I already have a particular building in mind."

"And the Bank will finance that too?"

"Certainly. It's clever of the Commercial to lend to smaller business ventures—none of the other banks are doing it, and there is serious money to be made." He pulled a Commercial banknote from his pocket and held it up. "Wonderful," he said, pointing to the Chinese characters that ran down the sides. "It says '*New Mountain of Gold*', the Chinese epithet for Australia. I like that. It just about sums up the position, don't you think?"

"Indeed I do," said Buchanan. He looked up as one of his assistants entered, carrying a covered tray. "Tea, Edward?"

"Thank you, yes," said Cole. He nodded his thanks to the assistant, who poured for him and passed him a delicate china cup and saucer before she left the men to their business once more.

"These are excellent ginger biscuits, if you'd care for one," Buchanan said, indicating the plate on the tray. "My cook makes them."

"Thank you, no," said Cole. He patted his stomach. "Have to watch the waistline, you know." He grinned. "Besides," he added, "I shall have to leave ample room for your dinner at the Club this evening. Your menus are always splendid. I must thank you, by the way, for obliging me by extending an invitation to Mr Pitman—he's a most interesting man. I'm anxious you should meet him while he is in Melbourne. His visit is to be brief—this will be by far the best way to establish contact."

"My pleasure," said Buchanan. "I'm happy to make his acquaintance. How do you know him?"

"He wrote to me after I published my *Discourse in Defence of Mental Freedom,* my first work on the philosophy of religion. We have corresponded ever since. He is the head of the Swedenborgian Church in Australia, and thoroughly opposed to dogma of any kind. He is a man after my own heart."

"I see," Buchanan said warily. "Is that why I am giving him dinner, Edward?"

Cole laughed. "Gracious no," he said. "Jacob Pitman is a successful architect and engineer in Adelaide. He works with government contracts, and has some most interesting inventions that I think may be of commercial value," he said. "He's a useful man to know."

"Ah," said Buchanan. "That's better. It is to be a business dinner, after all." He paused. "I've also invited Mr Woo," he added, a little too casually. "The Chinese business community has invested a lot of resources in our enterprises. I thought it only proper to ask a representative to dine with us."

"Capital," said Cole. "The famous Chang Woo Gow: I shall enjoy meeting him. One hears so many stories. Is he really eight feet tall?"

"Wait and see," Buchanan replied.

Cole frowned. "Obviously your guest list is entirely your own affair," he said, "but between friends: will you to permit me to enquire as to why you have chosen to invite Woo? Surely Louis Ah Mouy or Lowe Kong Meng from the Commercial Bank would have a larger stake in the consortium?"

Buchanan hesitated, deciding how much he might safely divulge. "Mr Spencer Valentine, the Bank's manager, will be joining us this evening to represent the Commercial's interests in our projects," he said at last.

"And?"

"And as for the rest, it's a delicate matter," Buchanan continued. "In the normal course of events, I would have asked Ah Zow Chan, with whom I have had business dealings these many years, as you know. He has helped the Chinese community to invest in a great many of our projects, but he is obliged to be in San Francisco at present on an urgent matter of business: he expects to be there for some time. Chang Woo Gow is now overseeing some of Mr Chan's more—shall we say *discreet*—Melbourne interests, and it was suggested that it would be opportune if I invited him along this evening. It will afford him the opportunity to meet some of the members of our consortium in congenial surroundings."

"That's intriguing," Cole said. "Woo's presence will certainly make for a most entertaining evening."

"I've decided to send Hector to escort him," Buchanan added. "The Melbourne Club can be so..."—he hesitated—"so *set* in its views. I think it best that Woo should not arrive alone, at least not on his first visit. Having my personal secretary with him to smooth the way should prevent any difficulties."

"Sensible," said Cole, chuckling to himself at the prospect of the stuffy concierge's reaction to the arrival of a Chinaman in this most conservative of privileged white enclaves, and, if rumour proved to be even half true, an enormous Chinaman at that.

"One does one's best," Buchanan said.

"Of course," Cole said. He leaned forward and helped himself to a ginger biscuit. "I know I shouldn't," he said, "but just the one won't hurt."

Buchanan smiled. "It's hard to resist good baking."

"And your cook is first rate," Cole agreed, munching happily. "But now, Alec," he said, "perhaps you'll be good enough to tell me what this meeting is really about."

Buchanan's smiled widened. "It's about this new printing venture of yours," he said.

"Oh?"

"I am wondering," Buchanan said, "about how best to present our new advances in telegraphic technology to the community at large. I understand you are commissioning new works?"

"Well, yes, but I don't publish newspapers, Alec. Surely *The Argus* or *The Age* would be better suited to that kind of publicity."

"I'm not so much interested in day-to-day journalism," Buchanan replied. "There will certainly be any amount of that."

"What, then?"

"Longer articles: interviews with the engineers, stories about families who have used the new relay, maybe even fictional stories about the Telegraph— that sort of thing," Buchanan said.

"But why?"

"Public opinion is swayed by such things," Buchanan replied. "We have had some—shall we say *unfortunate*—accidents during construction, and it would be well to focus attention away from that. We need to get people used to the idea that the Telegraph is a good thing, and here to stay. We need people to know that they can use it for personal messages." He shrugged: "You of all people know that we should not underestimate the value of popular reading. I'm certain that those scientific romances you sell are having an effect on the way people think—they certainly stir things up. And look how successful Mrs Seekamp has been with her campaigning, popping her politics in amongst the recipes in that women's journal of hers."

"*The New Day*," Cole said promptly. "I print it for her."

"There you are then," said Buchanan. "Perhaps Mrs Seekamp will write something in praise of the Telegraph—she is a shareholder in the consortium, after all."

"Indeed she is," Cole replied. "And I fully expect she will castigate us in her journal for not inviting her to dinner tonight."

"That was not possible," Buchanan said smugly. "The Melbourne Club has its rules. I'm sure the good lady will understand."

"I'm sure she will understand all too well," Cole replied.

Chapter 33

When McGill and Hector finally arrived at Buchanan's house on Wellington Parade, Morag Munro, dressed elegantly in a white-trimmed dove-grey dress that set off her shining copper curls, her wide grey eyes and her pale complexion, was waiting, nervously, in the front parlour. At the sound of the carriage she rose to open the front door herself, anxious that nothing should go awry.

McGill stepped down first and, as the door opened, strode across the gravelled drive. "Morag," he said as he quickly ascended the steps to the wide, covered veranda floored with tessellated tiles. He reached the doorway and took both of her hands in his own. "You look wonderful."

"So do you, James," she replied, blushing faintly. "You haven't changed a bit."

"Generous of you to say so," McGill replied. "Then let us say that the years appear to have been kind to us both."

"Won't you come in?" said Morag. "I expect you will need refreshment after your journey. I have ordered tea."

"Certainly," McGill said, smiling broadly. "And I really should pay my respects to Buchanan."

"He is in his city office today," Hector said, coming up beside McGill. "So it will be just the three of us for morning tea."

"Excellent," McGill said. "You can tell me all your news."

Morag led the way to the front parlour, where a splendid apple cake dusted with fine sugar sat on the top tier of a high silver stand, above layers of various smaller cakes and delicate sandwiches. The cook had been keeping watch for this special visitor: McGill had barely taken his seat in a chintz-covered armchair before a maid appeared bearing the tea tray.

"Thank you, Mary," Morag said firmly. "That will be all for now."

Mary bobbed her head in acknowledgement before she scurried back to the kitchen to report on what she had seen.

159

Morag rose and busied herself with the pouring of tea into fine gold-rimmed bone china cups.

McGill smiled. "This is an impressive house," he said, looking around. "I see you keep it in excellent order."

Hector grinned, watching his mother happily accept the compliment. He put down his teacup. "If you'll excuse me," he said, "I'll just pop out and have a word with the coachmen. I'll have them transfer Consul McGill's luggage to a dray for delivery, so that the carriage will be free for Sir Alec if he needs it this afternoon."

"Of course," Morag said. "I know you have a busy day today, dear."

Hector rose, kissed his mother lightly on the cheek and slipped quietly from the room, closing the door behind him.

"Your son has grown into a very capable man," McGill said. "It was kind of him to meet me, and to give us a little time alone together. You must be very proud of him."

"Very proud," said Morag. "He has had considerable difficulties to overcome, as you know, but things have worked out well in the end." She smiled again. "And you must tell me about your daughter," she added.

McGill extracted the creased photograph from his wallet yet again, and passed it to Morag. "There she is," he said. "That's Rosie."

"She's lovely," said Morag.

"She is," McGill replied. "And she faces much the same difficulties as Hector, having lost her mother." He hesitated. "Well," he said, "I know that's not exactly fair. Rosie has always had my mother to take care of her, and there has been no want of money to constrain her."

Morag looked down at her hands. "It wasn't easy for Hector when I took up this post," she said quietly. "It seemed temporary at the time. And yet…it has not been so uncomfortable. Sir Alec has been generous—he provided a first-class education for Hector, and immediately employed him in his company."

"But what of you?" McGill asked. "Now that Hector is grown, I imagine you would not always wish to remain a housekeeper—even in such a magnificent house as this."

"And I imagine that you would not always wish to live with your mother for your daughter's sake," Morag countered.

McGill looked at her, a huge smile suffusing his face. "Then have you given thought to the matter I wrote to you about?" he asked.

"I have thought of nothing else, James," Morag replied, her face lit by a smile as radiant as his own.

McGill reached inside his coat and withdrew a small black velvet box. "Then allow me to do this properly," he said. He crossed the room, dropped to one knee before her, and took her left hand in his right. "Morag Munro," he said, "will you do me the very great honour of becoming my wife?"

"Yes, James," she replied, smiling through the tears that somehow threatened to flow, "I will."

McGill opened the box and slipped the ring it contained onto her finger.

Morag looked down at her hand, tilting it to admire the large, square-cut emerald set in filigree gold that she now wore. The flawless stone was a fine, deep green that sparkled in the morning light. "James," she breathed. "It's beautiful. It fits perfectly. And emeralds are my favourite. However did you know?"

McGill looked relieved. "I hoped you would like it," he said. "I chose it for the colour: I thought it would suit your lovely auburn hair."

"It's perfect," was all Morag could manage to say around the lump in her throat.

McGill rose to his feet, still holding her hand as if he would never let it go. He drew her to him and kissed her deeply, tenderly. When they drew apart at last, Morag held up her ring again, wondering at its beauty.

McGill put his arm about her waist. "I bought the stone in New York," he said, "from a dealer with interests in a Columbian mine. He swore the world's finest emeralds are mined there. He also told me that the emerald is the colour of Venus, the goddess of love, so I had him set the stone in gold for you." He sighed. "That was years ago, my love. I've waited so long to be able to offer it to you, to offer it with all my heart."

"Then it has been worth the wait," Morag said. "It has found its home, at last."

"And we shall have such a lot to plan," McGill said, still smiling. "A wedding day, to begin with, and a home for us here in Melbourne—I daresay the Consulate will need refurbishing."

"And I shall have to find a new housekeeper for Sir Alec," said Morag.

McGill was suddenly serious. "Are you sure you will be prepared to move to America with me when my mission here is done?" he asked. "It will not be for some time, of course, but the time will come."

"I'm certain," Morag replied. "I moved from my home in Scotland to Australia all those years ago. I can move again. I am looking forward to meeting Rosie, and to us all becoming a proper family."

"It goes without saying that there is a place for Hector in my company if he chooses to come with us."

"Thank you, James," Morag said. "I'll admit I had hoped as much."

"Have you said anything to him?" McGill asked.

"No," Morag replied. "I would not have put you in such a delicate position. But I think Hector guesses, all the same."

"Guesses what?" said Hector, stepping back into the parlour.

161

"That I have asked your mother to become my wife," McGill replied, beaming. "And, I am delighted to say, she has given her consent."

"Congratulations," Hector said, stepping forward to shake McGill's hand. "I'm glad the matter is settled at last." He hesitated. "You will be my stepfather, then," he said. "I don't think I can call you 'Dad'."

"James will be fine," McGill said.

"Excellent, James," said Hector. "And now, if Mother can spare you, I have promised to deliver you to your new residence at the Consulate before noon. I believe a luncheon has been arranged in your honour."

"Of course," McGill replied. "I should not wish to inconvenience my new colleagues. Morag?"

"We have all the time in the world, James," she replied happily. "I have no doubt I shall see you later in the day."

"That you will," McGill said. "I can scarcely bear to be parted from you at all, on this of all days: we have a whole new life ahead of us now."

"A whole new life together," Morag echoed, bright-eyed and smiling.

"We'll be off, then," Hector said awkwardly, conscious that McGill was already running late. "And Mother will need some time to tell the staff," he added. "I must warn you, they are all agog in the kitchen, waiting for news."

"Then I'll leave you to it," McGill said. "Until later, my love."

"I'll walk with you to the carriage," Morag said, reluctant to let him go.

A s the carriage pulled away, McGill looked back. Morag was standing on the steps, her hair shining like burnished copper in the sunlight, her slim figure silhouetted against the doorway. She waved, and just for a moment McGill fancied that he had caught a glimpse of the girl she had once been, the girl who had journeyed to the goldfields full of hope and promise, the girl who had been denied her youth by the harshest of circumstances. *I will make this a new beginning, my love,* he thought, *for both of us.*

Chapter 34

At the end of a long day spent escorting McGill, reassuring his mother, and finalising the arrangements for Buchanan's dinner party, Hector was very tired. He returned to the house and changed into his evening clothes before he set out to perform the last duty his employer had requested of him before the function began: Hector was to escort the famous Chinese giant, Chang Woo Gow, to The Melbourne Club. Hector was more than a little nervous about the task—all he knew about the man had been gleaned from popular newspapers that delighted in the revelation that Woo had had an international career displaying himself in freak shows before arriving in Melbourne and marrying an Australian woman called Kitty. It was not encouraging information, but Hector would, as always, do his best.

The October night proved unseasonably chilly. Hector drew his cloak about him as he alighted from the Hansom cab in Spring Street, picked his way gingerly past seedy-looking pimps and their skinny whores, past importunate shills for bars and restaurants, and down the last few hundred yards into the dimly lit fog of Little Bourke Street. He tried not to breathe the dank, smoke-tainted air as he walked past alleyways that reeked of frying cabbage, of horse dung, of poverty. A filthy, ragged man made to brush against him. A pickpocket. Hector was ready for this. In a single, practised motion he slipped his knife from his sleeve to his hand: "I'm armed," he hissed. "Back off."

The man melted back into the shadows as if he had never been.

Hector slid his knife away, then patted his inside coat pocket, checking that his treasure was safe. He increased his pace, striding through the swirling fog until he paused, finally, at a nondescript red door with a brass dragon knocker.

He rapped twice. The door opened a fraction to admit him to a wide hallway. Hector was keenly aware of the sudden change in atmosphere as he stepped inside from the damp night air: the corridor was warm, its red-painted walls lit softly with lamplight, its air sweetened with sandalwood. The stocky man who bowed him inside was dressed in customary Chinese fashion—a thigh-length black cotton top over baggy black trousers, his hair drawn into a long pigtail that hung down his back.

As Hector was ushered along, he glanced through dark brocade curtains to a room heavy with the perfume of incense that failed to disguise the reek of opium. A den for the well-to-do, he realised, noting the scatter of delicately carved ivory pipes of the current fashion. He saw low divans, and gentlemen in evening dress sprawled upon them—attended by courtesans plying hard liquor, sex, and the ubiquitous opium. It was a scene of languid debauchery, the fires of lust damped by the drug.

Hector had no time to reflect on this revelation: he was directed, politely but very firmly, into a sitting room at the rear of the building. His host rose to greet him, offering a tight, formal bow from the waist.

"Mr Munro, I presume." Woo's English pronunciation was Oxford perfect, belying the effect of his splendid Chinese evening costume that featured a high Mandarin collar, a long brocaded coat with gold frogging, and loose black silk trousers. He was clean-shaven, and his black hair was drawn back tight into a very long braid that he wore draped across his right shoulder. The end of the pigtail was tied with thick gold thread which ended in a heavy gold tassel that swayed gently as he moved.

Hector, who stood six feet tall, was not accustomed to feeling short—but this man towered over him. He tried not to stare, hiding his astonishment by bowing in response. "Mr Woo," he said. "I am delighted to meet you at last."

Woo smiled slightly, gesturing Hector towards a cherry wood chair, finely carved with coiling dragons and highlighted in gold leaf. "Do sit down," he said. "You will take tea?"

Hector nodded, taking his seat as directed. He noticed that on Woo's right middle finger he wore a large ring of grass-green jade, carved into the shape of a rampant dragon and set in heavy gold. The ring shone in the lamplight as Woo clapped his hands, once.

A young girl glided into the room, silent on silk-slippered feet, demurely dressed in traditional embroidered robes of red and gold that accentuated her porcelain-pale skin, her dark almond-shaped eyes and her shining dark hair. She knelt at the low, dragon-carved table with her lacquered tray and looked up at Woo, silently seeking permission to pour tea.

Woo nodded.

Hector smelled the delicious, smoky scent of oolong, and, as the girl handed him the tiny cup, he could not help but marvel at her delicacy after the women he had seen in the opium rooms.

"Thank you," he said. "Oolong: The Black Dragon tea. I am honoured."

Woo nodded again, and the girl left them as silently as she had come.

Hector sipped politely, then replaced his cup on the table and reached inside the pocket of his frock coat.

Woo stiffened.

"A gift," Hector said quickly. He withdrew a slim, tissue-wrapped box, which he held out to his host, formally, using both hands as he had been instructed. "Please accept this small token of my employer's esteem. Sir Alec offers his felicitations, and hopes that you will accept my services as your escort to tonight's dinner party."

"How very thoughtful," Woo replied. He was unwrapping Buchanan's gift as he spoke. The tissue fell away to reveal a slim, carved ebony box. Inside the box, nestling snugly on a bed of red velvet lay a pair of exquisitely tapered ivory chopsticks, the upper ends cased in gold filigree depicting Imperial dragons. Woo inclined his head. "This is a generous gift," he said. "The dragons are most auspicious: my personal emblem. Your employer has chosen with care, and I thank him, and you, for your courtesy."

"We are honoured," said Hector, wondering what to do next.

His host rose once more to his impossible height. "I shall be with you directly," he said. He clapped his hands again, and the manservant who had opened the door reappeared, holding a long black topcoat. Woo slipped into it, donned his hat, and then turned back to Hector. "My man has brought the carriage to the door," he said simply. "This way."

Hector followed his host along a different corridor that led to a side door, held open by another of Woo's ubiquitous staff. As he stepped into the waiting carriage, he could not fail to notice that two heavily muscled Chinese retainers stepped silently up behind to ride on the footplate.

Woo was well guarded. Hector wondered, not for the first time that evening, exactly who was escorting whom.

Chapter 35

As Captain James McGill alighted from his carriage in front of the high, polished doors of The Melbourne Club, he could not help but marvel at the changes that had occurred since he was last in this city. The Club was frankly opulent. A liveried doorman opened the panelled doors, bowing McGill into a marble-floored reception area that glowed with soft light and gleamed with polished brass. The concierge stepped forward to greet him, discreetly consulted the guest list and verified that McGill was indeed the American Consul before beckoning a second attendant to take the guest's coat to the cloakroom. These procedures concluded, McGill was ushered into the Sitting Room, where pre-dinner drinks were being served.

McGill stepped into the room and accepted a glass of sherry from a formally dressed waiter who stood unobtrusively just inside the door with his laden silver tray.

Buchanan was standing by the mantelpiece, ready to greet his guests. "McGill!" he said. "Delighted you could join us. It has been a long time since you graced our shores. Welcome back."

"The pleasure is all mine," McGill replied, shaking hands with his host. "I must say, your Club is splendid."

Buchanan smiled. "We like it," he said. "Come along and meet Mr Edward Cole. He's been wanting to make your acquaintance ever since he learned that you were returning to Melbourne."

"How so?" McGill asked.

"Cole is our biggest bookseller and publisher, among other things," Buchanan said. "And he confesses to a certain fascination with the events of Eureka. I expect he wants to ask you about the California Rangers."

"That was such a long time ago," McGill said.

"And yet," said Buchanan, "I think you'll find that the effects of that day still resonate here with us."

He led McGill across the room to where a plump, fair-haired man was carefully examining the leather-bound books that filled the shelves of the comfortable room. "Edward Cole," Buchanan said, "allow me to introduce the American Consul, Captain James McGill."

"Oh," said Cole, turning around, caught unawares. He held out his hand. "I'm delighted to meet you, Captain McGill. I have been looking forward to making your acquaintance."

"It's a pleasure," McGill replied, shaking the hand Cole offered.

"I'll leave you two to chat for a moment," said Buchanan. "I must greet Mr Valentine—I see that he has just arrived."

Cole grinned happily at McGill. "Mr Valentine is the manager of the Commercial Bank," he explained.

"I see," said McGill. "Then he will be a most useful acquaintance."

"Indeed," Cole agreed. "I hope you won't mind," he continued, "but I have asked Sir Alec to seat me beside you at dinner. It will be such a rare opportunity to converse with the two leaders of the California Rangers together."

"The two leaders?" McGill said. "Is Ferguson coming to dinner?"

"He is," said Cole. "He has been deeply involved in the copper consortium. He has been much in the public eye, one way and another. In fact," he added, "when Buchanan helped to finance the ill-fated Burke and Wills expedition to search for a suitable route from Melbourne to the north coast for the telegraph line, Ferguson went along in charge of all the transport animals." He grinned. "He's a lucky man, your friend. Ferguson left the expedition at Balranald: only one of those who went all the way north survived."

"I don't know much about the expedition," said McGill. "But you're right about Ferguson—he has always had a charmed life. He's come through any number of conflicts unscathed."

"I daresay you've had your own share of luck," Cole observed. "Your timing in heading back to the States after Eureka was perfect: Governor Hotham had half the police force out searching for you! He was worried you might lead another uprising."

"I had heard," McGill said wryly.

Cole chuckled.

"In any case," McGill continued, "it will be wonderful to see Ferguson again, after all this time. I had hoped to look him up tomorrow. I have good news to share with him."

"Concerning your impending nuptials, no doubt," said Cole. "Congratulations, by the way: Mrs Munro is a splendid woman."

McGill hesitated, taken aback. "Thank you," he said at last. He shook his head. "Is there no privacy in this town?" he asked.

Cole grinned. "None at all," he replied. "Melbourne has the airs and graces of a city, but it gossips like a village." He shrugged expressively. "We were all looking forward to meeting the new American Consul, of course," he said, "and delighted to discover that the post was to be filled by the former leader of the famous California Rangers. But your arrival today has been thrilling: you set the tongues wagging when you appeared on the docks in the company of the infamous Madame Montez, and then in the course of the same morning you became engaged to the beautiful Mrs Munro. We can hardly wait to see what you will do next."

"I hope I don't disappoint, then," McGill said ruefully.

"I scarcely think that's possible," Cole replied.

Buchanan rejoined them, bringing with him a nervous, bespectacled, balding man whose shiny head gleamed pink in the lamplight. "Allow me to introduce Mr Spencer Valentine," he said. "I think you know Mr Edward Cole, but you will not have met our new American Consul, Captain James McGill."

"Delighted," said McGill.

"It's a pleasure to meet you, sir," said Valentine, his light voice a higher register than McGill had somehow expected from a man of his bulk.

"Mr Valentine is here tonight representing the Commercial Bank," said Buchanan.

"And are you also a member of the consortium, Consul?" Valentine asked.

"My personal company is about to be," McGill replied. "But in a way I am also here as a representative of another stakeholder: Mr George Train has asked me to act as his agent here in Melbourne."

"You know the inimitable Mr Train?" Cole asked.

"Certainly I do," McGill replied. "We go back a long way, and I have had a great many financial dealings with him over the years. He's a shrewd investor, and most pleased with the way the copper consortium has developed."

"And what's Mr Train doing these days?" Cole said genially. "Apart from developing his famous railroads, that is."

McGill grinned. "He's campaigning to be the next President of the United States," he said.

"Good Heavens," said Buchanan. "Is he likely to win?"

"Very likely," McGill replied.

"Against Ulysses Grant?" Cole said incredulously. "Grant's a war hero."

"People are tired of war," McGill replied. "They think there should be a better way, and George Train is offering them a genuine alternative. I was with him when he toured the country by railroad in his personal carriage. He is very popular. By all accounts, Train *could* take the Presidency. He was the front runner when I took ship for Melbourne."

"Well that's a piece of unexpected good news," said Cole. "Bravo for Train. I hope he wins."

"Yes," Buchanan agreed. "It certainly won't do our consortium any harm at all to have the President of the United States as a major investor."

"Indeed it won't," said McGill. He paused, turning to Buchanan. "And that reminds me, Sir Alec," he said. "Mr Train bids me ask you whether he has won his bet."

"Unfortunately, he has," Buchanan replied. "You may inform him that I owe him the princely sum of twenty pounds."

"How so?" Cole asked, scenting gossip.

Buchanan shrugged eloquently, raising the shoulders of his perfectly tailored evening coat the merest fraction. "When our copper consortium was in the process of being formed," he said, "Mr Train and I had a long conversation about the relative merits of independence for this colony in relation to matters of business. I was of the opinion that our copper mining enterprise could proceed unhindered to develop our own smelting factory, but Train insisted that the English government would block any such move. We wagered twenty pounds on the outcome. He was right: our political masters back in England have insisted that our copper ore be shipped to Swansea, the copper smelting centre for the Empire. So, here we only reduce the ore for shipping. Then all the copper goes to Wales to be refined, and must be shipped back again before we can use it."

"Not very efficient," said Cole.

"Indeed not," Buchanan replied. "It is most inconvenient, not to mention expensive—every merchant who handles the goods along the way makes a profit."

"Then perhaps you might begin to think differently about independence after all, Sir Alec," McGill said in his soft American drawl.

Cole gave him a curious, appraising glance. "I knew you would liven things up here," he said. "You really must let me ask you about the Eureka Stockade."

Chapter 36

Outside in the entry, two things happened at once to disturb the dignified marble silence of the reception area. The commotion spread to disrupt the polite murmur of conversation as Buchanan's guests sipped their sherry and exchanged pre-dinner pleasantries.

"You must excuse me," Buchanan said hurriedly, heading for the door.

Cole winked incorrigibly at McGill. "I'll just take a peek," he said, moving to open the door of the Sitting Room a fraction wider while the waiter affected not to notice. "I have an idea what this might be about."

McGill followed, intrigued.

In the foyer, the unbelievably tall Chang Woo Gow towered majestically over a flustered doorman, waiting with inscrutable patience while Hector tried to get a word in edgeways around the black-clad scarecrow of a priest with whom the concierge was currently arguing. The priest was tall, but completely overshadowed by Woo, whose presence appeared to make him angry.

Hector, whose temperament was usually easy-going, disliked the priest on sight. Everything about the man grated on his tired senses, triggered his anxieties. Concerned to avoid a scene, he tried a direct appeal to the doorman: "I'll just take Sir Alec's guest through, John, if I may," he said.

The doorman shook his head, indicating that he would not admit Hector and his most unusual guest without the consent of his superior. He opened his gloved hands wide: "Just doing my job, sir," he said apologetically. "I know you, Mr Munro, of course I do. But the Club is very particular about its rules. It's more than my job is worth to break them. The guest list must be checked, sir. I hope you'll understand."

"Of course," Woo replied, his Oxford accent clearly surprising the beleaguered doorman. "I would not wish it otherwise." He crossed his hands at his waist and deliberately tucked his manicured fingers inside his long sleeves, the very picture of irritating oriental serenity.

The doorman nodded, relieved but cautious.

Hector found the situation upsetting, but took a pace back to stand beside his guest, preparing to wait out the altercation. The priest was insisting in a loud Irish brogue that he had every reason to be admitted. The concierge thought otherwise.

Buchanan strode into the reception hall and up to the concierge. "Allow me to identify my *guest*," he said, nodding a greeting to Woo. "This commotion is most unseemly."

"My profound apologies, Sir Alec," the concierge replied. "But this man," he waved his pencil in the direction of the priest, "is not on your guest list. He pushed his way in here past the doorman and is now demanding to be admitted to your dinner."

Buchanan glanced casually at the intruder, and then looked again, hard. He was too practised a businessman to show his shock. His face remained as inscrutable as Woo's as he said smoothly: "If you will oblige me by stepping aside for a moment, Father, I shall just see to my guests and return to you directly."

"You know me, Buchanan," the priest grated. "I was explaining to your man here," he pointed a bony finger at the concierge, "that I am present as the delegate for the Bishop, who finds at the last minute that he is indisposed, and so has sent me in his place to be his representative."

"That's as may be," Buchanan replied politely. "But in all courtesy I have other matters to attend to. I shall escort Mr Woo to join my other guests in the Sitting Room, and then I shall return to deal with the matter of your admittance, without further inconvenience to others."

"I won't stand aside for a Chinaman," the priest said.

Buchanan lost patience. "Then you won't dine with me tonight," he replied. He crooked his index finger to summon the doorman. "Shall I call the men to escort you from the premises?"

The priest looked around. The sound of his altercation had clearly reached the street: two heavily muscled Chinese bodyguards had appeared silently and now stood a little behind Woo and Hector, ready for trouble. The Club's own guards also stood quietly on the steps, waiting.

The priest shrugged. "It seems I must give way," he muttered. He stalked to a leather chair in the lobby and sat, glowering at the Club's staff.

"Good," said Buchanan. "Mr Woo, do accept my apologies for your inconvenience."

"Not at all," Woo replied. "It has been most entertaining."

The concierge merely nodded as he ticked Woo's name on the guest list. An attendant stepped forward to whisk their coats away to the cloakroom,

THE FIVE STAR REPUBLIC

and Hector ushered his charge into the Sitting Room, at last. The effect of Woo's arrival was dramatic: the buzz of urbane conversation died, and all eyes turned to Buchanan as he entered a pace behind his guest.

Unfazed, Woo accepted a glass of sherry from a waiter who was clearly trying hard not to stare.

Cole and McGill, standing closest to the door, were first to be introduced. "Mr Woo," Cole said, bowing. "We have all been waiting to meet you. And you must allow me to introduce the new American Consul, Captain McGill."

"Delighted," said Woo.

"The pleasure is all mine," McGill replied, his soft American drawl a sharp contrast with the Chinaman's clipped English accent. "I see that Mr Munro has been taking good care of you."

"Indeed he has," Woo answered. "He has been most solicitous."

"Captain McGill led the California Rangers at the Eureka Stockade, you know," Cole said.

"How interesting," said Woo. "A great many of my countrymen were there, on the diggings."

"But they did not take sides, as I recall," McGill said.

"It has never been in our best interests to take sides," Woo replied. "We Chinese do not interfere in matters of Western politics: we stick to business."

"And will you always trade with the victors, whoever they are?" McGill asked.

"After the way we were treated in Hong Kong, in our own country, would you have us do otherwise?" Woo countered.

"Point taken," McGill said. "But there may come a time when you can no longer sit on the political fence. What then?"

Woo smiled. "If such a time should come," he said, "we shall of course consider our position."

"And do you think the Telegraph will change the political landscape?" Cole asked.

"I don't doubt it will change the way we do business," Woo said. "As for the rest—who can tell?"

Hector, who had been hovering nervously on the edge of this exchange, now moved smoothly through the room to bring Mr Valentine into the circle, neatly preventing further political discussion—at least for the moment. Just as the banker was being introduced to Woo, another man entered the Sitting Room.

Cole's face lit up into a broad grin as he recognised the newcomer. "Jacob," he said, shaking his friend's hand vigorously. He turned back to the group. "Allow me to introduce Mr Jacob Pitman," he said. "Mr Pitman is a leading architect and engineer, and he is joining us from Adelaide this evening." He paused, then added: "I fear you've missed the fun, Jacob—Mr Woo made a splendid entrance a moment ago."

"Then I'm delighted to make your acquaintance, sir," Pitman said, smiling in turn.

Woo bowed slightly and smiled back. The pleasantries were effortlessly resumed as Pitman was introduced to McGill and Valentine. Around the room the buzz of conversation arose once more: business was being done.

Buchanan squared his shoulders and strode back to the entry, where the priest waited impatiently. Buchanan didn't mince his words: "Really, O'Hanlon," he said, "your manners have not improved at all in your absence."

"I knew you'd be pleased to see me," O'Hanlon replied. "I've not long returned from Rome. When the Bishop mentioned your dinner this evening, I persuaded him to let me come in his stead."

"Did you indeed," Buchanan replied.

The Bishop of Melbourne was a gentle man: urbane, witty, and a welcome guest at table. Buchanan had no doubt that O'Hanlon had bullied his superior into giving up his seat tonight.

"And why would you do that?" Buchanan continued. He made a mental note to find out just what hold this devious priest had over the Bishop.

"I have an interest in your copper consortium, if you'll recall. So if you'll just have a word with your man there,"—O'Hanlon gestured towards the concierge—"we can go in to dinner."

Buchanan thought for a moment. "I don't appreciate your manner," he said. "I shall most certainly discuss it with your Bishop tomorrow."

O'Hanlon shrugged.

Buchanan spoke quietly to the concierge, who made a show of reluctance as he amended his guest list.

Buchanan returned to the priest. "I've admitted you, tonight, but only to avoid any more unpleasantness for my guests." He looked O'Hanlon straight in the eye. "You and I will talk later," he said, "after my guests have departed. There are matters we shall have to discuss."

O'Hanlon smiled thinly: being allowed in at all was a small victory. "Then let's go in," he said, making for the Sitting Room without further invitation.

Chapter 37

In honour of Sir Alec, and of the auspicious occasion, chief butler Clement had decided to attend to tonight's guests in person. He checked the magnificent Dining Room one last time and, seeing that all was in readiness, approached Buchanan as he returned with the priest to the Sitting Room.

"Dinner is served, sir," he said, bowing.

"Then you may proceed," Buchanan responded.

At a nod from Clement, one of the waiters struck the dining gong where it hung on its carved stand in an alcove. Two more waiters swung open the double doors to the Dining Room, and Buchanan led his guests in to dinner.

Clement himself personally ushered the men to their comfortable leather chairs at the long cedar dining table that dominated the richly decorated room with its dark wainscoting and sparkling central chandelier. A fire had been lit tonight, and blazed cheerfully in the elaborate fireplace with its finely carved mantel and high ornate mirror.

"No sign of Ferguson," Cole whispered to McGill as they were shown to their seats.

"Not yet," McGill replied. "I have no doubt he'll simply arrive late: some things never change."

"He'll have to hurry, then," said Cole, noting that waiters were now carrying in covered silver dishes and placing them on the sideboard in preparation to serve the first course.

McGill saw Buchanan speak quietly to a waiter. The empty place setting beside Cole was left, in case Ferguson should arrive after all.

"I'll say grace," O'Hanlon said, pushing his chair back and making ready to stand.

Buchanan cut him off. "Thank you, Father," he replied, "but no."

"No?" O'Hanlon frowned, perplexed.

"This is a very particular business occasion, Father," Buchanan replied firmly. "Tonight I propose to offer the Scottish Grace." He rose from his seat

175

at the head of the table before the priest could offer any further objection. "Gentlemen," he said, "I give you the Selkirk Grace."

The dinner guests shuffled to their feet and bowed their heads while Buchanan spoke, his deep baritone resonating in the panelled room:

> Some hae meat and canna eat,
> And some wad eat that want it;
> But we hae meat, and we can eat,
> And sae the Lord be thankit.

"Amen to that," Cole said loudly, while the others muttered their responses. "It's a fine sentiment for a fine occasion."

O'Hanlon, upstaged, glared at his host.

Woo observed the moment closely, mentally filing it away for future use, together with the curious fact that Valentine, the banker, had studiously avoided eye contact with the priest. A careful businessman, Woo always liked to know where the cracks in any structure might be, collecting all manner of information to be used for leverage.

The guests re-seated themselves as Clement unobtrusively directed his staff to move around the table, ladling the first course—a fine asparagus soup—into bowls, offering bread rolls still warm from the oven, filling wine glasses with a German Riesling. The conversation around the table turned to generalities suitable for a dinner party.

Buchanan, anxious to avoid any further conflict that might mar the event, chose a safe topic. "Have you all decided who will win the Melbourne Cup?" he asked amiably. "The race is only a fortnight away—the odds are shortening."

"I'm not a betting man," Valentine said primly.

"But everyone has a flutter on the Cup," Cole said cheerfully. "It's almost a national institution: it's a half-holiday for banks—including yours, Mr Valentine—and for public servants."

"That sounds serious," McGill said. "Do you really have a public holiday for a horse race?"

"Indeed we do," said Cole. "For all sixteen furlongs of it."

Woo spoke: "I have heard that a bay stallion by the name of The Quack will be the favourite," he said. "His trainer is the excellent Mr John Tait. He has five horses entered this year."

"And how do you know so much about horse racing?" O'Hanlon asked, an edge in his voice.

"I'm a man of business, Father," Woo replied equably. "Information comes my way."

"It would, in your kind of business," said O'Hanlon. "The opium trade must be difficult now that its import has become illegal."

"I import many things," Woo said, unruffled.

"I had thought that tea was your major business," Valentine chimed in.

"And so it is," Woo replied. "But I diversify where I can. In any case, I make it a matter of principle to know what my employees are talking about. And right now they are talking of little other than the Cup."

"Most of Melbourne is talking of little else," said Cole. "You should listen more to your flock, Father." Before the priest could respond, Cole turned to McGill. "You must allow me to invite you along to the big race," he said.

"I'd be delighted," McGill replied. "With your permission, I shall bring my fiancée along."

"Capital," said Cole. "We'll make a day of it. I shall make it my business to organise a suitable picnic."

"Nevertheless," said Buchanan, "people must still be talking about the Telegraph. Faster communication around the world will change everything."

Cole laughed. "In business circles, yes, you're in the right of it, of course," he said. "We are all agog at the prospect. But the man in the street is less concerned: he wants a meal, a beer, and a bet. You can't bet on the Telegraph!"

"Not yet, at least," said Buchanan, glancing across the table at Woo.

Woo smiled back at his host, his expression thoughtful.

The dinner progressed smoothly enough. The soup plates were cleared and the guests moved on to the fish course without undue incident.

"Still no sign of Ferguson," Cole observed. "I did so want to talk to you both about the stockade." He smiled. "I was there myself," he said, "but only in the background."

McGill returned the smile. "I have fond memories of your lemonade, Mr Cole," he said. "I trust it was a profitable venture."

"Very," said Cole. "But I'd still be intrigued to hear your account of the Eureka events: it was such a momentous day."

"There will be time at a later date, I'm sure," McGill said. "I shall be certain to arrange it."

"Thank you," said Cole. "In that case, let me ask you about the Civil War. You are West Point trained—you must have fought."

McGill considered his answer. "I must ask you to be discreet, Mr Cole," he said. "My government had, let us say, *other* uses for my services during that unfortunate conflict."

Cole was delighted. He tapped the side of his nose with his finger: "And now you are appointed our Consul, to oversee our terms of trade. Enough said," he replied. "I knew you were a man of many layers."

McGill turned smoothly to Pitman. "And I have not enquired about your latest architectural project," he said.

Pitman began a long, technical discourse, safely deflecting Cole from further questions of an inconvenient nature.

Chapter 38

The main course was ready to be served, and Ferguson had still not arrived. The waiters moved unobtrusively around the table, filling crystal goblets with a fine, aged claret that shone ruby-red in the candlelight.

In a practised performance worthy of the theatre, Clement wheeled in the carving trolley, deliberately sharpened the long carving knife with the steel, and lifted the silver dome to reveal a side of perfectly roasted lamb. The mouth-watering aroma of hot meat filled the air, and the guests watched with keen anticipation as Clement carved expertly, making the pink juices run down the blade and pool in the guttered carving tray as he sliced.

"For such fine food," O'Hanlon said unctuously, "the Lord be praised."

"Behold," Cole said sharply in reply, "the perfect example of the shepherd and his flock."

"Well put," said Pitman.

"What do you mean?" Valentine asked, idly swirling the claret in his glass.

"I mean," said Cole, "that the shepherd has it all his own way. Look at the fate of the flock, poor lambs. The shepherd takes away their liberty: he pens them up and milks them, he fleeces them, and ultimately, he eats them." He smiled mirthlessly at O'Hanlon. "What's in it for your flock, Father?"

"Salvation," O'Hanlon replied shortly.

"From whom, I wonder," said Cole.

"It's all about control, Edward," Buchanan said. "It's always about control."

"I agree," Woo said unexpectedly. "It's a question of who is to be master—nothing more."

O'Hanlon frowned angrily at Cole, but his reply died on his lips as Ferguson burst unceremoniously into the dining room. He was, by now, very, very late. He crossed the room in a few short strides and sank, dramatically, if a little out of breath, into the vacant dining chair beside McGill that Clement moved swiftly to hold for him.

"My apologies, Sir Alec," he said. "I was, shall we say, unavoidably delayed by circumstances beyond my control." He grinned, mischievously—rapidly regaining his composure. His blond hair was a little more tousled than usual, his dinner jacket decidedly rumpled, and his snowy-white shirt was marked with a spatter of bloodstains. He sported a long cut above his left eyebrow—a cut that still oozed blood. Ferguson distractedly wiped it away with his hand.

Clement was completely unfazed. Wordlessly, he dampened a linen table napkin with cold water from the silver pitcher on the sideboard and offered the compress to Ferguson.

Ferguson held it to his forehead, staunching the trickle of blood that beaded there. "Thanks," he said, wiping his bloodstained hand on the napkin: "most appreciated."

Clement merely nodded and returned to the sideboard to fill a plate for the latecomer.

It was Buchanan who spoke first. "Welcome, Ferguson," he said. "Better late than never, as they say. I'm afraid you've missed the soup, and the fish course."

Ferguson smiled at his host. "No matter," he replied. "I'm very glad to be here at last. I hope I haven't also missed the telegram."

"Not at all," Buchanan replied. "It hasn't arrived as yet. But I can see you have been having adventures."

Ferguson merely nodded, turning his attention to the claret that Clement was pouring for him.

It was Edward Cole who spoke up. "Come along, Ferguson," he said. "What on earth happened to you? You can't arrive looking like this and tell us you were merely delayed."

"I wasn't aware I appeared quite so dramatic," Ferguson replied. "It was nothing, really. I was visiting an acquaintance in Emerald Hill earlier this evening, and had occasion to hail a carriage to bring me here to the Club." He paused, taking an appreciative sip of his wine. "As luck would have it, another gentleman hailed the carriage at the same time, and, as it transpired that we were travelling in much the same direction, we agreed that we would share the ride. He introduced himself as Orsini. He seemed a decent enough chap."

O'Hanlon drew a sharp breath.

"Do you know him?" Ferguson asked.

"I've heard the name," O'Hanlon replied. He glanced meaningfully at Valentine. "The Orsini family are bankers."

Valentine said nothing, avoiding O'Hanlon's gaze.

Woo watched the silent exchange, intrigued.

"That's interesting," said Cole, "if a trifle unremarkable." He smiled. "Really, Ferguson: you *must* tell us what happened next. You do look a sight!"

"Well," said Ferguson, settling in now and beginning to enjoy his narrative,

"I was already running a little late, so I'm afraid I told the driver to be as quick as he could about it, and offered him a bonus to do it."

"Nothing unusual in that," Buchanan observed wryly.

"No," Ferguson agreed, "nothing at all. In any case, the driver decided to take a short cut. He was driving a little too fast through one of those narrow lanes in the city. It's foggy tonight, down there. We collided with another carriage heading in the opposite direction. The cabs scraped each other badly, and ours splintered as it toppled over onto its side."

"Was anyone injured?" Cole asked.

"Only cuts and bruises," Ferguson replied, dabbing at his forehead once again. "It was very fortunate that the horses weren't hurt. The carriage, alas, was a different matter." He shrugged. "The driver was furious: he let fly a string of curses that would make a sailor blush. I must admit I had to admire his vocabulary." He smiled at the recollection. "In any case," he went on, "he accused me of causing the accident and demanded compensation—you know the sort of thing. It was all nonsense, of course: the passengers can't be responsible for his bad driving."

"Indeed not," said Buchanan.

"After that," said Ferguson, "I decided to walk the rest of the way, but Mr Orsini chose to wait for another carriage. Between us we gave the driver a quite reasonable sum, to cover the fare for the distance we had travelled and to compensate him for the damage to the woodwork. We all shook hands and parted amicably enough. I then had a very brisk walk, across town and up the Collins Street hill—and here I am."

"Bravo," said Cole. "I always enjoy a good story."

"So one would hope," Ferguson replied. "Since you own the biggest book emporium in Melbourne, it would be a terrible shame if you didn't."

"Well," Cole replied cheerfully, "you must come to me if you decide to write your memoirs. I hear you have had rather a lot of interesting adventures, one way and another. I am publishing books under my own imprint now, you know." He grinned. "In fact, I am about to release a novel by a friend of yours, Celeste de Chabrillan: *Les Voleurs D'Or*—the translation is titled *The Gold Robbers*. The book has been hugely successful in Paris. Celeste penned it after her time here. I have no doubt you could write something yourself."

"I'll bear it in mind"' Ferguson said. "I might just do that—write my memoirs, that is."

"Capital," Cole replied, beaming. "Capital."

Chapter 39

The diners were finishing their main course when a liveried attendant slipped into the room and tapped Hector on the shoulder. "If you'll just follow me, sir," he said softly. "Your telegraph message is coming through now."

Hector excused himself and left the room.

"This will be interesting," Cole said.

"But probably not as dramatic as your own appearance, Charles," McGill said to Ferguson. "I doubt anything could beat that." He grinned at his friend. "It's so good to see you at last."

"And you, James," Ferguson replied. "I daresay we'll have time to chat properly over the port and cigars."

"If Mr Cole here can spare us," said McGill.

"Of course, of course," said Cole. "But remember, you have promised to tell me about the Eureka uprising."

Ferguson looked enquiringly at McGill.

McGill shrugged. "The tale may not be the one you expect, Mr Cole," he said.

"All the more reason to hear it," Cole replied, turning aside as the waiters cleared the dinner plates.

All eyes turned to Hector as he re-entered the room, carrying the precious slip of paper on a silver calling-card tray he'd borrowed from the butler to add to the sense of occasion. He crossed the dining room to offer the tray to Buchanan, where he sat at the head of the table: "Your telegraph, sir," he said.

Sir Alec was enjoying the moment. The room was charged with anticipation. He accepted the proffered telegraph, read it, then took his time to refold the flimsy paper and drop it onto the tray. He motioned for Hector to leave the tray, noting, with some satisfaction, the barely restrained curiosity that showed on the faces of the powerful businessmen who graced his table this October evening.

"Gentlemen," he said at last. "I believe a toast is in order."

Taking his cue, a waiter moved quickly around the table with a crystal decanter, refilling the goblets.

Sir Alec raised his glass. "I give you the first direct telegram," he said. "Gentlemen, we are now fully connected to the mother country."

The dinner guests raised their glasses, responding dutifully: "The first telegram."

It was O'Hanlon who broke the decorous silence that followed the toast. "Come along, Buchanan," he said, his tone snide. "Tell us what this wondrous message says. I, for one, expect the usual platitudes and greetings from Queen and Empire to mark this momentous occasion."

Pitman laughed. "Doubtless you're in the right of it, Father," he said. "I can't imagine English officialdom passing up the opportunity to patronize us poor colonials."

There were assenting nods from one or two others as the guests relaxed.

Buchanan, feeling the moment slip, took up the telegram once more. "You couldn't be more wrong, Father," he said. "The first news, gentlemen, is of a national coal strike in England." He paused for effect, then added: "And of the mounting tensions with the new German Empire." He smiled slowly. "It seems that all is not well in England, and no one there is in any position to condescend to any of us today."

The dinner guests sat for a moment in shocked silence, but then everyone started to speak at once, shaken by the unexpected news.

"Well I'll be damned," said Cole.

"Almost certainly," said O'Hanlon.

Cole returned the priest's hard stare. "I don't think you quite see the implications, Father," he said. "This is serious. A national coal strike could cripple England: it is so reliant on coal—for its industry, for its domestic heating, for everything."

"Surely the army will break the strike," Valentine ventured.

"Like they did at Eureka, you mean?" said Ferguson. "And what happens if the government forces don't win this time?"

"Then inevitably the Empire's control will slide," Buchanan replied.

"And the wolves are already circling," said McGill. "The second part of the telegram concerns the new German Empire, does it not?"

"Indeed it does," said Buchanan.

"Then the Germans will be watching the situation very closely," McGill continued. "Wilhelm I has been installed as Emperor of Germany. His Empire is only just emerging, so the Germans won't be able to act quickly—but they will prepare against the chance."

"Do you really think some kind of attack is a possibility, *Consul* McGill?" Cole asked, emphasising the title.

McGill paused, considering: "I do, yes," he said, "in the longer term, if England's power is curtailed in some way."

"A German attack?" said Cole.

"Possibly," said McGill. "Bismarck has made no secret of his ambitions. I recall something he said recently: *Let us put Germany in the saddle—it already knows how to ride.* That's hardly a declaration of peaceful intentions."

"It sounds like the plot of one of Mr Cole's more lurid scientific romances," said Pitman, attempting to turn the conversation to lighter matters. "What was the one about Germany's invasion of England, Edward?"

"*The Battle of Dorking*," Cole replied promptly. "I published it last year. It's by the eminent Sir George Tomkyns Chesney, no less." He looked around the room. "It's not so far fetched as all that," he said. "If Germany has designs on England, the *Dorking* scenario is not so impossible after all. What do you think, Consul?"

"I have no idea," McGill replied. "I haven't read it."

"Perhaps we could leave the realms of fiction for the moment," Buchanan said tartly. "We have enough facts here to worry us, without inventing more plots to frighten ourselves with."

"My apologies, Sir Alec," said Cole. "I always tend to get carried away by my literary projects." He turned back to McGill. "Should we really be worried about the possibility of a German attack?"

"That wouldn't be my only concern," McGill replied. "It's a question of opportunity. The British Empire has made a lot of enemies," he said. "France is still smarting from its recent defeat by Prussia, but I guarantee you it will nevertheless be looking for opportunities to inconvenience its traditional English enemies. And we should not forget that the Russian fleet is still in the Pacific. If England fails, the colonies will all be vulnerable, and Victoria more than most."

"I say, that's a bit far-fetched, isn't it?" Valentine said.

"Not at all," McGill replied. "The gold deposits here are bigger than those in California, Mr Valentine. Right now, Victoria is still the richest prize on earth."

"True," Cole said thoughtfully. "All the gold goes to England, so we don't really see the value of it. But when you put it like that, I can see our situation. Do go on, Consul."

"Well," McGill continued equably, "when my ship sailed into the Port of Melbourne this morning, I could not help but notice that the city is largely undefended."

"But there are gun batteries at the heads," Buchanan said.

"I doubt that would be enough to stop a war fleet," McGill replied.

"And we have the ironclad monitor, HMVS *Cerberus*, one of the most modern and powerful warships in the world, moored just inside the heads near Portsea," Ferguson added. "It's a floating gun platform. You wouldn't have seen it from your ship as you came in to dock."

"That's better," McGill conceded. "The monitors are first-rate—I've met the man who designed them, Captain John Ericsson. He's a brilliant engineer." He shrugged. "But if you only have one of his warships, it still wouldn't be enough to destroy a fleet if you were to be attacked."

"The Russian Fleet was anchored off San Francisco during the recent Civil War wasn't it, Captain McGill?" Cole asked.

"Certainly," McGill replied. "That was no secret."

"And so if England had officially entered that war, our colony here might have been attacked while the British forces were engaged elsewhere?"

"That was always a distinct possibility," McGill replied. "If England had declared war, you would automatically have been at war too. As a colony, you have no choice in the matter."

"True," Buchanan said.

"And that being the case," McGill continued, "as combatants you would have been fair game. As I said, Victoria is a rich prize." He turned to Woo. "You have been very quiet, Mr Woo," he said. "Are you contemplating the Chinese position in all of this?"

"I hardly know what to think, as yet," Woo replied. "British trade companies have already been severely affected by the opening of the Suez Canal: that was less than three years ago, but now warehouses are closing in London and Liverpool. The world is changing." He spread his hands wide. "I cannot tell what the outcome will be. But Sir Alec is right about one thing: if the coal strike continues, British control may falter, even if only a little. And that most certainly will have implications for Hong Kong, and for our trade there."

"Of course it will," Cole said thoughtfully. "I believe, Mr Woo, your countrymen have a suitable phrase for a situation such as this." He raised his glass in salute. "Gentlemen, I believe we can safely say we now live in interesting times."

"You may have to choose those sides after all, Mr Woo," McGill added with a smile.

"Perhaps," said Woo. "We shall see."

"Well I, for one, shall be most interested to see first-hand how this brave new future unfolds," said Buchanan. "But in the meantime, gentlemen," he added, smiling broadly, "I can predict with some certainty that our pudding is about to be served."

If Buchanan's guests were disconcerted by the news from England, they were more than willing to set their concerns aside in favour of the Club's excellent rhubarb and apple crumble, duly followed by port and cigars.

As the evening drew to its close, the concierge entered and spoke softly to Hector.

"Mr Clement bids me tell you that cabs have been arranged," Hector announced to the group at large, "for those who need them."

A murmur of thanks filled the room, and the company rose to make ready to depart.

As they waited in the reception area to retrieve their coats and scarves, McGill turned to Ferguson. "Would you care to come back to the Consulate for a nightcap, Charles?" he asked. "We have a lot of catching up to do."

"Another time, James," Ferguson replied, grinning. He winked. "I have a prior engagement," he said, "of a private nature."

McGill grinned back at his friend. "Another time, then," he agreed. "That will suit me as well—I'll admit to being tired."

"You've had an eventful day," Ferguson replied.

"As indeed have you," said McGill.

"Though for less edifying reasons," Ferguson said ruefully. "My head still hurts."

"Then you should get some rest."

"All in good time, my friend," Ferguson replied. "All in good time."

Suitably attired for the night air, they walked across the lobby to the entry hall, where the doors were immediately held open for them.

"Your carriage, sir," the doorman said, addressing McGill.

"Thank you," McGill replied. "May I offer you a lift, Charles?" he asked Ferguson.

"No, thank you," Ferguson replied. "I've not far to go."

As McGill settled himself for the short drive back to the Consulate, Ferguson waved cheerily before he turned and walked swiftly into the foggy night, leaving his friend to wonder who the object of this late-night assignation might be.

Chapter 40

When Buchanan's guests had departed, O'Hanlon remained behind. "You wanted to speak to me, Buchanan?" he asked.

"I want to know what you mean by appearing here tonight: uninvited, unannounced, and unwelcome," Buchanan replied, coming straight to the point.

"That's no way to speak to me," said O'Hanlon. "You've done well enough out of me to give me a decent dinner."

"Out of you?" said Buchanan. "You overestimate your worth, Francis."

"It's *Father* O'Hanlon."

"It's *Sir* Alec."

The men stared at each other for a long moment.

O'Hanlon blinked first. "I know that the copper lease I brought to you has proved valuable," he said at last.

"And you will have your reward," Buchanan replied. "I am a man of my word."

"Well, then?"

"I will do as we agreed," said Buchanan, "but that does not give you leave for your insolence."

"Oh?"

"Your behaviour here tonight was inappropriate. You barely managed to be civil at dinner. You certainly did your best to insult Mr Woo."

O'Hanlon shrugged. "I don't care to be in the company of heathen Chinamen," he said.

"A word to the wise," said Buchanan. "Woo is a powerful man, more powerful than you can know. He is a good friend, and a dangerous enemy. I would strongly suggest that you don't insult him any further—he has a long memory, and a very long reach."

O'Hanlon said nothing, but Buchanan noticed that a muscle twitched uncontrollably in the Irishman's jaw.

Buchanan rose from his seat and strolled to the fireplace, casually unbuttoning his trousers. Without warning, he pissed into the fire: the flames hissed and spat sparks, and the stink of hot urine and woodsmoke filled the elegant dining room.

O'Hanlon held his handkerchief to his nose. "What did you want to go and do that for?" he said. "Someone will have to clean that up. It's disgusting."

"No more disgusting than your behaviour has been tonight," Buchanan replied, rebuttoning. He walked deliberately to where O'Hanlon sat, and stood over him, his hand on the back of the priest's chair. "I'm the richest man in this city," he said. "I all but own this club. The staff will clean up after me."

"Meaning?"

"Meaning that you should take great care, Francis, that you do not become a mess in need of cleaning up. You may believe me when I say that I have the means to take care of such inconveniences."

O'Hanlon swallowed hard, shifting in his seat. He tried a different tack: "You'll not yet be aware, *Sir* Alec," he said, "that I am now in a position, authorized by Cardinal Antonelli himself, to make certain financial investments on behalf of the Church."

"Antonelli?"

"Cardinal Antonelli is the man who now controls foreign relations and finances for the Vatican," O'Hanlon replied. "You can ask your friend Valentine: he already has dealings with him."

"I shall certainly do just that," Buchanan replied. "And I might add that if a professional banker such as Valentine is involved I shall hardly have need of your services."

O'Hanlon shrugged. "Since Rome was annexed by Italy last year, the Banco di Santo Spirito is looking for suitable assets in other areas of the world," he said. "I am part of that search. I can arrange for the Vatican to invest in your enterprises."

"And how does a poor Irish priest from the Ballarat goldfields come to be in such a position?" Buchanan asked, not bothering to hide his scepticism.

O'Hanlon bridled at the question. "Let me just say that the Vatican has had occasion to find my *particular* skills of use," he replied, his voice grown cold as catacombs.

Inquisition, Buchanan thought suddenly. O'Hanlon was capable of anything. At that moment, Buchanan knew instinctively that the priest was being paid off by the Cardinal for services rendered—special services of the secret kind, services on the wrong side of whatever law the Church admitted. He shuddered at the thought.

O'Hanlon took advantage of Buchanan's momentary hesitation to continue his proposal: "We already have substantial holdings in the American railroads," he said. "I was recently in New York, to broker certain important deals. I'm sure you'll understand that some arrangements require, shall we say, a personal touch."

Buchanan frowned.

O'Hanlon didn't even pause for breath. "I was on my way back to Australia," he said, "so my visit to the United States was convenient. The system of land-grant railway construction there has proved most profitable for my bank. And I have heard that similar projects are under negotiation here. I can put substantial investment funds your way, if I choose."

"Can you now, Father?" said Buchanan, recovering his equanimity. "And why would you do that?"

"Let's just say that I believe I have a vested interest in seeing your consortium succeed," O'Hanlon said.

"And in return?"

"A seat on the board," O'Hanlon replied promptly.

"You're not a shareholder," Buchanan countered with equal speed. "And as a priest, you cannot be a shareholder."

"No indeed," said O'Hanlon. "But I believe you would find me useful."

"Perhaps," Buchanan replied. "But you cannot seriously imagine that any of my major shareholders would countenance such a thing. You deliberately insulted some of them this evening."

"It's a question of who's to be master," O'Hanlon said, mimicking Woo's Oxford accent.

"And that won't be you," Buchanan said firmly.

O'Hanlon stretched his lips into a thin smile, a smile that suggested he would bide his time. "What do you propose, then?"

"A promotion within the Church might suit you, perhaps?" Buchanan said. "That should be possible, given the right connections."

"Melbourne already has a Bishop."

"But Melbourne is growing, O'Hanlon." Buchanan paused, thinking quickly. "Ballarat is building a cathedral," he said at last. "The city must be large enough to have its own Bishop. And I have a great deal of influence there."

O'Hanlon scowled. "You want me banished to the country, out of the way," he said.

"On the contrary," Buchanan replied. "Ballarat is a major centre. If you were to become its Bishop, you would be very comfortable. There will be a new residence and all the trappings of wealth, of course. But most importantly, you would gain a useful social power base."

"And then?"

"I could appoint you to the board *ex officio*." He allowed himself a tight, grim smile. "Government bodies approve of religious appointees in circumstances of shared official projects like the development of railways: they imagine it lends a moral dimension to decision making."

O'Hanlon smiled slowly in return. "I like the sound of that," he said.

"Then leave it with me," said Buchanan.

"For how long?"

"For as long as it takes," said Buchanan, remembering his first meeting with this troublesome priest. "Nothing changes."

"Very well."

"And Father," Buchanan continued: "I shall soon have to make a very substantial contribution to the Ballarat Cathedral Building Fund to set the wheels in motion. I imagine that this investment—an investment, shall we say, in your future—is one that Cardinal Antonelli will approve?"

"Undoubtedly," said O'Hanlon. "I understand completely."

"I thought you would," said Buchanan. "You will let me know when the funds become available?"

"Of course," said O'Hanlon.

Buchanan stood, indicating that the interview was over. "I'll just see you out," he said. "Clement will hail a cab to take you back to Abbotsford."

"No need," O'Hanlon replied, quickly rising to his feet. "I have another meeting tonight."

Buchanan consulted his gold fob watch and glanced enquiringly at O'Hanlon. "At this hour?" he said.

"The Church's work is never done," O'Hanlon replied. "Good night, Buchanan."

"Good night."

Buchanan watched the black-clad priest make his ungainly exit, hearing the faint click of the long-legged man's joints as he strode towards the entrance hall. *"Too much time on his knees,"* Buchanan mused. *"But I doubt the time was wasted in prayer."*

Chapter 41

When Hector finally returned to Buchanan's house, his mother had already retired to bed and only the butler remained on duty. Hector bade him good night and headed for his own room, glad to be alone at last. He undressed at once and sank gratefully into his narrow bed, exhausted but relieved that this very long day had been a success—if one did not count the disconcerting news brought by the Telegraph. The speculation had been alarming, but Hector reasoned that any consequences that might flow from the English coal strike were still a long way off. He felt bone weary, as if he could sleep for a week: but since he had duties to perform next morning, he would make do with the scant few hours left to him by this evening's events.

He was soon asleep, but not peacefully.

The nightmare came. The nightmare was always the same, though it had troubled him less often as he had grown into manhood. The nightmare had first come to him on the day of his father's death. It had haunted his childhood, and it came tonight, with all its terror and horror and pain amplified by the events of the day.

In the dream, Hector watched as his father leant against a rough wooden counter, intent on something that lay beyond, out of Hector's sight. Hector was certain that the figure was his father, although the dream had never once revealed the man's face. The room was filled with terrible noise—shouting, roaring, whistling, screaming, and an explosive percussion that drowned out Hector's attempts to warn his father as the menacing black scarecrow man advanced upon him from behind. As Hector stood frozen, rooted to the spot with horror, the scarecrow man drove a long knife into his father's body. His father jerked violently and then fell limply to the floor. In an instant, as is the way of dreams, Hector was face to face with the black scarecrow man. The scarecrow man's face was close to his, so close it almost touched his own. Hector saw each bristle on the unshaven jowls, each red vein in the bloodshot blue eyes, each sweat-darkened strand of sparse sandy hair; he smelled sweat, and stale beer and old tobacco on the man's reeking breath. Hector wanted to scream, but no sound came. The tumult seemed to fade, and he heard the scarecrow man say: *"You saw nothing. Do you understand? Nothing."*

Hector had seen that face, in waking life, earlier that evening. He knew, with the certainty of dreams, that he had identified the man who owned it. The scarecrow man finally had a name.

Hector woke, drenched in sweat, to find his mother kneeling beside his bed. A candle burned brightly in the holder she had placed on his night table.

"You were crying out in your sleep," she said gently. "I didn't want you to wake the rest of the household. Is it the old nightmare?"

Hector could only nod. He was still shaking from the intensity of the dream.

"Then I'll just slip into the kitchen and make you some warm milk to help you sleep," Morag said. "Perhaps I'll put a wee dram of scotch into it. You've had a long, hard day—you deserve your rest." She kissed his cheek, drew her dressing gown more tightly about her, and tiptoed from the room.

Hector lay still for a moment, trying desperately to recall the last seconds of the nightmare. He knew, he just knew, that tonight it had finally revealed something very important. Tonight, it had revealed a name. But what that name might have been had slipped from his mind at his mother's touch. He shivered. The dream, as always, faded faster than the fear it brought.

194

Chapter 42

A little after sunrise next morning, Consul McGill was roused from his bed by an insistent knocking at the front door.

"Police! Open up!" a man shouted.

The butler, bleary-eyed, hastened to open the door.

"We're looking for Ferguson," one of the blue-coats said without preamble.

"Lieutenant Ferguson?" the butler asked.

"The same," the man replied.

McGill hastened downstairs, tying the cord of his dressing gown as he went, tucking his pistol out of sight. "What's all this about?" he asked briskly, emerging barefoot but wide awake into the tiled reception hall.

"And who are you?" the policeman asked.

"I should ask you two the same thing," McGill replied.

"This is the American Consul," the butler said hurriedly. "Captain McGill."

"Begging your pardon, sir," the man replied. "I'm Constable Baines, and this is Constable Bellamy."

"And what are you doing here, waking my staff at dawn?"

"We're looking for Lieutenant Ferguson, sir," Baines replied. "We have reason to believe he is here."

"Then your belief is mistaken," McGill replied. "Lieutenant Ferguson has his own house, in St Kilda, I understand."

"He's not there," said Bellamy. "His man said he was meeting you last night—said he was all excited that you were back from America."

McGill was suspicious. "And you thought he would be here?"

"Yes, sir. It seemed likely, sir."

"And why do you want to locate him so urgently?" McGill asked. "If you thought he was here, you might have waited until a civilized hour to ask to speak to him."

"Afraid not, sir," said Baines. "Ferguson is wanted for murder."

The butler gasped. "What did you say?"

195

"Murder," the constable repeated, enjoying the effect of his announcement.

McGill was unfazed. "That's preposterous," he replied calmly. "On what evidence do you accuse Lieutenant Ferguson of such a serious crime?"

"On the evidence of the corpse, sir," Baines replied. "The body of a Mr Joseph Orsini has been found in Spring Street. Orsini was stabbed through the heart. And we have a witness who saw Ferguson getting into a carriage with him yesterday evening, in Emerald Hill."

"Sharing a carriage with a murder victim doesn't mean *Lieutenant* Ferguson is guilty of the man's death," McGill said sternly, thinking rapidly back to the story his friend had told to explain his late arrival at last night's dinner. "There could be any number of innocent explanations."

"Perhaps, sir," Baines replied. "But Orsini is dead. And Ferguson is missing. It looks mighty suspicious to us."

"I'm sure you have jumped to the wrong conclusion, Constable," McGill said. "This will be cleared up in no time when Lieutenant Ferguson appears."

Baines appeared unconvinced. "*If* he appears," he said.

McGill considered for a moment. "When did you say this murder is supposed to have taken place?" he asked.

"Last night, sir," Bellamy replied. "It happened some time after Ferguson— Lieutenant Ferguson, that is—got into the carriage with Mr Orsini."

"Obviously," said McGill, losing patience. "If the man was alive when he got into the carriage, his murder must have been subsequent to that event."

"That's what I said, sir," Baines replied, shaking his head as if to dislodge the thought.

"Have you talked to the driver?" McGill asked.

"Our colleagues are looking for him now," Bellamy said. "We two are just supposed to locate Lieutenant Ferguson."

"Of course," McGill said. "In that case, since he is not here, you'll want to be on your way."

"Yes, sir," said Bellamy. "But before we leave, would you mind telling us if Lieutenant Ferguson did meet you last night, as his man said he had planned to do?" He took a notebook and pencil from his top pocket and licked the pencil's tip to moisten it in preparation for taking notes.

"As a matter of fact," McGill said calmly, "he did. But he did not come here to the Consulate. Lieutenant Ferguson was a guest last night at Sir Alec Buchanan's dinner party at The Melbourne Club, along with myself and a number of Melbourne's leading businessmen."

"I see," said Bellamy, labouring to write it all down. "And can you tell us who else was present, sir?" he asked.

"Certainly not," McGill replied. "That would be most improper. It was a private function. You will need to apply to Sir Alec for his guest list, if you deem it necessary to speak to the other attendees."

"I see, sir," said Baines.

"And let me remind you both," said McGill, "that Lieutenant Ferguson is an American citizen, and therefore my responsibility. I insist that you inform me the moment he is located."

"I don't know…" Baines began.

"But I do," McGill said. "I shall of course speak to your Commissioner— Mr Henry Moors, I believe—and to Governor Manners-Sutton this morning. And remember," he said, "that you cannot question an American citizen without a member of the American Consulate being present. And in this case, the official person to be present will be me. Is that clear?"

"I…"

"*Is that clear?*" McGill repeated.

"Yes, sir," the constables said in unison.

"Good. And now, if you'll excuse me, Wilson here will show you out."

"This way," the butler said, unnecessarily pointing the way to the front door.

The constables left unsatisfied. "He knows something," Baines said, as they crunched their way back down the gravel drive.

"Maybe, or maybe he just thinks he does," Bellamy replied. "He's the American Consul. All I know is he's a powerful man, and it's not worth our while to upset him."

Baines sighed. "And now we shall have to wake up another very powerful man, Sir Alec Buchanan, if we want that guest list."

"Do we really need it that much?" Bellamy asked. "It sounds as though Ferguson has a whole room full of influential alibis if he was at The Melbourne Club last night."

"Depends how long he was there," said Baines. "But you're right. Maybe we could leave Buchanan's guest list for a while. We could keep looking for Ferguson in all the likely places."

"Maybe we should look down by the markets," said Bellamy. "We haven't had our breakfast yet."

"Good idea," said Baines. "I could do with some breakfast: they make a good bacon sandwich down there."

Chapter 43

"That was close," said Ferguson, entering through a side door. "Good morning, McGill." He smiled. "I had to duck back around the corner of the drive as those two left: I didn't fancy meeting the constabulary on an empty stomach. Lucky for me they were making so much noise about it." He nodded a brief "good morning" to Wilson as he headed for the sitting room, still wearing his evening clothes and looking even more dishevelled than he had been the night before. The bloodstains on his shirt had dried to a reddish-brown. "Is there breakfast to be had, by any chance?"

"Charles!" said McGill. "Why on earth didn't you just walk in by the front door?" He shook his head. "The police will think you've been here all along."

"Let them think what they like," Ferguson replied. "And be damned. I've done nothing of interest to them."

"They're accusing you of murder," McGill said quietly.

"Murder?" said Ferguson, looking blankly at his friend. "Are you sure?"

"Perfectly sure, sir," Wilson said.

McGill pulled his dressing gown closer. "Perhaps we'd better go in and sit down and talk this through," he said, following his friend across the entry hall, feeling the tiles cold on his bare feet. "Wilson will bring us some breakfast, while we think of a way to clear up this whole mess as quickly as possible."

"Very good, sir," Wilson replied, obviously disappointed at being banished to the kitchen while the juicy details were discussed.

"Whom exactly am I supposed to have murdered?" Ferguson asked, sinking into an armchair and rubbing his forehead where a bruise was beginning to darken around the cut over his left eye.

"You haven't heard?"

"I wouldn't need to ask if I had," Ferguson replied wearily. "What's this all about, James? I don't understand."

"All I know," said McGill, "is that the body of the man with whom you shared a carriage last evening, a Mr Joseph Orsini, has been found in the vicinity of Spring Street. He was stabbed to death."

"He was well and truly alive when I left him," Ferguson replied. "You know my story."

"Yes," said McGill. "But the police don't. As far as they are concerned, you were seen getting into a carriage with a man they subsequently found murdered."

"That doesn't mean I killed him."

"No, but they have no other suspects as yet. They won't look for anyone else while they think you are the killer. Nothing much has changed since Eureka: these police like their solutions easy."

"True."

McGill smiled at his friend. "There must have been witnesses who saw you part from Orsini before Buchanan's dinner—the carriage driver, for one: you told us you had both paid him off."

"We did," said Ferguson. "Handsomely—he'll be bound to remember."

"Then all you have to do is find him. When he has confirmed your story, you just need to tell the constables where you have been since we parted at The Melbourne Club last night until the time the body was found, and you'll be wholly in the clear. They already know that you weren't at home: they interviewed your man."

"I can't do that," Ferguson said flatly.

"Do what?"

"Say where I have been, of course."

"Why not?"

"You should know why not," Ferguson replied. "I was with a lady—a married lady. I cannot give her name. Her reputation would be compromised, and she would be ruined. It's out of the question."

"And no one else saw you?" McGill asked. "Her servants, perhaps?"

Ferguson gave him a long look. "Of course not, James," he said. "I know how to be discreet."

"Then we have a problem," McGill said.

"Breakfast, sir," said Wilson, entering the room with a large butler's tray that he set down on its stand. He lifted a high domed cover to reveal eggs, bacon, toast, dishes of jam and butter, and a steaming pot of hot coffee.

Ferguson sniffed appreciatively. "That smells good," he said. "There's nothing like freshly brewed coffee to clear the head."

Wilson laid out plates and cutlery and poured the coffee into china cups, taking as long as possible about the task. "Will that be all, sir?" he said at last.

"Thank you, yes," McGill replied. "And you'd best close the door behind you, Wilson," he added. "We don't want the staff eavesdropping, do we?"

"No, sir," Wilson replied, resigning himself to kitchen gossip fuelled by a complete lack of information. He sighed as he left, softly closing the door to the sitting room.

"What to do then, Charles," McGill said. "My staff saw you arrive—we can't pretend you weren't here, and we can't stop them from gossiping. We'll have to notify the police."

Ferguson sighed deeply. "I suppose you're right," he said. "Things were so much simpler on the goldfields."

McGill lowered his voice. "What happened about that...incident?" he asked.

"Absolutely nothing," Ferguson replied. "It was exactly as I predicted. Nobody was much interested in pursuing the disappearance of a drunken sergeant, especially one as vicious as Dunn. On the whole, his men were glad to be rid of him."

"Well that's a relief," said McGill. "I always wondered."

Ferguson shrugged. "It's ancient history now," he said. "Ironic, isn't it?"

"What is?"

"Now it's your turn to take care of me."

McGill smiled. "I guess it is," he said. "But the only thing I can think to do right now is to send a man to the police. We'll allow the constables to come back here and interview you, with me as your witness." He smiled at his friend. "That will give you time to wash and tidy up. I'll give you a change of clothes: those bloodstains on your shirt won't help your cause. And it'll look better if you aren't still in evening dress when they get here."

"Thanks," said Ferguson. "Once again, history repeats—I had to do a quick change to avoid prosecution after Eureka, as I recall."

"So you did," said McGill. "Strange how things play out."

"Very." Ferguson sighed.

"Anyway," McGill continued, "if the police charge you—and they probably will—the Consulate will post bail."

"And then?"

"We'll find your carriage driver and set the record straight."

"But the murderer is still out there."

"True. And the police will have to find him. It's their job. You could hardly have spent the evening at Buchanan's dinner and then caught up with Orsini, a man you had met only once and whose final destination you did not know, in order to murder him, now could you?"

"Someone caught up with him," Ferguson said darkly.

Some hours later, an exhausted Ferguson had told his story to two disbelieving constables, their doubtful sergeant, and finally to a sceptical magistrate. Bail was set at a staggering one hundred pounds, which amount was duly posted by the American Consulate. Ferguson was released into McGill's care.

"You'll need to move into the Consulate, at least for the time being," McGill said as they left the Courthouse. "We must be seen to comply with the conditions of your bail. Fortunately, we have plenty of empty guest rooms."

"No problem there," Ferguson replied. "My place in St Kilda is rented on a short lease."

"And your staff?" said McGill. "Do you want me to try to place them?"

"There's only my manservant," Ferguson replied. "And frankly, he was far too free with my personal affairs when the police came calling. He should have been more discreet. I'll let him go."

"As you wish," said McGill, privately agreeing with the sentiment. "I'll send Wilson to collect your things. He seems reliable enough: he didn't turn a hair when you arrived this morning."

The two men travelled in sociable silence back to the Consulate. When they repaired to the sitting room once more, finally alone, McGill turned to Ferguson and said softly: "I'll put my cards on the table, Charles. The magistrate made the position pretty clear—unless the real murderer is found, this will not be easy for you. If you want me to put you on a ship, it can be done quickly and quietly. I'll take the blame for your disappearance. And as for the bail money, I can stand the loss well enough."

"Hell no," said Ferguson. "I'm innocent."

"Innocence isn't always enough, I seem to recall," McGill replied.

"Then we'd better do something about finding the killer ourselves," Ferguson said grimly.

"If all else fails, you do still have an alibi," McGill said gently.

"I won't hear of it," Ferguson replied. "Not if my life depended on it."

"It very well may, Charles," said McGill. "It very well may."

Chapter 44

"Have you seen this?" Clara stormed into the room brandishing a newspaper. Her face was flushed with anger, her hands shaking. "How dare he!"

"Dare who?" Lola replied, looking up from her breakfast toast in Clara's peaceful morning room. Sunlight streamed in through an open window that admitted soft air from the garden outside, a gentle breeze that carried the scent of flowers and the sounds of birdsong and bees. "What is it?"

"Some horrible priest, name of O'Hanlon, that's who," Clara all but shouted. "Have you seen what he said about you—about me—in this morning's *Argus*?"

"Obviously not," Lola replied, calmly spreading marmalade.

"You won't be so composed when you read it," Clara said. "The nerve of the man! Recently returned from Rome, the paper says. He should have stayed there. He should have saved his breath to cool his tea!"

"I assume this means he has said the usual unflattering things about my past," Lola replied. "The papers reported my arrival a few days ago, and this sort of thing tends to happen, I'm afraid." She sighed. "Don't concern yourself too much, Clara. I'm used to it."

"It's worse than that," Clara said. "Someone at the paper decided to interview this priest about the changes he has found upon his return to Melbourne—the usual social page stuff—and he's taken the opportunity to slander you, and me, before he gets on to slandering women in general. Misogynist bastard!" She slammed the paper down on the table, dropping the rest of the morning's mail with it.

Unperturbed, Lola poured tea into a fine, gold-rimmed china cup and handed it to her friend. "Here," she said.

"I don't want tea."

"Yes, you do. It will soothe you. You can tell me all about it while you sip."

"I suppose," Clara said, reaching for the cup. She took a deep, steadying breath. "The thing is," she said, "he describes your performances as immoral and a public disgrace, and says that decent people should boycott the theatre when your season opens."

"Nothing new there," Lola said. "And he's out of date—he doesn't realise that I don't dance now—I just manage the group." She shrugged. "Theatre patrons will ignore that kind of tedious moralising nonsense—they always do. Trust me: it won't affect my box office sales."

"That's just the start," Clara replied. "O'Hanlon attacks me, too. He says you are staying with me because we both have what he calls 'theatrical backgrounds'—he practically calls us whores!" Her voice was rising again in indignation. "And then he disparages *The New Day*, says he is shocked to find that respectable Melbourne society allows my women's journal to flourish—because my 'theatrical' past makes me an unfit person to publish it!"

"Oh dear," said Lola. "That will put the cat among the pigeons, won't it?"

"My women readers will be outraged, of course," Clara said. "But you have to understand, my dear, that I have been so successful because the journal is mostly about the usual things—fashion, recipes and the like—so no one sees it as threatening, and men mostly disregard it as a women's thing. But if I'm branded as morally unacceptable, some husbands could take it into their heads to ban it from their houses, and I'll lose my subscribers."

"Then we must find a way to counter it," said Lola. "I could allow someone from a rival paper to interview me, perhaps?"

"I know one or two people at *The Age*," Clara said thoughtfully. "They'd jump at the chance—you rarely give interviews." She shook her head. "But what good would that do?"

"Quite a lot, I should think," Lola replied. "I'll make sure the journalist realises that the priest is out of date and out of touch—he doesn't really know what my theatre group is doing, that much is clear. I'll be a picture of sweetness and light while I discredit him as an interfering old man who can't cope with change."

"Excellent," said Clara, cheering up for a moment. "I'll arrange it this afternoon. Nobody likes a wowser." She sighed heavily. "But I don't understand why he wants to attack us at all. What have we ever done to him? We don't even know him."

"We exist," Lola replied, "and we are both successful. For men like him, it's enough." She thought for a moment. "There have been plenty of scandals in Rome in recent years," she said. "Maybe I'll just hint that this priest was involved in one of them. We all know that there's many a man has been shipped out here to the colonies to avoid disgrace."

"He wants something," Clara said suddenly. "He must do. The question is: what can it be?"

"That depends who he hopes to impress with his opinions," Lola replied. "Maybe he just wants a promotion in the Roman Church: maybe he's proving he thinks like his masters?"

"Maybe," said Clara. "But I like your idea that he is covering up his own past by attacking ours," she added, finally getting back to her normal, stubborn self. "That rings true. And I, for one, won't be used as a diversion! So perhaps I'll just do some digging of my own. Two can play at this game: I still publish a journal, after all. If he's implicated in anything, I'll find it. I want to know what this priest is really up to. And when I do, I'll print it for everyone to see."

"Good idea," said Lola. "I'll help. Nobody gossips like the theatre: I'll see if anyone has heard anything useful." She looked up as Charlotte entered the room. "Good morning, my dear," she said.

Tall and angular, with honey-blonde hair that resisted all efforts to smooth it into fashionable shape, seventeen-year-old Charlotte Seekamp's only physical likeness to her mother lay in her cornflower-blue eyes, though her fiery temper and quick wit marked her clearly as her mother's child.

"'Morning, Lola. 'Morning, Mother. What's all the fuss about?" she asked, deftly lifting a piece of toast from the rack and buttering it with short, quick strokes. "I could hear Mother shouting all the way upstairs." She slid into a chair beside Lola and spooned marmalade onto a side plate.

"We've been libelled in this morning's *Argus*," Clara said shortly. She tossed the offending paper to her daughter. "Here, you can read it for yourself."

Charlotte poured her tea and settled in to read, munching her toast.

"Is there anything else interesting?" Lola asked, gesturing vaguely at the pile of mail Clara had left, forgotten, on the table.

Clara picked up the envelopes and shuffled through them. "This one looks promising," she said, selecting an embossed envelope and using a knife on it. "Ooh," she said, "you'll like this, Lola. The charming Mr Edward Cole invites both of us to join his picnic-party at the Melbourne Cup."

"Is that a horse race?" Lola asked.

"A very important horse race," Charlotte replied, looking up with sudden interest, "with the richest winner's purse in the country."

"All Melbourne's fashionable society will be there," Clara added.

"Excellent," said Lola. "But I might need to shop for something to wear."

"So might I," Clara replied, brightening up.

"Can I come too?" Charlotte asked. "To the Cup, I mean? I'd love to see the big race."

"I'll ask Mr Cole," Clara replied.

"Thanks," said Charlotte. "He's bound to say yes—he's such a nice man."

Clara turned back to Lola. "We can both look for materials this morning," she said. "We mustn't forget that we have promised to take Morag shopping for fabrics for her wedding clothes." She turned to her daughter. "Perhaps you'd like to join us," she said. "I could order a new dress for you to wear to the Cup." She looked Charlotte up and down, noting her grubby brown skirt and plain linen blouse. "And what *is* that you are wearing?"

"Riding clothes, Mother," Charlotte replied, unfazed. "I am going to Sir Alec's stables directly after breakfast. Hector has promised to take me riding on the trail for an hour." She paused. A defiant note crept into her voice as she added: "And no, I would not care to join you on a boring expedition to the stylish shops. I'm sure I can have something of yours taken in if Mr Cole allows me to join his party."

Clara sighed. "As you like, my dear," she said. "Although I do wish you would take a little more pride in your appearance."

Charlotte, wisely, did not reply. She contented herself with spreading marmalade on a second piece of toast, relieved that she was to be spared a shopping trip with her mother's friends.

"In any case," Clara continued, "it won't hurt that Lola and I are seen going about our normal business on Collins Street while people are reading this—this *rubbish*," she said, tapping the paper with her forefinger. "We can, at the very least, brazen it out today."

Chapter 45

By eleven o'clock the women were out and about, "doing the Block" in fashionable Collins Street in search of suitable fabrics for Morag's wedding ensemble. The fine weather had encouraged a crowd, and the stylish Melbourne ladies promenading the long Block spent as much time smiling and bowing to acquaintances as they did in attending to their shopping. There was, inevitably, some nudging and whispering when Lola and Clara appeared on the scene, but nothing of an unpleasant nature occurred to mar Morag's happiness at sharing such a joyful task with her friends.

After much discussion, she chose a watered silk fabric in eau-de-nil, the palest of pale greens, which Clara and Lola both insisted would look very well with her coppery red curls. A further hour was spent turning over ribbons and laces under the watchful eye of Mr Hicks, the proprietor, and in consultation with the highly regarded dressmaker attached to his establishment.

"I'm bushed," Clara suddenly declared. "It must be time for lunch."

"I agree," said Lola. "We all need some refreshment."

Morag laughed. "Come along then, both of you: we'll go to Moubray's." She turned back to Mr Hicks. "The material and trimmings should stay here with Mrs Rowan," she said, "and the account may be forwarded to Sir Alec Buchanan's house on Wellington Parade."

"Very good, madam," the man replied.

"And I'll return in a week for my first fitting, if that will be convenient for you, Mrs Rowan," she said.

"Perfectly convenient," the dressmaker replied.

"That's all, then," Morag said. "Shall we?"

The three women left the store and strolled down the hill to the Arcade, where Moubray's Tea Rooms famously provided dainty sandwiches and cakes for its select clientele. The place was almost full today: elegantly dressed ladies sipped tea while outside their servants dealt with the mountains of boxes and parcels that their employers had acquired in the course of a morning's fashionable shopping.

Clara made a beeline for an empty table by the window, waving at a waiter to follow.

"Three teas, mixed sandwiches, scones and cakes," she said when he approached. "That should be sufficient," she added.

"Goodness," said Morag, settling herself into her chair and taking off her gloves. "That was very quick."

"It's all they serve, really," Clara laughed. "This way they'll bring us a selection."

"And I'm sure it will do very well," said Lola.

Morag leaned forward. "Those women over there," she said. "They're staring."

"They probably read the piece in *The Argus*," Clara said ruefully.

"Not a bit of it," said Lola. "It's Morag they're looking at. It's her first public appearance since her engagement to McGill was announced. And your stunning engagement ring, Morag: it's easily the finest emerald any of us has ever seen. See how it is catching the light from the window—no wonder the women are staring."

"She's right," Clara said, glancing at the women. "They're all intrigued now that you are to marry the American Consul. I must say, you've probably spiked the plans of more than one Melbourne matron who hoped to marry off a daughter in that direction when it was learned that the new Consul was single."

Lola laughed. "You're a celebrity in your own right today, my dear," she said, "and for all the right reasons."

"Good heavens," said Morag. "I never gave it a thought."

"Of course you didn't," Clara said loyally. "Have you and McGill set a date, by the way?"

"Next Valentine's Day," Morag said, blushing slightly.

"How very romantic," Lola said.

"It's practical as well," Morag said defensively. "February will suit all of us. Sir Alec's new housekeeper will take up her position in the new year, and there will be time for the Consulate to be refurbished before the wedding. James has decided the place needs a thorough renovation."

"Splendid," Clara said. "You will let me write a piece about you, and your redecorated residence, for *The New Day*, won't you?"

"If you like," Morag replied. "But I don't think your readers will find me very interesting."

"They'll be all attention, I promise you," said Clara. "You've carried off one of Melbourne's most eligible bachelors, and you'll be hostess for all the

American Consular balls and dinners once you are married. They will all want to know you, believe me."

"And they'll all be waiting to see what you wear to the Melbourne Cup,'" Lola added mischievously. "You might start a fashion trend."

"Oh my," was all Morag could manage before the waiter interrupted, bringing tea and a tiered stand of sandwiches and cakes.

Chapter 46

November 7th, the day of the big race, dawned clear and bright: summer had come early this year. By mid-morning, excited crowds were gathering at the track. When Morag and Hector set out with Buchanan in his stylish four-in-hand carriage, they found the roads to the racetrack clogged with every kind of horse-drawn conveyance: Hansom cabs jostled with buggies and open carriages, while faster sulkies dodged around, somehow managing to avoid delivery vans and drays, all heading towards the same event. The journey was slow, but Buchanan's driver managed it without incident, arriving at the gates just as the American Consular carriage, carrying Clara, Lola and Charlotte as well as McGill and Ferguson, rolled to a stop.

"Well met," said McGill, swiftly alighting and stepping forward to hand Morag down from Buchanan's the carriage. "You look lovely, my dear," he said.

Morag smiled. "Thank you, James," she replied.

Charlotte, eager to be away, was first from McGill's carriage. She accepted a helping hand from Hector and stood impatiently brushing the creases from her plain blue skirts.

"You look charming," Hector ventured cautiously. "Will you walk with me?"

"Thanks, Hector," she replied. "Can we have a look around before we go in?"

"I think I can manage that," Hector replied, grinning suddenly. "Sir Alec does not need me at the moment, and our mothers will both be busy talking pleasantries for a little while—would you like to take a look at the mounting yards?"

"Please," Charlotte said, picking up her long skirts. "Let's go."

As Ferguson assisted Lola, and then Clara from McGill's carriage, he could not help but notice that several other race patrons paused to admire the new arrivals. The ladies were elegantly dressed for the day: Morag wore her dove-grey tailored dress, with a darker grey jacket, scarf and hat to complete the outfit; Clara had chosen a dark blue ensemble trimmed in fashionable astrakhan, while the famous Lola—always the object of curious attention—wore her trademark red with a black jacket, hat and gloves. Together, they made a fashionable showing as they walked towards the enclosure where Edward Cole, true to his word, had arranged a splendid picnic. Cole had had a large tent erected in a choice position on the grass, and had deployed his household staff to cater to his guests.

The scene that greeted the party as they headed for Cole's tent had a carnival atmosphere: people of all nationalities and all classes milled about, vendors of everything from skewered meats to snake oil plied their wares, larrikins lounged on the fences offering loud commentaries on the proceedings, and above the din the bookies shouted their odds. The air was full of the smells of horse dung and cooking smoke, mingled with the heady scents of roses and fresh cut grass.

"How divine," said Lola, pausing dramatically beside a rose bush laden with heavily perfumed red blooms. "These match my dress."

"Allow me," said Ferguson, taking the too obvious hint. He picked a single red rose, and bowed gallantly as he presented it to Lola. "For you, ma'am," he said: "a lovely flower for a lovely lady. I hope it brings you luck."

Lola smiled and pinned it to her jacket with the gold brooch she wore. "Thank you, Charles," she said. "I'm sure it will."

"You're in good form, Charles," said Clara, not to be left out. "Are you sure you're allowed out?"

Ferguson grinned. "I'm out on bail, as you know," he responded. "And besides, I have my chaperone with me—haven't I, McGill?"

"Indeed you do," McGill laughed. "I'll be sure to see that you don't get up to any mischief."

"Impossible," Lola said, laughing with him.

"But seriously," said Clara. "Have the police found the driver of the carriage yet?"

"Not yet," Ferguson admitted. "The man seems to have taken my money and vanished into thin air."

"Probably not his own equipage, then," said Clara. "He was almost certainly just hired to drive. And after the accident, you paid for repairs: so he has cheated the rightful owner, and now he's lying low."

"It seems very likely," Ferguson said. "But it makes it hard for me to establish the truth."

"I'll ask around," Clara said. "I have my sources, especially among the women. Someone must know something."

"I'd appreciate it," Ferguson replied. "I must admit, I've drawn a complete blank. And the police seem to think I'm the only one of Sir Alec's guests that evening whose destination after the dinner was unknown. They claim it looks suspicious—the Club isn't all that far from Spring Street, after all."

"But that's not true," Buchanan said, joining in the conversation for the first time.

"Oh?" said Ferguson. "Which part?"

"That everyone is accounted for," Buchanan replied. "After you had left, I talked with Father O'Hanlon. And I distinctly recall that he refused a cab. He said that he had to meet someone. He was secretive about it. I remember thinking it a very late hour for a priest to have arranged a meeting." He shrugged. "It may mean nothing, of course. But it may help convince your accusers that there was nothing sinister about your own affairs that night."

"Well," said Ferguson, "at least it shows that I am not alone in preferring to walk!" He paused, then added: "O'Hanlon was unpleasant to almost everyone at that dinner. I'd certainly be curious to know what he was up to at such a late hour."

"And so would I," said Clara. "I've no reason to trust that horrible priest."

The discussion of Ferguson's predicament was dropped, as if by mutual consent, as the party reached the tent. Cole's butler held the flap open with as much ceremony as if he had been at Government House. The guests entered an interior furnished with a long table set with crisp linen; there were formal dining chairs, and casual seating set around the perimeter. The cook was preparing luncheon, and McGill observed that there were oysters packed in seaweed and sacking, cold collations in wooden boxes, and large quantities of champagne set in a trough of cold water.

"Welcome, welcome," said Cole, beaming at his guests. He signalled to his butler, and the popping of champagne corks announced the beginning of the day's festivities. Minutes later, when the guests were all holding crystal glasses of chilled French champagne, Cole proposed a toast: "To good friends, good food, and good fortune."

"Well said," Buchanan replied. "Let us all hope Lady Luck favours us today."

"Hear, hear," Ferguson responded, drinking deeply. He set his empty glass down on a side table. "And if you'll excuse me," he said, "I'll just take a turn around the betting enclosure to see what's what."

"Let's all go," said Clara. "I certainly want to put a bet on the main race: it won't be any fun if we don't have a horse to cheer for."

"Good idea," said Cole. "I'm thinking of backing *The Quack*, the horse Mr Woo was so interested in—depending on the odds, of course."

"He's odds-on favourite," Ferguson said.

"No matter," Cole said airily. "I'll see what I can get. The favourite often wins." He beamed at his guests, happy to have such company on such a fine day. "Come along, everyone," he said. "We'll stroll down to the enclosure and back: it'll give the staff time to lay out our luncheon."

"I have one or two people to see," Buchanan said. "You all go ahead—I'll rejoin you shortly."

"As you wish," Cole replied. "Luncheon will be served at one o'clock."

"Very good," said Buchanan, already on his way out.

The rest of the party finished their drinks and trooped back out of the tent and down to the track, where the early races were underway.

Chapter 47

At the Melbourne offices of the Commercial Bank, its manager, Spencer Valentine, waited while the last of the clerks finished closing up for the Race Day half-holiday. The bank employees were excited, chatting happily as they all headed off to watch the big event. Valentine chose a different direction, walking across town to Lonsdale Street. His pink face was sheened with sweat by the time he reached St Francis' Church. He liked the quiet, shadowy peacefulness of the church's high, vaulted ceilings and cool, tiled floors. He often came here when he wanted to be alone, to think. He pushed open a heavily studded door, just enough so that he could slip inside, thankful to be out of the heat. He was just sinking gratefully onto a pew to rest his legs when a priest accosted him.

"I want a word with you," the priest hissed in Valentine's ear.

The bank manager pulled back in alarm.

"No, you can't leave." The priest grabbed Valentine by the arm. "This way." His grip was like iron as he marched Valentine towards an empty confessional. "In here," he said, giving the bank manager a push. "Nobody will interrupt us in here."

Valentine protested. "This is outrageous, O'Hanlon," he said, forced to sit.

"We need to talk," O'Hanlon replied, squeezing into the cubicle. His bony knees pressed hard against Valentine's plumper legs.

The bank manager, a fastidious man, recoiled from O'Hanlon. The priest needed a bath, and his breath was foul in this airless space.

"Well?" Valentine asked. "What's so urgent that you should accost me like this?"

O'Hanlon leaned even closer to Valentine, his words heavy with menace. "What did Orsini tell you?"

Valentine flinched. "Why? The poor man is dead. Murdered. His killer is still at large."

"I know that. Everybody knows that. What *I* need to know is what he told *you*."

Valentine shook his head, attempting to regain his composure. "Any conversation I may have had with Mr Orsini is entirely confidential," he replied. "The more so since his untimely death."

"Don't play that game with me," O'Hanlon said. "I know Orsini came to see you. He must have."

"Of course he came to see me. His bank has dealings with mine."

"Where the Banco di Santo Spirito is concerned, Valentine, you only deal with Antonelli through me."

"Cardinal Antonelli is the Finance Minister for the Vatican. He doesn't control the Bank."

"Nor does the Orsini family. Now, what did Joseph Orsini tell you?"

Valentine folded his arms and sat back as far as he could, saying nothing. The silence stretched, uncomfortably.

"Very well," O'Hanlon said at last. "Let *me* tell *you*: he told you that the Bank's accounts are seriously deficient. He told you he suspected that the Cardinal has been diverting money for his personal use. He asked you to check your records for any unusual transactions."

Valentine was shaken. "If you knew already, why ask me?" he said at last.

"I needed confirmation. You just gave it to me."

"My duty is clear," said Valentine. "I must report Orsini's suspicions to my superiors."

"But you haven't done it yet, have you?"

"I am waiting for our next scheduled board meeting. There's no need to cause undue alarm. In the meantime, I intend to do some checking of my own."

"You'll do no such thing," O'Hanlon said.

"I beg your pardon?"

"You heard me."

"I don't see…"

"What would the directors of the Commercial Bank think if they knew about your gambling habits?"

"What? That's preposterous! I don't gamble. You know I don't gamble. I'm probably the only man in Melbourne who doesn't have a bet on today's horse race."

"You gamble on the share market."

"That's investing. That's different."

"Is it? What would your superiors say if they knew that you're already channelling funds for Antonelli? If they knew that you're using their money to speculate on the American railroad boom?" O'Hanlon paused, letting the

THE FIVE STAR REPUBLIC

implications register. "In the event of an enquiry, it would be my duty to tell them."

"You wouldn't dare! It was you who talked me into it. I trusted you. You assured me I was doing the work of the Church."

"And so you are," O'Hanlon said. "And you will continue to do it. Let me spell this out for you, Valentine. The Cardinal wants to expand his interests here in Australia. He doesn't want distractions. So you will oblige him by disregarding Orsini's unfortunate visit. There will be no enquiry. There will be no scandal. Do you understand?"

Valentine swallowed hard, then nodded.

"Be sure that you do." O'Hanlon rose. "I'll be on my way. I'll see you at Mass, Valentine." He paused. "Remember, I'll be watching you."

The priest slipped back into the church.

Valentine stayed a moment longer in the dark confessional, massaging his temples. He shivered, despite the heat. He could feel the headache starting behind his eyes. He realised, too late, that he had been duped. He knew he was in trouble. He knew he was in for a sleepless night.

Chapter 48

Excitement at the racetrack was growing when Edward Cole's guests re-gathered for luncheon. With only two hours to go before the big race, the odds on the favourite were shortening. Cole's guests had all placed their bets.

"Which horses did you decide to back?" Buchanan asked the group as the oysters were being served.

"Oh," said Clara, "we girls all played safe and bet on *The Quack* with Mr Cole."

"Favourite or not," Cole said, "he's a beautiful animal: he's a shining bay stallion, tall and strong. He looks like he could stroll it in."

Ferguson laughed. "Maybe," he said. "I've spread my bets, but I'll admit I have some money riding on him—and some on trainer Tait's other horses: sometimes I follow the trainer, not the horses."

"Interesting," McGill said. "So we'll all be rich if the favourite wins."

"Satisfied, at least," said Cole, tucking into his oysters. He turned to Charlotte. "Did you place a bet, Miss Charlotte?"

"No, Mr Cole," she said. "But I did like the look of the horse you've chosen."

The lunchtime chatter continued gaily as the oysters were replaced by a main course of smoked ham, cold chicken and various vegetables, all served with a smooth mustard sauce of the chef's own devising. The atmosphere was happy, and Cole's guests relaxed. When, for a moment, the conversation lagged, swamped beneath the popping of corks and the clatter of cutlery, it was Consul McGill who turned the talk to matters other than horse racing and fashion.

"So what's the latest news from the Telegraph?" he asked Buchanan cordially.

"Not good, I'm afraid," Buchanan replied. "Every day brings darker tidings from Britain. The coal strike continues. Industry is beginning to grind to a halt."

"November is such a bad time of year for coal supplies to run short in

Britain," Cole observed. "Winter will be well and truly setting in now."

"Indeed," Buchanan replied. "The London papers say that the coal strike is set to become a general strike: and that will lead inevitably to a total shutdown."

"And what of the army?" Ferguson asked. "Surely the government will try to use force?"

"The army has already refused to fire on the strikers," Buchanan replied.

"Then the soldiers must be only one short step away from mutiny," said Cole. "I've read that they haven't been paid all of their wages for some time now. So why should they fire on their countrymen, if they're in the same predicament?"

"Why indeed," McGill said thoughtfully. "It sounds to me as though the situation is becoming dangerous, and quickly. What will you do, Sir Alec?"

"Do?" said Buchanan. "What can we do?"

"Prepare ourselves for a big change in circumstances," Cole replied.

"It seems to me," McGill said, "and I hope you'll forgive me if I am speaking out of turn, that there will soon be real opportunities here for astute businessmen. Even if Britain is only out of action for a short while, there's a lot you could do to capitalise on the situation."

"Such as?" said Buchanan.

"Stop the gold shipments," McGill replied promptly. "Britain takes all the gold you mine. Think of the advantage to this colony if the gold stayed here, as it does in California."

"I don't see how that's possible," Buchanan said. "We have a colonial government, after all. It would enforce the shipments, in the end."

"Delay them, then. And put the gold to good use in the meantime," said McGill. "Stockpile your gold reserves: at least that would protect your banks."

"That could be done," Buchanan conceded.

Hector, who had been listening intently, finally managed to get a word in. "How would holding back the gold protect our banks?" he asked.

It was Edward Cole who answered. "Banking isn't about people's savings," he said. "It's about debt. Bank notes represent that debt. When you present a banker's note, the bank pays you in gold sovereigns, does it not?"

"Yes, I know, but…"

Cole was not to be interrupted. "So the bank, in theory, must have enough gold to cover its debts, to cover the notes it has issued," he said.

"If things get worse," McGill added, "there is a real risk that everyone will try to cash out their notes at once. If there's not enough gold to go around, the banks will collapse. That's why the gold reserves are Victoria's great strength: as long as everyone knows they are there, your banks will be safe."

"I hadn't thought of it quite like that," Hector said.

"We could stop the copper shipments as well," said Cole, suddenly intense. "Think of it, Buchanan: we could build our copper smelter to refine the ore after all, and make our own copper wire. It'd be better than a gold mine."

"That's more like it," said Ferguson. "We already own the copper ore."

"That certainly bears thinking about," Buchanan said. "If a general strike interrupts our supplies of essential manufactures—like copper wire—then the government officials can hardly object if we keep their projects viable by making our own."

"I like the way you are thinking," said McGill. "If you refine your own copper you will gain a permanent measure of independence from your political masters."

"And we should be thinking about new technology too," said Cole, warming to his theme. "I've been reading about some amazing developments in the scientific journals."

"Not another of your romances, I hope, Edward?" Buchanan said.

"Not a bit of it," Cole replied. "It's the talk of our copper that made me remember." He turned to address McGill, his pink face glowing with enthusiasm and champagne. "You said that you had met Captain Ericsson, the engineer who designed the ironclad warship—the *Monitor*—did you not?" he asked.

"Indeed yes," McGill replied. "He's a brilliant man. Why do you ask?"

"Well," said Cole, "I'm asking about his credentials because it happens that I read an article in *The Technologist* about a new invention of his, called the *Sun Engine*."

"And what is that?" Clara asked, unable to stay quiet any longer.

"It's a prototype solar engine," Cole replied. Seeing the puzzled looks that greeted this announcement, he added quickly: "It's a steam engine that uses the power of the sun to superheat the water to make the steam. It doesn't need coal at all. And the best part is"—he paused for effect—"it's mostly made of copper."

"Impossible," said Buchanan.

"I'd have thought that iron-clad gunships were impossible," said Ferguson, "but we have one out in the bay, invented by the same man."

"Point taken," said Buchanan. "I suppose it's one more thing to think about. And I have to say I like the idea of building our own factories, if we get the chance. We've been paying far too much for far too long for just about everything."

"My thoughts exactly," Cole said.

"Well," McGill observed, "I for one shall be keeping a close eye on the situation in Britain as the strike unfolds. The implications for international trade and relations are enormous." He paused. "But I fear we are neglecting the ladies," he said.

Buchanan seemed suddenly to remember that the ladies included Clara, owner and publisher of a ladies' journal. "I do hope you'll regard these discussions as entirely confidential, Mrs Seekamp," he said. "They are mere lunchtime speculation, after all."

Clara took offence at his tone. "I wouldn't dream of publishing, if that's what you mean," she said sharply.

"I should hope not," said Cole. "You're a shareholder in the copper consortium, after all."

"I'm glad you remember that, Mr Cole," Clara replied. "I'm still part of the enterprise, even if I'm not invited to the shareholders' dinner."

Buchanan made as if to speak, but stopped at a warning glance from Cole.

"But you are here today, Mrs Seekamp," Cole said, "and in much more congenial surroundings, if I may say so. Perhaps we can overlook the strictures of The Melbourne Club for the moment—at least long enough for dessert? My chef has prepared something rather special for the occasion." He smiled his most winning smile.

Clara relented. "Just this once, then, Mr Cole," she said. "You are quite right. We are all here friends today, enjoying your generous hospitality. It would be such a shame to spoil it."

"Thank you," Cole said, relieved. "I'm much obliged."

Chapter 49

As the clock ticked towards three o'clock, excitement at the track was reaching fever pitch. The bookies placed last bets and closed their ledgers, people abandoned the amusement tents and drifted towards the railings, and in the stands the sun flashed on hundreds of field glasses as wealthier race patrons scanned the marshalling yards. Cole and his guests moved outside to stand on the hill, which afforded an excellent view of the barrier. As the horses breasted the machine, warm sunshine shone bright on muscles rippling beneath coats brushed until they gleamed, and highlighted racing silks of every colour and design.

As the horses readied for the jump, a strange silence fell over the waiting crowd. But then the gong boomed, the horses were off, and the roar of the crowd cut through the warm afternoon air. The lightweights forced the pace at first, and Lola bit her lip as the field entered the turn.

"There's our horse," she shouted to Clara above the din. "He's too far back."

"Wait," said Ferguson. "There's a long way to go yet. The jockey is holding him back. I can see the effort it takes to rein that horse in—he's heavy, but he's strong." He linked arms with Lola and Clara, walking them closer to the finish line. "We'll get a better view down here," he said.

McGill followed, with Morag clinging happily to his arm in all the excitement of the moment.

As the horses thundered into the straight, metal-shod hooves kicking up divots of the grassy track, a huge black stallion was leading the pack, with *The Quack* close behind him, sticking to the rails.

"Here we go," said Ferguson.

As he spoke, *The Quack's* jockey finally let the horse have his head, and plied the whip for good measure. The field flashed past the winner's post, with the big bay, *The Quack,* outpacing the black stallion by a head.

The crowd went wild: the favourite had won the Cup.

"We've won," said Lola, her eyes shining with excitement. She hugged

Clara and Morag in turn. "We've won. How thrilling!"

Clara just grinned back at her friend, sharing the pleasure of the victory.

"I think this calls for a celebration," Ferguson said, checking his betting slips. "We've won a tidy sum. I'm sure Cole has more champagne left."

As the jockeys rode back to the weighing yard, the cheering crowd surged closer to the railings, carrying McGill and Ferguson and the three ladies to the front. In the exhilaration of the moment, Lola unpinned the red rose from her jacket and tossed it to the jockey. "Bravo!" she called.

"NO!" McGill and Ferguson shouted together.

It was too late. The jockey's reflexes got the better of him. He caught the rose.

"Drop it, man!" Ferguson shouted. "Drop it!"

A look of pure horror crossed the jockey's face as he realised what he had done. He let the rose fall from his fingers, to be trampled beneath the hooves of his proud, race-winning horse.

There was an audible hiss from the crowd. Cheers and whoops of delight gave way to mutterings and curses.

"Stupid bitch!" one man spat at Lola.

"We have to get her out of here," McGill said to Ferguson. "This will turn ugly in a minute."

"Right," said Ferguson. He seized the bewildered Lola firmly by the elbow and began to push a way through the hostile crowd, protecting her from the press of outraged punters.

McGill followed, shepherding Morag and Clara, keeping their little group in a tight knot.

"What's happening?" Morag asked.

"We need to get you back to Mr Cole's tent," McGill replied. "You'll be safer there."

Clara started to protest. "Why?" she began.

"Not now, Clara," McGill replied grimly, shouldering his way through the throng. "Just stick close to me."

By the time Ferguson and McGill had finally pushed and shoved a way through the surging mob, clearing a way for the ladies, they were all hot, perspiring and dishevelled.

"Good Lord," said Cole, greeting them as they came in. "What happened out there?"

"Madame Montez happened," McGill said shortly. He strode to a side table and poured a glass of water for Morag.

"We'll be lucky if there isn't a riot," Ferguson said. "Better warn your staff, Cole."

"Already in hand, sir," the butler replied. "Shall I arrange for your carriage, Consul?"

"That would be best, yes," McGill replied. "Ferguson and I will take all the ladies home—if we can get the carriage out through the gates."

"I don't understand," said Lola. She set her jaw, and her eyes flashed with anger. "Why are they shouting at me?"

For answer Ferguson merely opened the tent flap and pointed to the stand, where instead of the red flag signalling that the race had been declared and the winner of the Melbourne Cup was clear, a yellow protest flag had been raised.

"The jockey of the horse that ran second will have lodged a protest," Ferguson said. "And before you ask, Clara, he is entitled to protest on the grounds that *The Quack*'s jockey was interfered with before he was weighed in." He struggled to keep the anger from his voice. "Lola's rose has probably cost him the race, and cost all of us a great deal of money."

"But it was just a rose," Lola said. "People throw roses at me in the theatre all the time. I was applauding him."

"You interfered with him," Ferguson said shortly. "Before the race was officially declared."

"As if you applauded before the performance was over," Clara said, suddenly comprehending. "It is as if you had interrupted the finale." She turned to Ferguson. "What will happen now?" she asked. "And where is Charlotte?"

"Right here, Mother," Charlotte replied, coming quickly into the tent. "Hector and I were watching from the hill."

"Thank you for taking care of her, Hector," Clara said. "I'm relieved you are both back, safe and sound."

"My pleasure, Mrs Seekamp," Hector said. "We didn't have too much trouble getting back here, though the crowd is getting lively now."

At that moment, Buchanan strode into the tent, his face flushed with exertion. "There will be an urgent committee meeting to decide the protest," he said. "This will be very difficult—the winning horse is heavily backed. There's a lot of money at stake, for bookies and punters alike." He accepted a glass of water from the butler and downed it at a gulp. "I'm on my way there now."

"You're on the committee?" asked Cole.

"No," Buchanan replied. "But I know the men who are. I've just been speaking to some of them, to see which way the land lies."

"Why?" Cole asked.

Buchanan held up his hand to forestall further questions. "Madame Montez is your guest today, Edward," he replied. "And I am of the same party. A scandal would reflect badly on us both, and on our business ventures."

"Then let me come with you," Cole said.

"Best you stay here," Buchanan replied. "I'll take care of this. Hector will accompany me." He straightened his jacket, preparing to brave the crowds once more.

Wordlessly, Hector checked the knife in his sleeve before he followed his employer out into the sunshine that shone benignly on a very angry mob.

Chapter 50

McGill was sitting with Morag in the front parlour, keeping her company until Buchanan and Hector should finally return. The evening shadows were beginning to lengthen in Buchanan's garden, and Morag had already lit the lamps. A tawny owl hooted in the background, already hunting for hapless mice.

"May I ask you something, Morag?" McGill said.

"Of course."

"It's about Clara's daughter, Charlotte."

"What about her?"

"I saw her sitting beside Ferguson in the carriage today. I hope I am not speaking out of turn, but I must say the family resemblance is striking."

"Ah," said Morag. "I'm not sure if I should answer that, James."

"You just have," he replied. "There's no need to say anything else, my love. I understand. It's just that I find it curious he hasn't mentioned it."

Morag looked down uncomfortably at her hands, twisting her handkerchief in her lap.

McGill hesitated for a moment. "He doesn't know, does he?" he said at last.

Morag shook her head.

"How can he not see?" McGill said.

Morag found her voice at last. "Clara has never said a word to anyone," she said softly. "She gave her his Christian name, but Charles Ferguson assumes, like everyone else, that Charlotte's father was Seekamp. Ferguson has watched her grow up, so he doesn't really look at her, if you know what I mean."

"But he should be given the chance to acknowledge her," McGill said, "at least to his own family back home."

"Surely that would just stir up trouble, for everyone concerned. Charlotte is perfectly happy as she is," Morag replied.

"Ferguson comes from an old family, a very *wealthy* family," McGill said.

"There will be a large inheritance, in the natural course of events. The child should not be deprived of what is hers by right."

"Oh," said Morag. "I never thought of that." She paused, conflicted. "But James, if you say anything to Ferguson, Clara will think I betrayed her."

"Then I won't mention it, at least for the present," McGill said quietly.

"Best not," Morag replied. "And definitely not at the moment: I think I hear footsteps on the drive."

At the sound of the front door, McGill looked up enquiringly, in time to glimpse Buchanan dump his hat and coat unceremoniously in the entry hall and stride towards the parlour to join his guest. He slumped into the nearest armchair, his face grim. Hector followed, looking tired and drained.

"Well, that's done," Buchanan said at last. "Drink, McGill?"

"Thank you, yes," McGill replied. "Whisky."

"And me," said Buchanan. "Hector, will you do the honours?"

"Certainly." Hector crossed to the drinks tray and began to pour from the crystal decanter.

"And you'd best have one for yourself," Buchanan added. "You've earned it."

Hector poured a sherry for his mother, handed the whiskies to Buchanan and McGill, before taking his own to a chair by the window.

"To damage limitation," Buchanan said, raising his glass in salute.

The men drank.

"What happened?" McGill asked at last. "We've been waiting to hear."

"The committee finally ruled in favour of *The Quack*," Buchanan said. "After a long debate, common sense prevailed: it was decided that the jockey only touched the rose for a second, and that a stupid mistake by a reckless foreign woman should not cost him the race." He shrugged. "It was a near thing."

"Was it so important to you?" McGill asked softly.

"As I said, the horse was heavily backed," Buchanan replied. "A lot of that backing came from Woo's Chinese business associates in Hong Kong. And others."

"Ah," said McGill. "The telegraph link. I understand."

Buchanan nodded. "Precisely. It was a matter of honour. The Montez woman is associated with us, and therefore with our consortium. If her actions had caused large financial losses in the business community, both here and abroad, the repercussions could have been catastrophic."

"You protected her," Morag said. "Thank you."

"I was protecting all of us," Buchanan said tersely. "The new telegraph link has only been in operation for a very few weeks. We cannot afford any loss of confidence in our business arrangements. This was a very expensive afternoon."

"How expensive?" McGill asked.

Buchanan shrugged, leaving it to Hector to answer.

"Sir Alec is to finance a new members' pavilion at the track," he said quietly.

Later that evening at the Consulate, McGill recounted Buchanan's story to Ferguson over a quiet drink before dinner.

"A whole new pavilion—that's what I call a decent consideration for the right result!" Ferguson said.

"Indeed," McGill observed.

"And Woo is already using the Telegraph to facilitate gambling on the Australian races for his associates in Hong Kong," said Ferguson. "I must say, he's quick off the mark."

"Very," McGill replied. "It makes me wonder what else he's using it for. I think our Mr Woo will bear watching, just quietly."

"I can see, now, why Buchanan might feel threatened by the events of the day," Ferguson said. "I must say I'd like to be a fly on the wall when he tells Lola what her little dramatic gesture cost him!"

"Do you think he will?" McGill asked. "Would it be quite the thing?"

"Buchanan's a man of business, first and foremost," Ferguson replied. "He's a strategist, and he takes his opportunities where he finds them. And he knows that Lola manages her own business affairs very nicely. So yes, I think he will tell her, when the occasion arises." He laughed. "I have no doubt they'll come to some arrangement."

"What's so funny?"

"I seem to recall that Madame Montez has unusually interesting ways of paying her debts. Buchanan may get more than he bargained for."

"Whatever do you mean?" McGill asked.

Ferguson shrugged. "Just don't offer to buy her a dress, James," he said.

Chapter 51

Two weeks later, Edward Cole was again meeting with Buchanan in his elegantly furnished Collins Street office.

"I wrote to Jacob Pitman immediately after our discussion at the Cup," Cole said. He fished inside his coat pocket. "And he replies that there is a suitable site for a copper smelter not far from the mine, beside the plant where we reduce the ore for shipping."

"That was fast," Buchanan said approvingly.

"He's an astute engineer," Cole replied, "and well connected. He's felt for some time that we should be refining our own copper for manufacture."

"And how does he propose to circumvent interference from England?"

"He is of the opinion that the South Australian Governor is far less likely to object than the officials here in Melbourne," Cole said. "The colony there is much less well developed, and most amenable to projects that will bring growth."

"I see," Buchanan said, stroking his chin thoughtfully. "And do we have an idea of costs?"

"Pitman is calculating some estimates for us," Cole replied. "And he says that, given our consortium's involvement with government projects here, it's quite likely that we can also negotiate to build a rail link that will suit everyone."

"Now that is interesting," Buchanan said. "Rail is the coming thing."

"Undoubtedly," said Cole. "It's also very useful that Consul McGill is so strongly connected to George Train and his American railroads, isn't it? Handled properly, we might be able to wangle additional funding from American investors."

"Indeed we might," Buchanan replied. "Train is in partnership with Thomas Durant—that's Union Pacific Railroads."

Cole whistled. "That's huge," he said.

"Indeed it is, Edward," said Buchanan. "Their construction management

231

company is Credit Mobilier—McGill tells me that they have already built the transcontinental railway lines from Missouri to the west, from San Francisco to the east. And now they are looking further afield. A project such as ours, with government backing and a guaranteed outcome, would be likely to appeal to their investors."

Cole grinned. "Most certainly," he said. "It's high time we had our own transcontinental rail link."

"It will come," Buchanan replied. "We just have to give it a push."

Cole grinned. "Is there any more telegraph news from Britain?" he asked.

"More of the same," Buchanan replied. "It's hard to believe what's happening there. The General Strike is getting worse, factories are closing, and the government in England is running out of funds to pay its wages bills. The army and navy haven't been paid at all this month."

"Then Whitehall is hardly likely to be bothered with us," Cole said, still smiling. "McGill is right: we should get going, Buchanan. If—or when—the British government regains full control, it will be hard for them to stop us if we are already underway and no objection was raised at the outset."

"True," said Buchanan, "particularly if they don't hear about the development until it's too late to argue."

Cole's face creased into a grin. "They'll be relying on the telegraph link for information, won't they?" he said slowly.

"And we own the telegraph stations at Alice Springs and Darwin," Buchanan replied. "It's a closed system, Edward. It only connects at certain controlled points with the rest of the world."

"And we control two of those connection points," Cole said, almost jumping up with glee. "I should have realised the implications a whole lot sooner."

Buchanan couldn't help grinning back at Cole. "I recognised the potential at the outset," he said, "but I thought it would just provide business security and give us early warning of anything that might affect us. But circumstances change, Edward. All of a sudden I find it's amazing how misinformation can find its way into the telegraph system. And of course," he added blandly, "messages in the other direction from the British government to their agencies in Melbourne and Sydney also pass through our stations."

"So the likelihood of any immediate investigation of our activities can be limited?"

"Severely limited," Buchanan replied.

"How can you be sure?" Cole asked.

"At the outset I issued a simple directive to our employees at the relay stations," Buchanan said. "The Telegraph operates on key words and codes. Any message that contains mention of our consortium or the names of our directors, or our nominated clients, is put aside for checking by my personal operatives. It's company policy, for security reasons."

"Brilliant," Cole said. "You put a loop in the system."

"The messages are only briefly diverted," Buchanan said. "On the surface, everything is as it should be." He shrugged. "My little loop provides a special level of security for sensitive business transactions," he said.

"Like Woo's operations?" Cole asked.

"Certainly," Buchanan said. "But not exclusively. It's important that all our clients have confidence in our credibility."

"I see," Cole said.

"I'm sure you do," said Buchanan. "To anyone else using the system, it's business as usual within the Empire." He paused, briefly. "That's what upsets the Americans so much," he added thoughtfully. "They can't access the Empire's telegraph system."

"And entrée into that system is a very valuable commodity. So we have a bargaining point with McGill's government as well," Cole said.

"And a very useful one," said Buchanan.

"Are we talking revolution, Alec?" Cole asked quietly, grown suddenly serious. "Will it come to that?"

"I think not," Buchanan replied. "And no matter what McGill tells us, revolution is bad for business. In the end, the old structures reassert themselves— with different people at the top, to be sure—but underneath it stays pretty much the same. Real power is so much more than political power, Edward. It will be better for us if the British government stays in place, and our officials here go on governing unchallenged. That way, we can control things: we go hand in glove with them as it is, and weakened input from England will make them even more amenable."

"And if the Empire falls?"

"We'll cross that bridge when we come to it," Buchanan said firmly. "For now, I'll assume it will continue, in some form, and I'll take whatever advantage there is."

"Which is why I think we should proceed with our copper smelter as fast as we can," said Cole, returning to his earlier position.

"Very well," Buchanan said. "I agree. But supposing that we get the thing built, how will we get the right workers?"

"We'll import them," Cole said. "We have plenty of time in hand. And there'll be no shortage of unemployed workers at the Swansea refinement smelters after this general strike. The Cornish miners are already desperate. They'll all be begging us to take them."

Buchanan nodded. "I've also been thinking about something else McGill said."

"Oh?"

"He mentioned that he knew that engineer, Ericsson," said Buchanan. "The one you were talking about. I expect that McGill might be able to contact him for us."

"About developing his Sun Engine?" Cole asked.

"Why not?" Buchanan replied. "If there's one thing this country has, it's blazing hot sunlight. And it's free."

"That depends what it costs to build the engine," Cole replied.

"True," said Buchanan. "But we'll be building steam engines of one sort or another to power our plant. The brown coal here in Victoria is no good. Why should we pay to ship black coal from another colony if we can use the sun for free?"

"It's worth a try," Cole said, no longer trying to hide his enthusiasm. "I'd really like to see it work: it would be a beautiful thing to see a steam engine running without belching horrible greasy black smoke over everyone and everything."

"I hadn't thought of that," Buchanan said. "But you're right—it would be clean. And that would save us even more money on the plant."

"How so?"

"We wouldn't have to shut down for days at a time to clean the soot out of the engines," Buchanan replied. "There wouldn't be any."

"How wonderful," Cole said.

Buchanan looked thoughtful. "You know, Edward, ever since we established the telegraph station at Alice Springs, I've considered that it would be the perfect place for controlled manufacturing. But the problem has always been that there's no coal there to power the steam engines. It occurs to me now that if Ericsson's engine proves viable, we *could* build a factory out there, or more than one."

"And a new rail link to Port Darwin would transport the goods?"

"My thinking exactly," Buchanan said.

Cole couldn't contain his excitement: he paced about the room, gesturing as he spoke. "That's breathtaking, Alec," he said. "I can see it: a model factory town, powered by steam and sunlight. We could commission Jacob Pitman to build it. We could name it *Helios*—a modern-day Heliopolis. It's perfect: a city in the desert, a city of the sun."

"Let's not get too carried away, Edward," Buchanan said. "It's just an idea."

"It's brilliant," Cole replied. "Would you like me to approach McGill?"

"I do think it would be better coming from you," Buchanan said. "You could write to Ericsson to sound him out. Then, if the thing appears to be at all likely, the Consortium can become officially involved."

"And in the meantime," Cole said, grinning from ear to ear, "it'll look like I'm simply pursuing yet another of my crack-pot scientific publishing schemes?"

"Something like that," said Buchanan. "We don't want to tip off the competitors, do we?"

"Indeed we do not, Alec," Cole replied. "Indeed we do not."

Chapter 52

"**I**'m sorry to interrupt, sir," one of Buchanan's clerks said, nervously venturing a scant few feet into his employer's office, "but there's a lady to see you."

"I was just leaving," Cole said, rising to his feet.

"No need to rush, Edward," said Buchanan. "Does she have an appointment?"

"No, sir, but she insists that you will see her."

"Does she indeed," Buchanan said. "And does this lady have a name?"

"Madame Montez, sir," the assistant replied. "She's…"

"I know who she is, yes," Buchanan said. "You may show her in, Roland."

"Yes, sir." The clerk edged towards the door.

"And order tea, would you?"

"Yes, sir."

A moment later, Lola was ushered into the office. She was demurely dressed today in a high-necked black lace blouse teamed with a dark red skirt and jacket. She walked in confidently, but stopped short when she saw that Buchanan was not alone.

"Oh. Good morning, Sir Alec, and Mr Cole," she said. "I hope I am not interrupting anything important."

"Not at all," Cole replied. "I was just leaving."

"Will you stay for tea, Edward?" Buchanan asked.

"Much as I value your cook's excellent ginger biscuits, no," Cole replied. "I have another engagement." He held a chair for Lola, who sat gracefully. "It's always a delight to see you, my dear," he said. "But I must be on my way." He kissed her hand. "Until next time," he said.

"Goodbye Mr Cole," Lola said, smiling. "Thank you."

As Cole turned to leave, he shot a curious glance at Buchanan, who shrugged ever so slightly in return.

As the door closed behind Cole, Buchanan turned to Lola. "This is an unexpected pleasure," he said. "Forgive me, but am I correct in assuming that since you have come to my office this is not a purely social call?"

Lola nodded, but before she could speak one of Buchanan's assistants knocked discreetly, then entered, bearing the tea tray. She made a fuss of pouring tea for Lola and then Buchanan, trying unsuccessfully to hide her burning curiosity about this most unusual visitor.

"Will there be anything else, sir?" she said at last.

"Thank you, no," Buchanan replied. He stood, waiting patiently until the door closed once again.

"And now," he said, "may I make so bold as to enquire the reason for your visit?" He chuckled: "As you can see, you've brightened the day for my staff—they'll be gossiping for hours."

"Oh dear," said Lola. She put down her cup and saucer. "I should have made an appointment."

"No matter," Buchanan replied. "But I really should like to know what brings you here to beard me in my den."

"Morag told me," Lola said quietly.

"Ah," said Buchanan. "I see." He held up his hand. "It's brave of you to come to me, but there really is no need for you to apologise. The matter is taken care of."

"Apologise?" said Lola, bridling. "I assure you that that was not my intention."

Now Buchanan was wrong-footed. "What, then?" he asked, startled.

"I came to discuss terms," said Lola.

"Terms?"

"For settling my debt to you," Lola replied impatiently.

"I assure you there is no such requirement on my part," Buchanan replied. "I understand that you meant no harm—yours was a gesture made in the heat of the moment. I was fortunate enough to be in a position to avert the unpleasant consequences that may have ensued—for all of us. That is all."

"Precisely," Lola replied. "I am an independent woman, Sir Alec. I take responsibility for my actions. And I am in your debt. So I am here to talk terms with you, if you'll be good enough to tell me what would please you."

Buchanan, for once, was speechless.

Lola stood. She deliberately crossed the floor to where Buchanan was still standing by his desk, and, reaching on tiptoe, kissed him full on the mouth, kissed him hard. "Now do we begin to understand each other?" she asked.

Buchanan took a deep breath and stepped back. "It was never my intention to compromise your virtue," he said.

Lola laughed. "My what?" she said.

Buchanan, surprised, laughed too. "I had not expected such candour," he said, steering her back towards her seat. He pulled up another chair, sat close beside her, and took her hand. "Perhaps we should talk."

"Yes," said Lola, "we should. I find it's best to have these discussions at the outset. That way there can be no misunderstandings later."

"Then let us consider our position together," Buchanan replied, recovering his equanimity. "I must say I find your approach refreshingly honest. What do you have in mind?"

Lola smiled coquettishly. "There are options, Alec," she said. "Obviously, I'm a single woman, in need of a patron."

"A husband?"

"Perhaps," Lola agreed.

"Just as a matter of interest, how many husbands have you had?" Buchanan asked, his voice carefully neutral.

"Well, let me see," Lola replied, counting on her fingers. "There were six that I actually married, I think."

"Good Lord," said Buchanan. "What happened to them all?"

"They died," Lola said simply.

"I'm not usually a gambling man," Buchanan said. "I must say I don't like those odds. Do all your lovers die?"

"Of course not," Lola said indignantly. "But I always say, in matters of the heart, you can't help bad luck. And I've had my share." She trapped the hand that held hers with her free one. "I didn't marry dear King Leopold," she said cheerfully, "even though he asked me. And he's alive and well."

"That's something, then," Buchanan said. "But Lola, you must know that marriage is out of the question."

Lola pouted. "I do now," she said. "Don't you like women?"

"Of course I like women," Buchanan responded. "I'm no monk."

"Then you don't like me?"

"Of course I like you. I just don't plan on marrying you. It would be too complicated."

Lola sighed. "But you don't deny you want me?" she said, looking into his eyes.

"No, I can't deny that."

"You don't think I can satisfy your needs?"

"I have no doubt that you can do that, and more," he said, smiling at the thought.

"And I hope you can, perhaps, satisfy mine," she replied.

Buchanan, once more taken aback, raised an eyebrow.

"Come now, Alec," she said. "You can't seriously think that sex is a one-sided transaction?"

"No, but…"

"But you are not accustomed to a woman being frank about it," Lola finished for him.

Buchanan smiled ruefully. "You have me there," he said.

"And if we are agreed on that point," she said, "perhaps we can come to an understanding after all. Obviously, I'll need a place of my own."

"Ah," said Buchanan, "now we come to it. You would prefer no longer to be the guest of Mrs Seekamp?"

"Oh, Clara is lovely," Lola replied, "and her daughter is a pet. But I meant simply that I cannot entertain you at her house. And your house is impossible, at least until Morag marries. And even then, the gossip would be hard for both of us."

"True," Buchanan replied. "I could always take an hotel room. That would be much less expensive than buying you a house."

"In the short term, yes," Lola conceded. "But a place of my own would be so much nicer for both of us."

Buchanan disengaged his hand from hers. "Let me get this straight," he said. "You are offering to recompense me for my financial losses with sexual favours," he said, "but it will cost me a house to enjoy them?"

"In a nutshell, yes," Lola said equably. "It seems like a good deal to me."

"For you, you mean," Buchanan replied, laughing.

"That too," said Lola.

"I'll admit you have style," Buchanan said, "but I have a better idea: one that may turn a profit for both of us."

"Yes?"

"Yes," said Buchanan. "I believe our partnership will be best handled as a business transaction, after all."

"I don't quite take your meaning," said Lola, suddenly less confident of her bargaining position.

Buchanan smiled. "I have just acquired a large house at the Spring Street end of Bourke Street, close to Parliament House," he said, "with the intention of creating a Supper Club there. My plan is that a very exclusive membership—politicians and businessmen—will be able to enjoy a bohemian atmosphere there, away from prying eyes."

"Sounds intriguing," said Lola.

"Well," said Buchanan, "you manage your theatre company, do you not?"

"Of course I do. We are very successful."

"My point exactly," said Buchanan. "So it occurs to me that I could refurbish the upper floor of the Supper Club as an apartment for you, in return for which you would agree to manage the club. And receive me, of course, when it is convenient."

"Of course," Lola said, smiling.

"And the famous Lola Montez will be quite a drawcard for the Supper Club," Buchanan went on, warming to the idea. "We would, it goes without saying, keep our private arrangements strictly between ourselves. As far as the world is concerned, ours will be simply a business relationship for mutual profit."

"That could work," Lola said, considering her options. "What kind of entertainments did you have in mind for your members?"

"In addition to the usual champagne and light collations, I had thought to include music and dancing and perhaps some special performances from time to time."

"And do you think that members of my theatre group might be included in that?"

"Possibly," said Buchanan. "But I don't think we should get ahead of ourselves just yet."

"What, then?"

Buchanan consulted his gold fob watch. "I suggest that we should go and inspect the building," he said. "It's not far to walk."

"I'd like that," Lola said.

"And then," Buchanan continued, "I'll take you to lunch at the White Hart Hotel. The chef there is very good."

Lola smiled. "And then?"

"I might just book that room." He stood, and offered his arm. "Shall we?"

Lola rose. "It will be my pleasure," she said.

Chapter 53

Christmas had come and gone with the usual festivities, the worthy citizens of Melbourne town indulging valiantly in traditional English fare despite the summer heat. The season was busy with social events, but otherwise it had passed without undue incident. On a warm January morning in the New Year of 1873, McGill and Ferguson were eating breakfast in the Consulate conservatory, away from the decorators already hard at work in the main house—but even here the smell of fresh paint assailed their senses, overriding the aroma of their freshly brewed coffee.

Wilson tapped softly at the door. "I'm sorry to disturb you," he said, "but a parcel has just been delivered for Lieutenant Ferguson. I thought you'd want to know."

"Bring it in then, by all means," McGill said.

"It's rather large, sir," Wilson replied. "I really do think you should come and see whether you will accept it, sir."

"Well, I'm intrigued," said Ferguson, getting to his feet and dropping his linen napkin onto the table. "Lead on, Wilson."

McGill also stood, abandoning his breakfast with regret. "Let's take a look, then," he said. "This sounds interesting."

"You might say that, sir," Wilson replied, his face a mask of propriety.

As McGill crossed the hallway, he looked up to see two heavily muscled Chinese deliverymen deftly propelling their cargo on a porter's trolley into the centre of the entry vestibule.

Ferguson stopped short, staring in disbelief as they set down a tall, neatly wrapped brown paper parcel, criss-crossed tightly with strong twine. From the bottom of the parcel protruded a pair of booted feet; from the top a dirty face with shifty eyes, yellow teeth and a weedy ginger moustache peered out. The face was clearly terrified, and the parcel crackled as it shook.

"Good Lord," Ferguson said, turning to McGill. "It's the driver of the carriage!"

243

"There's a note, sir," Wilson said, his demeanour as impassive as that of the deliverymen.

McGill stepped forward to remove the envelope pinned to the chest of the human parcel.

"It's addressed to you, Ferguson," he said, noticing the perfect copperplate handwriting and the red chop seal as he passed it to his friend.

Ferguson tore open the envelope, which contained a single sheet of ivory notepaper embossed with a pair of Chinese dragons, rampant, and the legend: *With the compliments of Chang Woo Gow*. Black ink Chinese characters scrolled down the left side of the page.

"It says," Ferguson read out:

> *"Dear Lieutenant Ferguson,*
>
> *It has come to my attention that the enclosed is an item that you have been missing. My agents located it this morning. Please accept my felicitations on its return. It has been my pleasure to assist you in this matter: I trust that as our future unfolds you will remember who your friends are.*
>
> *Yours sincerely,*
> *Chang Woo Gow."*

"Will there be any reply, sir?" one of the Chinese retainers asked.

"My compliments to Mr Woo," Ferguson replied swiftly. "Tell him Lieutenant Ferguson is sincerely grateful for his help in this most pressing matter."

"Thank you, sir," the men said in unison, bowing their way out of the entry hall.

McGill nodded to Wilson, who quickly followed them outside.

"Wilson will tip them handsomely," McGill said. "It's customary—we must observe the courtesies, especially where Woo is concerned."

"Oh Lord, sorry," Ferguson said. "I'm so surprised I clean forgot to tip."

"No harm done," McGill said. "It's all taken care of now." He paused, considering. "I must say," he added, "Woo's note is direct. No question that he expects a favour for a favour. Quid pro quo."

"Under the circumstances," Ferguson replied, "I can't say I have a problem with that."

"Perhaps not," McGill replied.

"What about me?" the parcel said, speaking up for the first time. The man had stopped shaking, recovering his composure now that his Chinese captors had gone. "You can't leave me trussed up like this."

"Can't we?" said Ferguson. "You were perfectly prepared to let me hang for a murder I didn't commit. The police have been advertising for you to come forward for weeks now."

"You do recognise this man, do you not?" McGill asked.

"Yes, sir, I remember him from the accident last month, sir."

"Then why haven't you come forward?" McGill said. "The advertisements were clear enough, asking for the driver involved in that particular accident to identify himself to the police. You must have realised that the other passenger was the murder victim."

The man cleared his throat. "I, er, didn't go back to driving work, like," he said.

"You mean you pocketed the damages money and left the mess for the owner to sort out."

"I took care of the horse, sir."

"Well that's something, at least," said Ferguson, wondering how much the poor animal had fetched on the black market.

Ferguson shared a long look with McGill, before he spoke again. "Let's be clear about this," he said. "I want you to make a statement to the police to confirm that Mr Orsini was alive after the accident, and that you saw me leave on foot."

"That's no more than the truth, sir. But..."

Ferguson held up his hand to forestall the inevitable plea. "I understand your situation," he said. "I'll see you right for any financial loss that comes to you through this."

The weasel face smiled thinly, anticipating profit to be had.

"But you also need to understand me," Ferguson continued. "I'm a fair man. Do right by me, and I'll do right by you." He leaned closer to the man, lowering his voice. "Cross me, and there will be nowhere to hide."

"I wouldn't..." the man began.

"Of course you would," Ferguson said equably. "But it really wouldn't be worth your while. If Woo's men have to parcel you up a second time, I'll have them throw you into the sea. Do you understand?"

The man swallowed hard, then nodded. "Yes," he muttered.

"Good," said McGill. "That's settled. I'll have the coach brought around and we'll escort Mr...?" he hesitated.

"Smith, sir."

McGill gave him a hard look. "That had better not be a lie," he said, "for your sake."

The man said nothing.

"We'll escort Mr Smith to the police station," he continued, "and we'll wait while he gives his testimony."

"Good idea," said Ferguson. "We don't want any more misunderstandings, do we?"

JANEEN WEBB AND ANDREW ENSTICE

"You going to untie me, or what?" said Smith.

"Or what, I believe," Ferguson replied. "You can't make a run for it trussed up like a chicken, can you? We'll unwrap you when we get you to the police, safe and sound."

Smith sighed in resignation. "No need for that," he said.

"Oh, I think there is." Ferguson grinned. "You've put me to enough trouble these last few weeks."

246

Chapter 54

"I have news," Cole said, dropping heavily into a chair in Buchanan's office and mopping his face with his handkerchief. "Heaven knows, it's hot out there," he said. "Is there any chance of a cool drink, Alec?"

"Certainly," Buchanan replied. "I'll just ring for some lemonade."

"Thank you," Cole replied. "That should hit the spot."

"My pleasure," Buchanan replied. "Now, what brings you out in all this heat to see me?"

"A letter from Ericsson," Cole replied. "He's actually interested in our project. He writes that he would consider a proposal, provided that he has free rein to develop his Sun Engine." He shrugged. "I must say I'm surprised."

"That's marvellous," Buchanan replied. "We'll have to consider a financial incentive great enough to induce him to travel. And of course he will have full control of building his invention," he continued. "It's not as if any of us would want to interfere."

Cole pulled a face. "I'm very interested in inventions, Alec," he said.

"And I'm interested in making money from them," Buchanan replied. "You can join Ericsson later, by all means, Edward—but please, don't put him off at this stage."

"Very well," Cole said. "But I can't help being excited about the project."

"Speaking of which," said Buchanan, "what news do we have from South Australia?"

"I've had another letter from Jacob Pitman," Cole said, "and a sheaf of architectural drawings and cost estimates. He writes that the Governor is amenable to our plan. The project can be underway as soon as we like."

"And Pitman himself will oversee the design of the smelter?"

"Yes," Cole said. He slid a slip of paper towards Buchanan. "But he won't come cheap."

"No matter," Buchanan replied, glancing at the precise rows of figures on the page. "We stand to make a great deal of money once this factory is

247

in operation, so I don't think our consortium should quibble too much about paying a competent engineer." He smiled at his friend. "Though we will, of course, charge some of his fees back to the government's development funds."

"Of course," Cole said, cheering up as one of Buchanan's assistants entered with a tray, upon which stood a cut-glass jug and two tall glasses: the jug was beaded with moisture, promising something cool inside.

Buchanan nodded his thanks to the assistant. "I'll pour," he said.

Moments later, Cole was sipping gratefully. "We need a plan of action, Alec," he said. "Clearly, the construction should begin at once: Pitman has already drawn up the plans. And McGill has assured us that our American investors are ready to go."

"That much is obvious," Buchanan said. "We start as soon as we can."

"But then," said Cole, "we need to be prepared to recruit experienced workers."

"Does Pitman have a time frame in mind?" Buchanan asked.

"As far as I can make out," Cole said, "he expects the initial stages of the building work to take about nine months. After that, the more complex work can begin."

"I see," Buchanan said. "So if we assume that work actually commences in February, we should be sending our representatives to America to meet with Ericsson, and then on to Great Britain to recruit copper workers, sometime around August. That way, arrangements could be put in place by the end of the year, give or take."

"That would be about right," Cole replied. "Have you thought of who you might send?"

Buchanan paused. "I'm thinking I might send Hector," he said at last. "His mother and McGill will be married next month, so the timing will be right. I feel it will be good for Hector to travel, broaden his horizons and all that."

"Capital idea," Cole responded. "Hector is a very capable young man. And the fact that his stepfather is the American Consul here in Victoria will stand him in good stead in any negotiations."

"Indeed it will." Buchanan smiled.

"But you won't ask him to go alone?"

"No," said Buchanan. "I am hoping to persuade Ferguson to go with him."

"Why Ferguson?"

"He's a bit of a loose cannon after all the unfortunate business with the murder of that Italian chap. I know Ferguson's a free man, now that the carriage driver has been found to corroborate his story, but the killer still hasn't been apprehended. Ferguson feels that he's still under a cloud, and he's right: the police raided one of Woo's brothels for no better reason than that they had followed Ferguson there—Woo wasn't best pleased."

"I can't imagine he would be," Cole replied. "Woo likes to keep his business concerns well away from the law."

Buchanan shrugged. "Ferguson just doesn't want to settle to anything," he continued. "And frankly, there are times when he's a little too hot to handle."

"Then it's time he took a break," Cole said. "And travelling with an experienced American—especially one so very well connected as Ferguson—would certainly smooth the path for Hector."

"The thought had occurred to me," Buchanan said dryly. "And Ferguson has always spent time with Hector—he taught him to ride and shoot—so they should travel well together. At least I hope so."

"When will you broach the subject?"

"Not until after the wedding," Buchanan said. "Once McGill and Morag are settled, Hector will be free from his obligations in that direction."

"And Ferguson?"

"Will agree, I trust."

Cole raised his lemonade. "It's all happening, at long last, Alec," he said. "Here's to our new copper smelter, and to the successful development of the Sun Engine."

"The Engine and the smelter," Buchanan toasted back.

"And let's not forget the City," Cole added. "I've asked Pitman to take a look at the Alice Springs site. It's best to be prepared."

"And has he agreed?"

"Of course he has: he is very interested in the whole project. He was one of the founders of the city of Adelaide, you know. Pitman is an architect as well as an engineer—he'll jump at the chance to build another city."

"In that case," said Buchanan, "the pieces are most definitely falling into place." He raised his glass once more: "Here's to a prosperous future," he said, "for all of us."

"Amen to that," said Cole.

Chapter 55

A few short blocks away, McGill slipped quietly into the Chinese quarter in Little Bourke Street.

Woo was waiting. "Thank you for coming, Consul," he said, ushering his guest into the cool, sandalwood-scented interior of the tea room he had chosen for this meeting.

"My pleasure, Mr Woo," McGill replied.

The two men were shown to a private table tucked away behind an exquisitely carved screen. At a nod from Woo, the waiter withdrew, bowing.

"I assume you want to speak to me about the safety of Chinese investments in America," McGill said, settling comfortably into one of the carved rosewood chairs.

"Among other things, yes," Woo replied. "As Consul, you must be aware that the new American anti-Chinese legislation is causing, shall we say, certain difficulties for my people in San Francisco. They are becoming most anxious."

"I had hoped," said McGill, "that if George Train became President we might have overcome those particular obstacles."

"But sadly, Train is now out of the Presidential race," Woo said.

"Alas, yes," said McGill. "It was most unexpected. I shall of course make every effort on behalf of your community, but I must warn you that the incoming administration is likely to prove intransigent on this matter."

Woo nodded. "My agents have said as much."

The attendant returned. He poured jasmine-scented tea into delicate little porcelain cups for the two men, and retired discreetly.

McGill, always the diplomat, was acutely aware of the need to offer his Chinese host a way to broach what was obviously a delicate subject. He sipped his tea politely, and smiled.

Woo smiled back.

"As American Consul," McGill resumed, "I am most grateful for your help in the matter of Lieutenant Ferguson."

251

Woo waved the compliment aside. "It was nothing," he said. He took another sip of his tea, appearing to savour the scented steam. "But on the subject of American issues," he added, "I might just mention that my business associates are experiencing some difficulties in the transfer of our San Francisco investment funds to the *City of the Sun* project. We are keen to invest: Mr Cole has been most persuasive on this point." He paused. "I like the name, *City of the Sun*. It is most auspicious. It reminds me of the Commercial Bank's phrase for Victoria—*Mountain of Gold*."

"Indeed," McGill said cautiously. "Mr Cole has a clever turn of phrase."

"And I know that you yourself have an interest in seeing this particular development proceed," Woo added, pursuing his advantage. "My associates find the American investment most encouraging."

"I'll do what I can to facilitate investment."

"Thank you." Woo sat back in his chair.

McGill changed tack. "I cannot help but feel that such matters would progress more smoothly if the Colony of Victoria attained its independence," he said.

"My concern about such an eventuality," Woo replied, "is that an independent Victoria might choose a similar anti-Chinese path to that taken by the United States."

"But that would be most unlikely," McGill countered. "An independent Victoria would have everything to gain from promoting the interests of its Chinese *citizens*," he said, emphasizing the last word.

"Is Independence likely, then?" Woo asked softly.

"In my view, yes," McGill replied. He shrugged. "George Train has always said it will come from economic pressures, and I am beginning to think he may be right."

"Perhaps," said Woo. "But I am sure you will appreciate that my business interests are best served by a stable political situation. I must know what—and whom—I am dealing with."

McGill leaned forward. "It will be important for all interested parties to make their intentions clear," he said.

"I fully understand your position," Woo replied. He nodded thoughtfully. "I shall await the outcome with great interest."

Chapter 56

Valentine's Day dawned clear and bright, and Morag awoke to find that Hector had been up early. He knocked softly and entered carrying a breakfast tray: on a white linen cloth, he had set out tea and toast, a dish of butter, strawberry jam, and a single red rose in a bud vase. Beside the rose lay a square, flat parcel, wrapped in tissue paper and tied with red ribbon.

"How lovely," she said, reaching up to kiss her son. "Thank you."

"I thought you should be pampered on your wedding day," Hector said, smiling at her and setting the legs of the tray firmly on the bed. "You've waited a long time for this."

Morag felt a faint echo of apprehension. "You don't mind, really, do you?"

"Of course not, Mother," Hector replied. "This is the best thing for all of us. I want you to be happy."

"I'm sure I shall be," Morag replied. "Will you take your tea with me?"

"I knew you'd say that," Hector said. "I brought two cups."

Morag poured tea, happy to sit quietly with her son in the peaceful morning light, listening to the chorus of magpies outside in Buchanan's garden.

"Does it feel strange, that this is your last morning here?" Hector asked.

Morag looked around. Her belongings were already packed. All that remained in her room were the essentials that she would need for her morning toilette. Her wedding clothes hung behind the door. McGill had arranged to have the last of her things collected while they were at church. All was in readiness.

"A little strange, perhaps," she replied at last. "I've been here a long time— much longer than I ever thought to be. But change isn't always a bad thing, and this will certainly be a change for the better."

Hector smiled at his mother. "The gift is from McGill," he said. "He asked me to give it to you this morning."

"Oh," said Morag. "I wonder what it can be."

"Open it and see," Hector replied.

Morag set down her teacup and untied the ribbon. The tissue fell away to reveal a black leather box, hinged at the back. She opened it slowly, and caught her breath as the contents were revealed. "It's beautiful," she said at last. "He must have planned this all along."

Hector's curiosity got the better of him.

"May I see?" he asked.

Morag turned the open box towards him to reveal, nestled in a bed of black velvet, a gold filigree necklace set with a large square cut emerald and smaller emeralds to either side, and a pair of emerald earrings to match. The stones sparkled with green fire, catching the sunlight that streamed through her window.

"Goodness," Hector said. "That must have cost a fortune."

"It matches my engagement ring," Morag said. "James must have had the stones all set together, and kept these aside for the wedding day." She wiped away a tear. "He told me he had bought the emerald for my ring from a Columbian dealer in New York. I might have guessed he'd buy more than one."

"Try them on," said Hector. "Here, I'll do up the clasp."

Hector set the breakfast tray aside and clasped the necklace about his mother's throat. She rose to stand before the mirror on her dressing table, laughing with delight. "Just the thing to go with my night-dress, don't you think?" she said, turning this way and that in her long linen shift to show off the jewels.

"Perfect," Hector replied, thinking he had never seen his mother so relaxed and happy. "Now come and eat your breakfast: this will be a long day." He sat on the little chair beside the dressing table and took up his tea.

Morag kissed him lightly on the top of the head. "Yes, dear," she said. "And thank you, for everything."

The wedding, a second marriage for both bride and groom, was to be a quiet ceremony, attended only by family and closest friends: Clara, Charlotte, and Lola were there, together with Buchanan, Cole, and Ferguson. Afterwards, there was to be lunch at the Consulate. In deference to McGill's position, the Bishop himself had decided to officiate.

The guests were already inside when Morag, accompanied by Hector and Buchanan, arrived at St Francis' Church on Lonsdale Street promptly at eleven o'clock. A small crowd of bystanders, alerted by the presence of the American Consul's splendid carriage at the curb, paused to watch as Hector handed his mother from Buchanan's stylish equipage. The matched black horses wore feathered plumes today, in honour of the event. There was an audible gasp from the women in the crowd as Morag alighted: she wore a strikingly cut dress and jacket of the palest green silk, with a matching hat—an outfit that perfectly set off her coppery-red hair and pale skin, and highlighted her exquisite emerald jewellery. The perfumed bouquet that she carried, a gift from her erstwhile employer, was a gorgeous mix of white roses, white trumpet lilies with pale gold centres, and fine trailing greenery. Today, Morag was truly beautiful as she entered the church and walked down the aisle on the arm of her handsome son, coming to marry the man for whom she had waited almost half of her life.

McGill, standing ready at the altar, looked around as the music swelled and his bride approached. His whole face lit up as he smiled—a smile that was for her alone.

The smile she returned was radiant.

The ceremony was underway and proceeding happily when a side door opened from an anteroom. Hector glimpsed the unmistakably tall, ungainly black-clad figure of O'Hanlon, about to enter. He stiffened.

Buchanan did not hesitate. He slipped smoothly from the pew where he sat with Edward Cole and, in a few short strides, caught O'Hanlon before he could intrude upon the wedding party.

"Not today, Father," he hissed. He took O'Hanlon firmly by the elbow and steered him back inside, closing the door quickly behind them.

"I have every right," O'Hanlon began.

"I will not have you interfere with these proceedings," Buchanan replied. "Not today."

"I'll do as I please," O'Hanlon grated, making for the door. "This is a church, and I am a priest."

"And you'll stay a priest forever if you cross me," Buchanan said quietly. "Your bishopric isn't guaranteed. Not yet."

"You wouldn't..."

"I assure you I would," Buchanan replied. "I own you, O'Hanlon. And if you want to prosper, you'll do well not to forget it."

O'Hanlon paled.

Buchanan pursued his advantage. "I know what you did," he said, dropping his voice to a tone of quiet menace. "Don't think to cross me."

He turned on his heel and slipped back into the church, leaving O'Hanlon to worry about just which of his crimes might have come to Buchanan's attention.

Buchanan straightened his jacket and re-joined Cole in the front pew, just in time to hear the Bishop pronounce McGill and Morag man and wife.

McGill kissed the bride.

Chapter 57

When the wedding party returned to the Consulate, they were surprised to find the surrounding street full of various cabs and coaches. As McGill handed Morag from their carriage, Wilson himself opened the door.

"Your luncheon guests await, sir," he said.

"But…"

"Lieutenant Ferguson assisted with the guest list, sir," Wilson replied. "It isn't often a Consul marries, and your staff insisted there should be a lavish luncheon in honour of our new Lady." He bowed, very slightly. "I trust it will meet with your approval, sir."

"I see," McGill said, laughing. "In that case, Wilson, I'm honoured. Lead on."

"Thank you, sir."

The wedding party quickly assembled in the entry hall. McGill took Morag's arm, and Lola immediately took up a proprietorial place beside Buchanan. Ferguson gallantly offered his arm to Clara, leaving Hector to accompany Charlotte.

"Don't wait for me," Edward Cole said. "I need to set up my photographic equipment."

"Don't be too long," McGill replied. "You don't want to miss the reception."

"I'll be right there," Cole said, happily fussing over the cases Wilson had placed carefully on a side table for him. "It's the latest equipment, you know," he added cheerfully, to nobody in particular. "Eadweard Muybridge himself recommended it—he's by far the world's leading photographer. I had it shipped across from San Francisco."

"Very good, sir," Wilson said, glancing warily at the complicated apparatus. "I'll make sure it isn't touched."

"Thank you," Cole replied. "In that case, perhaps I shall join the party after all."

The bride and groom entered the reception room to polite applause, followed by the unmistakable sound of the popping of champagne corks. Waiters began to circulate with trays of drinks and canapés, and the reception got underway.

Morag was immediately the centre of attention.

"My dear, those emeralds are perfect!" Lola said admiringly. "I've never seen a set so fine."

"They are a wedding gift from James," Morag replied, self-consciously putting her hand to her throat. "It's not too much, is it?"

"There's no such thing as too much jewellery," Lola replied firmly.

"You look lovely," Clara chimed in. "Just enjoy it." She glanced around. "And see, it is just as I predicted—everyone wants to know you."

"And those jewels have really given them something to gossip about," Lola added. "I'll wager none of them has anything to match them."

Clara was in the right of it: it seemed that half of fashionable Melbourne had been invited to the wedding lunch, and Morag was quickly caught up in a whirl of congratulations and invitations that she had no hope of keeping track of.

"Don't worry, Mother," Hector whispered. "They'll send cards to the Consulate to confirm arrangements. Just mention that the consular secretary keeps your diary."

"Thanks," she said, giving his hand a squeeze. "Whatever would I do without you?"

Hector smiled back. "I'm sure you'd be just fine," he replied. "Here, let me top up your champagne."

McGill found his way to her side. "Cole is ready to take the photographs, if you can spare him a few minutes," he said.

"Of course," Morag said. "It's so very nice of him to do this himself."

"It's his wedding present to us," McGill replied, steering her through the crowd. "He says he enjoys it. He's very good, you know. Did he ever tell you that after he lost his first fortune on the goldfields he recouped a lot of his losses by turning photographer?"

"No," Morag replied. "Did he really?"

"He certainly did. There are family portraits by Cole hanging all over the colony."

"Then I'm delighted he will do ours," Morag said. "We shall hang it over the mantelpiece, like an old married couple."

"Which is what I hope we shall be, in due course," McGill replied. "Shall we go through?"

Cole had set up his equipment in the morning room where the light was good, and had commandeered Wilson to be his assistant. The butler stood stiffly, awaiting further instructions: in his right hand he held the flash powder aloft on its little wooden stand, in his left he held the smouldering touch paper. Morag allowed herself to be seated while Cole arranged the folds of her skirt and directed McGill to stand behind her.

"There," Cole said at last. "You make a very handsome couple. Now, take a deep breath and stay very still." He ducked beneath the black velvet cloth that draped his photographic apparatus. "Ready?"

McGill nodded.

Cole emerged from the cloth, holding the trigger that would release the shutter to coincide with the flash. "Now, Wilson," he said.

Wilson touched the paper to the powder. The flash was blinding.

"Capital," Cole said. "Capital." He moved to change the glass plate and mix more powder.

"I'm seeing stars," McGill said. "What on earth are you using to make that flash?"

"Magnesium powder mixed with potassium chlorate," Cole replied happily. "Nothing to worry about. It makes a nice bright flare, doesn't it?"

"It certainly does," McGill replied, shaking his head.

"Now, I'll just take another, to be sure," Cole said, "then we'll have you both seated."

"And will you take a group photograph?" McGill asked, "as a keepsake for us?"

"Naturally," Cole replied. "Hector is rounding up your wedding party now. I must say, he is a most efficient young man."

Wilson, stoical in the face of his unexpected role in these proceedings, carried in more chairs before he resumed his task as flash assistant. Cole arranged and re-arranged the group to his liking for his photographs. At the last, Morag asked for her photograph to be taken alone with Hector. "My family back in Scotland have never seen my son," she said softly. "I should like to have a photograph to send."

"And so you shall," Cole said happily. "Come along, Hector."

The wedding party had been duly photographed and the guests were returning to the reception room, where luncheon was about to be served. Buchanan had already escorted Lola and Clara from the room when McGill said something in Cole's ear.

Cole gave him a sharp look, but nodded assent. "I'm just packing up," he said aloud. "But I find I have one unused plate. It seems a pity not to use it."

He turned to Charlotte: "Would you sit for me, Miss Charlotte?"

Charlotte beamed. "Of course, Mr Cole," she replied, slipping into the chair that he held for her.

Cole nodded his approval. Today, Charlotte had made an effort with her appearance and had dressed for the occasion in a pale pink silk ensemble trimmed with a darker shade in velvet ribbon—a combination that showed her blonde hair and blue eyes to advantage.

"You too, Ferguson," Cole said. "It will make a nice composition."

Ferguson shrugged. "If you wish," he said, moving to stand behind Charlotte until Cole was done.

McGill nodded his thanks, and turned to escort his bride to lunch, leaving Hector to bring up the rear with Charlotte, Cole and Ferguson.

Chapter 58

The Consulate's chef had surpassed himself today: the buffet luncheon was a resounding success.

"It'll be the talk of all Melbourne," Clara predicted happily. "I'm sure my subscribers will enjoy reading about it." She winked at Lola. "The ones who aren't here in person, that is," she added.

As Buchanan gave the toast to the bride and groom, Wilson wheeled in the sweets trolley, atop which stood a magnificent three-tiered wedding cake, iced in white, edged with gold ribbons around the tiers, and decorated lavishly with gold leaf. Wilson bowed as he handed a long, silver knife, tied with gold ribbon about the handle, to McGill.

"Your very good health, sir, madam," he said.

Morag held tightly to McGill's hand as they cut the cake together, to cheers from their guests.

Wilson deftly began to slice. "Coffee and cake will be served in the drawing room," he announced.

At this signal, the luncheon guests began the process of leaving the tables, and conversation ebbed and flowed again.

Cole found McGill. "What was that about?" he asked.

"What?"

"The last photograph," Cole replied.

"Just a whim, Edward," McGill replied.

Cole thought for a moment. "You're not usually a man for whims," he said. "But I won't press you, at least not on your wedding day."

McGill smiled at his friend. "Thanks," he said.

The reception drew to its close, and McGill and Morag had finally said goodbye to their luncheon guests, leaving the wedding party to themselves.

They gathered in one of the smaller reception rooms, where a long table had been heaped with wedding gifts. Wilson brought the tea tray.

"At last," Clara said, collapsing into a chair and slipping off her shoes. "I'm dying for a cup of tea."

Wilson poured silently and handed her a brimming cup.

Clara nodded her thanks, sipping gratefully.

"I must say, Mrs McGill, your renovations are marvellous," Cole ventured. "I didn't have the chance to congratulate you earlier."

"Thank you," Morag replied, smiling at his use of her new title. "I'm pleased you like them."

"We won't stay much longer, Mother," Hector said, "but I must say I'm intrigued to know what's in all of those wedding presents."

"Shall we open them, then?" McGill asked.

Morag smiled and nodded. "I'm astonished there are so many," she said.

"Clearly, the fashionable set means to wish you well," Clara said. "It bodes well for your tenure here."

"Indeed it does," Ferguson said.

Morag was delighted as she carefully removed the wrappings of a fine assortment of crystal and delicate china and embroidered linen from well-wishers. She held up a finely cut crystal bowl. "This is lovely," she said. "It's from Mr Valentine at the Commercial Bank. How thoughtful."

"I have financial dealings with him," McGill said. "I imagine a lot of the gifts are from business associates." He checked the card attached to another beautifully wrapped box. "See," he said, "this one is from George Train."

Hector had taken out his notebook. "I'll just keep a list," he said, "for the *thank you* cards."

"Good idea," Buchanan said.

"I told you that young man was a model of efficiency," Cole added. "He'll go far."

Hector said nothing, but Clara took up the thread of conversation. "And I must just make a note of all this for my readers," she said. "They'll be fascinated."

"Mother!" Charlotte admonished.

"What?"

"You're incorrigible."

"I don't mind, Charlotte, not really," Morag said. "This is the public face of the marriage, after all. All these gifts are as much for the Consulate as they are for me."

"Astutely put," Cole said approvingly. "But my intuition is that this one may be meant to be more personal." He handed a heavy parcel wrapped in bright red paper to McGill. "We don't have to guess who this is from, do we?" he said.

McGill laughed. "Indeed not," he said, taking out his knife to cut the string. "Nobody but Woo would send this colour."

"Oh my," Morag breathed as the paper fell away to reveal a Chinese lacquered box—red, the most auspicious colour for marriages. McGill opened it, to reveal a pair of exquisitely wrought cloisonné vases, their blue and green enamel-work outlined in delicate gold wire. Beneath them sat their dragon-carved rosewood stands.

"They are beautiful," McGill said.

"Very fine," Buchanan commented. "And now, if I may, I have a gift of my own for you," he said, smiling.

Taking his cue, Hector lifted a large, flat package tied with gold ribbon from where it stood against the wall. "Careful, Mother," he said. "This is heavy."

McGill helped Morag to untie the wrappings that protected a watercolour painting which shone with shimmering shades of gold, set in a heavy gilt frame.

"It's gorgeous," Lola breathed.

"Oh, thank you," said Morag. "It's exquisite: a whole city bathed in sunlight—how wonderful. And I have just the place for it."

Buchanan beamed. "Cole found it for me," he said. "It's called *The Golden City*. I thought it would appeal to you: I'm so glad you like it. It made me think of our plans for a City of the Sun."

"I think it's splendid," McGill replied. "I've never seen golden light like that."

"The painting is of Rome, seen from the Janiculum," Cole said. "The artist is Samuel Palmer. I saw it in the catalogue of this year's exhibition by the Royal Society of Painters in Watercolours."

"That sounds impressive," said Ferguson.

"What's the verse?" Clara asked, noticing the poetry inset at the bottom of the frame.

"It's from *Childe Harold*," McGill replied. "How appropriate: Cole knows my fondness for Byron."

"Indeed I do," Cole replied. "It's one of the reasons I pursued the purchase."

"I can't thank you enough," Morag said.

"My pleasure," Buchanan replied. He stood. "But now, I think, we should all be on our way. I shall be happy to accompany the ladies to their homes."

Hector rose and kissed his mother on the cheek. "I'll go back with Sir Alec," he said.

"Quite right," Ferguson said. "I'll make myself scarce." He turned to Cole. "Perhaps you'd like my company this afternoon, Edward?"

Cole took the hint. "Delighted," he said. "I could certainly use some help with my photographic equipment."

There was one more flurry of goodbyes. Morag was kissed and hugged by the women. Cole and Ferguson set out, and Buchanan's carriage finally rolled away down the drive bearing the rest of the wedding party to their homes, leaving McGill, at last, to lead his bride upstairs.

As the bedroom door closed behind them, McGill took Morag in his arms. He was about to speak, but she put her finger to his lips.

"No more talk, she said.

McGill smiled, pulling her more tightly into his embrace, putting his lips to hers in a passionate kiss, a kiss that wiped away the long years of waiting.

Morag sighed happily as she pulled away at last. "Perhaps, James, you could help me out of this dress?"

He nuzzled her neck, inhaling her perfume of lilies and roses. "It will be my very great pleasure, Mrs McGill," he said.

Chapter 59

Buchanan always enjoyed Chinatown, and the day after the wedding he was pleased to be taking lunch with Chang Woo Gow. The pair were seated at an elegant rosewood table by a window in one of Woo's restaurants in Little Bourke Street, and Buchanan watched with genuine delight the bustle of drays, deliverymen, street vendors and women haggling over vegetables. The narrow lane, with its overhanging buildings and pervasive smells of spices and charcoal smoke took him back, in memory, to his days in Hong Kong. He sipped contentedly from his tiny cup of jasmine tea.

"I've ordered for us," Woo said. "My chef is cooking a special Peking duck."

"Excellent," Buchanan replied. "Your chef never fails to delight."

Woo smiled at the compliment, but said nothing until the waiter had laid before them a brass pot of steamed rice and a wide dish of mushrooms with mustard greens. He served each of them a portion in a small porcelain bowl, and bowed as he left them to begin their lunch.

Buchanan picked up his ivory chopsticks. "I assume this isn't just a social occasion?"

"Not entirely," Woo replied. He leaned forward. "Some information has come my way. It may or may not be of use to you, but I consider it worth repeating."

"Do go on," said Buchanan, expertly selecting a slippery mushroom and popping it into his mouth. "These are very good," he added.

"It concerns the murder that so embroiled our friend Ferguson," Woo said.

"Ah," said Buchanan, shifting his attention into sharper focus. "It was good of you to locate that carriage driver. Poor Ferguson would still be under suspicion if not for you."

Woo waved a hand dismissively. "It was my pleasure to help," he said. "But the thing is, Buchanan, that since it has become known that I have an interest in the case, my men have been offered all sorts of details—some of them genuine."

"I see," Buchanan said carefully. "Information is a valuable commodity in any business."

"Indeed it is," Woo replied. "I make it my business to collect as much information as possible. It is often the best insurance against unforeseen circumstances—one never really knows what will prove useful."

Buchanan merely nodded, wondering where this was leading.

"In any case," Woo said, "I have been able to verify that the victim, Orsini, had only lately arrived from Rome. He was acting as an agent for the Banco di Santo Spirito, the Papal bank, in enterprises that would not, I fear, withstand too much public scrutiny."

"But Antonelli...."

"Is controller of the Vatican finances, and is also O'Hanlon's patron, yes," Woo said quietly. "And my sources tell me that Antonelli's corruption is breath-taking."

"I don't see..." Buchanan began.

"Neither do I," said Woo. "Not yet, at least. But I also heard a whisper that the very righteous Mr Valentine—the banker who never stoops to gamble—is on the take from Antonelli. Valentine's mixed up in this somehow."

"With O'Hanlon?"

"It appears so. I noticed that Valentine was careful to keep his distance from the priest at your dinner party: he was clearly surprised when O'Hanlon joined us, and he avoided confirming O'Hanlon's recognition of Orsini when Ferguson first mentioned the name."

"That's interesting," said Buchanan.

"Do you think O'Hanlon knew Orsini?" Woo asked.

"It's certainly possible," Buchanan replied. He hesitated.

Woo nodded encouragingly, waiting patiently.

"O'Hanlon was meeting someone after our dinner at The Melbourne Club," Buchanan went on. "He was very cagey about it. He refused a cab, so he was on foot, which means his destination was fairly close to the Club."

"Somewhere like Spring Street, perhaps?" Woo said. "There are plenty of hotels and bars along there—plenty of places for a private meeting."

"Perhaps," Buchanan conceded. "But that doesn't prove anything."

"Of course not," Woo said. "But it doesn't look good. I don't believe in coincidences. Do you?"

"No," Buchanan said shortly. "I don't."

"In any case," said Woo, "whether O'Hanlon was involved in business dealings with Orsini or not, the priest's name keeps cropping up in connection with the murder. And O'Hanlon's avowed involvement with Antonelli and the 'black nobility' in Rome makes him more dangerous than we had thought. He's a treacherous man, Buchanan."

"I know," Buchanan said.

Woo leaned even farther forward, speaking so that nobody could overhear. "Shall I have O'Hanlon—ah—*removed?*" he asked softly. "A permanent solution might be best."

Buchanan considered his alternatives. "It's a tempting thought," he confessed. "We can't trust him an inch."

"Then let my people take care of it."

"Not just yet, I think," Buchanan said at last. "Much as I despise the man, I still have use for him."

"As you wish," Woo said, settling back in his chair. "The option always remains open if you change your mind."

"I appreciate that," Buchanan replied. "And I might just whisper a word in Ferguson's ear. Forewarned is forearmed, as they say."

"Indeed," Woo said, nodding judiciously.

The waiter reappeared, this time bearing a silver-domed serving dish. As he lifted the lid, the delicious aroma of spiced poultry filled the air.

"Ah," said Woo. "The Peking duck: let us forget business for a while, my friend, and talk of other things while we do justice to the culinary arts."

Buchanan smiled in anticipation. "You're joining us for the opening of Lola's Supper Club, of course?"

"I wouldn't miss it for the world," Woo replied.

Chapter 60

The Bohemian Supper Club held its gala opening on 15th March. The renovations had taken longer than expected, but Lola was at last satisfied with the result and had organised a glittering occasion. New and potential members had received gold-embossed invitations to enjoy a late supper and "a little taste of paradise". Lola had been careful to let it be known well in advance that only a very select few would be invited, so curiosity coupled with exclusivity ensured that the rich and influential men of Melbourne had been vying for her attention. The press, of course, had been excluded, which was encouragement enough. Lola agreed, after much prevaricating, that journalists could interview her and inspect the venue before the festivities began, on the strict and very public understanding that they would be gone before the guests arrived—and the private understanding that a champagne supper would be provided for them, free of charge, in a back room.

Edward Cole arrived early, to find Buchanan casting a proprietary eye over the Club before the festivities began, leaving Lola to deal, adroitly, with the press. As with so many of the business interests he controlled, Buchanan preferred to remain in the background. Lola, on the other hand, adored the limelight: in that respect, the partnership was a good one.

Cole, in proper black evening dress but sporting a splendid gold brocade waistcoat for the occasion, was brimming with enthusiasm as he noted the appointments. Two huge Chinese urns flanked the formal entry hall, and a long oriental runner in reds and blues led to the concierge's desk and the cloakroom. But beyond these necessary formalities, intricately carved double doors opened into a large room decorated to resemble an Arabian scene from *The Thousand and One Nights*: Persian carpets woven in silks of vibrant reds and blues and golds shone in the light from hundreds of candles set in sconces on the red-painted walls that were hung with matching silken tapestries. The room was furnished with low couches and tables. Carved Chinese screens created private nooks to encompass low divans scattered with bright silk cushions, and intimate sitting areas were arranged near windows curtained and tasselled in red and gold. At the end of the room, a small curved stage promised entertainment. And to create the feeling of a tent fit for a potentate, Lola had had the ceiling draped in endless yards of white muslin, pinned at the cornices, draped and then gathered to a circle held in place by an enormous chandelier. The air was heavy with the perfume of rose and musk. The tables were set with silver bowls containing exotic salted pistachios, and crystal glassware that sparkled as it caught the candlelight.

Cole breathed in deeply. "It's like Aladdin's cave," he said enthusiastically. "It's gorgeous. I feel that there should be a genie."

"All in good time, my friend," said Buchanan, unusually expansive in this atmosphere. "Come and see the rest."

Cole allowed himself to be led through an arched opening and into a long room that contained a dance floor, polished and slippery and ready for use. The members of a string quartet were tuning their instruments on the dais provided for them, and Cole noted with satisfaction that Lola had thought to provide drinks for them on a side table. Nobody would be neglected tonight, it seemed. A further arch led to a supper room, hung with long silk tapestries depicting hunting scenes. Small tables were already set with white linen, fine china and gleaming silver, and each held a single candle in its own carved brass stand. The waiters were already setting out domed silver serving dishes under the watchful eye of a black-suited butler.

"We have a surprise in store for you tonight," Buchanan said.

"As if this isn't a surprise," Cole laughed. "Melbourne has never seen anything like this. I doubt anywhere has."

"True," Buchanan said. "I let Lola have free rein: she said it would be like a living stage set, and she was right."

"It must have cost an absolute fortune," Cole said, running his hand appreciatively across one of the silk hangings.

Buchanan sighed. "Well, yes," he said, "but I have imported most of the fittings Lola required through my Chinese associates. Woo has been most helpful in procuring the carved pieces—they are all rosewood, you know."

"I can see that," Cole replied. "What's the surprise?"

"Between ourselves, Lola has employed several dancers from her company to act as hostesses tonight," Buchanan said, "and they will perform for us, later."

"Capital," said Cole, following Buchanan back towards the main reception room. He noticed the thick, red-tasselled silk cord that stretched across the bottom of the staircase, denying entry. "What's upstairs?" he asked.

"Ah," said Buchanan. "In the end, I decided that, like most Clubs, I should provide rooms for those members who require them, from time to time."

270

"I see," Cole said slowly.

"I'm sure you do," Buchanan replied. "And I'm sure you understand that this arrangement is strictly private."

"I won't breathe a word," Cole said, winking theatrically. "Can I see them?"

"Certainly," Buchanan agreed, lifting the heavy cord for his friend. "This way."

The bedrooms were opulently fitted with red and gold brocades and silks, fine Persian carpets covered the floors, washstands stood ready with fine china and linen towels.

"Marvellous!" Cole exclaimed as he walked from room to room, seeing variations on the theme. He paused idly to look at one of the framed Japanese woodblock prints that adorned the walls. He stopped, and then looked again, hard. "Where on earth…" he began.

"My Chinese importers acquired the set for me," Buchanan said. "Good, aren't they?"

"Very fine, very—shall I say—explicit," Cole replied, now touring the prints from room to room to observe more closely the range of sexual positions they depicted, some more athletic than others. "I've seen prints such as these in specialist books," he said, "but never mounted for display. I have clients who would pay a great deal for these: the tinting and the brushwork are impeccable."

"I doubt it's the brushwork that most club members will be interested in," Buchanan chuckled.

"Probably not," Cole said ruefully. "Still, if you should ever come across another set…"

"I'll give you the name of the importer," Buchanan said.

"Most appreciated," Cole replied. "And I shall immediately forget that I have seen these."

"Most appreciated," Buchanan echoed.

"But Alec," Cole said, "now that these rooms are reserved for Club members, what has become of Lola's accommodations? Wasn't she to have the upstairs for her apartments?"

Buchanan shrugged. "Well, yes," he said, "that was the initial arrangement. But in the event, I have purchased the rather fine house next door, and it has been furnished to her taste."

Cole laughed. "She won, after all. You said she wanted a house."

"It'll be useful if I need to expand the Club," Buchanan replied. "It just so happened that it came on the market at the time the Club was being decorated."

"And I'll lay you odds the owners were heavily encouraged to sell by Madame Montez," Cole said.

"Undoubtedly," said Buchanan. "But despite her wiles, Lola will be a good manager for me. This will be a profitable venture, Edward, mark my words. I'm happy to indulge her, and it doesn't hurt to let her win once in a while."

"You're a cold man, Alec," Cole observed.

"I'm a businessman, like yourself," Buchanan replied. "Shall we go in and try the champagne?"

"Excellent idea," Cole replied.

Chapter 61

A buzz of voices greeted them as they reached the bottom of the staircase, and Cole realised that guests had been arriving steadily while he toured the bedrooms. The reception area was now busy with a throng of gentlemen in evening dress, all wandering about to admire the appointments. He easily identified Mr Woo, towering above the rest, chatting animatedly with the Chinese founders of the Commercial Bank, and Valentine, their manager, who seemed nervous in the crush of people. Consul McGill was there, deep in conversation with the new French Consul. Judges, lawyers, members of parliament, and any number of Buchanan's business associates had all attended the opening, rubbing shoulders with stage celebrities, writers and artists. The guest list was extensive: Lola had excelled herself tonight.

"It seems everyone who's anyone is here," Cole said, happily scanning the crowd. "The only one I can't see is the Mayor."

"You won't see him here," Buchanan replied. "He tried everything he could to block the Club. And now that it's here to stay, Lola won't allow him to set foot in the place."

"Quite right," Cole replied. "It's his loss."

"My thought exactly," said Buchanan. "But I'm afraid I must leave you to your own devices for a moment. I'll be right back, Edward," he added. "I just have one or two things to attend to. One of the girls will bring you a drink." He beckoned to an attendant.

Cole caught his breath. A beautiful young woman was bearing down upon him, carrying a silver drinks tray. She was dressed as an odalisque, in diaphanous silk trousers cuffed at the ankles, a short, fitted brocade top that left her midriff bare, and a transparent red silk veil that hid nothing of her dark-eyed beauty. Beneath the veil, her black hair was piled high on her head. She wore silver earrings, and silver bells at wrists and ankles, bells that tinkled as she moved gracefully in her golden ballet slippers.

"Champagne, sir?" she asked, offering him a crystal glass filled to the brim with bubbles.

Cole nodded. "You're American?" he asked, recognising her accent. "One of Madame Montez's dancers, I would guess?" He reached out and took the proffered glass, sipping gratefully.

She smiled at him. "That's right sir," she said. "We are all playing our parts, for this evening. Madame Montez has worked so hard for this—we all want it to be a success for her."

"It could hardly be otherwise," Cole observed, "if the dancers are all as spectacular as you."

"You're very kind, sir," she answered, still smiling as she moved away to the next patron.

The room was filling fast with dignitaries. Cole found himself almost shouting to be heard above the happy din, when Ferguson tapped him on the shoulder.

"Good show, don't you think?" said Ferguson, grinning boyishly as he snared another glass of champagne from a passing odalisque.

"Capital," Cole replied, wondering how Ferguson always managed to look so relaxed, so slightly tousled, in any company. "Shall we try the food?"

"Trust you to have found the supper room already," Ferguson replied. "Lead on."

Cole threaded his way through the crowd, holding his champagne out of harm's way, until he reached the archway that led to the supper room. He had only begun to contemplate the tempting arrays of seafood—lobster, prawns and oysters heaped on silver platters—when a huge cheer followed by spontaneous applause burst from the room he had just left.

"I'll come back for this," Ferguson shouted, making a beeline for the archway.

Cole followed, curiosity for the moment outweighing culinary temptation. He could hear Eastern music playing, and he joined the clapping crowd in time to see a tall, dark-skinned male dancer ascend the corner stage. One of the odalisques was there already, carrying a smoking copper lamp, which she mimed polishing. The man wore only baggy trousers tied at the waist with a red sash—his bare, muscled torso had been oiled so that his body shone in the candlelight. Incense poured from the lamp's long spout as the girl danced, adding notes of sandalwood and myrrh to the rose-scented room, drawing the big man closer to her. He began to turn, flexing his oiled muscles, gracefully spinning as he danced the story of the genie of the lamp.

"Be careful what you wish for," Ferguson whispered in Cole's ear.

Cole could only nod, entranced by the performance. He watched as other costumed dancers, playing various roles, brought gold and jewels, precious unguents in golden pots, ropes of pearls. The tale of Aladdin's tribulations and triumph was played out in mime and dance, and the crowd broke into thunderous applause as the dancers took a final bow—the tall genie centre stage, surrounded by smiling odalisques.

"Bravo!" Cole shouted. "Bravo!"

Buchanan somehow appeared beside him. "You wished for a genie, Edward," he said. "I trust that was satisfactory?"

"An exquisite piece of theatre, Alec," Cole responded, still applauding enthusiastically. "I must congratulate Lola."

The opening was a triumph. The journalists waxed lyrical in the morning papers: by the end of the next day The Bohemian Supper Club had become known—to the cognoscenti—as *Lola's*. The Club's membership books were already closed, and a waiting list had been established. Its future was assured. The Mayor, uninvited, was furious.

Chapter 62

"I think we can count the Club's opening a success," Buchanan said, settling into an armchair in Cole's opulently furnished office.

"Certainly," Cole replied. "The whole thing was splendid, and the newspaper reports have been nothing less than ecstatic all week."

"All Lola's doing," Buchanan said. "She fed the journalists an excellent champagne supper, and pretended not to notice when they sneaked back inside to take a look at the entertainment. I expect they're all panting to be asked back."

"I'm sure they are," Cole said, laughing.

"So we can concentrate on the bigger picture," Buchanan said. "What news from Pitman?"

"He writes that the building work proceeds at a good pace," Cole said. "And tells me that a number of manufacturers have already asked to be included when our refined copper comes on line."

"They must be as worried about supplies as we are," Buchanan remarked.

"Yes," said Cole, "but we're ahead of the game. Things are so bad in Britain that we'll be able to name our price as soon as we can begin operations."

"Have you heard from Ericsson?"

"Yes—he writes that he will be happy to oblige us by talking with our representatives. Have you discussed the travel arrangements?"

"Hector and Ferguson have both agreed to our plan," Buchanan said. "They'll leave for San Francisco in August. I've had a word with McGill. He's arranged for them to go straight to meet George Train there, before they take the railroad across to New York. It's all falling into place."

"And I have a further piece of interesting information to add," Cole said. "Pitman has a brother, Isaac, in Bath: he's famous for having invented a very useful shorthand system, among other things. But the point is, he's well connected and has agreed to help out our representatives with business contacts. He's also suggested that he is prepared to help with the recruiting, which would speed things up there."

"Excellent news," said Buchanan.

"And Bath is the home of master craftsmen," Cole said. "I acquired the clockwork automata for my Book Emporium from a Mr Ellett, who manufactures them there, in his shop in Princes Street."

"They are pretty toys, I'll admit," Buchanan said, "but I don't quite see how they would be of use."

"Not the toys," Cole said, "but their maker." He smiled. "It's true that my customers always enjoy the artifice of the mechanical creatures in my window," he said. "They draw a crowd. But it's the nature of their manufacture that I think we shall find useful. If we are to build Ericsson's Sun Engine, not to mention whatever new machines will become necessary for our City, I imagine we shall need to create whole new operating mechanisms. And who better to do that than a skilled toymaker?"

"I see," Buchanan said. "That's well thought of, Edward. Do you plan to invite the toymaker to join us?"

"That is my intention, yes," Cole replied. "Or one of his guild if he is not amenable himself. What do you think?"

"I think it's a first-rate idea," Buchanan responded. "Shall I leave you to write to Mr Pitman?"

"It will be my pleasure," Cole responded cheerfully.

Chapter 63

"That miserable priest!" Clara stormed into the sitting room, waving a newspaper. "He's done it again!"

"Who exactly has done what, Mother?" Charlotte asked, looking up with mild interest from the book she was reading. She was used to her mother's outbursts.

"O'Hanlon, that's who. And he's attacked Lola in *The Argus*, that's what."

"Why would he do that?"

"I think he hates women—successful women, at any rate. He's taken another swipe at my journal as well."

"If he's so awful, why does the paper keep interviewing him?"

"Papers like to stir up public sentiment," Clara replied. "And the Church has contacts at *The Argus*. There's always some little event they want to publicise, and it fills in the social pages for the paper. So O'Hanlon gets himself interviewed about other things, and then sticks a knife into us whenever the opportunity arises."

"And what is it this time?"

"He is being touted as the most likely candidate to become the first Bishop of Ballarat," Clara replied. "God help the poor women of his parish if that happens. He'll be a tyrant, you mark my words."

"So how did he bring Lola into it?"

"He's prattling on again about public decency," Clara said. "And since The Bohemian Supper Club has been the talk of the town for the past few weeks, he uses it as an example of the moral decay of the City of Melbourne."

"Well," said Charlotte, "the Club is hardly public: it's the most private supper club there is."

"That's probably it," Clara said savagely. "They'd never let him in."

Charlotte giggled.

"Anyway," Clara went on, "O'Hanlon's done the usual thing: he declares Lola's past makes her an unfit person to run a respectable business. Then he goes on to suggest that her Club is a modern version of Sodom and Gomorrah and that anyone who belongs to it is mired in sin—you know the sort of thing." She sighed. "Then he says that no woman should be allowed to run any business venture, and that my *New Day* is subversive and should be closed down forthwith."

"He sounds crazy," Charlotte said.

"Not really—that kind of malicious vitriol always finds an audience," Clara replied. She sighed heavily. "But two can play at that game," she said. "I have a little surprise in store for Father O'Hanlon."

"You're writing an article?" Charlotte asked. "Wouldn't it be better to just let it all blow over? It did last time. You'll look as bad as he does if you attack him back."

"I'm still checking facts," Clara replied. "But what I have in mind is more of a feature article—on the Roman Inquisition. And on how it has mistreated innocent children: the sort of thing that would horrify any mother."

"And you think O'Hanlon was involved?"

"I know he was," Clara replied. "I know it in my bones. I've been reading all the back issues of the papers, looking for clues. There was a shocking scandal not so long ago, and O'Hanlon's name is mentioned—just once, but once is enough—and the dates fit. He was in Rome, then—he says so himself in his interview."

"Be careful, Mother," Charlotte said. "The Church is a dangerous enemy."

"Yes, but what else can I do?" Clara replied. "My readers have a right to know if the Church is about to appoint a man with a murky past as their new Bishop."

"But your readers have no say in the appointment, do they?" said Charlotte.

"True," Clara replied. "They don't. But they can agitate for a better result with their own priests. And the women of Ballarat can at least be forewarned."

The April edition of *The New Day* carried a small but provocative article. Under the heading "Items of Religious News", Clara wrote:

Inquisitor in Melbourne?

It has come to the attention of this editor that a priest who now lives among us, a certain Father O'Hanlon, has been named as one of the perpetrators of a crime that should outrage any mother— indeed, any woman—the unlawful abduction of a child from its rightful parents.

    The scandal occurred in Rome at a time when Father O'Hanlon, by his own admission in The Argus, *was in residence at the Vatican and working for one Cardinal Antonelli, whom he now owns to be his patron. The appalling action in question involved a little Jewish boy, who, having been secretly baptised a Catholic by his nurse, was stolen away from his parents by agents of the Roman Inquisition—including Father O'Hanlon. The poor child was then placed in a Catholic orphanage, and found himself at the centre of lengthy controversial negotiations: in the end, the Pope himself ruled that the boy would not be returned to his parents—and that the child should be considered dead to them.*

Father O'Hanlon, a child stealer, is now being touted as the most likely candidate to be appointed as the first Bishop of Ballarat. I ask you, Ladies, is he fit to take up such an important post?

Chapter 64

Father O'Hanlon bustled into the vestry of St Francis' Church, intent on the business of the day. The door swung closed behind him, too quietly. The priest hesitated: a split-second later he felt cold steel pressed against the back of his neck, heard a sharp click as the hammer of a pistol was cocked. He eased his stiletto from his sleeve to his hand.

In answer, his assailant delivered a vicious, well-timed kick to the elbow. Bone grated on bone.

O'Hanlon yelped, and dropped the knife.

"Don't even think of taking *me* on," an American voice said softly. "I'm much better trained than you, not to mention younger and fitter. A knife in the back is more your style, or maybe a quick thrust between the ribs when your victim mistakes you for a true man of the cloth."

"Ferguson!" O'Hanlon said. "You can put down that gun. You know you won't use it. Not here."

"Probably not," Ferguson replied. "Just wanted to be sure I have your undivided attention."

"You have it," O'Hanlon muttered. "What do you want?"

"Right now," said Ferguson, "I want more than anything to kill you. Perhaps you'd oblige me by going for your knife?"

O'Hanlon did not move.

"Didn't think so," said Ferguson. He kicked the stiletto and sent it spinning across the polished floorboards and under a chest of drawers that stood against the wall.

"What do you want?" O'Hanlon asked again.

"We need to talk," said Ferguson. He holstered his pistol, grabbed O'Hanlon by his bony shoulders and dumped him unceremoniously on the couch. "Sit!"

O'Hanlon breathed a little more easily now that the immediate threat had

ANEEN WEBB AND ANDREW ENSTICE

eased. He reached with his left hand to massage his right elbow. "That hurts," he added.

"Be grateful I didn't break it."

"So what do you want to talk to me about?"

"About your future," Ferguson said. "About the wages of sin—yours, that is." He paused. "The word on the street is that you killed Orsini," he said quietly. "And set me up to take the blame. I must admit you're quick: my little accident in the carriage was certainly convenient for you."

"You can't prove anything," said O'Hanlon. "I'm a priest. I'm above suspicion. And I answer only to Rome."

"You're a murdering son-of-a-bitch," Ferguson said.

"If you had proof, I'd be in jail by now," O'Hanlon replied equably.

Ferguson laughed. "What makes you think I'd run to the law? As you say, they'd only send you back to Rome."

O'Hanlon almost smirked. "I heard," he said, "that Woo's Chinese thugs located the carriage driver for you."

"That's not all they located," Ferguson replied, ignoring O'Hanlon's tone.

"So what do you want?" O'Hanlon said. "Money? I can arrange any amount through my banking contacts."

Ferguson shrugged. "Orsini's family has posted a huge reward," he said. "You're worth much more dead than alive. If it were money that I wanted, you'd be dead by now. And I'd be an even wealthier man."

O'Hanlon paled. "What, then?"

"I want you to exercise a little social decorum," said Ferguson. "Lay off Mrs Seekamp and Madame Montez: if I see any more public attacks on them from you, I swear I'll tip the wink to the Orsini family. Antonelli can't protect you from them: he'll look the other way—you know he will. In any case, it's simply a matter of time before the so-called 'black nobility' catches up with you. You're only alive now because Buchanan is protecting you. I can't imagine why, but that's his business."

O'Hanlon did not reply. His urge to smile had vanished. He just sat there, stony faced, trying frantically to calculate the odds, trying to work out just how much Ferguson—and Woo—had found out.

"You didn't know," Ferguson said, suddenly realising the true position. "Did you really think you could play a double game with the Vatican banks and the Chinese business clans? Did you really think they wouldn't work it out?" He grinned. "It seems, *Father*, that you're in much deeper than I thought. That's cheered me up enormously!"

Still, O'Hanlon said nothing.

"Right," said Ferguson. "I'll be off then. I just wanted to be sure that the rumours are true. I just wanted to ask you about the murder: man to man, face

284

to face. You deny nothing—and that's good enough for me. Remember what I said: leave the women alone, or face the consequences."

O'Hanlon stood, recovering his equanimity. "If you're done threatening me," he said, "I'll see you out."

"Don't bother," Ferguson replied. "I know the way." He turned, then added: "and O'Hanlon—don't forget, I'll be watching you. And I won't be the only one."

Chapter 65

"**W**ell," said Cole: "it's official—it's been announced that O'Hanlon is to be Bishop of Ballarat. I hope you know what you're doing, Alec."

"He'll be safer in a position like that," Buchanan replied. "He'll have more to lose."

"Still, that article Clara published last month stirred things up a bit," Cole remarked. "I did wonder if his candidacy would survive a revelation like that."

"Clara misunderstands the machinations of power," Buchanan said. "In the end, she only made his superiors in Rome more determined to protect him. The final decision was made in the Vatican, not in Melbourne: his superiors here merely proposed his election. Clara should have known that Cardinal Antonelli would promote him to keep him quiet. Why else would he have sent him out here under his patronage? I'm sure that O'Hanlon knows more than he should, and he certainly wouldn't be above using that knowledge to his advantage. The man is totally unscrupulous."

"And you helped to make him a *Bishop?*"

"As I said, Edward, he'll be more governable in this role. He knows I can break him, should I choose to do so. He'll behave himself."

"Then for heaven's sake, watch your back, Alec," Cole said earnestly.

"Believe me, I intend to do just that, Edward," Buchanan said quietly. "But we have bigger things to worry us just now."

"What's happened?" Cole asked, clearly alarmed.

"The Vienna stock market has crashed," Buchanan said quietly. "The European newspapers are blaming it on what they call 'The American Commercial Invasion'."

"We know that America has been undercutting European production costs for some time," Cole said. "Grain from the mid-west has been flooding the market, and Britain has abandoned her traditional European suppliers for cheaper American wheat."

"Indeed," said Buchanan. "The Americans have been exporting everything from kerosene and manufactured food to beef and flour for less than it costs the Europeans to produce the goods. Something had to give. Continental banks are tumbling—the inter-bank lending rates have gone through the roof. It seems to me that commercial panic has already set in."

"Bad news for O'Hanlon and Cardinal Antonelli, then," said Cole. "The Banco di Santo Spirito must be in trouble."

"Luckily, we have absolutely minimal exposure there," Buchanan replied. "I never trusted O'Hanlon. But the whole thing bodes ill for European businesses."

"Do you want to bring forward Hector's departure for America?" Cole asked.

"I think not," Buchanan replied. "I did consider it, but our plans are very well advanced at this stage. We don't want to be seen to be too anxious about events in Europe. And McGill agrees with me that America seems stable enough. On balance, it will be best if Ferguson and Hector travel in early August, as planned. It's May now—a few more weeks won't make much difference to our long-term plans."

Cole sighed. "I'm sure you're right, Alec," he said. "But I must admit I find the whole thing very worrying."

"True," Buchanan replied. "But remember, as things stand, business losses in Europe may very easily become gains for us." He paused. "Fortune favours the brave, Edward," he said. "We have only to hold our nerve."

Chapter 66

McGill was having a quiet, pre-dinner drink in his study with Ferguson, with just a week to go before Ferguson was due to depart for America on August 11th.

"I must say I'm relieved you'll be travelling with Hector," McGill said. "San Francisco can be a dangerous place."

Ferguson grinned. "I'll wager that Hector can take care of himself," he replied. "I've taught him well. But I must admit I'm glad of the diversion. I find I'm weary of Melbourne, tired of all the finger-pointing. I'll never be truly in the clear until the murderer is exposed—if he ever is."

"Exposed?" McGill echoed. "You sound as if you know who did it."

"I might," Ferguson replied. "I've heard a whisper, from a reliable source."

"But?"

"But there's no proof."

"Whispers of that sort run both ways," McGill said. "You'd better watch your back."

Ferguson concentrated on his whisky for a long moment before he raised his eyes to his friend's face. "That thought had occurred to me," he said softly.

"Then it really is just as well you'll be away for a while."

Ferguson shrugged. "I've wound up my affairs here," he said. "No loose ends."

"But you are coming back?"

"I don't really know," Ferguson said. "Probably. There's nothing to keep me at home—not really. I burned those bridges long ago."

"But you will visit your family while you are back home?" McGill asked.

"I plan to," Ferguson replied. "Mother writes that all is well, but I'd like to see for myself all the same. I may be the black sheep of the family, but I still stay in touch with her."

"In that case," McGill said, "I have something for you." He slid open the top drawer of his desk, and withdrew a slim envelope.

"What's this?" Ferguson asked.

"Your photograph," McGill replied. He took a deep breath. "This is a bit delicate, Charles," he said at last. "I know you're not one for social conventions, but even so, I've been debating in my mind whether I should tell you or not. But in the end, I feel it's my duty, as a friend. I hope you'll forgive me."

Ferguson turned the envelope over in his hands, looking puzzled. "What on earth is it, James?" he said.

"Look at the photograph," McGill replied. "Tell me what you see."

Ferguson opened the flap of the envelope and took out the sepia photograph. "It's me and Charlotte," he said at last. "What of it?"

"Look again, Charles."

Ferguson stared again at the photograph, seeing himself posed behind the seated, smiling Charlotte. "She's a pretty girl, James," he said. "But I'm no good at guessing games. You'll have to tell me what this is about."

McGill swallowed. "She's your daughter, Charles," he said softly. "Surely you can see the resemblance."

Ferguson was thunderstruck. He gazed intently at the photograph, lost for words.

"I noticed the family likeness the first time I saw you together, at the Melbourne Cup," McGill said in a rush. "Please don't think that Morag told me — she didn't. I worked it out for myself. But she couldn't deny it when I taxed her with it."

"Are you sure?" Ferguson said at last. "I can see a resemblance — but Clara has never once said a word to make me think the child might be mine."

"Might?" McGill said. "Think about it, man. Seekamp was in prison."

"But why wouldn't Clara say anything?"

"She probably thought it best. She was, after all, a married woman: her child is legitimate. She'd see no point in causing unnecessary scandal."

"But...?"

"Would you have wanted to marry her?"

"No."

"And Clara must have known that. She's no fool. She chose the best path for both of you."

"So why are you telling me now?"

"Because you are going home, Charles: the child is yours, and you should acknowledge her to your family. There will, eventually, be an inheritance. Would you deny your daughter her birthright?"

"I see your point, James, but why would they believe me?" Ferguson asked. "I've never married, after all."

"They have only to look at the photograph," McGill said. "Your family will see what I see. It's obvious."

Ferguson sighed. "I suppose I'll have to have it out with Clara," he said at last.

"That's entirely up to you," McGill replied.

"The first thing my mother will do is write to her grandchild," Ferguson said ruefully. "If I'm to acknowledge Charlotte—Oh!" he said. "The name. I never thought about it."

"No, but Clara did," McGill said.

"I shall have to own her here first," Ferguson continued, completing his sentence. "It wouldn't do to have her learn the truth—if it is the truth—any other way." He shrugged. "That's going to be one hell of an encounter."

"I suppose so," said McGill.

"But at least I'll have an escape route: by this time next week I'll be on a ship, San Francisco bound," Ferguson said, cheering up slightly.

"True," McGill said.

"Then I guess I'm for it," Ferguson said. "I'll talk to Clara—she's not likely to lie if I ask her outright."

"You're right about that," McGill replied. "When it comes to confrontation—if it comes to that—Clara is fearless."

"I'll have another drink, if you don't mind, James," Ferguson said, contemplating Clara's likely reaction. "I don't think I'm quite ready for fatherhood."

"Charlotte's turned eighteen," McGill remarked dryly.

"I know," Ferguson said, "but I feel she's bound to resent me."

Chapter 67

Morag was sitting quietly at her writing desk in the morning room, dealing with her correspondence, when Clara flounced in.

"You told him!" she said without preamble.

Morag looked up in surprise. "Whatever is the matter, Clara?" she asked.

"You know what the matter is," Clara said. "You told him."

Morag shook her head in puzzlement.

"You told your husband about Charlotte," Clara said.

"I promise you I did no such thing," Morag said, beginning to understand the situation. "James saw it for himself. When he told me his thoughts, I asked him not to say anything."

"I don't believe you," Clara said flatly. "Men aren't that perceptive."

"I'm afraid James is, especially when it comes to family matters."

"I still don't believe you—you must have told him, or at least confirmed his suspicions," Clara said.

Morag looked guilty. "I couldn't deny it," she said quietly. "But I didn't tell him."

"Anyway," Clara continued, "McGill told Ferguson, and Ferguson came to my house last night and asked me outright."

"And you said…?"

Clara shrugged. "I couldn't lie," she said. "I had to admit it."

"Oh dear," Morag said. "What happened?"

"We had a row, of course. Charlotte learned the truth in the worst possible way, with Ferguson and I hurling accusations at each other."

"And then?"

"Charlotte was shocked. She told me her whole life was a lie, accused me of denying her a father. And now she has locked herself in her room and won't speak to me at all."

"She'll come around," Morag said. "But Clara, she must have asked about her father before now. You must have told her something."

"Only that Henry and I separated before she was born," Clara replied. "I never actually said he was her father, but I never said he wasn't."

"Understandable," Morag said. "Sit down, Clara. I'll ring for tea. We'll find a way through this."

"You've done enough damage, thank you very much," Clara said. "I don't want your tea and sympathy. You've wrecked Charlotte's life—and my reputation. I suppose the news is all over town by now."

"How could it be?" Morag replied, exasperated. "I keep telling you, I haven't said a single word to anyone."

"I'll be ruined when this gets out," Clara said stubbornly.

"But how can it possibly get out?" Morag asked. "The only thing that has changed now is that Ferguson and Charlotte know—and it's their secret too, isn't it? Neither of them is likely to make a public fuss about it."

"Then why did McGill have to go and tell Ferguson at all?"

"If my husband told Ferguson the truth," Morag said gently, "it would be because he felt it his duty to have Charlotte properly acknowledged. You know that Ferguson comes from an extremely wealthy family—there is the matter of Charlotte's inheritance to be considered."

"That's exactly what Ferguson said," Clara replied angrily. "I knew it: you made it up between you, you and your husband, to damage me." She turned on her friend, shaking. "And just because you married your Mr Perfect, it didn't give you the right to betray my private life to him. I thought you were better than that."

"Clara…" Morag began.

"Don't you *Clara* me. And you needn't think your husband is so perfect, either. I know for a fact that he had sex with Lola on that ship, on his way to propose to you. How perfect is that?"

Morag was stunned. "You can't…" she began.

"Lola as good as told me herself," Clara said, "the morning she arrived with him. I asked her outright, and she didn't deny it."

"I think you'd better leave," Morag said, rising from her seat and gathering what shreds of dignity she could. "This has gone far enough. We'll both say things we'll regret if this conversation goes on much longer. You need to calm down."

"I won't stay where I'm not wanted," Clara replied, heading for the door. "And don't think you can make it up with me, Morag *McGill*," she said, with heavy emphasis on the surname. "No one likes a traitor."

Clara slammed the door behind her, and Morag sank back into her chair, crushed. She held her hands tightly in her lap to stop them from shaking.

"What was all that about?" McGill asked, coming into the room. "I saw Clara leaving with a face like thunder." He paused, realising that his wife was crying, her shoulders heaving. "Morag, what has she done?"

Morag lifted her gaze to meet her husband's. "You told Ferguson about Charlotte," she said. "And Clara is convinced I betrayed her secret to you."

"Oh," McGill said. "I'm so sorry, Morag. I judged it best to tell him before he sets sail for San Francisco. I gave him the photograph that Cole took of him and Charlotte, to show his mother."

"You should have warned me."

"I meant to: I only told him yesterday evening."

"And he went straight around to confront Clara," Morag said. "It's typical of Ferguson, really, to meet the situation head on."

"I should have realised he would do that," McGill said. "I'm sorry, my love. You've been caught off guard, and it's my fault." He moved to put his arms around her.

She pulled away.

McGill hesitated. "There's something else, isn't there?"

Morag nodded miserably.

"Come on, out with it," McGill said. "It can't be that bad."

Morag's gaze was bleak as she weighed her options. "Very well, then," she said at last.

McGill felt a shiver of anxiety. He had never seen Morag like this. "Tell me," he said softly.

"Clara said that you had intercourse with Lola," Morag blurted out through her tears, "on your way to propose to me."

McGill was staggered: he had not expected this. "No, my love," he said at last, as gently as he could. "That's nothing but a malicious lie."

Morag stared at him, wanting to believe him, not quite daring to. "But Hector said she was with you when you arrived at the docks," she said, hiccupping.

"That much is true," McGill said. "We were on the same ship, and I spent time in her company. But Morag, you must believe me when I say that nothing untoward happened between us. I swear it on my life." He opened his arms to enfold his wife, feeling her tears wetting his shirtfront as she wept against his shoulder. "How could I, when I was coming to be with you?"

Morag clung to him, still sobbing. "Then why would Lola say you did? Clara said she asked Lola outright, and she didn't deny it."

McGill hesitated. "I would never speak unkindly of a lady," he said, "but you need the truth today: Lola offered me her body, and I refused."

"You turned her down?"

"Yes." He shrugged ruefully. "I must say she was surprised."

"She would have been," Morag said, brightening a little.

"So she wouldn't have wanted to admit that to Clara," McGill finished. "I think your friend has gotten hold of the wrong end of the proverbial stick, my love: it wouldn't be the first time, would it? I can only guess that Lola prevaricated and Clara assumed that something happened when it didn't. She said what she said to hurt you."

"She succeeded in that," Morag replied.

"I'm sure it will all blow over," McGill offered. "Let me ring Wilson for some tea."

"Thank you," Morag said, "for the tea, that is. But you don't know Clara. She can bear a grudge for a very long time."

"Then we'll get by without her," McGill said firmly.

Morag shook her head. "But what about Hector," she said, "and Charlotte? They spend such a lot of time together."

"Hector is leaving next week," McGill said. "This morning's drama will be forgotten by the time he returns. You'll see."

"I hope so," Morag said. "Clara's still my best friend—I'd hate to lose her over this."

"You won't," said McGill. "Trust me: it will all work out for the best."

Chapter 68

Two days later, Charlotte met Hector at the stables, dressed for their usual ride. As she entered, Hector looked up from the saddle girth that he was tightening, his face lit by a huge smile.

"Charlotte," he said, straightening up from his task. "It's you. I wasn't sure whether you would come today."

Charlotte smiled back at him. "It's a lovely day, Hector," she said, a little too brightly. "It's perfect for riding. Why wouldn't I come?"

"You know why," Hector replied. "For the first time ever, our mothers aren't on speaking terms. I have no idea what happened: all I know is that there was a terrible row."

"I know," Charlotte said quietly.

"Do you know what it's about?" Hector asked. "Mother is totally miserable, but she won't tell me anything. She says it's not hers to tell."

Charlotte looked stricken.

Hector gave his horse a quick pat and closed the stall. In two strides he was beside Charlotte. Her took her by the hand and led her outside into the sunshine and motioned to a wooden bench beside the stable wall. "Here," he said. "Sit with me, Charlotte. I can see you're upset. You don't have to tell me if you don't want to."

Charlotte burst into tears.

Hector felt helpless. "I'll get you some water," he said, standing up again and making for the pump. He filled the tin cup that always stood there, and carried it back slowly, giving Charlotte time to regain her composure.

"Here you are," he said, bending down to hand her the over-full cup. He slopped water on her riding dress.

Charlotte jumped up, brushing at it—and knocked the cup from his hand.

Water went everywhere. They both laughed. The tension was broken.

"Here," Hector said, "take my handkerchief."

"Thanks," Charlotte said, mopping at her skirt. She managed a weak smile.

"At least the other end of the bench isn't wet," she said. "We can sit there: the sun will dry my skirt."

They settled themselves companionably, and sat in silence for a while, watching the bees droning away in the flowerbeds, listening to the chirruping of the brilliant blue fairy wrens that flitted about busily. When Charlotte seemed calmer, Hector ventured a question: "Is there anything I can do to help?" he asked.

"No, Hector," she replied. "There's nothing anyone can do. The damage was done long ago."

"Then it shouldn't affect us," Hector said hopefully. "We can leave them to work it out for themselves. We don't have to be involved."

"But we do," Charlotte replied, her lower lip trembling. She took a deep breath. "You might as well know, Hector," she said. "You'll find out anyway." She looked up at him, trying hard not to cry again. "Promise you won't hate me?"

"I could never hate you," Hector said. "But you've got me really worried now. What on earth is the matter? What has upset you so much?"

"Lieutenant Ferguson is my father," Charlotte said softly.

"What?"

"Lieutenant Ferguson is my real father. There, I've said it aloud." Her fragile composure crumbled. She looked down at her lap, watching her hands crumpling Hector's sodden handkerchief into a tight ball. "Mother never told me, and she never told him either," she said bitterly. "All these years, she just let everyone think that Henry Seekamp was my father. She left him before I was born, so it was easy for her to do. I'm eighteen, Hector—I'm not a child— she could have told me."

"Nobody knew?"

"Your mother did, but she never said anything either."

"Then how...?"

"Captain McGill worked it out," Charlotte said. "And apparently your mother couldn't deny it when he asked her directly. That's what *my* mother is so angry about: she thinks her closest friend betrayed her."

"She wouldn't..." Hector began.

Charlotte dismissed his protest with a gesture. "I know," she said. "Mother is just angry that her secret is out. She wants someone to blame, and she's fixed her sights on her best friend." She shrugged. "Anyway, McGill told Ferguson—he gave him the photograph that Mr Cole took of us at the wedding." She shrugged. "We *do* look like father and daughter, when you see it in that light."

"But that's wonderful news," Hector said.

Charlotte rounded on him. "How can it be wonderful?" she asked. "I've been lied to all my life, by my own mother."

"Yes," Hector said. "But Lieutenant Ferguson turns out to be your father. You like him. Isn't that better than being the daughter of a man your mother left because he was a dangerous drunkard?"

"I suppose so," Charlotte said grudgingly. "But I could have had a father all my life. I always thought I didn't. You don't know how awful that feels."

"Don't I?" Hector said. "It's not exactly the same, but I do know how it feels to grow up without a father. I saw my father killed." He stopped short, realising what he had just said. "I saw him die," he amended quickly. "I wasn't quite seven years old. I still have nightmares about it."

"Oh, Hector," Charlotte said. "I'm so sorry. I had heard that your father was killed at the Eureka Stockade, but I never thought you were there. Nobody ever said."

"It seems there's a lot they never told either of us," Hector replied. "I guess we'll just have to stick together."

Charlotte smiled up at him. "I guess so," she replied. "But you're going away next week," she added, "with my..."—she hesitated— "my father. That's bizarre, isn't it?"

"Very," Hector replied. "But I won't be away for long. I'm coming back."

"It will seem strange without you," Charlotte said. "You've always been here. And you've never lied to me."

"And I never will," Hector said. "I hadn't realised just how much I'm going to miss you." He took both of her hands in his and looked earnestly into her eyes. "Will you allow me to write to you, Charlotte?" he asked.

"Of course," Charlotte replied. "Oh," she added, as understanding dawned. "You mean..."

"As a suitor, yes," Hector replied, blushing to the roots of his red hair. He was still holding her hands in his. "I felt so empty this morning when I thought you might not come," he said. "And I have to leave next week. Please say you will let me write."

"Yes," Charlotte replied. "I'll miss you too. But Hector, there's a problem."

"What is it?" Hector asked, his heart suddenly pounding in his chest.

"Letters will take too long," Charlotte replied. "You'll be gone from one place to the next before I can reply."

Hector breathed again. "Then we'll use the Telegraph."

"I don't know how."

"It's easy—I'll show you." He smiled at her. "We'll need our own code," he said happily, "if we don't want nosy clerks reading our private messages."

"Can you do that?" Charlotte asked. "Arrange a code, that is?"

"Of course," Hector replied happily. "I do it all the time for Sir Alec's clients. Don't worry, I'll see to it today."

"That will be marvellous," Charlotte said. "Are we still going riding?"

"I think we should," Hector said. "I've saddled our poor horses already—they've been waiting a long time for their exercise. And it's such a beautiful day: it would be a pity to waste it."

"Yes, it would," Charlotte replied, feeling as if a weight had somehow been lifted from her shoulders. "Let's go."

Minutes later, they rode out of the stable yard together, heading towards the bridle path than ran beside the Yarra river. The path was shaded by towering red gums, and the wattle bushes were in flower, dusting the track with yellow pollen. The air was full of birdsong: they heard the liquid notes of a native thrush, the chirruping of a yellow robin, the sharp crack of a whip bird, the carolling of magpies. Out in the middle of the river, a big silver fish jumped high, scattering bright droplets of spray before it fell back with a huge splash. Hector laughed at the sight. At that moment, Melbourne seemed far away. Today, at least, he and Charlotte could be happy.

Chapter 69

The final few days before Hector's departure seemed too short for the flurry of last-minute organisation. Morag fussed about, offering nervous advice about packing, until McGill reminded her that Hector would need to travel light, and she reluctantly left her son to his own devices. Hector had a million details to attend to, and some of his mother's anxiety seemed to have penetrated his usual calm. He wanted to spend more time with Charlotte, but found it difficult to arrange amongst all of the demands on his time: he snatched what moments he could with her, taking secret delight in the planning of their personal telegraph code.

Buchanan was all business: the international financial news that flooded in daily via the Telegraph was unrelentingly bad, and he was worried. He had a seemingly endless list of last-minute instructions to go with the satchel of letters to be hand-delivered to various recipients.

"You'll need to keep your wits about you, Hector," Buchanan said, handing a last few items to him on the evening before his departure. "The American bond prices are weakening, and short-term lending rates are rising faster than any of us expected. The situation may become very unstable. You will make sure that these are all delivered to the right people, won't you?"

"Yes, Sir Alec," Hector replied. "Please don't worry. Everything is in order."

"Very well, then," Buchanan said. "I'll wish you good night, and God-speed," he said.

The men shook hands. Hector's journey had officially begun.

Ferguson had remained, as usual, unfazed: if he was surprised, the day before he was due to leave, to receive a small package wrapped in red velvet with written instructions and a request from Woo that he deliver it to a certain address in San Francisco's Chinatown, he didn't show it.

"Do you have any idea what might be in it?" McGill asked.

"Best not to enquire," Ferguson replied. "I owe Woo a favour: acting as courier for his package is little enough for him to ask of me."

"I suppose so," McGill replied. "But be careful, all the same."

"I'm always careful," Ferguson replied.

When the morning of August 11th finally dawned, McGill and Morag rode in the Consular carriage to the docks with Hector and Ferguson, where the steamer *Nevada*, in the charge of Captain James H. Blethen, was making ready to catch the morning tide. Hector inhaled the familiar smells of salt and fish and tar, hardly even noticing the screech of the silver gulls that squabbled over scraps where a fisherman was clearing his nets at the end of the pier. After all the fuss of the last few days, Hector just felt relieved to be on his way at last.

When all was in readiness, Morag clung to her son. "Promise me you'll be careful," she said, hugging him to her.

"Yes, Mother," Hector replied, kissing her lightly. "We'll be back before you know it."

McGill shook hands with Ferguson, and then embraced Hector. "Look after each other," he said.

"Will do," Ferguson said nonchalantly. "Come on Hector—time to go."

The two were just about to set foot on the gangplank when Charlotte arrived, hatless and out of breath. "My cab was late," she said, "but I simply had to come to wish you both *bon voyage*."

"Very kind of you," Ferguson said stiffly. He was, it seemed, still a little uncomfortable in her presence.

But Hector's smile lit up his face. "Thank you," he said. He kissed her hand. "I'll miss you."

A meaningful look passed between McGill and Morag.

A whistle sounded from the steamer.

"They're waiting for you," McGill said.

"We're off," Ferguson replied.

The two men sprinted up the plank, just in time. Before long, they were standing companionably at the rail, waving farewell to McGill, Morag, and Charlotte, who watched them out of sight.

"May we offer you a ride home?" Morag asked Charlotte.

"Oh, thank you," Charlotte replied. "I'd appreciate it, if it wouldn't be too much trouble."

"No trouble at all," McGill said. "You know you're always welcome in our house, Charlotte: you and Hector are close, and you'll want to hear the news of his progress. So don't let your mother's ill temper make you a stranger to us."

Charlotte smiled. "Thank you," she said: "I promise I won't let that happen."

"Good," said McGill. "I'm glad that's settled."

PART III

1873: The Great Panic

"Merchants will look on with encouragement, and the diggers are ever ready to give their vote and support to a change of administration. We must think, and then act, if the other colonies hesitate. Victoria must take the lead, and she is prepared to set the example.

The moment our flag is at the masthead we shall run the race of nations."

George Train, *An American Merchant in Europe, Asia and Australia.* (1857)

Chapter 70

The steamer arrived in Sydney on the afternoon of the 14th of August, and departed again next day on the afternoon tide, San Francisco-bound. The crossing was calm and uneventful: Ferguson made a tidy sum at the poker tables, by way of keeping himself amused, but Hector spent most of his time reading, glad of the chance to relax after the frantic efforts that had preceded his departure. The fair weather held, and the voyage was completed without mishap. On the afternoon of Saturday September 13th, Hector and Ferguson disembarked in San Francisco, rested and ready for business.

When they deposited their luggage at a convenient dockside hotel, they had no difficulty in establishing that George Train's mansion stood at the top of the Nob Hill district.

"The new cable car runs up Clay Street towards Nob Hill," the hotel clerk said. "It's only been open for a couple of weeks."

"Excellent," Ferguson replied. "We can ride that. It'll take us close to Train's house."

"Great idea," said Hector, looking about him in amazement. "Mr Cole told me there were engineers planning to build a cable car line here, but I never thought I'd get to ride on it."

"Then you're in luck today," Ferguson answered, grinning. He consulted his map. "It looks to me as if it goes right past Chinatown. We can make a brief detour to deliver Woo's little package on the way to Train's house, and that will be all our obligations taken care of."

"Suits me," Hector replied. "I'd like to take a look around—who knows when I'll get another opportunity."

"Let's go then, while we still have daylight," Ferguson said, heading for the door.

Chapter 72

"That won't be necessary," a new voice said, its owner's English clipped accent cutting across the guttural grunts that echoed in the alleyway.

Ferguson did not take his eyes off his assailants. "Ah Zhow Chan, I presume?" he asked.

"The same," Chan replied.

The remaining attackers wasted no time weighing the new threat. They melted silently into the alleyway, disappearing as quickly as they had come, the leader still nursing his bleeding arm.

Hector and Ferguson held their defensive positions, fearing a second assault.

"Come, come," Mr Ferguson, the new voice said. "You are safe, I promise you. My men are here now."

"We could have taken them," Ferguson replied. "Easily."

"I can see that for myself," Chan replied, "but there is no threat to your safety now. I must apologise for your welcome. I was expecting you, but..." he gestured at the carved lintel—"you chose the wrong black dragon."

Ferguson shrugged. "The directions weren't exactly clear."

"Again, my apologies. Will you follow me? My house is just another block away."

"Very well," Ferguson said. "But I'll need the agreed identification."

"Of course," Chan replied. He extended his right hand and turned the gold ring on his middle finger to face outward, revealing a carved jade dragon, the twin of Woo's own magnificent ring.

Ferguson nodded. "That seems to be in order," he said.

"Do you have my goods?"

"Of course."

"Then please, come with me."

When Ferguson sheathed his weapons Hector followed suit, feeling more than a little wary, prepared to defend himself again at the first hint of trouble.

313

"One moment," Ferguson said, bending to retrieve his knife. He put his boot on the dead man's chest, steadying himself as he pulled the blade free and wiped it casually on the man's tunic. "No sense wasting a nicely balanced blade," he remarked, to nobody in particular. "Let's go."

They were escorted to a much larger building which stood, as promised, a scant block away. Its door carvings depicted a pair of huge, rampant black-enamelled dragons decorated with gold leaf; its sides were flanked by rather more salubrious pawn shops.

"This is more like it," Ferguson said.

"Will you take tea?" Chan asked, ushering them into a small, traditionally furnished room. The first evening shadows were falling, and the lamps had been lit.

Ferguson nodded. "Fighting's thirsty work," he said.

Chan signalled to an assistant to bring tea, and motioned his guests to sit. "I must say, the criminals who attacked you were not prepared to encounter two such well-trained fighters," Chan remarked. "Most Europeans who wander into these areas are easy prey."

"Nobody but a fool would come here unarmed," Ferguson said, patting his revolver in its shoulder holster.

Chan merely nodded.

"What happens about the injured?" Hector asked.

"My men have already taken care of it," Chan said airily. "Your attackers were not an organised gang—just opportunists, probably related to the old man who summoned them when he realised you were carrying something of value."

Ferguson sighed. "My fault, then: I told the old man I had a package for you."

"That would explain it," said Chan. "We live in a cutthroat world."

His assistant reappeared to pour tea, and the smoky scent of oolong filled the room.

Hector inhaled the fragrant steam from his cup. "Mr Woo uses the same oolong blend," he said appreciatively.

"Indeed he does," Chan replied. "We have the same supplier. We used to share this tea often when I resided in Melbourne."

"And have you moved back to San Francisco on a permanent basis?" Ferguson asked.

"It is a matter of business," Chan replied. "My interests, like Mr Woo's, span the globe." He nodded encouragingly at Hector. "In any case," he added, "it's always good to meet another connoisseur."

Hector smiled at his host, recovering his equanimity.

Ferguson sipped perfunctorily. He put down his cup. "Do you have the paperwork?" he asked Chan.

Chan passed him a slim envelope.

Ferguson read swiftly and checked the banker's draft, then reached inside his jacket and withdrew the red velvet package. He handed it to Chan. "Mr Woo sends his compliments," he said.

"And I return mine to him," Chan replied, observing the formalities. "Do you know what you have carried all this way?"

"No," Ferguson replied. "I don't open other people's mail."

"An honourable man," Chan mused, "and a fighter: you are a true warrior."

Ferguson brushed the compliment aside. "We should be going," he said.

"My men will escort you," Chan said, "when you have finished your tea. You're both marked men now. You stand out here,"—he nodded to Hector—"especially you, with that red hair. It wouldn't do to leave you to find your way back unguided, especially at nightfall."

"Thank you," Hector replied.

"Much appreciated," said Ferguson.

Chan smiled, slowly unwinding the velvet. Inside the fabric was a further layer of fine parchment, covered in closely written calligraphy. As Chan unrolled the parchment, he stared intently at the letters for a few moments, reading the Chinese characters before he smoothed the parchment fully open to reveal a single layer of white silk. This, too, he unwound, until, at the last, he held aloft a superb strand of large, evenly matched pearls that shone with soft lustre in the lamplight.

"These are from our pearling operations off the western Australian coast," he said, caressing them. "I believe they are the finest pearls in the world."

"They're stunning," Hector said appreciatively.

"Indeed they are," Chan replied. "And they'll fetch a princely sum in the right market."

"I wish you joy of them," Ferguson said formally. He stood. "Thank you for your hospitality, Mr Chan, but I'm sure you will understand that my friend and I really must be on our way."

"Of course," Chan replied. "I'll summon my men immediately."

Chapter 73

With Chan's bodyguards to escort them, Ferguson and Hector soon found themselves out of Chinatown and back at the respectable front of California Street. Safely delivered, they had no chance to thank their guides: Chan's men simply bowed and departed, leaving their charges once again to their own devices.

Hector took a deep breath, savouring the clean salt air after the fetid fumes of Chinatown.

"Well, that was interesting," Ferguson said.

"Yes: those pearls really are very beautiful," Hector replied, thinking wistfully of how much Charlotte would have liked them.

Ferguson smiled enigmatically. "As Scheherazade has it, *the key to the treasure is the treasure*," he said.

"What does that mean?"

"It means," Ferguson replied, "that we have just delivered a document, more precious, obviously, than the pearls."

"The parchment?"

"Exactly." Ferguson chuckled. "You have to hand it to Woo," he said. "He's cunning. That was as good a triple blind as I've ever seen: anyone other than Chan would assume that the pearls—which *are* exceedingly valuable—were the treasure. I did not know what I was carrying; if I had opened the package, I might have realised the truth, but I couldn't have read the Chinese characters; if the package had been stolen, the wrapping would most likely have been thrown away in the thief's greed for the pearls."

"Clever," said Hector. "Mr Woo must value the document very highly, to use such a treasure as a decoy."

"Indeed," Ferguson replied.

"Do you have any idea what the scroll might be?"

"Not really," said Ferguson. "But given Woo's business interests, I can guess." He patted his pocket. "The banker's draft Chan gave me for Woo is for a very large sum indeed, drawn on a Hong Kong bank. Given that the US government is blocking Chinese business here, I would say that Woo and his associates are quietly getting their money out. The scroll could be instructions of some kind."

"That would make sense," Hector said. He sighed, glancing up at the sky. "The light is fading fast," he said. "I've just realised how tired I am. I vote we forget Woo's enigma for the moment. I think we'd better find Train's house while we can."

Ferguson grinned. "That shouldn't be a problem," he said, pointing up the hill: "that enormous two-storey thing with all the fancy trimmings is bound to be it—Train loves to make a show."

"After you, then," Hector replied. "It's getting cool out here."

"Delighted," Ferguson replied. "At least Train will give us a proper drink—I could use one after all the excitement."

Train's mansion dominated the hill, dwarfing its opulent neighbours in what was clearly a precinct of millionaires: beside it stood a turreted mansion, but the sheer size of Train's home overshadowed it. Ferguson led the way to the front door, through a tall portico framed with elegant Corinthian columns. The theme continued around the massive bulk of the building: every doorway had its fluted columns; every window was dressed with intricate cornices and coping.

"It looks very grand," Hector said, trying belatedly to straighten his jacket.

"It will be," Ferguson replied, ringing the bell. "George Train has always had a taste for the finer things in life."

A butler appeared, in full livery.

"Lieutenant Ferguson and Mr Munro," Ferguson announced. "Mr Train is expecting us."

"Indeed, sir," the man replied. "If you'll just follow me, gentlemen."

Hector couldn't help but stare as they were led along a hallway lined with carpets so thick he could not hear his footsteps. "These ceilings must be sixteen feet high," he whispered to Ferguson.

"Try not to be too impressed," Ferguson whispered back.

The butler ushered them into a grand sitting room. Tall white marble Corinthian columns graced the walls, echoed by a pure white chandelier designed to contrast with the oak-grained woodwork. A fire burned in the marble fireplace, and deep red carpets covered the floors, matched by the plush red velvet of the chairs.

"Very nice," Ferguson said.

"Do you like it?" Train said, bustling into the room. A head shorter than

Hector, Train was fussily dressed with a heavily brocaded red waistcoat under his black suit. His fingers flashed with rings: diamonds and rubies. "I have forty-four rooms here, you know," he said, "and rather beautiful gardens."

"Hello, George," Ferguson said, hugging him affectionately. "I'm pleased to see you too. It's been a long time. Do allow me to introduce Mr Hector Munro."

"Delighted, I'm sure," Train said, shaking Hector's hand vigorously. "I've heard such a lot about you from your stepfather. McGill is very proud of you. I've been expecting you." He crossed to the silver tray that sat waiting on a heavily carved sideboard. "Would you care for a drink?"

"I thought you'd never ask," Ferguson laughed. "Hector and I have been having adventures in Chinatown."

"Goodness," Train replied, casually pouring large measures of single malt whisky into cut crystal glasses. "Whatever possessed you to go in there? It's a den of thieves."

"I had a commission to deliver," Ferguson said.

"Ah," said Train. "Enough said." He handed the drinks to his guests. "Your very good health," he said, raising his glass.

"And yours," Ferguson responded, sipping gratefully.

"I've arranged dinner here this evening," Train said. "And the guest rooms are in readiness. I assume you'd like to freshen up before we dine?"

"Thank you," Ferguson said, "but we have left our luggage at the Commercial Hotel, down by the docks. We are to leave for New York first thing Monday."

"I know," said Train. "I have had a telegraph from Buchanan to that effect." He paused. "I find I must now travel to New York myself—I have urgent business there. So I hope you will not object when I tell you that I have taken the liberty of booking my journey to coincide with your own. I have engaged a private carriage on the train, in the hope that you will join me."

"We'd be delighted," Ferguson replied. "That will make the journey much livelier. You can tell us what's been happening here in San Francisco."

"Excellent," Train replied. "Now, if you'll excuse me a moment, I'll send someone down to collect your things from the hotel."

"Something's wrong," Ferguson said softly, when Train had left the room.

"What should we do?" Hector asked.

Ferguson shrugged. "Stay with it," he said. "He'll tell us when he's ready."

A moment later, Train was back. "All taken care of," he said airily. "Would you like the grand tour while you are waiting for your things?"

"That would be wonderful," Hector replied.

"Then come along—I'll just top up our drinks before we go."

The appointments of the house were breathtaking. Train led his guests into a ballroom where huge bouquets of hothouse flowers stood in massive urns atop white marble pedestals, augmented by beautifully wrought artificial flowers in gold. The air was full of birdsong, as imitation canaries and warblers sang their clockwork hearts out.

"Mr Cole would admire this," Hector said. "He enjoys miniature inventions of all sorts: he has automata in the window of his Emporium."

"I know," Train replied. "We have corresponded about it. I hope he may visit someday. I share his passion for new technologies: he is a most fascinating source of information. I look forward to his letters." He ushered Hector along. "Now, let me show you the dining room. It can seat two hundred guests," he said proudly.

"Magnificent," Ferguson admitted, glancing admiringly around the room.

"My dinner service is all new," Train went on: "all solid silver, and crystal, and the finest porcelain. My guests here want for nothing." He smiled. "I even have Church and Clarke to furnish my orchestras when I entertain."

Hector wandered away to admire the paintings, and Ferguson took the opportunity to speak to his friend. "What's wrong, George?" he said.

"Nothing," Train began.

"You're not your usual self," Ferguson replied. "Are you ill? Are we imposing?"

"Not at all," Train replied. He turned to look Ferguson in the eye. He sighed deeply. "You've caught me at an awkward moment, Charles," he said at last. "All is not well in the business world."

"You don't need to entertain us if you have pressing affairs to attend to," Ferguson said. "We'll understand. We can take care of ourselves."

Train smiled. "I must confess it's good to see a friendly face," he said. "You are not imposing at all, Charles. Things are not going my way, but it may be that this will prove an opportune meeting for you. Would you care to come into my study?"

He led Ferguson and Hector towards the back of the house, where a beautifully proportioned room looked out onto the gardens, now shadowed in darkness.

"What's up?" Ferguson asked, glancing around at the drifts of paperwork that festooned every flat surface.

"We're in trouble," Train said simply. "You might as well know: I doubt the company will last much longer when word of our losses gets out."

"You mean Credit Mobilier?"

"The same: we've been under investigation since January, after the newspapers revealed allegations of fraud within the company. It was all a campaign tactic in the Presidential race, of course, but mud sticks." He shrugged. "You know I lost, of course?"

"Consul McGill did tell us, yes," Ferguson said. "Such a pity—you'd have made a most interesting President."

"Much appreciated," said Train. "Anyway, the point I was making is that we've lost some major investors." He grimaced. "When connecting me in the press with Victoria Woodhull and the feminist agitators wasn't enough to ruin my reputation, my enemies went after my financial dealings. They've done a lot of damage."

"So what will you do now?" Ferguson asked.

"I'm getting all my personal holdings out of the railroads," Train replied. "I'd suggest you do the same."

"My word," said Ferguson. "That is serious."

"I'd better telegraph Sir Alec for instructions," Hector said.

"No," Train said bluntly. "I'm telling you this within these four walls, for the sake of friendship. Act for Buchanan, by all means, but don't use the Telegraph—it isn't secure here. If word gets out you'll start a run on the market, and we'll all be sunk."

"I'll think on it," Hector said.

"Take my advice," Train replied. "Don't think too long."

Chapter 74

Hector and Ferguson boarded the transcontinental railroad carriage on the morning of Monday 15th September, New York bound. True to his word, George Train had engaged a private first class carriage, ensuring they would travel in comfort and style.

"Just the ticket," Ferguson said, settling back into his plush armchair in the oak-panelled car.

"It's very comfortable," Hector ventured, looking around at the polished woodwork with its brass trimmings.

"I thought you'd like it," Train replied, checking the French champagne that sat waiting in its silver bucket. "I've instructed the chef to prepare something special for luncheon today, in your honour."

"Splendid," Ferguson replied. "I think I'm really going to enjoy this part of the trip."

By the time they arrived in Omaha, late on the afternoon of Thursday, 18th September, there was a telegram waiting at the Railroad Hotel for George Train. The colour drained from his face as he read it.

"Bad news?" Ferguson asked.

Train nodded. "It's from my brokers in New York. They tried to warn me. Jay Cooke's company has collapsed: they are about to declare bankruptcy." He consulted his gold half-hunter fob watch. "But the Stock Exchange has closed now. We're an hour behind New York here in Omaha. I'll have to salvage what I can first thing in the morning. You'd better do the same."

"Why is Jay Cooke so important?" Hector asked.

"He's our financier: his company controls the main investment bank for funding our railroads," Train replied wearily. "Union Pacific can't survive this."

"Oh," said Hector. He turned to Ferguson. "I can't possibly get instructions from Sir Alec before nine o'clock tomorrow morning when the Exchange re-opens."

"Eight o'clock here," Train corrected automatically.

"It would take an absolute minimum of twenty-four hours to telegraph him and receive a reply, assuming there were no delays," Hector said, working it out.

"Too long," Train said, "even if it was safe to do it—which it isn't. As I said before, the Telegraph here isn't secure. We can't risk a run on the market."

"But..." Hector began.

"My interaction with my brokers is a private code, heavily encrypted," Train explained.

"I understand," Hector replied. "We do the same for sensitive transactions at home. But I don't have a code for a situation like this."

"We'll have to decide for ourselves, then," Ferguson said.

"It's up to you, of course," said Train. "I can instruct my brokers to act for you, if you can authorize the transactions."

"I can," Hector said.

"Then, for God's sake, do it!" Train said. "Do you want to lose your shirts on this?"

Hector hesitated.

Ferguson touched him lightly on the arm. "I'll see you right," he said. "If Buchanan kicks up a stink, I can cover the losses."

"Thank you," Hector said. He squared his shoulders. "I appreciate that. But I have to make this decision. And I say we do it. We'll salvage what we can."

"Good man," Train said. "We'll sell every bit of stock Buchanan and his Consortium hold in Union Pacific and Credit Mobilier the minute the exchange opens in the morning. That should minimize the losses. I'll telegraph my brokers now."

"What about McGill's company?" Hector asked. "What about Edward Cole? They are both heavily invested."

"Can you sign for them?" Train asked.

Ferguson turned to Hector. "McGill is your stepfather now," he said. "You're family. You can authorize the transaction."

"In that case yes, I will," Hector said.

"I'm sure that will be in order," said Train. "That just leaves my old friend, Edward Cole." He hesitated a moment. "If you'll stand surety," he said to Ferguson, "I'll authorize it myself. Cole would trust me on this."

"Done," said Ferguson.

It took hours before all of the instructions to Train's brokers were complete and verified by telegraph, using his private code. Train seemed to have aged considerably in the course of the evening.

Hector looked pale and shaky. "I hope we've done the right thing," he said.

"Too late now," Ferguson said cheerfully. "Let's go and eat. The hotel will make something for us, even if it's only a sandwich. And a drink: I think we could all use a stiff drink."

"Well said," Train replied, visibly pulling himself together. "We've done all we can, for now."

Chapter 75

When the New York Stock Exchange opened at nine o'clock on Friday 19th September, the sales were swiftly completed. The size of the holdings Train dumped on the market had the effect of reducing the price, at which point there were plenty of willing buyers. By ten o'clock, Buchanan, Cole, McGill and the Consortium had been divested of their holdings. Train's hotel suite now resembled his San Francisco study, with slips of paper strewn over every surface.

Ferguson turned to Hector. "Have you telegraphed Buchanan?" he asked.

"Yes," Hector replied. "I've just done it. I also sent messages to Cole, and McGill." He shrugged. "I was very circumspect. I said only that I have sold off their railroad stocks this morning. They'll understand." He smiled inwardly: his final telegram had been entirely personal—a private message for Charlotte, using their own secret code.

"Not too bad at all," Train muttered, holding the latest telegram that had just arrived for him from his brokers. "The prices started to slide towards the end of our run. I took a chance, and sold short—not too much, under the circumstances, but it has softened the blow. I reckon our combined losses average less than twenty per cent. This calls for a celebration."

"Celebration?" Hector said, paling at the news. "We made a loss."

"But we're out and clear," Ferguson said. "This could be very bad."

"We'll know by the end of the day," said Train. "By the time we leave for New York, I'll have another telegraph message from my brokers."

True to his prediction, Train received a telegram just before their evening train was about to depart from Omaha station.

"What's the news?" Ferguson asked, as they once again boarded their private carriage.

Train was shaken. "It's worse than any of us could have predicted," he said. "By the close of trade today, fifty-five railroad companies had gone bankrupt, including Union Pacific."

Ferguson let out a low whistle. "That's amazing," he said.

"There's more," Train replied. "A number of smaller companies have gone to the wall in their wake. The Stock Exchange has been declared closed, indefinitely." He sighed. "There will almost certainly be a run on the surviving banks."

"Then you gave us good advice, Mr Train," Hector said. "I withdrew our travelling funds this morning, as a precaution."

"Very sensible," Train replied. "McGill said you were an intelligent man."

He looked out of the window. "I think we're off," he said. "At least we'll get a bit of peace until the next stop."

"True," said Ferguson, settling back in his seat. "None of us got much sleep last night." He smiled at Train. "And another good thing," he said: "the press won't be looking for you in a railway carriage."

Train managed a small smile in return. "They'll catch up with me eventually," he said. "They always do." He sighed. "And then I'll be in for a rough ride."

The engine whistle sounded, and the train began to pull away from the station, building up steam.

By the time Hector could no longer see the glow cast by the lights of Omaha, the 1873 Depression had well and truly begun.

Chapter 76

On the following Monday morning, Edward Cole's face was ashen when he walked into Buchanan's Collins Street office. "Have you heard the news?" he said, dropping into his usual chair beside the desk. "It's the talk of the town. The American stock market has crashed. We're ruined."

"Perhaps not," Buchanan replied calmly. "I'll admit I've had a sleepless night, but this telegram has just arrived from Hector." He held up the slip of paper, re-reading it. "Have you received one too?"

"I don't know," Cole replied. "I haven't been to my office this morning. I came straight here when I saw the papers."

"Then I'll send one of my clerks to check," Buchanan said, ringing the bell on his desk. A junior clerk appeared, and was promptly dispatched to Cole's nearby office.

"Why?" Cole asked. "What's Hector got to do with this?"

"I'm not entirely sure," Buchanan said, passing the telegram to Cole.

Cole read it, and then read it again, slowly, as comprehension dawned. "He says he's sold off your railroad stocks," he said, incredulously. "Did you give him instructions?"

"No," Buchanan replied. "But Hector was visiting George Train just before the crash. If he had warning, he used it well: he was authorized to act for me. This message isn't coded, so he can't say very much."

"I hope you're right," Cole said fervently. "I hope he has sold short."

A knock at the door heralded a second visitor. "Excuse me, sir," another of Buchanan's clerks said. "The American Consul is here."

"Show him in," Buchanan said, rising from his chair.

"Good morning," McGill said, striding into the room. He held up a slip of paper. "This telegraph from Hector has just been delivered to the Consulate," he said. "Do you have any idea what it means? I gave him no instructions of that sort."

"I hope it means that your stepson has saved you from financial ruin," Buchanan replied.

"I always said he was clever," Cole said. "Sir Alec has a similar telegram: we're checking my office now."

The first clerk reappeared in the doorway, holding an envelope. "Your message, sir," he said to Cole. "Will there be anything else, Sir Alec?"

"You could bring tea," Buchanan replied as the young man made his exit.

Cole's hands shook as he tore open the envelope. "He sold my railroad stocks," he said, his voice almost cracking with relief. "Look at the time on this: he sold just before the crash."

"Train must have warned him," Buchanan said. "And Hector must have used Train's own brokers in New York—there would have been no other way to get the thing done so fast."

"Whatever he did, we owe him our futures," Cole said fervently. "Though I don't really see how he could have acted on my behalf."

"Could Train have authorized your transactions?"

"Yes, I suppose he could," Cole replied. "He's acted for me before."

"Then Hector must have asked him to include you in the arrangements," Buchanan replied. "There's no mystery about Hector acting for you, McGill—he's your stepson. That would be good enough for Train's people, in an emergency."

"I should hope so," McGill replied. "And it certainly was an emergency! But it appears that Hector has won us a reprieve."

"We still have to get our money out of America," Buchanan replied, "and Hector must have sold at a loss. There's a lot to be done, but broadly speaking, yes, gentlemen, we have a reprieve."

The tea arrived, and the men busied themselves for a moment with the practicalities of milk and sugar.

"I'll have to contact Hector," McGill said, drawing up a chair beside Cole. "I must tell him he has my gratitude. If I know him, he'll be worrying because he made a loss, even if he did it saving our skins."

Cole laughed. "Probably," he said. "We will all congratulate him. And we must plan a suitably generous reward of some sort."

Chapter 77

When the door had closed once more behind Buchanan's assistant, McGill spoke up: "The implications for this crash are international, aren't they?" he said.

"There can be no doubt about it," Buchanan replied. "Short-term lending rates have been climbing very rapidly in Britain and Europe as well as in America: they are now impossibly high. And that will almost certainly have been the cause of Jay Cooke's insolvency. There's no way for anyone to borrow enough to trade out now—the markets are panicking everywhere. The only ones who will be safe are those with huge cash reserves."

"Then Victoria will have to act quickly," McGill said.

"What do you mean?" Cole asked.

"I mean that you will have to declare your Independence," McGill replied. "And do it soon."

Buchanan was speechless. He simply shook his head.

"Why?" Cole asked. "I know that Independence is close to your heart, McGill, but why pursue it now?"

"Because the moment is upon you," McGill replied. "You are solvent, and your masters are not. If you don't cut the cords that bind you to England, the Empire will drag you down with it. You'll never recover."

"I see your point," Cole said.

"Listen to me," McGill said earnestly. "You know that the German Empire has recently moved from silver to a gold standard, like Britain, and we in America are following suit. You have the largest gold deposits on earth: that's the biggest cash reserve there is. If you keep the gold here, you can develop your enterprises while the rest of the world is starved for funds. But if you let Britain go on taking your gold, it will drain you dry for its own ends. The English banks are busily issuing bonds, amassing debt against the gold they expect to extract from you. You can't seriously imagine that England's powerbrokers care about you, or this colony. They'll be looking out for themselves, at your expense."

"That's true," Cole replied.

"If you keep your gold," McGill went on, "your banks can guarantee the safety of their investments. International bankers are already looking for a safe haven. Your banks can provide that: Melbourne will be in a strong position to become an important financial centre." He turned to Cole. "And the Commercial Bank will be able to guarantee funds on the scale that you need to build your City of the Sun."

"What about our supplies?" Buchanan said, engaging with McGill at last. "The Melbourne Mint is already striking gold sovereigns, so we have currency. But the question of the supply of manufactured materials remains: almost everything is imported."

"England won't be able to continue providing the goods you need," McGill said. "Now that the Indian armies and navy have mutinied, the British Empire can no longer guarantee its shipping routes. America can supply you—but not if you remain a British colony."

"Why not?" Cole asked.

"Because England won't allow you to broker your own deals," McGill said. "Look at the situation you had with the copper smelter, then multiply it across every industry. England will try to use you to support what remains of its own manufacturing, and that means inflated prices and delayed deliveries: you'll be last in line here."

"And America?" Cole asked.

"America is already supplying most of Europe," McGill replied. "We have a surplus of almost everything. And the European markets are about to dry up for want of funds. We are perfectly placed to provide everything you need. I tell you this as Consul: America *will* support you. I can make the trade offer as official as you like."

"So you supply us while we develop our own manufacturing capacity," Buchanan mused. "And, in exchange, Melbourne becomes a free port."

"Exactly," McGill said. "It's mutually advantageous."

"If Victoria did declare Independence," Cole added, "there would be nothing Britain could do about it. We are too far away, and they have too few resources." He thought for a moment longer: "McGill's right," he said to Buchanan. "It's now or never. I say we do it."

"But I'm not the government," Buchanan protested. "This isn't something I can just decide."

"No, but you are very well connected," McGill replied. "Talk to your parliamentarians," he said, "talk to your fellow businessmen. This is more about business than politics: it's about economic survival. I would be willing to support you at a public meeting if you wish."

"Whoa!" said Buchanan. "You're moving too fast for me."

"We have to move fast," Cole said. "Choose a date for a meeting, and I'll print up some posters and organise some materials for the papers."

"There would probably have to be a referendum," Buchanan said, stalling. "Parliament won't want to just vote on a private Member's Bill on something so momentous."

"So hold a referendum," said McGill. "Things haven't changed all that much since Eureka: there's many a man would like to see the back of English rule here. And this time, they don't have to fight: they have merely to vote." He shrugged. "And they will all see that Independence now is in their best interests. You could offer to reduce all their taxes, for a start—a large part of that money goes back to Britain, one way or another, so the Colony would lose nothing."

"The Governor..."

"Will certainly oppose it," McGill finished for him. "Bowen is new to the post, and he's a professional colonial administrator. He'll side with his British masters."

"But Bowen is already caught up in the conflict between the Legislative Council and the Legislative Assembly," Cole said. "The Upper House is blocking payment to members of the Lower House, and blocking their reform bills to boot."

"Then the Lower House members will be for Independence," said McGill. "The squatters in the Upper House may prove more difficult: they already have substantial reserves in landholdings."

"But many of them also have other investments," Buchanan said.

"We have to accept that there will always be some in parliament who will put their petty concerns before the general good," McGill said. "We'll have to work around them, or spike their guns."

Cole grinned suddenly. "They're clients at Lola's Supper Club, to a man," he said. "I have no doubt that she can furnish us with any amount of scandal, if we should happen to need it."

"Edward!" Buchanan said. "That's privileged information."

"Of course it is," Cole replied. He held up his hands in surrender. "I'm not saying we should use it, Buchanan—I'm just mentioning that the option is there, if we need a little extra leverage."

"I don't think we are anywhere near that point yet," McGill said. "Let's think this through for a moment. What's the first thing your Governor will do when he gets wind of the proposal?"

"Send a telegram to Whitehall for instructions," Cole answered promptly. He grinned boyishly. "And that telegram will have to go through Alice Springs."

"Why is that amusing?" McGill asked.

"We control the telegraph stations at Alice Springs and Port Darwin," Buchanan replied, straight-faced. "We control the messages in both directions. We can control his information—messages can be lost, messages can be delayed, messages can be changed: it happens all the time."

"I see," McGill replied, suddenly reminded of Woo's gambling syndicate. "How very useful."

"Isn't it?" said Cole.

"Now that I think about it," Buchanan said, "a Petition would be faster than a referendum, and easier to organise: a Petition doesn't require enabling legislation, so the Upper House couldn't stall it."

"That's better," McGill said. "What do you need for that?"

"It's just a short, formal statement that the petitioners sign," Buchanan replied. "Signatures are collected and the document then goes to Parliament, in support of proposed legislation."

"Is that all?" Cole asked.

"As I understand it," Buchanan replied, "a Petition can only be presented by a Member of Parliament, and once presented there can be no debate on the Petition itself—the only question to be entertained by the House is whether it is received or denied. It's quite straightforward."

"And then?"

"The Lower House would vote on previously tabled Legislation, drafted to reflect the Petition."

"Then let's do it," Cole said. "A simple *yes* or *no* question for the Parliament is exactly what we need."

"Could you arrange for a member to draft legislation and present a Petition?" McGill asked Buchanan.

"Certainly," Buchanan replied. "I could speak to the Premier: he's been instrumental in enabling the construction of our railways."

"Capital," said Cole. "Mr Francis is just the man we need: he's a businessman, a pragmatist where financial matters are concerned. His Education Act last year was nothing less than visionary, and very hard fought. He's a sound man."

"Indeed," said Buchanan. "James Francis has clashed often enough with the Upper House over issues of constitutional reform. He may very well be persuaded to support us in this. Everyone knows he's a moderate reformer, not some extreme radical: the public will listen to him. If he'll champion our cause, Victorian Independence will have a better than even chance of succeeding."

"In that case," Cole said, "if you will undertake to have a Petition drawn up, Buchanan, I'll undertake to get it printed and circulated." He grinned. "This will be the biggest Petition they've ever seen. We'll start it off at a public meeting, arrange lots of press coverage, and take it from there. The groundswell of public opinion will carry it forward, you mark my words."

McGill nodded.

"I've just thought of something else," Cole said. "Anyone can sign a Petition. Ordinary working men who aren't eligible to vote can sign, and they will sign—they'll be the ones who'll lose their jobs if England drags us down into depression."

"That would certainly increase the pressure," Buchanan said. "The members of the Lower House are always bleating about listening to their public." He turned to Cole. "It would be best if you speak at the meeting, Edward," he added. "Can you do that?"

"I'm no orator," Cole replied, "but I've done my share of public speaking. I'll be happy to do it."

"Good," said Buchanan. "I'll be much more effective in dealing with the politicians if I am not overtly associated with the initial meeting."

"If I may make a practical suggestion, Edward," said McGill, "I would counsel that you simply declare, at your public meeting, that you will keep all of your current structures in place. The Governor will still sign Bills; Parliament will still control the Colony; public servants will continue as usual—the only difference will be that there will be no English overlords with power to veto their decisions and siphon off their profits. Every official from the Governor down will have more power; every investor will keep more of his profits: I can't see why that wouldn't be attractive, especially as everyone can see that the British Empire is about to crash."

"Excellent idea," said Cole. "That will appeal to both vanity and greed: there's no shortage of either in our government."

"And nobody will have cause to feel threatened," Buchanan added. "Everyone wins. Yes, I think I could sell that to my friends in high places."

"Good," McGill said. He smiled ruefully. "I can't help but recall that after my failure to protect the miners at the Eureka Stockade George Train insisted that Independence should be won by economic development, not force of arms. It pains me to admit that he may have been right all along." He squared his shoulders. "I promise you, gentlemen, I have no intention of failing a second time. Call on me for whatever you need, Sir Alec: I will answer for America."

"Thank you," said Buchanan.

"Capital," said Cole.

"But remember: you have to act quickly, while everything is in flux."

"I do understand, McGill," Buchanan said, suddenly feeling very weary. "The world is changing, and we must change with it." He sighed. "I'll call on Mr Sinisgalli this afternoon. I'll ask him to make an immediate start on drafting the Petition."

"Sinisgalli?"

"My lawyer, Edward," Buchanan replied. "He's sound: he was part of the Italian contingent at Eureka. He'll be in favour of Independence, and he'll be discreet."

"He fought at the stockade," McGill added. "When the English troops attacked, the famous Carboni was asleep in his bed—but John Sinisgalli was up at the barricade, fighting beside Ferguson. He's a brave man. I'd trust him with my life."

"We can certainly trust him with this, then," Cole replied.

"My point exactly," said Buchanan.

"I'm glad that's settled," McGill said. "I'll wait to hear from you both, but for now, gentlemen, I'll bid you good day: I have a great deal to do to organise my own business affairs. Hector has given us a head start—but we have yet to weather the coming storm."

Chapter 78

A short distance away, at The Bohemian Supper Club, a housemaid screamed. Lola pulled out her tiny silver and mother-of-pearl inlaid pistol and dashed up the stairs towards the sound. She stopped short in the doorway, appalled at the sight that greeted her. She did not need her pistol: she tucked it out of sight, strode across the newly-stained rug and put her arm around the hysterical young girl, firmly coaxing her out of the room.

"Go down to the kitchen, Annie," she said. "Tell Cook to give you a hot cup of tea, with plenty of sugar. I'll be down directly. Don't look: I'll deal with this."

The maid left, sobbing, and Lola began the grim task of checking the blue-faced, swollen corpse that swung from the chandelier, turning gently in the current of air created by the maid's departure. The room stank of whisky, and shit: the man's bowels had evacuated when he hanged himself, ruining his tailored suit. Lola moved swiftly to open a window, then turned back to look at the mess: an overturned chair lay on its side where the man had kicked it away, a pile of telegrams had been strewn across the still-made bed, and, on the night table, an envelope in the Club's signature lavender stationery had been propped prominently against the cut-glass water decanter.

Lola did not hesitate: she opened the envelope, read quickly, and then tucked the note inside her jacket. She checked the man's pockets, and carefully opened every drawer and cupboard to make sure there was nothing else of an incriminating nature before she left the room. She locked it firmly behind her.

Downstairs once more, she sent the maid home before she wrote a note for the police and summoned a footman to deliver it. The man was wide-eyed with curiosity—news of the suicide of a prominent Club member had spread fast.

"Here, Jim," she said. "I want this delivered to the police headquarters." She dropped a coin into his hand. "This is for your trouble, and for your silence. I don't want word of this getting out before the police enquiry."

"Yes, milady," the man replied, smiling at his good fortune. "Mum's the word."

Lola surprised him. "And this," she continued, giving him a second coin to match the first, "is for you to take your time in delivering it. There's something I need to do before the police get here. Do you understand?"

"Yes, milady," he replied, his smile broadening into a wide grin. "I'll take the long way."

"See that you do," Lola replied.

As soon as the man had set off, Lola donned her walking jacket and hat, instructed the staff that nobody was to be admitted in her absence, and set off briskly for Buchanan's office.

McGill had left, but Edward Cole was still engaged in earnest discussion with Buchanan when the office door was flung open. Lola swept into the room, trailed by an agitated clerk.

"I'm sorry, sir," he began.

Buchanan waved the apology aside. "It's quite all right," he said. "Just close the door behind you."

"My dear, whatever is the matter," Cole asked.

Lola, pale and a little shaky, allowed him to help her to a chair.

Buchanan crossed to the drinks tray and poured a measure of brandy. "Here," he said, offering her the glass. "Drink this. You'll feel better."

"Thank you," Lola said, sipping gratefully. "I'll be fine in a moment or two."

Cole patted her free hand. "You look as if you've seen a ghost," he said.

"In a manner of speaking, yes," Lola replied. She looked up at Buchanan. "It's Valentine," she said. "He's dead."

"Dead?" Buchanan echoed.

"One of my maids found him," Lola said. "She's distraught, poor girl. I've sent her home."

"How did she come to do that?" said Cole. "Find him, I mean."

"Valentine hanged himself from the chandelier in the second-best bedroom at the Club," Lola said. "I locked the place up, and came straight to you."

"Surely you sent for the police," Buchanan said.

"Of course," Lola replied. "I've sent a man to fetch them, and paid him double to take his time about it."

"And why would you do that?" Cole asked.

For answer, Lola reached inside her jacket and held out the folded piece of lavender writing paper, embossed in gold with The Bohemian Supper Club's letterhead. She held it out to Buchanan. "I judged it best that this should not fall into the hands of the local constabulary," she said. "It mentions you by name, after all."

Buchanan took the suicide note and unfolded it carefully. His face was grim as he read:

To whom it may concern,

I am a ruined man. I am responsible for the extensive investment of the funds of the Bank, and of its clients, into the US railroad share schemes whose finances were underwritten by the Banco di Santo Spirito. These companies have now failed, and I have since learned that the investors have no recourse to recoup their losses. The funds are bankrupt. The guarantees are worthless. The investors are ruined. All who invested in American railroad shares must also be ruined. I who am about to die freely confess that I accepted certain inducements from the agents of Cardinal Antonelli, particularly Bishop O'Hanlon, to make these transactions. Nevertheless, I beg you will believe me when I say that I acted only in the interests of making a profitable return for my employers and for their clients. I have failed. I accept responsibility for my part in this most dreadful outcome, but I cannot accept the life of shame and the poverty that must follow my disgrace. I therefore bid you farewell. Forgive me.

I must also beg your pardon, Madame Montez, for the inconvenience my death in your most excellent establishment must occasion for yourself and for my old friend, Sir Alec. Forgive me.

Sincerely,
Spencer Valentine

"How very sad," Cole remarked. "Even in death, he sounds like a banker."

"He was a banker," Buchanan said shortly.

"And our own investments?" Lola said tentatively.

"Are safe," Buchanan replied. "Thanks to some quick thinking by Hector Munro, and Ferguson."

Lola sighed. "That's a relief," she said. "So not everyone was ruined. But poor Valentine could not have known that."

"No indeed," said Cole. "We've only just learned the truth of it ourselves."

"You did the right thing bringing the note to me," Buchanan said, slipping the paper into a drawer of his desk, sliding the drawer closed and turning the key in the lock. "Did you touch anything else in the room?"

"No," Lola said. "Valentine had a bottle of whisky—getting up courage, I suppose—and a whole pile of telegrams. They were all about the stock market crash. There's nothing to find that concerns the Club, or any of our patrons."

"Good," Buchanan said firmly. "Let's get you back to the Club. I want you to make sure that there's a newspaper with headlines about the New York crash for the police to find. They'll have their motive soon enough."

"Indeed they will," Lola said heavily. "I do wish Valentine had chosen somewhere else."

"Perhaps he was happiest at your Club," Cole mused.

"Perhaps," Buchanan conceded.

"The girls were fond of him," said Lola. "They'll be upset."

"I'm sure you can take care of the situation," Buchanan said. "It would be best if the girls don't gossip about it."

"They won't," Lola said. "They know my rules."

"Of course," said Buchanan. "And Lola," he added, "it would be a good idea to contact one of your reporter friends at *The Age*: you can offer an exclusive inside story in return for a guarantee that the Club will not be mentioned—the editor is a prominent member, after all."

"What you need is a lurid headline," Cole said. "Something along the lines of *Failed Banker Suicides After Stock Market Crash*—something that will focus on Valentine and draw attention away from the Club."

"Of course," said Lola. "I must be on my way, if I'm to return before the police arrive."

"Shall I escort you, my dear?" Cole asked solicitously. "You've had a nasty shock."

Lola managed a tiny smile. "Thank you, Edward, but no," she replied. "It's not far, and if I am alone I can always claim I took a short walk to clear my head if the police happen to see me." She stood. "I'll be on my way."

Buchanan rose to open the door for her. "I'll be along as soon as I can," he said. "I shall arrive at a respectable remove. Don't worry, my dear: everything will be handled with the utmost discretion."

"Thank you," Lola said. "Once the police have taken the body away, I'll see to the clean-up. No sense in leaving anything for the sensation seekers."

W hen Lola had departed, Cole turned back to his friend.
"I have to admire her spirit," he said. "She's cool in an emergency."

"She's an intelligent woman and a good business partner," Buchanan replied, careful, even in such a situation, to deflect attention from his private life.

But Cole was following his own train of thought. "This won't be the only suicide we hear of today, you mark my words," he said bleakly. "This crash has ruined a lot of people."

"Indeed," Buchanan replied. "But McGill is right: there are opportunities aplenty for the survivors."

"I was thinking more of men like Valentine," Cole said. "Small investors, bankers, brokers, who saw what looked like golden opportunity but could not survive a crash."

"We've had a lucky escape ourselves," Buchanan said thoughtfully. "And we, at least, avoided dealings with the Vatican—I never trusted that bank."

"To put it more precisely, you never trusted O'Hanlon," Cole replied. "With good cause. The man's a menace."

"True," Buchanan said. "But there have been rumours for some time that Valentine was taking bribes from Antonelli: his note confirms it."

"And he got in over his head, poor man," said Cole.

"I don't know about that," Buchanan replied. "He must have known what he was getting into."

"I doubt it," Cole said. "The man was a staunch Catholic: he'd have trusted the Church. His faith makes his suicide doubly shocking."

Buchanan sighed. "I can see O'Hanlon's hand in all of this," he said.

"And you made him a Bishop," Cole said, his voice heavy with disgust. "People who trusted him, like poor Valentine, are ruined. And O'Hanlon will get off scot-free. His sort always does. There's no justice in this world."

"None at all," Buchanan agreed calmly. "We must negotiate our own outcomes, as best we can."

Chapter 79

The morning of Monday 22nd of September dawned bright and clear. George Train was fiddling with his paperwork, but Ferguson and Hector were enjoying the scenery as they completed their long journey into New York. They arrived at Grand Central Station at midday.

The press was waiting. The minute Train was recognised on the crowded platform he was mobbed by reporters shouting questions.

Ferguson took Hector by the arm. "We'll leave him to it," he said under his breath. "No sense us getting involved. We'll collect our luggage—we're bound to catch up with him later at the hotel." He shrugged. "Train has booked us all into the Windsor Hotel on Fifth Avenue: it's only recently opened, and is reputed to be the best hotel in the city."

"That's George Train," Hector laughed. "Nothing but the best."

"It's a fortunate coincidence," Ferguson said, looking faintly embarrassed. "My mother is staying there too. Her telegraph message said she is combining a shopping expedition with the chance to catch up with me."

"Your mother is here?" Hector said. "How wonderful."

"I sent her our itinerary," Ferguson said. "She's a resourceful woman: when she learned I would be coming she simply decided to meet me here in New York."

"I like her already," Hector replied.

"I'd appreciate it if you'd make yourself scarce when we get to the hotel, while I take Mother to lunch," Ferguson said. "She and I have family matters to discuss."

"About Charlotte?"

Ferguson was taken aback. "You know?" he said.

"She told me," Hector replied.

"Does everybody in Melbourne know by now?"

"Certainly not. Charlotte told me in confidence. She won't say a word to anyone else." Hector hesitated. "She's really quite pleased, you know," he added.

Ferguson nodded. "Thanks for telling me," he said. "It was one hell of a way for her to find out, poor girl." He shrugged. "It was one hell of a shock for me, too. Clara didn't exactly make it easy for any of us."

"I can imagine," Hector replied, suddenly worrying about how Clara would react to the news of his own burgeoning relationship with her daughter.

Hector was glad of the opportunity to be alone. He spent the afternoon exploring the city and delivering Buchanan's commissions. His reception everywhere was the same: Hector was thanked for his time, offered coffee, told politely that no decisions could possibly be made before the stock market reopened—and who knew when that might be? Business had shut up shop, holding its collective breath. Hector had not expected anything else; nevertheless, he discharged his duties punctiliously. At the end of the day he went to the telegraph office to send updates to Buchanan, and was relieved to receive a sheaf of messages from home: the congratulations and thanks from McGill, Cole and Buchanan gratified him; but it was the message from Charlotte that warmed his heart. He was still smiling as he finally returned to his room to change for dinner.

George Train had engaged a private dining room at The Windsor, and was delighted to meet Ferguson's elegant, charming mother. The four of them sat down to a splendid meal, where, by unspoken consent, the talk was mostly limited to social pleasantries.

Train at last began to relax. "You'll have to cut your stay short, now," he said to Ferguson.

"Yes," Ferguson replied. "The stock market is closed. Hector has delivered his commissions, but he cannot transact any business."

"We are still engaged to meet with Captain Ericsson tomorrow morning," Hector said.

"The famous engineer?" Mrs Ferguson asked.

"Yes indeed," Hector replied. "Do you know him?"

"Not personally," Mrs Ferguson said. "I only know what I have heard: that the way he has been treated by the government that he helped to preserve is totally outrageous."

"Oh?" said Ferguson, scenting scandal.

"Ericsson has never been paid," she explained. "It's common knowledge, in certain circles, that the American government took advantage of his inventions, and left him to foot the bill."

"That's too bad," Hector said.

"I can't imagine ironclad warships come cheap," said Ferguson.

"They certainly don't," said Train. "And I too have heard that Ericsson has been left high and dry over the matter of costs. It's disgraceful! I'm a great admirer of his work. The man is a genius when it comes to new technologies—our mutual friend, Edward Cole, is very excited about Ericsson's latest inventions reported in the scientific journals, particularly the Sun Engine. Cole thinks it could revolutionize our manufacturing industries. I trust you will pass on my warm regards to Captain Ericsson when you meet him."

"Of course," said Hector. "It will be my pleasure."

"It's the Sun Engine we're meeting Ericsson to discuss," Ferguson said. "Our consortium hopes he will build it in Victoria. We'll see if anything comes of it."

"In that case, I beg you will not forget your friends," said Train. "After these past few days, I find that I'm in need of new investments."

Ferguson smiled. "I never forget my friends," he said. "Don't worry, George—you'll be the first to know if things get interesting."

"I mean it, Charles," Train said. "If you can persuade Ericsson to help your consortium, I can guarantee American investors for the project."

"Even after the events of yesterday?" Mrs Ferguson asked. "The newspapers are all calling the market crash *The Great Panic*."

Train pulled a face. "Newspapers are prone to exaggeration," he said.

"But surely the events *are* catastrophic," Mrs Ferguson countered. "The banks have closed their doors. Businesses are failing. People everywhere have lost their life savings."

"Even so, ma'am," Train replied. "The investment market is a strange beast, but I can assure you I know very well how to ride it."

Mrs Ferguson was unconvinced. "Then I wish you joy of it," she said sharply.

Hector tried to smooth things over. "Does that mean you'll be coming back to Victoria, Mr Train?" he asked.

Train shrugged. "Who knows?" he said. "It's unlikely, but it's not impossible."

Ferguson leaned back in his chair, swirling the wine in his glass, considering. "It's far too soon to tell how things will play out," he said. "But, to answer your question about our departure, George, there will be some small amount of organisation for us to attend to. But after that, Hector and I should be on our way. I'm quite anxious to discover what the effect of all of this will be in Britain."

"I can tell you what will happen," Train replied, his expression grim. "The Empire will fall—it's a foregone conclusion. It was already struggling: this last year has been one long sad story of strikes, mutinies and foreclosures.

JANEEN WEBB AND ANDREW ENSTICE

The British economy simply can't survive now—the remaining banks were already over-extended. You'll be lucky to manage to transact any business there at all."

346

Chapter 80

The momentous decision to make a bid for Independence had been taken: Buchanan no longer hesitated. He met immediately with John Sinisgalli, engaging the lawyer's help to phrase the Petition correctly. By the end of the day, the form of words had been hammered out. It read:

> *A PETITION*
>
> *To the Members of the Legislative Assembly of the Colony of Victoria:*
>
> *Whereas the recent events in Great Britain, Her Imperial Dominions, and other Nations, have rendered impracticable the assurance of Imperial assistance to the Colony of Victoria in time of need; and the Colony of Victoria having grown in stature, wealth and confidence sufficient that it now exercises in all but name the power and dignity of an independent Nation, and stands ready to take its rightful place among the Nations of the world:*
>
> *We, the undersigned, Residents of the Colony of Victoria, earnestly pray your Honourable Assembly to submit to Her Imperial Majesty Queen Victoria, her Ministers and Representatives, a Declaration of Independence by the Assembly of Victoria on behalf of its People; said declaration to be subject solely to the will of the People as represented by the Assembly, and not to any outside Power.*

"We need that final sentence," Sinisgalli said. "In 1855, Britain kept the right to veto our legislation, so the real power stayed firmly in its hands." He grinned. "When this has been printed, I hope you'll allow me to be the first to sign. This will be the most important document the Parliament has ever received. I'd like my name to be there, for my children, for all posterity."

"I appreciate the sentiment, Mr Sinisgalli," Buchanan replied. "I'll need you to check the first copies, in any case. I'd be delighted if you'd put your name to it."

"It will be an honour," Sinisgalli replied.

Chapter 81

Edward Cole, enthusiastic and energetic, had copies of the Petition printed the very next day. He also printed posters and handbills for the public meeting, which he planned to hold in the Town Hall on Saturday afternoon. In the matter of publicity Cole had excelled himself. The posters that now appeared all over the city were positively lurid, depicting a drowning England clinging to a struggling Victoria, dragging the colony down towards certain death. One of the *Punch* cartoonists had drawn the poster: there was no mistaking the threat it depicted.

Cole was attending to his correspondence in his office when a policeman rapped sharply on the door and walked in, uninvited.

"Sorry, sir," Cole's secretary said, peering around the constable's broad back. "I couldn't stop him, sir. He just barged in."

Cole looked up from his desk. "That's quite all right, Timothy," he said. "Is there a problem, Officer?"

"I'm Constable Bellamy, and I'm here on official business, sir," the man replied. "I'm here to deliver this, sir." He held out a cream-coloured envelope. "I was instructed to hand it to you, sir, personally like."

Cole accepted the letter, noting the official seal of the Mayor of Melbourne on the flap. "Thank you, Constable Bellamy," he said. "Do you require a reply?"

"I need you to sign for it, sir." Bellamy unfolded a sheet of paper from his top pocket.

"Of course." Cole glanced at the document, and then dipped his pen into the silver inkwell on his desk and scribbled a signature. "Thank you again, Constable," he said. "My clerk will show you out."

When Bellamy had gone, Cole slit the envelope and sat back to read the Mayor's letter. A worried frown creased his usually cheerful face. He ran his fingers through his blond curls, and read the letter twice. A minute later he was on his feet, reaching for his coat.

349

"I have to go out, Timothy," was all he said to his puzzled assistant.

Cole headed straight for the American Consulate, and Wilson the butler directed him to the conservatory, where McGill was taking morning tea with his wife.

"Edward, what a lovely surprise," Morag said. "Do come in. Your timing is excellent, as always. Would you care for a cup of tea?"

"Thank you, no," Cole said. He turned to McGill. "I'm afraid I'm the bearer of bad news." He handed the Mayor's letter to McGill. "See for yourself."

"Whatever is the matter, Edward?" Morag asked, her face a picture of concern. "What's the letter about?"

"It's from Mr John Thomas Smith, the Mayor," McGill replied. "He has banned us from using the Town Hall for Saturday's meeting."

"Can he do that?"

"Indeed he can, my dear," said McGill. "His letter states that he fears the meeting will incite public unrest. He is exercising his legal authority, as Mayor, to prevent such potentially unlawful use of City property."

"It's nonsense, of course," Cole said wearily. "But I own I was a fool to think that the authorities would not fight back with whatever weapons are at their disposal."

"And this particular Mayor has spent a lot of time ingratiating himself with the Governor," McGill said. "He'll want to show his establishment patrons that he is a reliable servant."

"True," said Cole. "I'm afraid this is just the opening round."

"But not one that men like Smith can be allowed to win," said McGill. "It won't be hard to change the venue."

"But the posters are already printed and distributed," Cole said.

"Can you print up a change of venue notice? One that can be pasted over the original?"

"Certainly."

"Then we'll have our volunteers put them up everywhere. We'll put signs around the Melbourne Town Hall and make sure some of our people are there to redirect anyone who turns up."

"But redirect them to *where*? We need to book another venue, and quickly. That may not be easy at such short notice."

"May I make a suggestion?" said Morag.

"Of course," said Cole.

"Why don't you hire the Princess Theatre in Spring Street? It's huge, and it won't be in use in the daytime."

"Capital idea!" said Cole. "Magnificent! My friend George Coppin owns it, and he is most sympathetic to the Independence movement. He's standing for Parliament, you know, right here in East Melbourne. I'm sure he'll be amenable to our using The Princess." He grinned. "Better yet, the theatre is right opposite Parliament House."

"That will certainly focus the attention of the authorities," McGill said. "We'll hold the meeting right on their doorstep."

"Mayor Smith will hate that," Cole said.

"I do hope so," said Morag. "He's an odious man. He has been unspeakably rude to Lola."

"Quite so." Cole made to stand. "I'll go at once to see Coppin," he said. "His house is not far."

"Let Wilson go," McGill said. "And allow me to make it an official request. I'm sure the Consulate will be delighted to foot the bill."

Cole smiled. "Thank you, James," he said. "Wilson can use my carriage. I'll wait here."

McGill rang for Wilson, and issued rapid instructions.

"It will be my very great pleasure to arrange it for you, sir," Wilson said. "I shall return as quickly as I may."

Cole finally began to relax. "Perhaps I'll have that cup of tea after all," he said.

"And may I tempt you to a slice of seed cake?" said Morag.

"I think I've earned a piece of cake this morning," said Cole.

"Indeed you have, Edward," said McGill. "And now, you and I can take the opportunity to talk tactics while Wilson sees to the venue."

McGill and Cole were still deep in discussion when Wilson returned.

"I've spoken to Mr Coppin, sir," he said. "Mr Coppin sends his compliments, and wishes to advise that he is delighted to offer the use of the Princess Theatre for the Independence meeting."

"That's wonderful news," Cole said.

"Indeed, sir," said Wilson. "Mr Coppin also wishes me to tell you that he will attend in person, and hopes that there will be an opportunity for him to speak."

"Better and better," said Cole. "A number of Lower House MPs have already offered to join us. I shall write to Coppin at once."

"Is there something else, Wilson?" McGill asked.

"One small thing, sir," Wilson replied. "Mr Coppin regrets that, for legal reasons, he cannot offer the venue free of charge."

"I wouldn't have expected him to do that," McGill said.

"No, sir." Wilson permitted himself a small smile. "Mr Coppin set the fee at one penny, sir. I've taken the liberty of paying the rent in advance."

"Well done, Wilson," Cole said. "That was very well done indeed."

"Thank you, sir." Wilson was still smiling as he left the room.

Chapter 82

ector Munro's meeting with Captain John Ericsson took place next day,
September 23rd, in the inventor's workshop down by the New York docks.
Ericsson was a large man, big-boned and broad-shouldered, standing some
inches taller than Hector.

"Mr Ferguson, Mr Munro: welcome," Ericsson said formally, his Swedish
accent still pronounced, even after half a lifetime in America. "I've been
expecting you. Won't you come inside?"

Hector gazed about him in amazement as they entered: there were benches
supporting strange-looking glass apparatus and littered with tools, there were
plans and drawings pinned to every wall, copper wires snaked across the
window sills, and fine metal shavings crunched underfoot on the floor. The air
produced an odd, chemical feeling at the back of Hector's throat. He reached
towards one of the stands.

"Don't touch anything," Ericsson said sharply. "My inventions are finely
calibrated."

"Sorry," Hector said. "It's just that this is all so interesting."

"And expensive," Ericsson said shortly. He cleared some paperwork away
and brushed off a couple of chairs, inviting his guests to sit. "Now," he said,
"with your permission we'll get straight to business. I'm a busy man."

"I can see that," Hector replied.

"You are here to discuss my Sun Engine," Ericsson continued. "I have
been corresponding with Mr Cole, as you know. I had a further telegram from
him just yesterday: it appears your consortium is most anxious to engage my
services. I warn you, I don't come cheap."

"When you get paid at all, that is," Ferguson drawled, settling himself
more comfortably.

Ericsson bridled. "And what would you know about my affairs?" he asked.

"My mother told us about your problems last night," Ferguson continued.
"She travelled to New York to meet me at the Windsor Hotel. When your

name came up in passing at dinner, she said that it's a great scandal that the United States government hasn't ever paid you for developing its warships, and isn't ever likely to."

"It seems your mother knows a great deal about me," Ericsson said sharply.

Ferguson shrugged. "My family is very well connected," he replied.

"Apparently so," Ericsson replied. He seemed to lose a little of his brusque demeanour.

"There'll be no chance of recovering whatever is owed you now," Ferguson continued, pressing his advantage. "The stock market has crashed, and the banks are failing. The American government has no money to pay its debts, or to finance new developments, if it comes to that."

"So much is clear already," Ericsson said.

"But we aren't here to talk about that," Hector cut in. "We're here to discuss Sir Alec's invitation for you to join us in Australia, to build your Sun Engine. We are all very excited about it."

Ericsson brightened a little. "How far has your project advanced?"

"The buildings to house the new copper refining process are well underway. We expect to be ready to begin installing machinery by the end of the year."

"And you want me to develop my Sun Engine to crush the ore?"

"That would be just the beginning," Hector said, almost stumbling over his words in his enthusiasm. "Mr Cole thinks you could develop it much further than that—he's already contacting the craftsmen who make automata so that he can provide you with whatever precision tools you might need. You'll have any amount of copper at your disposal, and the means to craft it into whatever you wish."

"Encouraging," Ericsson conceded. He pulled a sheaf of letters and telegrams from a drawer. "It says here," he said, "that you would agree to provide me with suitable accommodation, workshops and equipment."

"Yes," said Hector.

"And that I would have complete control of developing my inventions."

"Of course," Hector replied. "Those things are already agreed."

"It's a whole new opportunity to pursue your interests," Ferguson put in. "All we need is for you to agree to come: we'll undertake to arrange the rest."

"I'll admit I'm disillusioned by the way I've been treated here," Ericsson conceded. "But how do I know that your consortium will behave any better than the United States government?"

"We can only give you our word on it," Hector replied. "We won't cheat you."

"That's what they said," Ericsson replied, lapsing morosely into silence as he considered his position.

Hector and Ferguson waited.

Hector was trying not to fidget as the silence stretched out. He shifted uncomfortably in his seat, relieved when a blond, blue-eyed boy burst into the room. The child was clearly a replica of his father, raw-boned and ruddy-cheeked.

"Allow me to introduce my son, Karl," Ericsson said, smiling at the boy.

"Good morning, sirs," Karl said obediently.

"And how old are you?" Ferguson asked.

"Fourteen, sir," Karl responded. "Are you really from Australia?"

"Yes, really," Hector answered.

"And are we really going to visit there?"

"You'll have to ask your father," Ferguson replied.

"I would so like to visit Australia," Karl said. "I've read so much about the flora and fauna there. It must be very strange."

Hector smiled. "On the trail where I exercise my horse there are birds with feathers so bright we call them rainbows—rainbow lorikeets, that is; and then there are crimson rosellas and bright green king parrots everywhere."

"Could I see them?" Karl asked.

Ferguson laughed. "You could hardly not see them," he said. "Bright birds are as common as sparrows in Victoria. Even the garden wrens are as blue as the sky."

Karl's face lit up with a wide smile. "I'd like to see that," he said. "And are there many butterflies?"

"Millions of them," Hector said. "So many they haven't all been identified yet."

"Oh!"

Ericsson interrupted: "My son collects specimens," he said.

"So do I," said Hector. "May I see yours, Karl?"

Karl looked to his father for permission.

"Only one or two trays," Ericsson said. "These gentlemen are busy."

Karl headed straight across the cluttered room to stand before a specimen chest. Carefully, he pulled out a shallow drawer to reveal, mounted on thin board, a dozen rows of precisely ordered butterflies—each carefully pinned and neatly labelled. The collection was showcase perfect.

"These are mine, sir," he said solemnly.

Hector was surprised. "That's impressive," he said. "My own aren't nearly so well organised."

Karl beamed.

"My son has a natural talent for these things," said Ericsson.

"So perhaps you should bring him to Australia to further his education," Ferguson said.

"You have me there," Ericsson said. "My son is the main reason that I have been giving serious consideration to your offer. Ever since his mother died, I've worried about his upbringing. Let me ask you, Mr Munro: are there decent schools in Melbourne?"

"I was educated at Scotch College," Hector replied. "It's a fine school. I have no doubt that Sir Alec will arrange for your son to enrol there, if you wish. The school has boarding facilities, so his education will not be interrupted when you are away."

"That would be satisfactory," Ericsson said. He shook his head, as if to clear his thoughts, and lapsed into silence once more. "Well, gentlemen," he said at last. "I have made my decision. It appears we have a deal."

He rose to shake hands with each of them in turn.

"That's wonderful, sir," Hector replied. "I'll inform Sir Alec at once. How soon can you travel?"

"As soon as your consortium has arranged to transport all of my equipment," Ericsson replied, gesturing vaguely at the crowded workshop.

Hector's heart sank.

Ferguson surprised him. "That won't take too long at all," he said to Ericsson. "I can have a team down here to crate up everything you need by the end of the week."

"Then do it," Ericsson said, "before I change my mind." He shrugged. "I'll admit I was having second thoughts," he said, "but the market crash has changed all that: there's not much here for an inventor in the immediate future. It's time I tried something new." He smiled at his son. "Yes, Karl," he said: "we *are* going to Australia."

Chapter 83

On Saturday afternoon of 4th October, the Princess Theatre was full to bursting. Outside, Spring Street was packed with people from all walks of life, people pushing their way into the building, people trying to find vantage points—so many people that they filled the roadway between the theatre and Victoria's Parliament House, standing opposite. Street vendors were doing a roaring trade in cool drinks, and shysters and pickpockets were busily working the crowd.

The police were out in force.

Even before the meeting began, it was clear that the citizens of Melbourne were seriously worried: they wanted to do something, anything, to avert financial disaster. Hundreds had already signed the Petition; dozens of volunteers now carried copies for their workmates to sign. Copies had appeared everywhere, urging signature: on hotel bars, at the ticket offices of railway stations, on the counters of fashionable shops—one copy was displayed prominently on the hall table of The Bohemian Supper Club, and even The Melbourne Club sported a copy on the concierge's desk, despite the disapproval of several prominent members. The tide of public opinion was turning.

The country centres were not forgotten: meetings had already been arranged in Ballarat and Bendigo; the Mayor of Beechworth had offered to convene a meeting himself; a paddle-steamer captain had vowed to carry the Independence Petition to the towns along the Murray River.

Inside the Princess Theatre, the excitement was growing. The holiday mood was giving way to restless anticipation.

When Cole finally ascended the steps to take his place on the stage, ready to speak, he was greeted by loud applause.

Cole tried not to grin. He was enjoying himself immensely. He looked out over the sea of faces that filled the giant auditorium to overflowing. At the back of the hall, the doors were still jammed open by the press of bodies as more people tried to push their way inside from the crowded lobby. Cole glanced down, and saw that there were several influential citizens in the front row beside McGill: he smiled at the Premier, James Francis; at George Coppin, owner of the theatre; and at the lawyer John Sinisgalli, who was applauding vigorously with the rest.

Cole cleared his throat. "My fellow Victorians," he said.

The crowd erupted in a wild roar of approbation.

Cole held up his hand for silence. When the noise died down, he began again.

"My fellow Victorians," he repeated, "we are met here today to address the largest—the only—important question of the moment: are the citizens of this great colony finally to determine their own destiny?"

There were cries of "Yes!" and "About time!" from the back of the hall, and a few boos, clearly orchestrated. The objectors were immediately heckled and jostled by the people around them.

Cole held up his hand again. "Gentlemen, please!" he shouted. "Let's not descend into vulgarity. The matter at hand is far too important for that!" He took a sip of water, giving the crowd a moment to settle before he continued. "Some of you here today will recall, as I do, the events of almost twenty years ago at the Eureka Stockade—when a group of very brave men prepared to lay down their lives in the pursuit of justice and liberty. Among them was my old friend, James McGill—sitting here today in the front row."

McGill stood to acknowledge the cheers and catcalls from the crowd.

"At Eureka," Cole continued, "Captain McGill and his California Rangers supported the miners who fought for common justice. But today, *Consul* McGill is here to represent the support of his great nation, the United States of America, for our right and just cause."

More cheers interrupted Cole's speech.

"I trust he won't labour the point," McGill murmured as he resumed his seat beside Premier Francis. "I'm sticking my neck out just being here."

"I'm sure everything will be fine," Francis replied.

Cole, oblivious to McGill's discomfort, resumed. "My friends," he said, "the miners who fell at Eureka did not die in vain. The British Empire granted the Constitution upon which our current liberties are founded. Those of you who are now entitled to vote can thank those fallen men for the privilege. But," and here Cole smacked his right fist into the palm of his left hand for emphasis, "make no mistake: it is a privilege, not a right!" He paused to sip again at his water, letting that thought sink into the minds of his audience. "When our Constitution was framed," he continued, "democracy was not the concern of the men who wrote it. Indeed, you might well be forgiven for thinking that the reverse was true. A Legislative Assembly frames the laws, but these laws must then be approved by an Upper House—a Legislative

Council that represents the interests of our British overlords, and the squatters who support them. And beyond them there is an Imperial veto."

"Shame!" a man called from the back of the hall.

"Get on with it!" another shouted. "I didn't come here for a history lesson. What about our Independence?"

The crowd erupted into competing cries of agreement and dissent.

"Indeed," Cole said, pitching his voice above the noise, "as my rather rowdy friend reminds us, Independence is the key question. So what about Independence? What has history to do with the choice that faces us here today?" He looked around at the crowd. "Well, my fellow Victorians, let me remind you that the final approval or rejection of our call for Independence rests not with us here today, or even with the representatives we have elected to speak for us—many of whom, including our Premier, are here to address you today."

He paused, while Premier James Francis rose briefly to acknowledge the crowd.

"No, my friends," Cole continued, "the final decision rests with that same Upper House which was only ever intended to curb the democratic temper of our times. Across the road from this very theatre, in Parliament House, sit many men whose only interest is self-interest. Men who will oppose to the bitter end any move to Independence; men whose driving fear is the loss of their considerable privileges and power should we succeed in separating ourselves from the Empire." He sipped from his water glass again. "Indeed," he added, "if you take a good hard look at the Parliament building, you'll notice it has gun embrasures on the lower level—cannon installed after the Eureka uprising to protect those same men in case of any further trouble from the likes of us!"

"Outrageous!" someone shouted.

At the front of the auditorium, heads nodded in agreement.

At the back, a knot of uniformed police began to make their way forward. They pushed, they shoved, and occasionally they wielded truncheons. Behind them, they left a very angry mob.

Some of the mob began to chant: "Shame! Shame! Shame!"

McGill turned to Premier Francis. "Can't you do something?" he said. "The last thing we want is a riot."

Francis shrugged. "I can't intervene," he said. "They'll have their orders."

"And the President of the Legislative Council will be behind it, no doubt," McGill replied.

"William Mitchell," said Francis. "Now there's a man who doesn't care about due process."

The police, increasingly hot and flustered, were slowly getting closer.

Cole speeded up his speech, suddenly aware of the disturbance, and of the advancing constabulary.

"In Victoria today," he shouted, "we live in the richest colony on earth. But even we are not immune to the vagaries of international markets. The world trembles on the brink of economic collapse. The mighty British Empire is failing. Do we want to be dragged down with it?"

"No! Never!" the crowd responded. "No!"

The uniformed police edged closer.

Cole could hardly be heard now above the increasing noise. "Finders," he yelled, "should be Keepers! I ask you, fellow Victorians, would you rather be subjects of a failing Empire, or citizens of the wealthiest new nation on earth?" He was losing his voice: he gathered his reserves for one last shout. "We need Independence, and we need it now! It's time!"

The police reached the front of the theatre.

Cole stepped back to acknowledge the rapturous cheers of the crowd before he finally scrambled down from the stage.

The police were waiting—a dozen or so sweating, blue-uniformed men, armed with heavy truncheons. A senior constable stepped forward, clutching a piece of rolled parchment.

Several of Cole's supporters also deliberately moved forward, ready for trouble.

Cole waved them aside. "It's all right," he said. "Constable Bellamy, isn't it?" His smile was genial. "Have you come to join our cause?"

"Not exactly, sir." Bellamy looked slightly embarrassed.

"Well, then," Cole said, "what seems to be the trouble?"

"I'm sorry, sir." Bellamy looked nervously over his shoulder at the milling, excited crowd. "I have here a warrant for your arrest."

"What?"

John Sinisgalli moved smoothly to intercept the warrant. He leaned across to whisper in Cole's ear. "Let me handle this," he said. He turned to Bellamy. "I'll take that, Constable, if you please."

"And who are you?"

"I am Mr John Sinisgalli, Constable, and I have the honour to be Mr Cole's legal counsel. I shall speak for him in this matter."

"Oh," said Bellamy. "I still have to arrest him, sir."

"On what charge?"

"It's in this paper, sir."

"Give it here, then." Sinisgalli unrolled the document, reading swiftly. His expression was grim. "It appears that you are being arrested on a charge of seditious libel, Mr Cole. It's a serious indictment."

Cole shook his head. "Sedition?" he said. "On what grounds?"

"On the grounds that the petitions and posters that you have caused to be printed are calculated to excite disturbances in the Colony of Victoria," Sinisgalli said.

"I see," said Cole. "What happens now?"

"You have to accompany me to the police station, sir," said Bellamy.

"It would be best if we can do this quietly, Constable," Sinisgalli said. "You won't need the help of your colleagues over there." He gestured towards the waiting men. "We really don't want to start a riot."

"No," said Cole. "We most certainly don't. A riot is exactly what this police action is designed to provoke."

"Indeed it is," said Sinisgalli. He sighed. "Any disturbance over your arrest today will simply act to prove the case for the Prosecution."

"My thought exactly," said Cole.

Premier Francis had to push his way through the crowd to reach his friend. "May I be of assistance, Mr Cole?" he asked. He stared hard at Bellamy. "I've met this constable before, I think."

"Yes, sir," said Bellamy. "At Parliament House, sir."

"Then you know who I am."

"Yes, sir."

"It's all right, Mr Premier," Cole said quickly. "A small misunderstanding that needs to be ironed out." He gave Francis a straight look. "If you would be so kind as to continue the proceedings here, Mr Sinisgalli and I will take care of this other matter."

Francis took the hint. "Of course," he said. "There are other MPs waiting to speak. I shall be happy to direct the rest of this event."

"Thank you," said Cole. He turned back to the waiting police. "Lead on, Bellamy," he said. "The sooner we get to the police station, the sooner Mr Sinisgalli can arrange for my bail."

"Thank you, sir," Bellamy said, his relief showing plainly on his young, freckled face. "If you'll follow me, sir."

Cole was escorted from the theatre to the sound of loud cheering as Premier Francis ascended the stage to address the crowd.

The meeting was proceeding. The riot had been averted.

Cole chanced to look up at Parliament House—only to see Mayor Smith standing there on the steps, arms crossed, to observe the arrest. Mayor Smith smirked, not bothering to hide his pleasure.

"Don't react," Sinisgalli murmured. "At least we know who's behind your arrest."

Cole sighed. "I never doubted it for a minute," he said. "I warned McGill that Mayor Smith was beginning a dirty tricks campaign."

"Two can play at that game," said Sinisgalli.

"Whatever do you mean?"

"Lawyers hear a lot of things," Sinisgalli replied enigmatically. "Let's just concentrate on getting through the next part of this little charade, shall we?"

Chapter 84

McGill and Morag were sharing breakfast in the Consulate Conservatory: coffee, eggs and bacon for him, tea and toast for her. The room was warm with morning sunlight, lightly scented with the perfume of the potted tiger lilies and the Australian bush orchids that Morag nurtured among the more conventional parlour palms. Just outside the long window she had installed a wrought-iron birdhouse in the shape of an elaborate Chinese pagoda: this morning, a family of eastern rosellas with their gold and red and green plumage vied with their bigger blue and crimson cousins for a share of the crumbs with which the cook had just refilled the feeding tray. Beyond them, a flash of yellow, black and white stripes announced that the garden's New Holland honeyeaters were visiting the blossoming fuchsias.

"I always like this part of the day best," Morag said, happily spreading strawberry jam on her toast. "It's the only time we really have to ourselves."

McGill set aside the newspaper he had been reading.

"Was there anything interesting?" Morag asked.

"The papers are full of the news of Cole's arrest," McGill said. "There's a lot of speculation about the possible outcomes of his impending trial."

"Poor Edward," said Morag. "I am so dreadfully worried about him. It's a good thing that Mr Sinisgalli was there at the time to defend him."

"Indeed it was, my dear," McGill said. "Sinisgalli saw the situation for what it was—an attempt to provoke a public disturbance. His quick action almost certainly prevented a nasty brawl that would have played straight into the hands of the authorities. And Sinisgalli moved swiftly to arrange bail. The magistrate set it very high, but Cole has deep pockets. Buchanan has also offered to stand surety, so that side of things is taken care of."

"Well, that's a relief. I'd hate to see Edward in financial difficulties just for standing up for what he believes in."

"Quite so," said McGill. "But if the authorities thought that arresting Cole would silence debate, they couldn't have been more wrong. His arrest has served only to fuel the fires of debate." He tapped his pile of newspapers. "Arguments—for and against—are raging in *The Argus* and *The Age*, but no matter what political agendas are discussed, it's economics that is exercising the minds of the worthy citizens of Victoria. Mark my words, my dear: this movement is all about money."

"I know," said Morag. "It's like a new kind of gold fever in the colony. Everyone is using the new slogan: *Finders Keepers*. Little signs are popping up everywhere with just those two words: *Finders Keepers*. That's a good thing, don't you think?"

"Probably." McGill sighed. "But Cole's trial could still go either way—Judge Redmond Barry is hearing the case himself."

"Judge Barry?" said Morag. "That's dreadful news. He's the one who manipulated a jury into finding poor Henry Seekamp guilty of sedition, and that ended so *very* badly for all concerned. And now Edward is charged with the same crime, before the same judge."

"More or less," McGill agreed. "Barry is a very staunch defender of the *status quo*," he said, "but Buchanan tells me the judge is also increasingly volatile—it is possible that his theatrics will alienate a jury. I'm told that's what happened when the Eureka miners were acquitted."

"Then let's hope it happens again," Morag said. "It seems to me that Edward was unfortunately all too accurate when he said that the authorities would use whatever means they could to block the Independence movement. The Mayor tried to stop the meeting, and when that failed, the police charged Edward with sedition. He's been ordered to stop printing those posters."

"We have to expect opposition," McGill said mildly. "No public cause, great or small, ever succeeded unopposed."

"I expect you're right," said Morag. "But I do worry about Edward. And I worry about you too, my love. You're heavily involved in all of this."

McGill decided to change the subject. He turned to the paper's social pages. "I notice O'Hanlon has announced he is extending the Orphanage in Ballarat," he said.

"That horrible man is always in the news," Morag said. "He makes my skin crawl. I don't trust him an inch, and he certainly should not be allowed anywhere near children."

"I don't imagine he will be," McGill replied. "It'll be business as usual for O'Hanlon—the nuns will do the work, and he will take the credit."

"In this case, I hope you're right," Morag replied. She sighed. "It seems there's trouble everywhere—but at least things are peaceful enough here this morning."

"Don't speak too soon," McGill replied, seeing Wilson approaching with a small salver.

"This just arrived, sir," Wilson said. "I thought you'd want to see it right away."

"Thank you," McGill replied, smiling ruefully at his wife. His expression changed as he read the message. "It's from Ulysses Grant," he said.

"Good gracious," said Morag. "The President himself: whatever is the matter?"

"He's read my reports," McGill replied. "He confirms America's support for Independence here in Victoria."

"Sir Alec will be relieved," Morag said. "That's very good news."

"Yes," McGill said. "I can go to the next public meeting with the President's personal guarantee of uninterrupted supply."

"There's something else, isn't there?"

"I'm afraid so, my love. President Grant has extended my tenure here as Consul for a further five years: he requests that I oversee our American interests as the transition takes place." He looked earnestly across at Morag. "Will you mind terribly?" he asked.

Morag smiled. "Of course not, James," she said. "You are doing something very important, for all of us." She reached out and took his hand. "And besides," she said, "our home is very beautiful, and we are happy here."

McGill smiled back. "We are," he said, "and thank you."

"That's settled, then."

"It will be hard on Rosie, though," McGill said. "I really don't like to be away from her for such a long time."

"We could have her here," Morag said promptly. "We have plenty of room."

McGill looked thoughtful. "That would be wonderful," he said. "But she's only nine—she can hardly travel alone, and my mother isn't well enough to make the journey with her."

"And Hector is heading across the Atlantic to England," Morag said.

McGill laughed. "Hector could hardly take a child where he and Ferguson have to go: it will be dangerous enough for two grown men."

"I know," Morag said. "I worry about him."

"He'll be fine," McGill said. "He's done exceptionally well so far."

Morag sighed, returning her attention to the more immediate problem of her husband's child. "Could we ask that new engineer, Ericsson, to escort her?" she said. "Edward Cole tells me that Ericsson will undertake the voyage from New York to Melbourne soon, and he's bringing his young son with him. He might be amenable to the idea."

"It still wouldn't be proper," McGill replied. "A little girl can't be expected to travel with a man and a boy."

"Then we could hire a nurse," Morag replied. "Your daughter will be travelling first class: perhaps the steamship company can recommend someone suitable? If Rosie takes the same ship as Ericsson, we could hire a nurse for both of the children—surely he'd appreciate that."

"And we could then reasonably ask Ericsson to oversee the arrangement," McGill said. "That might work."

Morag beamed at him. "I'm sure it would work," she said.

"In that case, I'll telegraph Mother to ask her opinion," McGill said.

"Hadn't you better reply to your President?"

"That too," McGill said, smiling again at last.

Chapter 85

By the close of business on September 24th, Hector had completed the commissions that were still possible for Buchanan. His discussions with the New York agent who had provided engineers for the telegraph project had been very successful.

"Sir Alec will be pleased," he told Ferguson when they met for lunch. "Mr Delaney was quite keen to assure me that he can supply as many technicians as we need. He says that there are a great many engineers who have remained unemployed after the end of the Civil War, and the stock market crash will only make things worse for them. He says they'll be more than willing to take ship for Australia, especially as the consortium will bear the cost of their passage."

"Good result," Ferguson said. "And I, for my part, have arranged for the removal of Ericsson's effects."

"I can't believe you did it so quickly," Hector said.

"It was lucky Mother was here," Ferguson replied. "Her family owns several shipping concerns here in New York. It was a simple matter to have one of them send a team to have Ericsson's goods packed into crates."

"Ericsson says he'll be ready to leave by the end of the month," Hector said. "His passage can be booked by telegraph."

"Then there's nothing to keep us here any longer," Ferguson said.

"What about your mother?"

"We've said all that needs saying," Ferguson replied. "It was good to see her again. And she's actually quite pleased to find she has a granddaughter. She insists she will write to Charlotte to welcome her to the family."

Hector laughed. "I'd like to be a fly on the wall if she ever meets Clara."

Ferguson pulled a face. "In that event, I'd be planning to be as far away as possible," he replied, with some feeling.

Chapter 86

ector and Ferguson booked first class passage to cross the Atlantic to Liverpool aboard the Ocean Steamer *Massachusetts* for the following evening, the 25th September. The morning was taken up with errands, but by late afternoon they were on their way at last.

"I'll just make one last stop at the telegraph office," Hector said. "I want to check in case Sir Alec has sent any last-minute instructions for our arrival in Liverpool."

"Sure," Ferguson replied. "We've just about got time."

In contrast to yesterday's handful of messages, today the clerk handed Hector a single slip of paper.

Hector read and re-read the telegram, shaking his head in disbelief.

"What's up?" Ferguson asked.

"The Consortium has voted me a parcel of shares," Hector said. "They've offered me a partnership."

Ferguson clapped him on the back. "So they bloody well should," he said. "You saved all of their miserable hides. Congratulations."

"Thanks," Hector said, still dazed.

"Well," said Ferguson, looking up at the clock on the wall of the telegraph office, "time and tide and all that: our ship sails soon, and we can't leave here until you've sent your acceptance. You'd better do it."

"Right," said Hector. "I'll do it now."

hen they reached the impressive steamer dock, they picked their way through the chaos of embarkation, located their stateroom with its twin bunks and clean, economical appointments, and betook themselves back on deck for a last look at the city. All manner of people milled about, settling their last-minute arrangements. Finally, a bell sounded, and a steward walked the ship, calling "All Ashore", an announcement that prompted a final flurry of leave-takings—some in smiles and laughter, some in silence and tears. When the last visitors had left the ship, the great engines roared into life: the water at the stern became a whirlpool of boiling foam, the parting gun was fired, and the last lines were cast off. The sun was setting as the huge, hulking, smoke-belching steamship slipped down the Hudson River, and Hector bade farewell to New York.

"I never got to explore nearly enough of it," he said to Ferguson.

"Next time," Ferguson replied. "I have no doubt you'll be back before long."

The crossing took ten days. The steamer hugged the coast until it reached Newfoundland and headed into open water. Ferguson spent most of his time chatting easily with other passengers in the main saloon, a large chamber that served the purpose of parlour, study, dining room and drawing room for those hardy souls not confined to their cabins by seasickness. He was, as always, a great hit with the ladies, whiling away the hours flirting outrageously with one pretty widow in particular.

In the gaps between the five meals that constituted the daily routine of the steamer—breakfast, luncheon, dinner, tea and supper—and when the weather permitted, Hector preferred to walk the decks. Despite the raw winds, he preferred the fresh air to the warm fug of the saloon. He watched the sparkle of sunlight on the waves, allowing his mind to drift into pleasant imaginings of his future: now that he had a partnership, he had something substantial to offer Charlotte.

And if Ferguson, on occasion, failed to sleep in his own bunk, Hector affected not to notice.

Chapter 87

Clara's editorial in *The New Day* led with the headline: "Independence: Now or Never". Fired up once again by the prospect of political freedom, she wrote:

It has come to the attention of this writer that plans are afoot to Petition the Parliament of Victoria to declare this Colony's Independence from England. To those of us who remember the Eureka Stockade, the question of whether we need Independence hardly needs to be asked: good men fought and died there for the ideal of freedom from our oppressive masters. It is true that some small gains have been made, but we are still under the yoke. We know that the world economic situation is dire: if we stay tied to Britain, we will be doomed to extinction—Britain will take all of our resources, and leave us with nothing but the scraps from our own table: our businesses will fail, our menfolk will lose their employment, and all to prop up our masters on the other side of the world.

We cannot yet vote, Ladies, but we can sign a Petition. I urge you, for the sake of your children, for the sake of all of us, sign the Petition: say YES to Independence. It is high time we cut the apron strings and stood up for ourselves. We have a bright future, here in this new land, if only we are brave enough to seize it and make it our own. We need Independence, and we need it now.

Chapter 88

Bishop Francis O'Hanlon took another long pull from his silver hip flask as he stared at the accounts ledger spread out before him on his leather-topped desk. His tastefully panelled study was strewn with paperwork: dozens of telegraph messages had slipped from plush chairs and onto the red and blue Turkey rug. The place was a mess. The financial situation had gone from bad to worse, and O'Hanlon's masters at the Vatican were not disposed towards forgiveness where their money was concerned.

A sharp knock at the door roused this morose Prince of the Church from his reverie. He looked up.

"Come!"

Mrs Lafferty, the housekeeper, bustled into the room carrying a tray. "I've brought your morning tea, Your Grace," she said, "and this morning's post." She sniffed, frowned disapprovingly at the silver flask, and looked around her in dismay. "I'll be right back," she said.

Before O'Hanlon could object, Mrs Lafferty had marched out of the room, deposited the tray on a chair in the hall, and returned to clear a space on a cedar side-table. She bustled out again, re-entering a minute later to set out the tea things and a plate of fresh-baked shortbread dusted with sparkling sugar. Beside it she placed a small pile of letters and papers.

"There," she said. "That's better. Shall I open a window, Your Grace? It reeks in here."

"No, Mrs Lafferty," O'Hanlon said. "That will be all." He ran his bony fingers through his thinning, mousey hair. "Close the door on your way out. I'm busy. I do not wish to be disturbed."

"Very well, Your Grace." Mrs Lafferty's black skirts rustled accusingly as she swept, straight-backed, out of the room, radiating disapproval. She closed the door hard, not quite slamming it behind her. There was no love lost between the worthy women of Ballarat and their new Bishop.

"Bloody interfering woman," O'Hanlon muttered. He added a slug of Irish whiskey to his tea and picked up a piece of shortbread. He bit, and crumbs scattered onto his post. "Damn," he said, brushing bits of biscuit onto the carpet.

A slim magazine slid from the pile to join the telegraph slips on the rug.

There was another tap at the door and a plump, middle-aged priest entered the study.

"Good morning, Your Grace. Mrs Lafferty said I should come straight on in," he said cheerfully. "She said there's fresh tea in the pot. May I?" He picked up a cup.

"Help yourself, O'Brien," O'Hanlon said sourly.

"Thanks." Father O'Brien, moon-faced and amiable, did not need to be asked twice. He poured tea, added milk and three sugars, balanced two pieces of shortbread on the saucer, and looked around for somewhere to sit. He hesitated, but then moved a stack of papers from a chair, and settled himself comfortably. "I must say, Your Grace, this is an unexpected delight," he said. "Mrs Lafferty's baking is a thing of wonder."

O'Hanlon just glowered at the interloper.

The priest faltered. "I can see you're busy," he said. "I won't take up much of your time."

"Good."

"I've come about the Orphanage, Your Grace. I promised the nuns I would speak with you. We're very short of funds. We are rationing even the bare essentials—food and so on. The situation is becoming critical."

"Everything is short of funds," O'Hanlon replied, mentally calculating the odds that the priest would ever see the private accounts, would ever learn just how much had already been siphoned out of the Orphanage Fund to cover his other losses. "The Orphanage will have to wait its turn."

"But the nuns..."

"Damn the nuns," said O'Hanlon. "I don't care that the nuns hate me. I am their Bishop, and they *will* obey me." He laughed shortly, suddenly recalling his unpleasant brush with Mr Woo at The Melbourne Club. "I was once told by a heathen Chinaman that it's a question of who's to be master," he added. "The Chinaman was right about that. And *I* am master here. The nuns will do well to remember that."

Father O'Brien realised, belatedly, that the Bishop was in one of his legendary bad moods. It was equally clear that the Bishop had been drinking. There was no possibility of progress when O'Hanlon was like this. So the priest sipped his tea and stared at the floor, casting about for a way to change the subject. "I see you have *The New Day*," he said at last. He picked it up from the carpet. "All the parish women seem to read it."

"What?" O'Hanlon's already-mottled face darkened further. "That's the rag the dreadful Seekamp woman publishes, isn't it?"

"Indeed it is, Your Grace. But it's harmless enough—it's all recipes and frocks and women's things."

"Don't be stupid! That Seekamp woman is a public menace. Give it here!"

Quaking now, O'Brien handed over the journal.

O'Hanlon snatched it and leafed through the pages. His hand shook as he read the editorial. Finally, he slammed the journal down on the desk. "That woman!" he spluttered. "She's gone too far this time! She's urging her readers—our parish women—to sign the ludicrous Independence Petition that's circulating in the town."

"But you said it yourself, Your Grace: the women have no power."

"That doesn't stop them stirring up trouble," O'Hanlon replied. "I need to make an example of this one. I *will* make an example of her." He sat back in his chair, thinking. "There's one good thing," he said at last. "Ferguson is out of town."

"Who's Ferguson?" O'Brien asked.

"A rich bastard who protects her," O'Hanlon replied.

O'Brien concentrated on his tea, afraid to provoke the Bishop further.

O'Hanlon stood abruptly, towering over the hapless priest. "I have to go out," he said. He turned on his heel and stalked from the room, leaving the anxious Father O'Brien to console himself with tea and the rest of Mrs Lafferty's famous shortbread biscuits.

O'Hanlon grabbed his hat and coat from the hallstand, let himself out by the side door, and stalked down the gravel drive, his robes flapping against his bony shins. For all his new Bishop's finery, the man still looked like a scarecrow.

A porter answered the bell at the heavy oak door of the Ballarat Lunatic Asylum.

"I'm here to see Dr Grey," O'Hanlon said.

"Certainly, your Grace: I'll show you the way to his office."

"I know the way."

The porter could only attempt a clumsy bow as O'Hanlon strode across the hallway and up the curving staircase that led to the consulting room of Dr Grey, the asylum's director.

O'Hanlon did not knock.

Dr Grey, a thin, slightly stooped man whose hair was as grey as his name, looked up sharply. The fragrant bowl of roses on his desk did nothing to disguise the reek of furniture polish, bleach, and pungent medications—the pervasive smells of institutions for the insane.

"Is there a problem, Your Grace?" he asked.

O'Hanlon sat, uninvited, in the leather chair opposite the desk. "You might call it that," he said.

"If it's about the girl—Alice—I can assure you that she is behaving herself perfectly well. She's a model inmate, in fact. We no longer have to restrain her."

O'Hanlon shrugged. "Just as long as she is kept away from the other children in the Orphanage," he said.

"I wonder if that is entirely necessary," said Grey. "She was clearly hysterical when you brought her here, but she is calm now."

"She told one of the younger nuns that I had abused her," O'Hanlon said. "Father O'Brien had the story from the nun, and felt it his duty to report it to me."

"Quite right," Grey said. "O'Brien runs the Orphanage very well. It wouldn't do to have rumours of that sort in circulation. It could damage the reputation of the Church."

"Well, at least we have implemented a satisfactory solution," O'Hanlon said. "The child is clearly deranged."

"When the nun found the girl, Alice was bleeding from both her...forgive me, Your Grace...orifices," Grey said.

O'Hanlon pursed his thin lips in distaste. "And might I enquire how you know this?" he asked.

"Where children are concerned," Grey replied, "I am obliged to seek information from a reliable source. I could hardly expect a sensible answer from the girl, so I asked Father O'Brien to arrange for me to interview the nun. Father O'Brien remained in the room at all times—I assure you it was all quite proper."

"I see."

"The nun was deeply distressed by the incident. She is of the opinion that the child really was abused."

"I don't care one whit for the opinion of busybody nuns," said O'Hanlon. "I will not be accused by a crazy girl."

"Of course not, Your Grace." Dr Grey leaned forward. "But it is not uncommon for children to attribute their deepest fears to men in positions of power," he said. "If the girl was assaulted—say by one of the older boys at the Orphanage—she may have transferred the blame for her...ah...problem...to your good self."

"That's just more evidence that the girl is of unsound mind," O'Hanlon said. "I want her kept here. Permanently. Do I make myself clear?"

Grey spread his hands wide. "As you wish, Your Grace," he said. "You know you have the authority to commit difficult orphans to my care." He sighed. "It just seems a shame to keep this particular child locked up. The girl makes things, pretty things. She's good with her hands."

"Then perhaps you will find ways to employ her." O'Hanlon stared hard at the doctor, daring him to contradict his orders. "The subject is closed. The girl stays in the asylum. Let that be an end to it."

"Very well." Grey sat back, waiting for O'Hanlon to get to the point of his visit.

"I've come to arrange the committal of another woman," O'Hanlon said. "A dangerously deranged woman." O'Hanlon thumped his copy of *The New Day* down on Grey's desk. "I've come about the woman who publishes this filth. She must be locked up for her own good, and for the good of society."

Dr Grey stared at the Bishop in surprise. "Even you can't just have her committed at will, Your Grace," he said mildly. "She would have to be declared legally insane."

"I want *you* to make that declaration," O'Hanlon said.

"It's not that simple. I would have, at the very least, to examine the woman. And I don't imagine she would be at all inclined to submit to such an examination. Do you?"

"Then how else can such a thing be done?"

"There is a legal option," Grey said. "As I understand it, a person can be committed to an asylum if two doctors are prepared to swear in open court that the person in question is of unsound mind and likely to commit an indictable offence."

"Sedition is an indictable offence," O'Hanlon said. "She's obviously committing that one in her wretched journal. She's clearly urging the women who read it to acts of disobedience."

"I doubt that would be enough," Grey said.

"What would be enough, then?"

Grey opened a slim, leather-bound ledger that lay on his desk. "See for yourself, your Grace," he said. "These are the reasons for our recent female admissions." He slid the volume across the polished cedar desktop.

O'Hanlon peered at the neat, copperplate entries.

"*Hereditary predisposition,*" he read. "*Kicked in the Head by a Horse; Imaginary Female Trouble; Hysteria; Menstrual Derangement; Mental Excitement; Novel Reading; Overtaxing Mental Powers; Parents were Cousins; Periodical Fits; Deranged Masturbation; Gathering in the Head; Venereal Excesses; Eating Snuff.*"

"I don't think there's much to help you here," said Grey. He turned the page.

"This is better," said O'Hanlon. "*Fits and Desertion of Husband; Egotism; Immoral Life; Bad Habits and Political Excitement; Vicious Vices;*"

Greediness." He tapped his finger on the page. "This fits the Seekamp woman very nicely."

"Even so," said Grey, "all of these admissions were testified by a responsible male relative. Does Mrs Seekamp have a husband, by any chance?"

"She did, but she left him," O'Hanlon said. "The story is common knowledge: she fled to Melbourne because Seekamp is a drunkard. He kept all her money. She's been campaigning for women's property rights ever since."

"But are they legally divorced?"

"I doubt it," said O'Hanlon. "The Church would never allow it."

"And an Act of Parliament is far too expensive," said Grey.

"So?"

"So perhaps you should approach Mr Seekamp," Grey said. His relief was palpable. "He might prove amenable."

"Perhaps I'll do just that." O'Hanlon tucked the offending magazine back inside his robe and rose to his feet. "This has been most enlightening, Dr Grey," he said, not bothering to disguise his contempt for the doctor's scruples. "I trust you will remember your true position in this institution."

Grey chose to ignore the threat. "I shall, of course, do anything I can do to help the Church, Your Grace," he replied evenly, "anything *within* the law." He stood, indicating that the meeting was over. "Good day to you, Your Grace."

Chapter 89

O'Hanlon did not bother to reply. He stalked out of Grey's office, retraced his steps to his mansion, and collected a new bottle of Irish whiskey from the cabinet in his study before he set out once more. It was only a short walk into the town of Ballarat, and he headed straight for the office of the now defunct *Ballarat and Southern Cross Times*.

Henry Seekamp was sitting there, bleary eyed, at a kitchen table that served as his desk. He was dressed in grubby trousers, a collarless shirt, and shapeless boots. He smelled almost as bad as his fetid room.

O'Hanlon plunked the bottle of whiskey onto the middle of the cluttered table and got straight down to business. "I've come about your wife," he said.

Seekamp laughed. "You're too late," he said. He dabbed at his watering eyes with his shirtsleeve, and then scratched at the stubble on his unshaven chin. "She ran out on me years ago. I thought everyone knew that."

"But you are not officially divorced, are you?"

"I suppose not."

"In that case, you might be able to help me—and help yourself into the bargain."

"How?" Seekamp eyed the bottle longingly.

O'Hanlon moved it out of his reach. "I'll get right to the point," he said. "Your wife is a menace to society. I understand that a deposition from you will be enough to have her committed to the asylum."

Henry shook his head. "You want to commit her to the *lunatic* asylum? Why?"

"As I said, the woman is a threat to decent people. Think, man! You are not legally divorced. If your wife is committed you will have a claim on all her property. You'd have enough money to re-start your paper, if that's what you want. That much money would keep you in whiskey for a very long time."

Henry was immediately suspicious. He tried hard to focus his fuddled thoughts. "What's in it for you?" he asked. "Why come to me?"

O'Hanlon was exasperated. "I'm here because *you* can make the necessary deposition," O'Hanlon said. He was trying to be patient. "I'm here because someone has to shut down your wife's scurrilous publication. It goes against the natural order of decent society." He pulled out the journal and tossed it onto the desk. "You've seen the latest editorial, of course?"

"No," said Seekamp. "As a matter of fact, I haven't." He reached for the magazine, flipping pages until he found Clara's exhortation to her readers. A slow smile lit up his grubby, wrinkled face. "This is good stuff," he said.

"It's seditious rabble-rousing, that's what it is! Your wife is urging her readers to support the latest hopeless attempt at Independence that's being touted by enemies of the Church. She's stirring up trouble for everyone. She must be stopped!"

Henry straightened his shoulders. "I went to prison for sedition," he said softly. "I went to prison for supporting the miners at Eureka. That prison sentence cost me my health, my marriage, and my livelihood. But when all's said and done, I would do it again. I believed in Independence then, and I believe in it now."

"Then you're a fool."

"Undoubtedly," said Seekamp. "But not fool enough to take your thirty pieces of silver, O'Hanlon." He lunged forward and grabbed the bottle. "But I'll take your whiskey." He hugged the bottle to his chest. "You owe me that much."

"Owe you?"

Seekamp's voice took on a note of drunken cunning. "You just tried to bribe me into making a false declaration. I could go back to prison for that. So in return for the whiskey, I won't report you to the authorities."

"Nobody would believe the likes of you."

"Perhaps not." Seekamp shrugged. "But if you're done sneering at me, you can leave my premises. You'll get nothing from me."

"You'll regret this," O'Hanlon said.

"Probably. Thanks for the whiskey, O'Hanlon. You can see yourself out."

Henry Seekamp stood in the doorway and watched O'Hanlon stalk back down the dusty main street. When Henry finally went back to his worktable, he did not open the whiskey bottle. Instead, he scrabbled about for a clean sheet of paper, fitted a new nib, and refilled the inkwell. Then, for the first time in almost twenty years, Henry Seekamp sat down to write a letter to his wife.

Chapter 90

Hector and Ferguson arrived in Liverpool on the sixth of October. The steamer entered the river on the morning tide, churning its way between miles of wharfage, magnificent buildings and warehouses, to tie up, finally, at Princes dock. It was a morning of grey skies, chilly wind and falling leaves—autumn had come early this year. The port was busy, as if to give the lie to persistent rumours of the demise of commerce on England's shores: ships of all descriptions were engaged in a seemingly endless process of loading or unloading; carts and drays trundled about; brawny dock workers hefted heavy crates and bundles—all to be dodged by sailors, passengers and onlookers alike.

The Midland Railway Company's station was conveniently nearby, and Hector and Ferguson had no difficulty securing first class seats on the next service to Bath.

"No sense wasting time," Ferguson had said. "The train will reach Bath by later afternoon. Pitman will be expecting us."

The journey was mercifully uneventful, taking them through Birmingham and Gloucester and on to Bath. The country scenery had been pleasant, but Hector was shocked when, on the approach to Bath, the tracks cut through miles of heavily polluted industrial areas and past the crazily leaning shapes of a tent city that obviously housed the poor, the derelict, and the unemployed citizenry. The contrast could not have been greater.

"I thought Bath would be beautiful," Hector said, looking out of the window at the squalor through which they were passing. "When Mother learned we were coming here she read me Jane Austen's descriptions of the city: it sounded really grand, a noble place. This is disgraceful."

"It is grand, when we get to the expensive areas," Ferguson replied. "As it is in every industrial city, those who can afford it turn their backs on the poor, and make certain that they do not see the poverty on which their wealth is based." He shrugged. "It would be simply too depressing otherwise."

Hector did not reply, but stayed staring out at the view of the city's outskirts, as if to commit the scene to memory.

It was early evening when the train finally pulled into Queen Square Station—new, clean, and magnificently proportioned in contrast to the ramshackle buildings that lined the approach to it. As they alighted on the platform, Ferguson and Hector were immediately aware of a scuffle occurring at the back of the luggage van, where half a dozen scruffy men were dragging trunks and cases onto a cart.

"Stop! Thief!" one of the passengers shouted. "Help! Guards! That's my trunk!"

One of the miscreants—a big man, tall, broad-shouldered and heavily muscled for all that his belly was sunken from hunger—pulled a knife. "Out of the way," he grated, "if you know what's good for you."

"Hey, you," Hector shouted. "Get away from there."

Ferguson and Hector both drew their pistols and sprinted along the platform. They stopped short when they reached the luggage van. The would-be thieves scattered, all but the man with the knife, who stood his ground.

"I wouldn't do that, if I were you," Ferguson said in his soft American drawl. "I'd suggest you put that knife away, and leave the luggage where it is."

The man looked up desperately at the shining Colt revolvers, both pointed in his direction. "What's it to you?" he asked.

"That's my luggage on your cart," Hector replied, keeping the man squarely in his sights.

"And mine," said Ferguson. "And we want it back."

"You won't shoot."

"I assure you I will," Ferguson replied calmly. "Try me."

At that moment the station guards came running up, muskets at the ready. The would-be thief put up his hands.

"Seize him," the portly stationmaster said, red-faced from the exertion of catching up with his men.

Two of the guards grabbed the man, pinioning his arms behind him. He was strong: they struggled to hold him, until one of them held a knife to the side of his throat, and he sagged, defeated.

"We just want our luggage," Hector said mildly.

"And you've caught a thief for us into the bargain," the stationmaster said, still breathing heavily. "You have our thanks." He aimed a kick at the captive. "But you should have shot him," he added morosely. "It'd have saved us the price of the rope to hang him."

The man spat expressively at his captor's feet.

"But you can't hang him," Hector said. "He hasn't actually stolen anything."

"Only because you prevented him," the stationmaster replied.

"True," said Ferguson, "but Mr Munro is right. Maybe you can lock up the man for attempted robbery?"

"The jails are too full," the stationmaster replied. He gestured to his guards. "Let him go." He shook his fist at the captive. "And you, thief, make sure you don't come back here. If I catch you again, you *will* hang."

The man looked up, his greasy face a picture of disbelief as the guards released his arms and stepped away from him. Then, to everyone's surprise, he seized Hector's hand and kissed it. "God bless you, Mr Munro, sir," he blurted out before he turned, and ran.

"Well," said Ferguson, "that's not quite the welcome we were expecting."

"I daresay not," the stationmaster said. "May I ask where you are headed?"

"To Royal Crescent," Hector replied. "We are guests of Mr Pitman."

"Then allow me to suggest you hire a dray," the stationmaster said. "The trip will take slightly longer than it would on foot, but it will be a safer option."

"Can you arrange that?" Ferguson asked.

"Of course, sir." He beckoned to a waiting driver. "This way."

The luggage was quickly loaded and Hector was surprised to observe that they passed superb buildings as the horse plodded its way around two sides of Queens Square to exit north up the amazingly steep Gay Street, where the buildings were only a little less grand—though equally grimed with the all-pervasive soot from now-silent factories. They approached the spectacular Circus, and then turned left along Brock Street to the entry to Royal Crescent with its magnificent curve of houses.

"That's more like it," Ferguson said. "A little more like Jane Austen's Bath, I trust?"

"Absolutely splendid," Hector replied, gazing at the architecture in the twilight. "Mother would like this."

A cold mist was already rising, shrouding the lower parts of the town by the time the driver reined in the horse to halt outside a truly imposing building. The crescent was unnaturally silent: a few dispirited sparrows clung to the railings, but Hector could see no other sign of life.

"Here we are, sirs," the driver said. "I'll just unload your luggage, sirs."

Ferguson handed the man some coins, deliberately tipping too much.

"Thank you, sir," the man said, wide-eyed at the windfall. He pocketed it quickly and turned to leave, as if he feared Ferguson might reconsider and ask for his change.

Chapter 91

When Clara Seekamp arrived to take afternoon tea with Lola Montez, she brought with her a copy of *The New Day*, fresh from the printing press.

"I've written an editorial about Edward Cole's forthcoming trial," she said. She settled herself into one of Lola's plush red velvet armchairs. "I thought you might like to read it."

"Of course," said Lola. "But is that wise? Edward is charged with sedition just for printing copies of the Independence Petition."

"Someone has to speak up," Clara said.

"There's something else, isn't there?"

Clara sighed. "I've had a letter from Henry."

"Good gracious," said Lola. "What on earth prompted Henry, of all people, to write to you after all this time?"

"He wrote to warn me," Clara said. "It seems that after I published my last editorial urging women to sign the Petition, Henry received a most unwelcome visit from none other than Bishop O'Hanlon."

"And what could O'Hanlon possibly want with Henry?"

"He wanted," said Clara, "to have *me* locked up!"

"Locked up?"

"Committed," said Clara. "O'Hanlon was looking for a way to prevent me from publishing more articles. He wanted Henry to declare me of unsound mind, so that I could be locked up in the Ballarat Lunatic Asylum."

"That's preposterous," Lola said. "He can't do that. What possible grounds would he have?"

"Anything that looked plausible, I expect." Clara tried to laugh. "I've been doing some checking," she said bitterly. "Women have been committed there for as little as *political excitement*, whatever that is. It seems that men can have women committed for almost anything."

"But to approach Henry?" Lola said. "That's devious, even for O'Hanlon."

"True," said Clara. "He must have thought Henry still somehow had some

385

marital rights. But to Henry's credit, he sent O'Hanlon packing."

"Well, that's a turn up for the books."

"Yes," said Clara. "Henry may be a hopeless alcoholic, but he's not without his principles. He also wrote to tell me that he supports the Independence movement, and is already campaigning for it in Ballarat."

"A good outcome, then," said Lola. She smiled. "And that's what prompted your editorial?"

"In a manner of speaking, yes," said Clara. "O'Hanlon is after my blood. He takes every to opportunity to attack *The New Day*. And he's thick as thieves with Mayor Smith—and everyone knows that Smith is trying every avenue he can find to block the Independence movement. I'm as certain as I can be that it was Smith who complained to the constabulary that Mr Cole's posters were seditious."

"Smith is an appalling, pompous little man," Lola said. "I can just see him in cahoots with the odious O'Hanlon. They make a good pair."

"And both of them are tight with Judge Redmond Barry," Clara added.

"So is that what's in your editorial?"

"See for yourself."

Lola opened the magazine. "Oh," she said. "That's a wonderful cartoon of Judge Barry!"

"Isn't it?" said Clara. "*The Weekly Times* agreed to let me reprint it. It's from their *Masks and Faces* series."

"I like the caption: *O Wise and Upright Judge*." Lola giggled. "Barry must hate that."

"I certainly hope so," said Clara.

Lola turned her attention back to the magazine.

Under the headline: "Sedition or Free Speech?" Clara had written:

It has come to the attention of this correspondent that Mr Edward Cole is highly unlikely to be given a fair trial on the charge of seditious libel, which will be heard in the Melbourne High Court later this month before Judge Redmond Barry.

Mr Cole is a leading businessman, owner of the world's biggest Book Emporium, and a pillar of Melbourne society. He is an upstanding citizen and a gentleman of good conscience, a gentleman well known for his charitable works. His only offence against the law has been to support Independence and to speak his mind in these difficult financial times, as it behoves every good citizen to do.

But who exactly is this Redmond Barry who presumes to sit in judgement upon a man such as Mr Cole? This writer has undertaken some research, and can now report that Mr Barry attained his present position merely through luck and good old-fashioned ingratiation. Mr Barry was no more than a second-rate lawyer who could not get work anywhere that mattered, a man who had decided to try his luck in the colonies for want of anything better to do. He was running his practice out of a rented bedroom when Melbourne was yet a small town. But when the miners struck gold in Ballarat and people started pouring in from all over the world, the new Victorian government needed judges in a hurry. Barry just happened to be in the right place at the right time. And so he was appointed as a judge—a man with no judicial training, no experience, and no impartiality.

It is evident that Judge Barry's only intention is to please his political masters, a fact well proven in his conduct of the trials after the failed uprising of the Eureka Stockade. Some readers of this journal will recall that it was Judge Barry who convicted Mr Henry Seekamp, then editor of The Ballarat Times, *on the charge of seditious libel—the same offence of which Mr Cole now stands accused. It was also Judge Barry who attempted, unsuccessfully, to convict the Eureka miners on the charge of treason. There can be no doubt that this judge will, once again, act only to uphold the wishes of his political masters—those powerful men who seek to preserve their own privileged positions at the expense of everyone else in the colony of Victoria.*

Many readers will also be aware that Judge Barry, a close associate of Mr John Smith, Mayor of Melbourne, is also publicly allied with The Most Reverend Father O'Hanlon, the Bishop of Ballarat. But Barry is not a man who adheres to the moral strictures of the Church. It is no secret that he has an intimate relationship with one Mrs Louisa Barrow: they have never married, nor cohabited—yet they have four children, all of whom bear his name. I ask you, Ladies, is this acceptable behaviour for a man who sits in judgement upon the moral and ethical positions taken by other citizens?

Let me once again urge you, Ladies, to sign the Independence Petition. It is time for us to make a clean start, to be free from the political manoeuvring that has saddled us with men such as Judge Barry.

"Well done," said Lola. "That should put the proverbial cat amongst the pigeons. But don't you think it's a bit harsh to name the lady with whom Barry is involved?"

"I suppose it is," said Clara. "Personally, I applaud her for not marrying that man. As things stand, their relationship really is no secret: they are often seen dining together." She shrugged. "But I know my readers. I know that most of them will choose to take the moral high ground. I want them to disapprove of Barry, and they will."

"Then let's hope it encourages them to vote for freedom," said Lola.

Chapter 92

When McGill next met with Cole and Buchanan, he found Cole pacing up and down Buchanan's office.

"Is something amiss?" McGill asked.

"I'll admit that I'm more than a little worried about my imminent trial," Cole said. "The government forces are lining up against me: just this morning, *The Argus* has published a letter by William Mitchell, President of the Legislative Council, condemning the Independence Petition and all but demanding my conviction for sedition."

"He would," said Buchanan. "Mitchell was Chief Commissioner of Police at the time of the Eureka uprising. He's firmly opposed to reform of any kind."

"Even so," Cole replied, "there have been a lot of similar letters from other squatters—all of them powerful men."

"They're just protecting their own interests," said McGill.

"Of course they are," said Cole. "Any possible change in the *status quo* is bound to make them nervous. But these men have influence." He shook his head. "And speaking of influence, Bishop O'Hanlon is also against us: he's using the social pages in just about every newspaper to urge his flock not to sign our Petition."

"No mystery there," McGill replied. "The Catholic Church is eternally conservative. And O'Hanlon is always angling for advancement: he'll be trying to please his masters in the religious hierarchy."

"And please himself at the same time," Cole said sharply. "When he's not attacking *me* in print, he's denigrating successful women—especially Lola and Clara. This opportunity suits him very well."

"True," said McGill. "O'Hanlon is a nasty piece of work. I've never trusted him, not since the day I met him just after the Eureka uprising. I was trying to find out how Hector's father died, but O'Hanlon refused to speak of it." He paused, remembering. "And now that I think of it," he added, "O'Hanlon was incredibly rude to Mr Woo at Buchanan's Melbourne Club dinner, the day I arrived back here after all those years away. You must recall the scene he made, Alec?"

"Indeed I do," said Buchanan. "It was most inconvenient."

"Anyway," said McGill, "O'Hanlon clearly hates the Chinese almost as much as he hates women. He's a strong advocate for anti-Chinese legislation— he must be worried that a newly independent Victoria will extend citizenship to our Chinese residents."

"Or worse," Cole said, "that we might give back the right to vote to eligible women!"

McGill smiled. "That really would upset him! As it is, Clara goads him at every turn. And she never gives up campaigning for Women's Rights."

"All the same," said Cole, "I really do wish Mrs Seekamp would stop trying to help me." He sighed. "She's a dear lady, but she has an unfortunate knack of inflaming public opinion. Judge Barry has been against me from the outset—it won't help that Clara's latest editorial has now turned public attention toward his unconventional private life. By all accounts, the man is furious."

"Then let us hope he is furious enough to overreach his authority," Buchanan said, his tone severe.

"Sorry, Alec," Cole said. "I know we are here to discuss far weightier matters."

"Don't apologise, Edward," Buchanan said. "Your trial may be very important in the way the politics of this particular situation play out."

"It's certainly inspiring our supporters to greater efforts," McGill said. "Our Petition seems to have taken on a life of its own. The courts may have banned you from printing more copies, Edward, but lots of people are making their own. Handwritten copies are perfectly legitimate. The push for Independence is gathering momentum every day."

"It could hardly be otherwise," Buchanan said. "The citizens of Victoria can only watch as events unfold overseas. They feel helpless in the face of what looks like a relentless cascade of disasters. The New York stock market crash was terrifying, and any man who reads a newspaper must be aware of the effects of it in Britain."

"I did warn you," McGill said. "Britain was already weakened: it cannot hold against the tide. More banks have failed, more businesses have collapsed, and more workers have been laid off. The message is clear: the Empire is in decline."

"True enough," said Cole. "But there are still men prepared to argue that it is Victoria's duty to go down with the ship. Mitchell is clearly one of them."

"But I must believe they are in the minority," McGill replied. "Most Victorians are more than ready to abandon Britain to its fate: most have, after all, come to this Colony in search of a better life. Why should they give up on that hope, when they have already come so far? Why should they support a country that didn't want them in the first place?"

"Why indeed?" Buchanan said. "An Independent Victoria will eventually have a new Constitution, and everyone hopes that will mean better rights for all of our citizens." He shrugged. "But it's your original idea, McGill, that's really taken hold in the popular imagination: the notion that Victoria should keep its gold reserves for its own use is uppermost in their minds," he added. "The people here want their banks to be safe, want financial independence, want reliable currency. I can't say I blame them. It's no more than we all want for the future. And for that, we have to keep our gold."

Cole grinned. "The popular catchcry says it all," he said. "Just those two little words: *Finders Keepers*. It's everywhere: there are handwritten posters in shop windows and on street corners, there are ordinary workmen distributing handbills all over the colony. It's a simple message—and a very effective one too. It goes right to the heart of the matter."

"Then let's make it our business to see that it succeeds," McGill said. "Not all of the Upper House will be against us—there are businessmen there as well as squatters."

"I know," said Buchanan. "And it is to those businessmen that we must appeal."

McGill checked his fob watch. "I hate to hurry you, gentlemen," he said, "but I have an official luncheon to attend at noon. May I ask if there have been any other developments?"

"Things are moving," Buchanan said. "The other Colonies are watching events here very closely. New South Wales will sit on the fence—so to speak— as long as it can, but the some of the others will likely follow if we succeed."

"I've had a very confidential letter from Pitman," Cole added. "He's been approached by his friends in the South Australian Government to make contact with us. It is known already that Buchanan and I are managing the Independence Petition here."

"I see," said McGill.

"I'm not sure you do," Buchanan replied. "The point that Pitman makes is that if Victoria declares Independence, South Australia will follow suit. Moreover, the leaders have been giving serious consideration to the idea that South Australia would then vote to join forces with Victoria, thus creating an entity that will control the middle of the continent and the new rail link from Port Augusta in the south through Alice Springs in the centre to Darwin in the north."

"Which, coincidentally, will suit the interests of our consortium very well," McGill said, immediately realising the implications. "Gold and copper resources will be managed together, and control of the Telegraph will be complete."

"And our new City at Alice Springs will benefit enormously," Cole added.

"Precisely," said Buchanan. "As you said some time ago, McGill, the push for independence is about business, first and foremost."

McGill shook his head. "The scale of it is breathtaking," he said.

"But no more than we bargained for," said Cole. "This is not the time for half measures."

"Indeed it is not," McGill said firmly.

"Has something else happened?" Cole asked, catching McGill's tone.

"I've bought a railway," McGill replied, casually.

"Gosh," Cole replied. "Where?"

"Back home," said McGill. "My brothers and I have bought the Boston, Hartford and Erie Railroad, in partnership with another Boston company. It will be re-developed as the New York and New England Railroad."

"That's exciting," said Cole. "May I ask why?"

"To defend our other assets," McGill said. "My brothers have been watching the railroad market very closely. There's an oil millionaire, a Mr John D. Rockefeller, who is using his substantial cash reserves to buy up all the railroads he can get. He started almost immediately after Jay Cooke failed. It's rumoured that Rockefeller has done a deal with Cardinal Antonelli to acquire all the Vatican's failed railway assets for practically nothing. However he's doing it, he's buying at bargain basement prices."

"And that concerns you?"

"Of course: if he controls all the railroads he can push up freight charges as high as he likes."

"So you bought a railroad to ensure that you can keep your freight lines to New York operating at reasonable cost?"

"Precisely. And we can guarantee fair prices for other Boston companies."

"Capital," Cole said admiringly. "You never cease to surprise me, McGill."

Chapter 93

When Ferguson and Hector knocked, Isaac Pitman himself opened the door. "Hello, and welcome to Bath," he said cheerfully, leading the way indoors. "You can leave your luggage in the hall for now—we'll take it upstairs to your rooms later."

The house, surprisingly, was cold and damp; the curtains were drawn, but the lamps remained unlit.

Hector shivered.

"Come into my study," Pitman said. "I have a fire going in the grate: it's unseasonably chilly this evening." He led the way down a long, narrow corridor and opened a heavy door into an oak-panelled room dominated by a large, carved desk. The room was charming, made cosy by lamplight and firelight.

"I'll just fetch tea," Pitman said, bustling out again. "You must be in need of something hot."

"Thank you," Hector said, crossing to the fireplace to warm his hands.

"The house feels deserted," Ferguson remarked, just as their host reappeared, carrying a tray from the kitchen.

"Times are hard," Pitman said, re-entering the room and replying to Ferguson's comment. Pitman set the tea tray down atop a pile of paperwork on his untidy desk, where it wobbled precariously. "I've had to let most of the staff go," he said. "Luckily, my housekeeper and her husband have chosen to stay on. I can't pay them as much as I used to, but they are content, under the current circumstances, to keep a dry roof over their heads." He shrugged. "I must say I am grateful: Mrs Hatfield is a good cook."

"That's always a good thing," Ferguson replied. "But how have things come to such a pass, and so quickly?"

"Here in Bath we have never recovered from last year's General Strike," Pitman replied. "The local industries were forced to shut down when the coal supplies dried up, and then the workers lost their employment. Everybody

393

thought it would be temporary, but then the banks got into difficulties and the foreclosures began. Landlords evicted tenants who could no longer pay the rent, banks evicted landlords who couldn't pay their mortgages. Many a valuable house is standing derelict now—once the bankers repossessed the properties, they found there was nobody to sell to. Those, like myself, who do own properties outright, are trapped too: we cannot move, because there are no buyers to be found. There's simply no money to be had to re-start the big manufacturing concerns that were the lifeblood of the city. Their owners are holding tight to their cash reserves, and the banks aren't lending."

Ferguson sighed deeply. "It's a house of cards," he said. "Pull out the wrong piece and the whole thing comes tumbling down."

"We saw the tent city as the train arrived," Hector said. "It looked very bad."

"There are thousands of unemployed workers living there, cheek by jowl, in terrible conditions," Pitman said. "The place is full of disease—the death rate is appallingly high. It makes me very angry: bailiffs throw people out of their homes, then the homes are left to rot while the people starve in a tent and die in poverty."

"What would you do?" Ferguson asked.

"The banks could simply leave people in their homes—at least until things improve. At best, the people would work to pay off their debt; at worst, the property would be cared for—the tenants could always be evicted later," Pitman replied.

"Sensible," Hector replied.

"They'd never do it," Ferguson said. "It would look too much like charity."

"And no banker is ever guilty of that," Pitman snapped.

After a long moment, he shook his head as if to clear his thoughts. He rose to pour the tea. "Sorry," he said. "I have people at my door every day, begging. I can't help them. The whole situation is very upsetting."

"I can see that," Hector replied. "I was very disturbed by the camps." His jaw tightened at the raw memory of the stark realities of a city he had once imagined as a place of light and beauty. "You're describing a whole regime based on nothing more than inhumanity and injustice," he said. "Surely there has to be a better way than that!"

"I wonder where all of this leaves us," Ferguson said, quickly changing the subject.

"Very well placed, I should think," Pitman answered, glad to turn his mind to practicalities. "Our unemployment will be to your advantage."

"And theirs," Hector said quickly. "We're offering them a new start, in a new city."

"In a strange land," Pitman replied. "Some of us would find it very hard to leave our homes."

"Not if you've already been evicted," Ferguson said.

"No," Pitman conceded, "not then." He shrugged. "In any case, I have advertised on your behalf, as I promised Mr Cole I would."

"Thank you," Hector said.

"We had thought to go to Swansea when our business here is done," Ferguson added. "We need expert copper workers as well as clockwork engineers."

"Mr Cole explained all that, so I've advertised there, too," Pitman replied. "You'd have a lot of trouble getting down to Swansea, as things stand. There have been deliberate train derailments: the passengers have been robbed, sometimes killed; the trains have been cannibalised for their fittings, even for their metal. People are desperate: they survive on what they can beg, scavenge or steal."

"We could ride," Hector said, not at all averse to the idea of being on horseback for a while.

"Even for the two of you, it would be dangerous," Pitman replied. "The by-roads are infested with robbers; bands of unemployed and displaced brigands control the highways. You'd be taking your lives in your hands."

"Then what can we do?" Hector asked.

"The workers have come to you," Pitman replied. "As I said, I've already advertised for you. Bath is — or was — a major industrial centre, so unemployed craftsmen of all kinds have flocked here, seeking work. Once I circulated my advertisements in Swansea, large numbers of copper workers journeyed here, poor devils: they are waiting in the tent encampment, watching for your arrival, hoping you will offer them work."

Hector smiled, at last. "How soon can we meet with them?" he asked.

"I'd suggest tomorrow evening," Pitman replied. "The Marlborough Hotel would be best: the main refugee camp lies beyond it, and it's a convenient meeting place. I'll organise it with the landlord tomorrow morning, and Mr Hatfield can put up some posters in the town. You should get quite a crowd." He hesitated. "I must warn you, though: it will be dangerous. There have been fights already over just the prospect of work. Men have killed for less."

"I'm sure we'll manage," Ferguson said, patting his barely concealed revolver so that his host could see that he was armed.

If Pitman was concerned, he didn't show it. "You'll also want to meet Mr Ellett, the toymaker," he said. "You must have passed his shop on your way here: he lives at the bottom of Princes Street, on the south side of Queen Square."

"Certainly we must," Hector replied. "Though I'm sure he wouldn't have appreciated us arriving unannounced."

"The social niceties have slipped, somewhat," Pitman said wryly, "but I'll be happy to accompany you tomorrow morning. I always enjoy visiting him: his little shop is full of wonders."

Chapter 94

The morning of Edward Cole's trial was cold and blustery, but at least the skies were clear. A huge crowd had gathered at the Courthouse. The public gallery was jam-packed with Independence supporters long before the trial was due to begin, and many would-be onlookers were constrained to wait outside. It wasn't long before street urchins were weaving their way through the crowd, begging for pennies and keeping a sharp lookout for likely pockets to pick. Loud-mouthed larrikins lounged against the railings, drawing unwanted attention from the contingent of blue-uniformed police that Judge Barry, expecting trouble, had requested to attend. Before long, enterprising Chinese street vendors turned up, and the aromas of smoking charcoal and grilling meat began to mingle with the common smells of horse dung and the whirling dust and grit that permeated the windy streets of Melbourne. The immediate precinct of the Supreme Court of the Colony of Victoria soon began to take on a carnival atmosphere. Members of the press began to gather—they stood about, chatting amiably as they awaited scraps of news. And everywhere there were hand-lettered signs and banners bearing a single message of hope: *Finders Keepers*.

Inside, Lola Montez had sent her servants on ahead early to secure seats in the front row of the public gallery for herself and her friend Clara Seekamp. Now, as the appointed hour approached, the two fashionable women sat watching expectantly while courtroom clerks fussed about, preparing for the trial. Today, Clara wore a plain blue dress and coat, which made her appear unusually conservative beside the flamboyant Lola—garbed, as always, in her trademark red-and-black ensemble.

A court official rapped his staff for attention.

"All stand!" he said.

Clara nudged her friend. "Here we go," she said. "Fingers crossed."

All eyes were on Sir Redmond Barry, resplendent in his ermine-trimmed scarlet robes, as he took his place on the rostrum that was the focus of attention in the dark-panelled courtroom. Judge Barry's demeanour was almost as pompous as the likeness of him portrayed in Clara's cartoon: he returned the formal bows of the assembled lawyers and court officials with a condescending nod that barely disturbed the fall of his full-bottomed wig. He sat. The theatre of the courtroom arranged itself around him. The business of the day had begun.

Lola leaned across to whisper in Clara's ear. "All this is beautifully stage-managed," she said. "I couldn't have done it better myself."

"It reminds me of a Punch and Judy Show," Clara whispered back. "I half expect Judge Barry's common law wife to appear and start beating His Honour about his head."

"That'd be something to see," said Lola. "The crowd would love it."

The judge glared across the courtroom at her, almost as if he had heard.

"All sit," the official intoned.

Clara settled herself comfortably on a cushion before producing a notebook and pencil from her reticule. "I don't want to miss any of this," she whispered to Lola.

Edward Cole, impeccably dressed in a well-tailored grey morning suit, snowy white linen shirt and discreetly patterned dark blue silk cravat, resumed his seat in the dock. He looked around with interest. If he was overawed by this display of Imperial pomp and power, he certainly didn't show it.

"Proceed," said the judge.

The prosecutor rose to his feet. "If it please the court, my lord," he said, "the Crown calls upon Constable John Bellamy to confirm his deposition."

A nervous-looking Bellamy took the stand, stammering a little as he swore his oath.

"Take your time, Constable," Barry said. "I just need you to read out your statement."

"Yes, sir," said Bellamy. He unfolded the piece of paper he had been clutching, and began to read:

> *"In the Supreme Court of the Colony of Victoria, in the case of The Queen v. Edward Cole, I, John Bellamy, on my oath, say as follows:*
> *I am a Constable of Police. I arrested the defendant on Saturday the 4th October instant in The Princess Theatre on Spring Street, in Melbourne, in consequence of certain posters and printed materials which he had printed, and which are seditious and calculated to excite disturbances among the people of Melbourne. I produce the posters and papers referred to.*
> *The Defendant by his Counsel admitted that he caused the posters and petitions to be respectively printed and published*

*by him, and by the advice of his Counsel declined to make any
statement.*

*Sworn on Monday 6th October 1873, at Melbourne before
the Acting Chief Commissioner of Police, Mr. Hussey Malone
Chomley."*

"Thank you, Constable," said Barry. "That will be all. You may step down."

"Sir." As Bellamy hurried away from the stand, his progress through the
courtroom was marked by boos and hisses from the crowd.

Judge Redmond Barry was not in the mood to compromise his authority.
"Silence!" he roared. "I will not tolerate interjections."

The crowd fell quiet, but Clara observed their mutinous expressions and
made a quick note of them for her report.

Judge Barry turned his attention to Sinisgalli. "Your client has admitted
the offence," he said. "I cannot see any reason to delay the jury, but I am
bound to ask you, as his defending counsel, if you have anything to say."

"Thank you, Your Honour."

Sinisgalli rose to his feet, adjusted his robes, and turned to the jury.

"Gentlemen," he began, "my esteemed client, Mr Edward Cole, has
admitted to nothing more than causing a petition and some posters to be printed.
He is a famous publisher of books and pamphlets, he owns Melbourne's
largest book emporium: this is a man for whom publication of all manner of
material is a daily event. So, as men of good sense, let us ask ourselves why
these particular publications have so excited the interest of The Crown that Mr
Cole finds himself in the dock today."

Clara listened intently as Sinisgalli launched into an impassioned speech
about freedom of expression and the rights—indeed the duties—of all citizens
to speak out on matters of grave importance to the community. The jurors,
clearly, were heeding Mr Sinisgalli's arguments—but it was equally apparent
that Judge Barry, constrained to hear Sinisgalli out, could barely contain
his disapproval of this line of argument. Clara jotted down a note to tell her
readers that Judge Barry could not refrain from checking his fob watch from
time to time, waiting for Counsel for the Defence to finish.

When Sinisgalli paused to take a sip of water, Judge Barry seized the
moment.

"I'm sure the jury understands your client's position perfectly well, Mr
Sinisgalli," the judge said.

"But Your Honour…"

Barry held up his hand for silence. "Enough, Mr Sinisgalli," he said. "I
rule that the Court will now hear closing submissions. I trust, gentlemen, that
you will be brief." He turned to the Prosecutor. "The Crown may begin," he

said.

T he closing addresses duly completed, Judge Redmond Barry made everyone wait while he made a great show of consulting his notes. Finally, he looked up at the assembled crowd, and cleared his throat.

"This is it," Clara whispered to Lola. "He's about to sum up."

Both women leaned forward expectantly.

"Gentlemen of the Jury," Judge Barry said, "you have now listened to the proceedings of this case, and to the closing addresses from learned Counsel for the Prosecution, and for the Defence. Having heard all the evidence, it is now your solemn duty to retire and consider your verdict. Before you do so, however, it is my equally solemn duty to direct you in matters of law raised by this case."

He stared with ill-concealed contempt at Edward Cole, who was still sitting equally in the dock, apparently at ease with the proceedings.

Barry fixed his steely gaze upon the jurors. "Gentlemen," he said, "I have in the past been called upon to preside over other cases of seditious libel, notably one concerning the uprising on the Ballarat goldfields. In that instance, the verdict of the court was not, unfortunately, delivered in time to prevent the insurrection whipped up by the seditious writings of the newspaper proprietor in question."

He paused to take a sip of water, clearly enjoying the moment. His every gesture indicated he was completely confident of obtaining the outcome he wanted. He obviously did not intend to hurry.

"Self-righteous bastard!" Clara muttered under her breath.

Lola patted her friend's hand. "Hush," she whispered.

The judge resumed his oration. "Once again, gentlemen, we in Victoria face a crisis in our affairs. It is essential for the preservation of law and order that an example should be made of *anyone*,"—he glared at Cole again—"no matter what their position in society, who seeks to promote the overthrow of the established order of government. Only thus can we hope to prevent a repetition of the misery inflicted by violent men upon a peaceful community."

Clara was scribbling furiously. "The nerve of the man," she muttered, not missing a word of Barry's speech in her notes. "This is exactly what he did to bully the jury into convicting poor Henry."

"In the case that we have been hearing," Judge Barry continued, "the Defendant is not accused of penning the tawdry materials himself. He is, rather, the instigator and instrument of their publication. In law, it is as though he *had* uttered the words himself. Worse, for without his intervention these insidious posters and papers would not have attained the public notoriety that has forced the Government to act."

There was a rumble of disapproving voices from the public gallery.

Judge Barry ignored it. "The Defendant has not disputed that he caused these most offensive posters and papers to be printed. All that you have to decide, gentlemen of the jury, is whether these materials in question do indeed constitute seditious libel. And in my opinion, gentlemen, the Crown has proved beyond question that such is the case. By demanding the negation of the legitimate authority of our most gracious Sovereign, these materials challenge the very basis of our society. It is therefore my duty to instruct you, gentlemen, that you *must*—I repeat *must*—find the Defendant guilty as charged."

He sat back, savouring the moment. "You may now retire," he said.

"All rise," said the clerk.

Independence supporters in the gallery could no longer contain their anger. Murmurs of dissatisfaction became shouts and catcalls and boos.

"Shame!" a man yelled.

"It's an outrage!" another answered.

Someone waved a placard bearing the Independence slogan: *Finders Keepers*.

Clara was still jotting notes as fast as she could. Her face was pale, but her lips were set in a determined line.

"Silence!" roared Barry. "If this disturbance does not cease at once I shall clear the court!"

The angry cries subsided into mutterings, but the bearer of the placard still waved it vigorously, attracting Barry's attention.

"Officer, remove that person from my court," he said, pointing his shaking finger at the man.

Judge Barry waited, deliberately, while the unfortunate offender was escorted from the courtroom. Then he rose. He bowed briefly, and with a grim smile of satisfaction he swept from the courtroom—heading for his comfortable chambers to await the jury's inevitable verdict.

Chapter 95

Outside, on the steps of the Courthouse, word of Barry's unfavourable summing-up spread quickly. Anxious knots of Independence supporters milled around, earnestly discussing the effect a guilty verdict might have on their cause. On the other side of the street, the artist S.T. Gill was drawing rapidly, recording the scene in his sketchbook.

The Mayor, John Thomas Smith, took the opportunity to slip out of the courtroom to speak to the waiting representatives of the press.

A senior reporter from *The Argus* spotted Smith at the top of the steps. "It doesn't look good for Cole, does it, Mr Mayor?" he called.

Smith paused for effect, standing proudly beside one of the cast-iron columns that lent the architectural muddle of the Supreme Court buildings a little dignity.

"Indeed it does not, Mr Lang," he replied.

"Can you give me a statement, Your Worship?"

Smith tucked his left hand inside the lapel of his coat, adopting what he imagined was a dignified pose for the photographer who had now joined the journalist and was busily setting up his tripod. Behind him, an office junior carried a pole and the photographer's flash powder.

"I shall be happy to give you my views for your readers, Mr Lang," Smith said. "There can be no doubt about the outcome of these proceedings: Judge Redmond Barry has now *directed* the jury that they must find Edward Cole guilty of seditious libel, as charged."

There was a blinding flash as the photographer from *The Argus* took his picture.

The Mayor blinked, but resumed his carefully prepared speech.

"It is, as His Lordship has graciously remarked upon several such occasions, imperative for the stability of this colony that we put an end to this kind of dangerous rabble-rousing. There can be no doubt that the egregious petition promulgated by Cole and his supporters is designed purely to cause popular unrest and to undermine the established government. This cannot be tolerated."

"Can Mr Cole appeal the decision?" Lang asked.

Smith shook his head. "There would be no point," he said, unable to keep the smugness from his voice. "The Governor would be obliged to back Judge Barry to the hilt on a matter such as this." Smith paused for breath. "And furthermore…"

But before he could deliver his next pronouncement the Courthouse doors swung open. All manner of people spilled out, chattering excitedly. Among them were Lola, elegant and composed as ever, and beside her a hatless, breathless Clara, who was waving her notebook.

The reporters recognised her at once.

"Mrs Seekamp," Lang called, his loud voice carrying over the hubbub. "What's the news?"

"Not guilty!" she called back. "The jury found him not guilty!"

Lang abandoned the Mayor and pushed his way through the crowd to stand beside Clara. "But what about Judge Barry's direction?" he asked.

"The jury ignored it." Clara's blue eyes were sparkling with delight and mischief. "The jurors barely left the court," she said. "It was a wonderful moment when they returned. Judge Barry had retired to his chambers—he must have thought he had time to take his tea. He was most flustered when he was called straight back. And you should have seen his face when the foreman of the jury announced their 'not guilty' verdict. Barry couldn't believe what he was hearing: he made the foreman repeat it. Then the judge's face went as red as his robes. He was apoplectic! He couldn't contain himself. He ranted about law and order and social responsibility for a good five minutes. And when he had to tell Edward Cole that he was free to go—well, the judge could barely get the words out. He's ordered the courtroom cleared—he couldn't stop the cheering from the crowd." She patted her notebook. "It's all in here," she said. "It'll make a marvellous article."

"Then I trust I can persuade you to share it with *The Argus*?"

"Of course, Mr Lang," Clara said happily. "It will be my very great pleasure."

The Mayor wasn't finished yet. "It's a disgrace!" he boomed. "The jury has done the colony of Victoria a grave disservice!"

Clara couldn't help herself. "It's one in the eye for you and your mates," she retorted. "And for your friend *Bishop* O'Hanlon!"

Before the Mayor could frame a suitable reply the Courthouse doors swung open once again, and this time the surging crowd included Edward Cole and John Sinisgalli.

Cole was recognised at once. He was seized, and hoisted aloft by jubilant Independence supporters. He struggled briefly, but had no choice but to

THE FIVE STAR REPUBLIC

surrender to the demands of the moment.

"Friends! Friends!" Cole tried to address the crowd, but his voice was lost in the uproar until one of the burly workmen carrying him roared for quiet.

Cole began again. "Friends!" he said. "This is an historic moment. Faced with the awful power of the State, twelve good, decent men have today chosen to prefer justice and liberty to the demands of a corrupted law!"

Loud cheers rang out, but the crowd was quickly hushed when Cole raised his hand.

"In years to come," he said, "when your children and their children ask how Independence was won for Victoria, you will be able to say: *I was there when it all began. I saw the proud men of authority humbled.* I urge you, now, to carry on the noble work of fighting for a free Victoria, for a free future."

The cheering erupted again, and Cole was finally set down on the Courthouse steps—only to be mobbed by eager reporters vying for his attention.

Clara grinned at Lola. "Edward certainly knows how to sway a crowd," she said. "I had no idea he was such a good orator."

"This calls for a celebration," Lola replied. "I've ordered champagne and oysters for us all at The Club. My staff have everything in hand." She smiled. "Buchanan will be there, and Mr Woo. Mr Sinisgalli already knows—he will bring Cole along when they are done here."

"You planned this," Clara said.

"Of course I did," Lola replied. "It would never do for such a famous victory to go uncelebrated."

"And if we had lost?"

Lola shrugged. "It was always possible," she said. "In many ways, it was probable. If Edward had lost, I'd have been inviting you all to drown your sorrows with my excellent champagne."

"But he won," Clara said gleefully. "And I, for one, intend to thoroughly enjoy his success." She grinned at her friend. "Right after I interview him for *The New Day*, of course."

Chapter 96

On the other side of the world, in the ancient city of Bath, Isaac Pitman accompanied Ferguson and Hector to Ellett's house, leading them down the hill and across Victoria Park to Princes Street. At the bottom of the hill was a modest house, four storeys tall, but quite narrow. At street level, a small-paned bay window proclaimed, in faded gold lettering: *Ellett, Manufacturer of Toys and Automata.*

Hector paused by the window, peering in at the cluttered display: he saw brightly painted clockwork soldiers, each with its brass winding key; a model version of the Iron Duke steam engine, and another of the massive engine that had hauled the train from Liverpool to Bath; and in one dusty corner a caged, mechanical bird with impossibly bright plumage and a golden beak, open ready to sing. It was a child's paradise. He sighed as he pushed open the heavy wooden door, setting in motion a bell attached to a spring. The bell was still ringing as the three men stepped into a small shop space, no bigger than ten feet by twelve. The fireplace was clean but empty; the walls were equally clean, but their paintwork was shabby—and everywhere there were open shelves, lined with intricate automata. The room smelled of wood shavings, and paint, and machine oil.

Ellett was waiting to greet his visitors: a slight, sandy haired, bespectacled man who wore a leather apron tied neatly over plain work clothes. "Hello, Isaac," he said. "I see your guests have arrived at last."

"Mr Ferguson, Mr Munro," Pitman said, making perfunctory introductions.

"Delighted to meet you, sir," Hector said. "I see you have one of Mr Train's favourite songbirds in your window."

"Ah, yes," Ellett said, smiling. "You know Mr Train, then?"

Ferguson nodded. "We have just come from visiting his house in San Francisco. Your birds adorn his ballroom—I must say, the effect is spectacular."

The compliment had the desired effect: Ellett smiled at his guests. "He commissioned those birds specially," he said softly. "I'm glad to know they are working well."

"And Mr Cole sends his regards," Hector added, following Ferguson's lead. "I can also tell you that the automata you created for his book emporium are a huge success."

"It seems your creations are everywhere," Pitman said.

"It warms my heart to know they are out there, working away in the world," Ellett said, his almost childlike enthusiasm for his toys peeping through his otherwise quiet demeanour. "But you haven't come about that," he added. "I've had several letters from Mr Cole, offering me employment in Victoria. Cole tells me you are planning to build a whole new city. It's an amazing idea, but it's hard to contemplate when times here are so bad we don't even have the money to mend a roof."

"Yes, sir," Hector said. "I understand completely. Ferguson and I were shocked to find conditions so reduced here in Bath." He took a deep breath. "But we truly have come to make you an offer, sir, if you are interested in hearing it."

"I'm always interested in everything," Ellett replied, motioning them to sit.

"As you know, I am here to represent Sir Alec Buchanan and Mr Edward Cole," Hector said. "Our consortium is developing new technologies, and will need a skilled engineer—such as yourself—to design and make the tools and equipment that will drive them. Captain John Ericsson has agreed to join the venture: he leaves from New York at the end of this month."

"Ericsson," Ellett said. "Now that is interesting. I read about his designs in *The Technologist*. He's said to be brilliant."

"He is," Ferguson said simply. "We are about to build his Sun Engine." He gave Ellett a straight look. "We'd be honoured if you'd consider joining us, sir," he said.

"Well," Ellett replied. "I'll certainly think on it." He shrugged his narrow shoulders. "I can't imagine leaving Bath—but then I never imagined Bath would find itself in such dire straits."

"We can offer you first class passage," Hector said, "and Sir Alec will, of course, bear the cost of having your tools and equipment and personal effects crated and shipped to Melbourne."

Ellett smiled again. "That's encouraging," he said. "I'd hate to be parted from my tools—some of them have been handed down through generations of Elletts." He turned to Pitman. "Are you considering emigrating, Isaac?" he asked.

"No," Pitman replied. "I'm too old for that. But I'm happy to act as Cole's agent. My heart is here, in Bath, and here is where my old bones will be laid to rest."

Ellett hesitated. "When would you need your answer?" he asked Hector.

"You can take your time, sir," Hector replied. "We will not be here for more than a few days, but the necessary arrangements can be made by telegraph if you decide to accept our offer at a later date."

Ellett glanced wistfully around his workshop. "I'll make a decision before you leave," he said.

"We'd appreciate that, sir," Hector replied, rising to his feet. "We'll hope to hear from you soon. But for now, we'll take our leave." He hesitated. "If I may be so bold, Mr Ellett, I would very much like to buy one of your singing birds, for my mother. She has a beautiful conservatory, and she would enjoy your craftsmanship very much."

Ellett beamed. "Of course, of course," he said. "It would be my pleasure. Do come this way—you can make your selection and I'll arrange to have it shipped for you."

"Thank you," Hector said, following his host into the back room to make his purchase. "I'll only be a minute," he said to Ferguson.

"Take your time," Ferguson replied.

A short time later Hector re-emerged, grinning. "They are all so exquisite," he said. "I bought two: one for Mother and one for Charlotte."

"He chose my best work," Ellett said happily. "You have a good eye, Mr Munro."

"Excellent," said Ferguson, "but we really must be on our way. Thank you again, Mr Ellett."

"We have a meeting to arrange at The Marlborough," Pitman added.

"Be careful how you go up there," Ellett replied. "Don't touch the food— the place is full of disease. And remember, The Marlborough's not safe, especially after dark."

Chapter 97

McGill was in his office at the Consulate when the telegram from Ericsson arrived. The Consul rose immediately, and went to find his wife.

"Good news," he said, offering her the flimsy slip of paper. "Captain Ericsson has agreed to our request: he will escort Rosie, and her nurse, to Melbourne."

"That's wonderful," Morag replied. "When will they arrive?"

"By the middle of November," McGill said.

"Then I'd best see to her room," Morag said. "I have been thinking to have the walls re-papered in a pink flower pattern. What do you think, my dear?"

McGill laughed. "I leave such things entirely to you," he said. "I'll get on with arranging the details for Rosie. I'll just telegraph my mother."

"Very well," Morag replied, smiling back at him. "And will you also telegraph Hector?"

"I was about to do that very thing," McGill said. "I'll ask him to return as soon as he can. I'd like him to be here when the Independence Petition goes to Parliament: it will be a momentous occasion, one way or the other."

Chapter 98

In Bath, Isaac Pitman, true to his word, had sent his housekeeper's husband ahead: posters advertising the recruitment meeting—and offering work to experienced copper workers—had already been tacked to the wall when they arrived. As the three men made their way to the door, they picked their way through scattered debris and skirted a noisome channel of raw sewage that ran beside the pub.

A grubby child detached himself from the shadows to accost the visitors.

"Spare a copper, sirs?" he said, wiping his runny nose with a filthy sleeve before he held out his grimy hand.

Hector shuddered and tossed him a coin, trying not to stare at the open, weeping sores on the boy's face.

"Be off with you, now," Pitman said quickly.

The child ran, clutching the coin.

Pitman turned to Hector. "There'll be a crowd of them in no time, now that you've given something," he said.

"We won't be long," Hector replied. "How could I refuse a suffering child?"

"It's hard, I know," said Pitman. "Their need is great, and they are everywhere."

The landlord opened the door. "Mr Pitman, gentlemen, do come in," he said. "Tell me what you'll want for your meeting, and I'll do my best to oblige."

"We'll just need to speak to the men," Ferguson replied. "And when the business is done, I'll be happy to pay for beer for all of them."

"If word of *that* gets out, there'll be a riot," the landlord said, grinning. "I'll keep it to myself, until you give me the nod."

"Fair enough," Ferguson said. "We don't want any trouble."

The man laughed. "Hard to avoid it, down this way," he said shortly.

When Hector and Ferguson returned that evening, a crowd had already gathered at the pub. As they entered the main room, Hector tried not to gag on the smell of so many unwashed bodies packed into the small space. The pub reeked of slops, sweat and stale cabbage stew.

"I hope Sir Alec Buchanan has deep pockets," Pitman observed, holding his handkerchief to his nose. "There's easily a hundred skilled men out there, all waiting to take ship, if the price is right."

The landlord had set up a long bench for Hector. Ferguson walked across and plunked a ledger on its grimy surface, ready to sign up likely candidates. He was at the bar, preparing to ring the bell, when the trouble started.

One man put down his half-full beer mug; another picked it up and drained it in a single swallow. In reply, the first grabbed the other's arm and twisted it, setting off a scuffle that quickly turned into a bare-knuckled fistfight. The two brawny workers were soon slogging it out, overturning benches and toppling jugs. The fight spilled into the centre of the room, and Hector found himself surrounded by angry men. He slid his hand inside his jacket, exposing his Colt revolver, ready to use it if necessary.

The landlord waded in, wielding a long staff: "Come on lads, break it up," he shouted above the din. "This meeting is supposed to be for you."

The men separated, panting. One sported a cut above his eyebrow: his eye was swelling fast.

While all attention was focussed on them, a third man slipped behind Hector, aiming a short knife at Hector's unprotected back.

The stroke went wide, blocked by a brawny arm and followed by a heavy, left-handed punch that laid the man out cold on the floor, bleeding from a cut lip. "No," said the owner of the arm. "This one's alright—leave him be."

Hector spun around, to see the big thief from the railway station grinning at him. "I thought you might be wanting a good coppersmith," the man said.

"Indeed I do," Hector replied. "And thank you."

"One good turn deserves another, as they say," the man replied: "Samuel Tozer, coppersmith, at your service, sir."

"Hector Munro," Hector said, "and welcome aboard." He offered his hand to shake—the hand the man had kissed in gratitude only yesterday.

Tozer poked the man on the floor with his boot. "He was after your revolver," he said, by way of explanation. "Those things are valuable. A man could live well on the proceeds of a piece like that." He shrugged. "We're all desperate enough for anything around here."

"Understood," said Hector.

Another scuffle broke out behind the bar; the shouting began again.

Ferguson reached casually inside his coat, drew his revolver and fired a single, deafening shot into the air. Flakes of soot-blackened plaster showered the room, leaving a clean patch on the ceiling where the bullet had struck.

The crowd subsided into shocked silence—the only sound was the scuttling of a startled rat as it ran across the flagstone floor seeking shelter.

"Enough," Ferguson said. "Do you want to hear what we have to say or not?"

"Let's hear it then," the landlord said.

"Right," Ferguson replied. He did not re-holster his pistol. He stood there, ready and waiting for the first sign of trouble.

The crowd got the message.

"We need skilled copper workers in Australia," Hector shouted into the ensuing calm. "We are building a new city: we need smelters, smiths, wire workers, all sorts. Sir Alec Buchanan's company will provide passage for each of you, and your families, on a ship to Australia. In return for which, you will sign an agreement to work for him for five years." He looked back at his newfound friend. "Mr Tozer here has already volunteered."

There was a sudden racket of protesting voices.

"We'd be no better than indentured labour," one greasy-haired man shouted, louder than the rest.

Ferguson raised his pistol, and the uneasy silence resumed.

"If you'd just let me finish," said Hector. "The agreement is that if you leave Sir Alec's employment sooner, you will repay the cost of your passage. That option is always yours to take."

"As if we could ever earn enough to do that," another man muttered.

"The wages are better there," Hector said. "But the choice is yours—take it or leave it. It's all the same to me."

"I'll take it!" The man who spoke strode up to the front of the smoky room. "Where do I sign?"

"Right here," Ferguson replied, pointing at the ledger. "Mr Munro will write your name in the book and you can make your mark beside it."

"Me too," said a second man. "I've no loyalties to keep me here to watch my family starve."

The trickle of acceptance quickly became a flood: by the end of the allotted hour, Hector and Ferguson had signed on a whole crew of experienced copper workers, from smiths to smelters.

Ferguson signalled to the landlord: "Drinks all round," he said.

The crowd cheered.

The bargain was sealed, in beer and blood.

Chapter 99

"Tea?" said Woo.

"Thank you, yes," Buchanan replied, settling comfortably into one of Woo's magnificent rosewood chairs.

"I trust your Independence Petition is going smoothly, now that the business of Cole's trial is successfully concluded," Woo said, pouring his fragrant oolong blend for both of them.

"Indeed it is," Buchanan replied. "But Cole's arraignment was a warning to us all. There is a lot of resistance from powerful men."

"Bound to be," Woo said. "I understand that Judge Redmond Barry is searching for anything at all that will enable him to bring more charges."

"True," said Buchanan. "Barry is only Acting Chief Justice, after all. He wants to make his mark before Justice Stawell returns from England."

"Barry is a difficult man," Woo said. "Before Cole's trial I made some discreet enquiries, of course, but there is nothing to suggest Barry would be amenable to, shall we say, a financial consideration."

"There wouldn't be," said Buchanan. "Barry is conservative, unimaginative, pompous, and very harsh in his judgements. He has a bad temper, and he is prone to theatrics. But he has never been corrupt."

"Pity," said Woo. He took a tiny sip of tea. "But then, his actions have served us well: Cole's arrest has encouraged more people to support the Petition. The talk here is of nothing else."

"I hope *your* people have all signed," Buchanan said.

Woo smiled. "I could hardly stop them," he said. "We Orientals bring huge amounts of business into this colony, but still we are discriminated against. We hope Independence will change that."

"It will, if I have anything to do with it," Buchanan replied firmly. "Premier Francis hopes to introduce further reforms once the question of Independence is settled."

Woo merely smiled in acknowledgement. "In that, you have my unqualified support," he said.

"How are things in Hong Kong?" Buchanan asked.

"Stable, as far as anyone can tell," Woo replied. "Our business remains secure, and largely unhindered by administrators. It seems that Britain is concentrating its efforts on keeping control of India."

"Excellent," Buchanan replied. "In that case, its attention will be elsewhere when our Petition is presented."

Woo sipped thoughtfully for a moment. "I'm as certain as I can be now that Bishop O'Hanlon is Orsini's murderer," he said conversationally.

"Good Lord! We suspected him, of course. Do you have any new information?" Buchanan asked, surprised by the conversation's sudden change of direction.

Woo shrugged. "Nothing that would stand up in court," he said. "But my Italian sources have lately confirmed that Orsini's family is indeed a leading part of Rome's 'black nobility', key men in the Vatican and more heavily involved with the Banco di Santo Spirito than I had thought. The Orsinis are dangerous: they would not have taken kindly to O'Hanlon's interference here as Antonelli's personal agent—and I know now that the Cardinal is undercutting the bank's official rates."

"So you think Orsini really was meeting O'Hanlon that night?"

"In all probability, yes," Woo replied. "And O'Hanlon struck first." He paused. "O'Hanlon is always causing difficulties: when last we spoke of this you said you had a use for him. Let me ask you, Buchanan, whether that is still the case. If not, I have only to mention my suspicions to my Italian colleagues and the difficulties will disappear. For the Orsini family, vengeance is swift and final."

Buchanan hesitated. "O'Hanlon has killed before," he said softly.

"That wouldn't surprise me," Woo replied. "What have you heard?"

"A whisper, by way of one of Lola's girls: it seems that the unfortunate Mr Valentine heard the story from a client at the Commercial Bank, and passed it on." He paused. "Priests and bank managers—people tell them a lot of secrets."

"And whores," Woo added. "I get all sorts of information from my girls."

"True enough," said Buchanan. "Lola's Supper Club is useful in more ways than one."

"And Valentine's story?" Woo prompted.

"It seems O'Hanlon began as an ordinary schoolyard bully," Buchanan said, "but one day he went too far. He killed another boy—strangled him with his bare hands in a fit of rage."

"That rings true," said Woo. "We know O'Hanlon has a violent temper. What happened next?"

"The priests bundled him straight into their seminary and claimed he was a postulant," Buchanan said. "The law couldn't touch him then. The priests saved O'Hanlon from the noose, and he became one of them."

"He couldn't have done anything else," Woo observed.

"Indeed he could not," said Buchanan. "The official story was that O'Hanlon had reformed, had learned his lesson."

"But which lesson?" Woo said. "He got away with murder, and the Church protected him."

"And has been protecting him ever since," Buchanan added. "Valentine's informant said O'Hanlon caused trouble wherever he went. The Church moved him from parish to parish, and finally shipped him out here to Australia, out of the way." Buchanan spread his hands. "And that's all I know," he said, "except to add that Lola's girl had the impression that Valentine was afraid of O'Hanlon."

"With good cause, as things turned out," Woo said. "Let me ask you again: do you want me to take care of this murderous priest?"

Buchanan thought hard. "O'Hanlon does still have his uses," he said at last.

"As you wish," said Woo. "But I warn you, you'll be stuck with him: he won't dare return to Rome."

"True," Buchanan replied. "And there may yet come a time when your information about the Orsini family will prove useful after all. One never knows. Thank you for telling me."

"My pleasure," Woo replied. He sat back in his chair, still sipping his tea.

Chapter 100

After the meeting at The Marlborough, the business in Bath was swiftly concluded. Next morning, Pitman undertook Buchanan's commission to provide rail and shipboard passage for Buchanan's new copper workers: most were to leave the next week, as soon as the paperwork could be completed. Ferguson and Hector were to return to Liverpool on the evening train, ready to set sail for Melbourne the following day.

Hector was packing for the journey when he received an urgent message from Mr Ellett, asking him to return. Hector set out immediately, accompanied by Ferguson: they walked down to Princes Street, and found Ellett waiting nervously in his little shop.

"I've decided to join you in the colony of Victoria," he said quickly. "Can you arrange my passage?"

"Most certainly," Hector replied. "Mr Pitman is acting as our agent. You can take ship as soon as the formalities have been completed. It won't take long."

"And my equipment?"

"Can be crated up as soon as you like," said Ferguson.

"Has something happened?" Hector asked. "You seem very anxious."

"I've started getting threats," Ellett replied. "I have only the tiniest debt, for clockwork supplies, but a banker's agent is threatening to seize my stock and my personal effects if I cannot make immediate payment."

"Then we'd better get you out of here at once," Ferguson said. "Mr Hatfield will come this afternoon to start the packing, under your direction."

"Thank you," Ellett said.

"And if I may make a further suggestion," Ferguson continued, "you should stay at Mr Pitman's house until you are ready to embark. You two are old friends, after all. And it wouldn't do to have you arrested for debt at this point in the proceedings. We can make arrangements to clear your debt at a later date."

"Excellent idea," Hector said.

421

"What about my house?" Ellett asked.

"You'll have to board it up, for now," Ferguson said. "As long as it is secured, it can be sold off at a later date, when things improve."

"Or I return," said Ellett.

"Of course," Hector said. "That will be your decision, entirely."

Chapter 101

In the arena of public opinion, the question of Independence for Victoria was decided in the affirmative long before the Petition was declared closed and the organisers had begun to put the long lists of signatures together for presentation to the Lower House. When all was ready, Premier James Francis, leader of the Lower House in the Parliament of Victoria, rose to his feet to table the Petition for Independence.

"Gentlemen," he said, "in the Petition now before us, the people have spoken. Common sense must prevail: the man in the street wants independence, our voters need independence, and our businessmen must have independence. Even the voiceless have spoken: those residents who cannot vote—the poor, the women, the workers—all have added their signatures to those of our enfranchised citizens. We must not disappoint them. I urge you, for all our sakes, to accept the Petition."

The House decided to put the question without delay. There was no need for a division: the support was overwhelming.

"The 'ayes' have it. I declare the Petition for Independence received by this House," the speaker said formally.

Shouts of "Hear! Hear!" reverberated through the chamber as members voiced their approval.

The Speaker moved quickly to call a vote on the Legislation, while the optimistic mood lasted.

"I wouldn't get too confident just yet," Buchanan said, settling into his favourite armchair at The Melbourne Club. "The Lower House was always going to support the Petition."

"It was a unanimous vote," Cole replied, taking his seat opposite. "That should send a very clear message to the Upper House."

"Which will therefore strongly oppose it, as it has every other attempt at reform," Buchanan said. "William Mitchell has made no secret of the fact that he regards the whole Independence Movement as an inconvenience to be quashed as soon as possible. And as President of the Legislative Council, he has a great deal of influence."

"I thought he'd like the clause that allows the Parliament to relieve the Governor of his post if he fails to sign the Legislation," Cole said.

"Perhaps," said Buchanan, "but Mitchell is expecting to receive a knighthood in the near future. It's certainly not in his interests to allow Independence to occur."

"I see," said Cole. "No wonder he was pushing for my conviction: he wants the Independence movement quashed at any price. It's sheer self-interest—if Victoria ceases to be a colony, Mitchell loses his chance at a knighthood."

"Precisely," Buchanan said.

"Then we will need to consider our strategy where Mitchell is concerned," said Cole.

"Indeed," Buchanan replied.

"As I said at the Independence meeting," Cole said, "the real problem is that the Constitution granted to us after the Eureka uprising to satisfy the demands for democracy was written so that the Upper House would always provide a way to counter the democratic tendencies of the Lower House. In a word, it was put there to block reform."

"Precisely," Buchanan replied. "George Train pointed it out at the time. I argued with him then, but now I see the truth of what he said. The old men of the establishment *have* kept control: the Upper House is not at all democratic—it is there to represent the interests of the wealthy landowners and their English masters."

"Train has been right about a good many things," Cole said thoughtfully. "But if the Upper House is constituted to prevent democracy, what are we to do?"

"They would see it as preventing anarchy."

"Even so, it will make the next stage exceedingly difficult for us."

"Difficult, but not impossible," Buchanan said. "The businessmen in the Upper House will support us—they can see as well as the rest of us that staying tied to the Empire is financial suicide. It will come down to a question of self-interest—it always does." He sighed. "The Legislation will need an extra push: but we have not yet exhausted all our options."

Cole smiled at last. "And the Governor?" he asked.

"Governor Bowen has received absolutely no instructions from Whitehall on this issue," Buchanan replied blandly. "It seems that he has been abandoned by his political masters—he will have to make his own decision when the time comes."

"I knew that loop in the telegraph system at Alice Springs would prove useful," Cole said happily. "Do you have a sense of Bowen's position?"

Buchanan shrugged. "If the Legislation succeeds, he will have little option but to sign," he said. "If he accepts, the position will offer him dignity and power. If he refuses, he will be obliged to return to England in disgrace—to return as the man who lost the richest colony on earth."

"I can't see the latter option having much appeal," Cole said. "Especially as he married into aristocracy. I've met his wife, and I have to say she is ambitious enough for both of them. I have no doubt what her advice will be."

"Nor do I," said Buchanan. "As I said, our real problem is the Upper House. We shall have to study our position very carefully if the first reading of the Bill goes against us."

Chapter 102

When Hector and Ferguson finally arrived back in Melbourne, they found McGill waiting for them at the pier.

"Welcome back, both of you," McGill said, embracing each man in turn, American style. "I've brought the Consular carriage to collect you, and your luggage."

"It's good to be home," Hector replied. He smiled at McGill, suppressing a twinge of disappointment that Charlotte had not come to the docks, hoping that nothing was amiss between them.

McGill smiled back. "The others are all waiting at the Consulate," he said. "Your mother has arranged a private luncheon in honour of your return, so I persuaded her that it would be best if she stayed to greet our guests." He shrugged. "Otherwise, I'd have needed two carriages."

"Quite right," said Ferguson.

"And besides," said McGill, "it will give us a chance to talk before you are both caught up in the pleasantries of luncheon."

"And we have such a lot to tell," Hector said.

"Indeed," McGill replied. "And I also have news: in your absence, things here have certainly been moving apace." He paused as the Consular equipage rolled into view. "Our carriage, gentlemen," he said.

"It'll be a pleasure to travel on dry land," Ferguson said, mounting the step.

"It certainly will," Hector agreed.

The three men settled in to exchange news as the driver pulled away, taking them home.

"The recruitment was very successful," Hector said. "The situation in England is much worse than we had anticipated. I was shocked when we arrived—Bath has horrible camps where unemployed workers huddle together in the most appalling conditions. The hope of a better future was incentive enough: there were more men willing to sign on than we could take, so I trust the copper smelter is well underway by now. The workers we did sign on in Bath won't be far behind us. Pitman was arranging passage for them when we left."

Ferguson grinned. "The process was not without some excitements," he added.

"True," Hector said. "But we managed well enough. And I should add that in New York Mr Delaney has undertaken to engage American engineers for us. I expect that the first of them will be arriving here quite soon."

"Excellent news," McGill said. "The pieces are all falling into place. Ericsson arrived two weeks ago. I have to say he seems very happy—he and Edward Cole are closeted in Cole's office for days at a time, planning ways to develop the solar steam engine."

Ferguson laughed: "And that would suit Cole down to the ground," he said.

"He's certainly found a like-minded soul in Ericsson," said McGill. "Especially since Ericsson brought with him the most amazing pictures of his Sun Engine in operation. Cole's friend Muybridge took them himself when the engine was tested in New York. It's a whole new kind of photography—moving pictures—and Cole is determined to learn the technique."

"Of course he is," Hector said smiling. "I'm glad Ericsson has arrived before us."

"Whatever you said to persuade him, it worked a treat," McGill said.

"I had to promise decent schooling for his son, Karl," Hector said.

"Ah," said McGill. "Buchanan mentioned something about that. Karl seems a bright lad."

"He would be," said Ferguson, "if he takes after his father at all."

"I like Ericsson," McGill said. "He's an honest man, and passionate about his inventions. And he was kind enough to chaperone my daughter and her nurse on the voyage."

"Your daughter is here?" said Hector.

"Indeed she is," McGill replied. "The President extended my tenure as American Consul so your mother and I judged it best that Rosie should join us here. You'll meet her at luncheon."

"And how is Mother coping with your daughter?" Hector asked, suddenly anxious.

"They took an instant liking to each other," McGill replied, his relief evident in his voice. "Morag is treating Rosie like a China doll: the child has more new dresses and ribbons than I've seen in years. And Rosie loves it, of course—everything is new and exciting." He smiled. "I've promised her a pony for Christmas."

"That sounds entirely satisfactory," Ferguson said. "Dare one enquire about Clara?"

"Still not speaking to Morag, I'm afraid," McGill replied.

Hector looked stricken.

"But Charlotte has still been spending a lot of time with us," McGill hastened to add. "She'll be at luncheon, Hector."

Hector breathed again. "Thanks," he said. "It'll be good to see her."

Chapter 103

Morag had arranged a splendid homecoming for her son, inviting only the people she knew he would most wish to see. Buchanan and Cole were there, of course, with Lola and Charlotte. Ericsson had also been invited, and stood to one side with his son Karl as Ferguson and Hector entered the reception hall.

Hector embraced his mother with unfeigned affection. "Mother," he said, hugging her tightly. "I'm so glad to be back, so glad you are well."

Morag's smile lit up her face. "I'm relieved to have you back safe and sound after all your adventures," she said. "And you too, Charles, of course," she added, extending her hand to Ferguson.

"Delighted," said Ferguson, lightly kissing her fingers. He turned, and stepped forward to shake hands with Buchanan and Cole: "It's good to be back among friends," he said, bowing from the waist to acknowledge the ladies.

"It's good to have you returned to us," Buchanan said. "We all owe you a great deal."

"I'm glad you're home safe," Cole added. "I must admit there have been times when I was rather worried: the press has been full of lurid accounts of the unstable state of things in England."

Ferguson laughed. "Nothing we couldn't handle," he said. "But it's good to see you here, Edward. I hear you've been having adventures of your own."

Cole smiled ruefully. "You might say that," he said.

"There'll be time enough for legal and business matters tomorrow," Buchanan said. "Mrs McGill has decreed that this is to be a social occasion, and I applaud her wisdom."

"Hear, hear," said Cole. "Today is for homecomings. Let's enjoy ourselves."

"Excellent plan," said McGill. "Shall we all go in to the sitting room? We just have time for a sherry before lunch."

Morag had thought of everything: to Karl's delight, the drinks tray on the sideboard included a tall pitcher of lemonade, and the footman had already poured a glass for him.

"Capital," said Cole, accepting a tiny glass of amber sherry and settling himself in an armchair beside Lola. "And now, my dear," he said, "you really must tell me all the latest gossip from your club."

Hector turned to Ericsson, drink in hand. "It's good to see you again, sir," he said. "I trust you are settling in well?"

"Well enough, thank you," said Ericsson. "I find that I'm very interested in this project. I put my time on the ship to good use: I am thinking about redesigning my Sun Engine collector for larger-scale applications."

"Splendid," said Ferguson. "And may I enquire whether your scientific materials have arrived in satisfactory condition?"

"Most satisfactory," Ericsson replied. "Mr Cole has been helping me to arrange a demonstration for you all. We are planning to do it next week, when Mr Jacob Pitman will be visiting Melbourne. Consul McGill has kindly allowed us the use of his gardens for the purpose."

"How wonderful," Hector said. "You will not yet know, of course, that we have persuaded Mr Ellett, master toymaker from Bath, to join our project. He too will be with us next week. He sailed shortly after we did."

"Did you say Ellett is coming to join us?" Cole asked.

"Indeed he is," Hector replied.

Cole's face creased into a huge smile. "But that is the most wonderful news," he said.

Ericsson looked puzzled. "Should I know of this man?" he asked.

"Ellett is the maker of the automata at the front of my book emporium," Cole explained. "He is truly a master craftsman. He has a most uncanny knack of understanding the tiniest pieces of machinery. I'm sure he could make anything, if he once put his mind to it."

"I've actually brought some of his pieces with me," Hector said, feeling suddenly shy. "They are clockwork songbirds: there is one for your conservatory, Mother; the other is for Charlotte."

"I'm sure they'll be wonderful," Morag said. "I can't wait to see them."

Charlotte just smiled.

"We hope Mr Ellett will be able to make whatever precision moving parts you need for the manufacture of your Sun Engine," McGill added.

"Then I shall look forward to meeting him next week," Ericsson replied stiffly. "I have always been in the habit of making my prototypes myself."

Before the moment could become uncomfortable, Hector turned to Karl. "And have you seen many butterflies yet?" Hector asked the boy.

"Yes, sir," Karl said shyly. "I've started a new collection."

"Glad to hear it," said Ferguson. "Have you seen many strange animals as well?"

"Some, sir: we went to the botanical gardens and I saw a koala bear in a gum tree." Karl looked suddenly hopeful. "I've heard there are water moles, sir," he blurted out. "I've heard they are little furry animals that live in water and have webbed feet and bills like ducks. Is that true, sir?"

Ferguson laughed. "Of course it's true. They are sweet little animals," he said. "They are called platypuses."

"I can take you to see them, if you like," said Hector. "I know a spot on the riverbank where they can usually be found. Miss Seekamp and I often ride that way." He smiled at Charlotte. "You could ride with us one day, if your father will permit it."

Karl's face fell.

"He doesn't ride," Ericsson said softly. "We have always lived in the city."

"Then it's time he learned," Ferguson said. "Would you like that, Karl?"

The boy just nodded, taken aback by this sudden turn of events.

"I'm sure we can find a quiet pony for him in the stables," McGill added.

"That's settled, then," said Ferguson. "I'll teach him myself."

"And then we can show you a wombat burrow," Charlotte added. "You won't see wombats by daylight, of course, but they have burrows quite near the riding track, so you can see where they live."

Karl smiled up at her. "That would be wonderful, Miss Seekamp," he said. "I haven't seen a wombat yet."

Cole laughed. "There'll be plenty of time for that," he said. "I might even take you out myself one evening: I'd rather like to photograph one of the creatures."

At a nod from Morag, McGill checked his fob watch. "The hour is upon us," he said. "Since we are all assembled, we should go in to luncheon." As he spoke, a sweet-looking but solemn little girl, decked out for the occasion in ringlets and bows, joined them and reached up to take his hand.

"And who is this pretty child?" Ferguson asked.

"This is Rosie, my step-daughter," Morag said. "Rosie, this is Mr Ferguson, and my son, Mr Munro."

Rosie curtsied. "Pleased to meet you, Mr Ferguson," she said.

She curtsied again to Hector: "Pleased to meet you, Mr Munro." She gazed enquiringly up at him. "Will you be my brother now?" she asked.

Hector hesitated, looking across the child's head at his mother.

Morag nodded.

"Of course I will," Hector said. "Your father is my step-father, after all."

"So we shall be a family," McGill said, covering the momentary awkwardness.

"Indeed we shall," Morag agreed. "Shall we go in?"

Hector took the opportunity to escort Charlotte into the dining room. He offered his arm, and she walked a little closer than propriety demanded.

"Did you miss me?" Hector whispered.

"Every minute," Charlotte replied.

"I missed you too," he said. "I have presents for you, later."

"Having you back is gift enough for me," she said.

"Oh…" Hector began.

"But I'm dying to see what you've brought me," she added.

"That's all right then," he replied, holding her chair for her, delighted to find that his mother, tactful as ever, had seated him beside Charlotte. He squeezed Charlotte's hand beneath the table.

"Everything will be alright now you're home, you'll see," Charlotte said happily.

Luncheon was a huge success, and afterwards the guests repaired to the conservatory for coffee. Ferguson was happily regaling the company with tales of their adventures in Chinatown when Hector seized the moment to slip outside into the garden, following Charlotte.

"I'll just get some air," he muttered.

McGill made to rise, but Morag put a hand on his arm. "Let them be," she said softly. "Charlotte's been pining for him. And it's clear enough that Hector is desperate to speak to her. Let them have a little time together." She sighed. "I doubt Clara will make him very welcome: there's trouble ahead in that direction, to be sure."

"Perhaps not," Lola said. "Let us hope for the best: Clara's no fool."

"Indeed not," Morag replied. "But she's stubborn as a mule."

"True enough," Lola said ruefully. "We've all had occasion to see Clara dig her heels in."

"Will Mr Hector marry Miss Charlotte?" Rosie piped up unexpectedly.

"Whatever makes you ask that?" Morag replied.

"He likes her," Rosie replied. "He gave her his chocolate bonbon—I saw him."

"Well yes, he did," Lola said, smiling. "But that doesn't mean he will marry her."

"Karl says that he and I are to be married, when we are grown up," Rosie confided.

"I don't know about that, sweetheart," said McGill. "It will be a long time before you're ready for a big decision like that."

434

"I wonder," Ericsson said. "The two of them spent a lot of time playing together on the voyage. And Karl has always been very definite—if he once makes up his mind, nothing will move him." He glanced across the room at his son, who stood silent, but smiling confidently.

"Even so, deciding at the age of fourteen to marry my daughter may be precocious, even for Karl," McGill said, laughing it off.

Ericsson laughed too. "We'll see what we shall see," he said. "And in the meantime, Mr Cole and I have a city to build—with Mr Pitman's help, of course."

"A city?" Ferguson asked. "I thought you were engineering a solar steam engine."

"That too," said Cole. "The thing is, Charles, Buchanan and I have always thought that our telegraph station at Alice Springs would be the perfect site for manufacturing, if only we could power the machinery. Jacob Pitman has already drawn up preliminary plans for a site near the station."

"So once the Sun Engine is running at the copper smelter, we will be able to design new prototypes," said Ericsson. "We will build all manner of steam engines, driven by the power of the sun."

"And a model factory town to house them," Cole added enthusiastically. "Think of it, Charles—a new town powered by steam and sunshine."

Ferguson shrugged. "It's too much for my tired brain to comprehend just now," he said. "But you're talking about a city in the desert. I know the springs are there, but will you ever have enough clean water?"

"That's part of the beauty of our scheme," Cole replied. "The by-product of steam is distilled water: as the steam cools we can choose to channel the purified droplets away as they condense, stream off the clean water and leave the sludge at the bottom of the apparatus to be removed later. It means we can use brackish water to start the process. It's such an elegant solution, don't you think?"

"If it works," Ferguson said dubiously. He turned to Buchanan. "Is it possible?" he asked. "Can you really build such a thing?"

"It's not impossible," Buchanan replied. "Nothing is impossible. If you had asked me three months ago, I'd have said Independence for Victoria was not even remotely feasible—but here we are, waiting for the Upper House to decide our fate. So yes, Charles, I believe it may be possible."

"Well," said Ferguson. "Wonders will never cease."

"Let us hope not, Mr Ferguson," Ericsson replied. "Let us hope not."

Chapter 104

It was mid-afternoon, and sunlight streamed into Lola's private sitting room, making the polished rosewood furniture glow and lighting up the red velvet trimmings. The only sound in the room was the chattering of a pair of bright green budgerigars where they perched in their ornately gilded birdcage. Lola offered a chair to an obviously nervous Charlotte, and sat, waiting patiently until the girl should be ready to talk.

"It's lovely to see you, Charlotte," Lola said. "But you're nervous: would you care to tell me what this visit is about?"

Charlotte took a deep breath. "It's about Hector," she explained. "We want to marry, but Mother has forbidden it. I'm eighteen years old, so I need her permission. She says I'll have to wait until I'm twenty-one, if I want to marry him without her consent."

"That's a bit much," Lola said. "If I recall correctly, your mother was married at sixteen, and bore her first child shortly afterwards."

"I know," Charlotte replied. "But you know Mother: I can't argue her into changing her mind."

"So why come to me?" Lola asked. "Your mother is hardly likely to listen to my advice on matters of the heart."

"It's not that. The thing is, I've decided to give myself to Hector, married or not," Charlotte said defiantly. "If I'm pregnant, Mother will have to let us marry."

"Good for you," said Lola. "But why tell me?"

"I don't know what to do," Charlotte blurted out, blushing bright red to the roots of her honey blonde hair. "I can't ask Mother. I thought you might tell me."

Lola smiled kindly. "It was brave of you to come and ask," she said. "I understand completely."

Charlotte stared down at her hands in her lap.

"There's no mystery," Lola said. "It comes to every woman, sooner or

437

later. Hector will know what to do, for his part. I can certainly tell you what to expect. Do you know how to pleasure yourself?"

Charlotte shook her head.

"Well, then," said Lola, "first things first: you need to learn how to please yourself, so you can teach Hector." She sighed deeply. "I've had to teach all my husbands," she added.

Charlotte looked up, her whole face a question.

"I have an idea," Lola said. "I can see you are embarrassed to continue with me, but one of my girls can show you: Lily is here today, and she's about your age."

"Oh, thank you," Charlotte said, greatly relieved.

Lola left the room for a few moments, and returned with a dark-haired young woman, shorter and plumper than Charlotte, but vivacious and friendly.

"You come with me," she said, taking Charlotte by the hand. "Madame Montez has explained what's needed. We'll use one of the upstairs rooms — it's too early for the patrons to be about. We won't be disturbed."

Charlotte allowed herself to be led from the room.

Some time later, Lola tiptoed past the room, pausing to listen to the giggles on the other side of the door. *Well,* she thought, *that sounds very promising. Young Hector is in for the surprise of his life.*

Chapter 105

The large, private back garden of the American Consulate was a hive of activity as Captain John Ericsson, dressed more formally than usual for the occasion, made the final preparations for the demonstration of his Sun Engine. All was going well—even the weather was cooperating, and Ericsson was perspiring slightly in the hot sunshine of a November day in Melbourne. The air was full of the scent of flowers, and a flock of fairy wrens were busily hunting insects in the shrubbery around the garden's ornamental fishpond. A kookaburra laughed from high up in a flowering gum tree.

Ericsson ignored it. He was completely focussed on making his last-minute calibrations.

Inside the house, Morag McGill, dressed elegantly in a pale green silk dress, was busy with arrangements of her own: she had ordered an informal luncheon to follow the scientific proceedings, and was checking that all was in place.

She glanced up as Hector joined her. "Is there anything you need, dear?" she asked.

"No, Mother," Hector replied. "I've just been running a few last-minute errands. Mr Cole is setting up his photographic equipment to record the event. He says it is an historic occasion—and he's borrowed Wilson to be his assistant again."

"Poor Wilson," said Morag. "He didn't much enjoy holding the flash powder apparatus last time." She glanced through the Conservatory window at the shining copper machinery and the assorted bits and pieces of equipment that now dominated her manicured lawn. A little way back from the Sun Engine, she could see Cole fussing with an assortment of cameras and tripods, attended patiently by the stoic butler. At a safe distance from the Engine, a trestle table bearing trays of glasses and pitchers of lemonade had been set up under a shady tree, along with a semi-circle of canvas deck chairs arranged to give a good view of the Engine—even though Morag doubted anyone would want to sit once the demonstration finally got underway.

"Goodness," she said. "It looks very complicated. I hope it works, after all this." She glanced up at the wall clock. "Our guests will be here soon."

"I'm sure it will work, Mother," Hector replied. "The only question is how *well* it will work."

"I see," said Morag. She looked up sharply at the sound the sound of carriage wheels on the gravel drive. "Somebody is rather early."

"That will be Charlotte," Hector said. "I asked her to come a little ahead of time. I'll just go and meet her."

"As you like, dear," Morag said. "Is everything all right—between you and Charlotte, I mean?"

"Everything is fine," Hector replied, hurrying from the room to hide the rising blush that threatened to betray him.

An hour later, the invited guests were milling about on the lawns when Ferguson, relaxed as always, shepherded a rather slight, nervous-looking Englishman into the garden.

"Ah, Consul McGill," he said, spotting his host. "Allow me to introduce Mr Ellett, who has only just joined us from Bath."

McGill offered his hand. "Delighted to make your acquaintance, Mr Ellett," he said. "Your reputation precedes you. And may I introduce my wife, Mrs Morag McGill?"

"Charmed," Ellett said diffidently. He bent to kiss Morag's hand.

"I trust you had an agreeable voyage?" she asked.

"Agreeable enough, Mrs McGill," Ellett replied. "Though I must admit I'm no sailor."

"Well, you're here now, safe and sound," McGill said. "And just in time for Captain Ericsson's demonstration."

Ellett, obviously abashed at finding himself in company with the American Consul and a group of fashionably dressed guests, was at a loss for words. "Indeed, yes," he managed to say.

Morag took pity on him. "And I really must thank you for my wonderful clockwork songbird," she said. "It has pride of place in my Conservatory, and it is greatly admired by all who see it."

Ellett smiled at last. "I'm glad you like it, Mrs McGill," he said. "Your son has a very good eye—he chose my best work."

"I've no doubt he did," said Morag. She glanced around, but couldn't see Hector anywhere. She realised she hadn't seen him at all since Charlotte arrived. "My son is helping to arrange the demonstration," she said smoothly, "but I'm sure he will be here to greet you soon, Mr Ellett. But in the meantime, you really must meet Mr Cole. He is so looking forward to your arrival."

Ellett brightened up immediately. "Thank you," he said. "Mr Cole and I have corresponded for many years. It will be a pleasure to meet him properly at last."

Morag beckoned to Cole, who stepped forward and embraced Ellett as a long-lost friend. "Welcome, and thrice welcome!" he said. "I can't tell you how delighted I am to have you here today. We are all agog to see Captain Ericsson's invention at work. You really must allow me to introduce you to him."

Ericsson looked up distractedly when Cole tapped him on the shoulder. "I've brought Mr Ellett," Cole said cheerfully. "Mr Ellett, this is Captain Ericsson."

Ericsson shook hands with Ellett, sizing him up. "Cole here tells me you make automata," he said carefully.

"Among other things, yes," Ellett replied. "I have taken the liberty of bringing one of my replica steam engines for your son, if you will allow the gift."

Cole clapped his hands. "Capital," he said. "That is a precious gift indeed. A model train by Mr Ellett is a thing of wonder—perfect to the last detail. I own I am quite jealous. Karl is a lucky boy!"

Ericsson could hardly demur. "My son will be delighted to receive it," he said, "though perhaps we might leave it until after the demonstration?"

"Of course, of course," said Ellett. "I did not mean to intrude upon you at such a critical time. I am most intrigued to see the workings of the solar steam pump at first hand. I carried several technical journals with me for my sea voyage, and I have studied the reports of your invention very closely."

Ericsson began to thaw a little. "You must forgive me, Mr Ellett," he said. "I have much to do to produce this little demonstration."

"May I watch the final calibrations?" Ellett asked. He looked down at his hands. "I already have some thoughts about clockwork mechanisms that might facilitate the small movements your machine will require to stay aligned with the sun."

"Certainly you may observe," Ericsson said. "I'll be most interested in your thoughts."

"As will I," said Cole. "The whole enterprise is completely fascinating. I'll be taking the pictures for the City of the Sun consortium, of course, and I've promised to send George Train a full photographic record for our potential American investors, so I'll be really quite busy. But I still don't want to miss a thing."

"Nor do I," said Jacob Pitman, walking across the lawn to join them. "Hello, Edward: it's good to see that you have all your marvellous photographic equipment ready for the big event."

"Jacob, welcome!" Cole beamed happily as he began another round of pleasantries, introducing the architect to the engineer and the designer.

But Ericsson was impatient. He had work to do. "You really must excuse me, gentlemen," he said. "There will be plenty of time to discuss the technicalities once the engine is operating."

"Of course, my friend, of course," said Cole. "We'll leave you to it. I see that the redoubtable Mrs McGill has provided lemonade. Shall we join the others, Jacob?"

"Lemonade will be most welcome," Pitman replied.

"I'll stay here, if I may," Ellett said. "I promise I won't be in the way." He smiled shyly at Ericsson. "Perhaps I might even assist? I'm accustomed to managing finicky adjustments."

Ericsson nodded. "Thank you very much, Mr Ellett. That is most kind," was all he said.

Cole and Pitman headed for the refreshments, to join Ferguson and McGill and Morag. Buchanan had arrived now, with Lola, who had dressed for the garden party in a flowing red ensemble and an amazingly fashionable hat—a huge confection of gauze and feathers and flowers and beads.

"You look stunning, my dear," Cole said gallantly.

Lola smiled. "It wouldn't do to be outdone by a mere Engine, now would it?" she said archly.

"Not even a Sun Engine could ever outshine you," Cole replied, bowing from the waist.

"The demonstration is looking very promising, don't you think?" said McGill.

"I don't understand a bit of it," Ferguson said cheerfully. "But I must say I'm relieved that Ericsson and Ellett seem to be getting on together." He pointed back across the lawn, where Ellett was carefully holding wires while Ericsson tinkered with the machine. "I was worried they wouldn't."

"They are both men of science, but they aren't actually rivals," said Cole. "That's the beauty of this situation."

"Indeed," said Buchanan. "That's the beauty of the whole project of the City of the Sun: we bring together various experts, such as Mr Pitman here, and we let them get on with their jobs. It's by far the best way to get a good result."

"Amen to that," said Cole. "I have every confidence that we shall succeed."

Morag looked around again. "Oh," she said. "There's Hector, at last. And Charlotte."

Hector escorted Charlotte to join the group, and moved to stand beside

McGill. "It seems Captain Ericsson is nearly ready to begin," Hector said. "He asked me to tell you."

Morag spoke softly to one of the serving maids. "I've told Mary that the children can join us now," she explained. "I thought it best to keep Karl and Rosie out of the gardens until Captain Ericsson completed his preparations."

"Good idea," said Hector.

"And here come the children now," said McGill. "In that case, I think we are almost ready."

Hector hesitated. "Have you met Miss Seekamp, Mr Pitman?"

"Of course," Pitman said. "It's a pleasure to see you again, Miss Seekamp. And is your gracious mother also joining us today?"

"Alas, not," Charlotte said quickly. "She finds she is unable to attend. But I have promised to tell her all about it, and Mr Cole is taking photographs, so Mother may write an article for her journal after all."

"That's good," said Pitman. "I know she wouldn't want to miss an event such as this."

Morag bit her lip. She *had* taken the opportunity to invite Clara, but her overtures had been rebuffed once again.

Clara was sticking to her outrage, stubborn as ever. She had sworn never to forgive Morag for the imagined betrayal of her secret.

Lola caught Charlotte's eye. "You look radiant, my dear," she said softly. "Is everything going well?"

"Perfectly well, Madame Montez," Charlotte replied. She smiled. "Thank you."

Lola smiled back. "Then that is most satisfactory," she said.

McGill took Morag's arm. "I think we should all join Captain Ericsson," he said. "It appears that the moment has arrived."

"Capital," said Cole. "I'll just attend to my cameras. Wilson has everything ready. He's a good man."

Charlotte shared a private smile with Hector as the party set off across the lawns to witness technological history in the making.

Chapter 106

Captain John Ericsson was standing beside a polished copper half-cylinder that looked not unlike a drum sliced in half lengthways. The apparatus was mounted on a simple stand, which Ericsson had arranged so that the inner surface of the cylinder faced the brilliant late-morning sun. Beside the cylinder stood a small steam pump, no more than two feet high.

Ericsson adjusted his top hat and straightened his jacket as the dignitaries approached. When they were all assembled, he took a deep breath. "Ladies and gentlemen," he said, "thank you all for attending this little demonstration of my solar steam pump. As you can see, the solar collector is already operational."

"That's interesting," Pitman whispered to Ellett. "He's using a single cylinder engine."

"Allow me to demonstrate," Ericsson said. Deftly, he engaged the drive, and the wheel began to spin. There was a faint pumping sound, like a heartbeat, as the steam-driven cylinder rose and fell.

"Bravo!" Cole shouted from beneath the velvet cover of his camera. "Stand still, everybody!" There was a bright flash as Wilson lit the touch powder and Cole recorded the moment for posterity.

McGill led the applause.

Cole dashed from one camera to the next, taking more photographs.

When the polite clapping faltered into silence, Ericsson turned to the onlookers. "Do you have questions?" he asked.

"I must say I'm surprised, Captain Ericsson," Ferguson said. "When I first heard about your invention, I'll admit I imagined something larger."

"Something like a railway engine, perhaps?" Ericsson said drily.

Ferguson laughed. "Well no, not as big as that," he said.

Lola nudged Buchanan. "I must say I agree with Ferguson," she whispered. "I thought the Sun Engine would be more substantial."

Buchanan, tight lipped, did not reply: he was listening intently to the

445

exchange between Ferguson and Ericsson.

"Perhaps this is just a scale model, for the demonstration?" Ferguson ventured.

"No, Lieutenant Ferguson, it is not," said Ericsson. "Let me explain. Others have built enormous apparatuses to capture the sun's power. Monsieur Mouchot in Paris has developed his device to the point where it can successfully generate steam. But to do so he requires a gigantic dish-shaped collector and condenser array, fully fifteen feet in diameter, requiring skilled engineers to assemble it, and skilled operators to make it work. It is a delicate construction that must be handled with the utmost care."

"I comprehend the difficulty," Ellett said, forgetting his shyness in his enthusiasm for this small, elegant Sun Engine. "I have read about this. Such an unwieldy device would also have to be pointed directly at the sun, or it would rapidly lose efficiency."

"Exactly so," said Ericsson. "If such a device is even a few degrees off it becomes effectively useless."

"Are you saying that your smaller cylinder is less precise and therefore more efficient?" McGill asked.

Ericsson shook his head. "It is a question of practicalities. My machine, as you will see, can be operated by almost anyone, and with minimum instruction. A blacksmith can assemble it. It can be transported on a small cart—or even, if necessary, on the back of a mule."

"That certainly makes it an attractive proposition for our remote locations," Pitman observed. "The machine will be almost ready to go from the moment it arrives at its destination."

"Precisely," said Ericsson. He smiled at last, his initial annoyance giving way to his enthusiasm—to the passion of a true inventor. "I, too, began with a dish-shaped collector," he said, warming to his impromptu lecture. "It seems obvious, given that it is the most effective manner for concentrating the sun's force on a single point, and so for generating the greatest heat. But what appears obvious in theory must be tempered by practicality."

"I understand," said Ellett.

"I'm not sure I do," Ferguson said.

Ericsson pointed to his engine. "This half-cylinder focuses the sun's rays along this line of water-filled pipe," he said. "The energy is more dispersed than it would be if focussed on a single point, but it is only necessary to track the sun in one direction, over the course of a day."

"And that can be done by a simple clockwork mechanism," Ellett said.

"Or even an unskilled man with a hand crank," Ericsson added.

"Extraordinary," said Cole, joining the group. "I've left Wilson to take care of the photographic equipment," he added. "He's becoming quite skilled at it.

But this is much more fascinating. The energy this small collector generates really is enough to power a steam engine. Who'd have thought it?"

"I'll concede I believed that there might be difficulties, given the advances in steam technology in recent years," Ericsson said. "The new engines are much more efficient than their predecessors, but they also require much higher pressure to operate."

"But surely that would make Mouchot's system more desirable, would it not?" Pitman asked.

"Not at all!" Ericsson's tone was triumphant. "I simply reverted to the earlier form of engine. It is less efficient, but it requires far less energy to operate. My small device here can pump water all day without pause, so long as the sun shines."

Cole could not contain his enthusiasm. "Well then," he said, "what are we waiting for? There's a pond over there." He pointed to the ornamental fishpond. "Let's see the engine pump!"

Ericsson looked across the lawn to the fishpond. He nodded. "Very well," he said. He took up a length of flexible hose that lay nearby, and handed it to Cole. "If you would be so good as to immerse this in the pond, so that the tube fills with water, then bring me the end with the coupling," he said, "you shall have your demonstration."

"Capital," said Cole, heading at once for the pond.

In a matter of minutes he had returned, holding out the end of the hose to Ericsson.

"Thank you." Ericsson deftly attached the hose coupling to a valve on the machine.

The speed of this unexpected development alarmed Morag, who feared for her garden. "Please, Captain Ericsson," she said, "have a care for my fish."

"Eh? What?"

"My ornamental fish," Morag repeated. "They'll die if you pump them out onto the lawn."

Ericsson shrugged impatiently. "Then how am I to demonstrate the pump?"

Ellett spoke up. "Do you have some kind of open weave material, or some form of netting, Mrs McGill?" he said. "We could make a filter to protect your fish."

"You could use my butterfly net, Father," Karl said. "I always have it with me in the garden." Shyly, he held out his treasured net.

"Well done," said Cole. "Thank you, Karl: that is a most useful suggestion."

The boy beamed as Cole took the net and slid it over the open end of the hose.

"Perfect," Cole said.

"Thank you, son," Ericsson added. "That was quick thinking."

Karl stood straighter. He felt taller. Public praise from his irascible father was a very rare thing indeed.

Ericsson fiddled with the coupling, making minor adjustments. "And now," he said, with the air of a conjurer about to produce a rabbit from his hat, "I give you the solar steam water pump."

There was a collective gasp from the onlookers as water began to trickle, and then flow freely from the pipe onto the lawn.

"Splendid," Pitman said. "It works perfectly."

"A machine like this could provide water for almost anything," Cole said happily. "This is a most miraculous device."

Charlotte looked up at Hector, standing close beside her. "It's wonderful," she said. Her eyes were shining. "This will change our whole future."

Hector squeezed her arm. "I believe you're right," he said. "I'm so relieved that my journey was not wasted. This will take us in a whole new direction."

Buchanan finally broke his silence. "I grant this is an impressive device," he said. "But I'm afraid I still don't see how we could use it to power a city. And that is, after all, our objective in all of this."

"All in good time, Mr Buchanan," Ericsson replied. "I have been working on design blueprints that will meet your needs."

Buchanan looked unconvinced, but before he could argue, Morag spoke:

"Perhaps you could discuss the plans over luncheon?" she said quickly. She glanced with dismay at the amount of water still being pumped from the fishpond. "A light collation has been prepared for us in the Conservatory, and my cook will be quite anxious about it by now."

McGill responded immediately to the distress in her voice. "Of course, my dear," he said. "By all means let us go in. Such a resounding achievement calls for champagne! And Cook has been kept waiting long enough. We can continue our discussions in cooler surroundings."

"Thank you," Lola said gratefully. She plied her black lace fan with renewed vigour. "I shall certainly be glad to be indoors, out of this heat."

"Of course," said Ericsson. "My apologies, ladies: I had not meant the demonstration to take so long." He bent to disconnect the hose and uncouple the drive shaft. "I'll just leave this to cool," he added. "I shall disassemble it after lunch." He glanced around anxiously.

"Your equipment will be perfectly safe," McGill said. "I'll have one of the grooms keep watch."

"Thank you," said Ericsson. "One must be so careful."

"Quite so," said McGill.

"But I'll pack up my photographic gear now," Cole said. "It won't do at all to leave it out in the sun."

"Shall I help, sir?" Wilson asked. "I have already wrapped the exposed plates, and capped the lenses, as you instructed."

Cole looked relieved. "That would be best, yes," he said. "Thank you, Wilson."

"My pleasure, sir," the butler replied, straight-faced as always. He turned to Morag. "And I've sent a man to order the water cart, ma'am," he said. "The fishpond will be refilled this afternoon."

Morag smiled. "Thank you, Wilson," she said. "Much appreciated."

She took her husband's arm as they led their guests across the muddy lawn, picking their way over soggy bits and pieces that had somehow been strewn about in the course of the demonstration.

"Sir Alec doesn't look at all happy," Morag remarked.

"I don't think this demonstration was at all what he had expected," McGill said. "Buchanan has every right to be worried. He has invested heavily in this project, and has already paid a very substantial sum to bring Ericsson and Ellett here to Melbourne, not to mention all their expensive equipment."

"I know," Morag said. "But..."

"The proposed new city is a very risky venture, especially in the current economic climate," McGill said. "The more so since our political future is uncertain: the Independence vote could still go against us—its passage through the Upper House is by no means assured."

"But the development of the new technology could still go ahead, couldn't it?"

"In a limited way, for the copper smelter, yes," said McGill. "But without Independence, it will be impossible to build the proposed city. If the Independence vote is lost, Britain will siphon off Victoria's gold, and our banks will no longer have the wherewithal to guarantee such a huge undertaking."

"Oh," said Morag. "I hadn't thought of it quite like that."

McGill sighed. "And besides," he added, "Cole's enthusiasms are all very well, but Buchanan will need more than a small solar powered water pump to convince him to provide more capital for such an experimental project. The city will be the biggest capital investment Victoria has ever seen. I understand Buchanan's position all too well: I myself am very wary."

"Then let us hope that Captain Ericsson will explain his plans more fully at luncheon," Morag replied.

McGill smiled. "I'll make it my business to ask the right questions, my dear," he said. "After all, we too are invested in Buchanan's consortium."

Chapter 107

The popping of champagne corks greeted the guests as they entered the Conservatory, where the tiled interior was cool after the warmth of the sunlit garden.

"This is much better," Lola said, accepting a glass from one of the consulate's serving maids. "I was beginning to feel quite faint in all that heat."

"Would you like to sit down?" Buchanan asked.

"I'm fine now," Lola replied.

McGill clapped his hands for attention. "Friends," he said, "today we have witnessed the workings of a truly remarkable apparatus." He raised his glass. "I give you a toast: to Captain Ericsson, and the Sun Engine."

"The Sun Engine," the guests echoed, sipping champagne.

"And now," McGill continued, "an informal luncheon has been provided." He gestured to the buffet table, where staff stood ready to carve slices of ham or dish up seafood and salad from the heaped platters that filled the sideboard.

"Your mother has done us proud," Charlotte murmured to Hector. "The food looks wonderful."

"She always puts on a good spread," Hector replied. "Let's hope it helps our guests to relax." He gestured to the small tables dotted around the room, each set for a small number of diners. "She thinks of everything—she told me she set up the round tables for small groups so that the inevitable technical discussions don't bore the rest of us to death. And the guests are at liberty to move about as they wish."

"She's an experienced hostess," Charlotte observed. She glanced across the room to where Morag had deftly placed Ericsson and Cole at a table with McGill and Buchanan. "That's clever: I couldn't help noticing Sir Alec was less than impressed by what he saw."

"I'm sure McGill will sort it out," Hector replied. "Let's leave them to it: today we can enjoy ourselves." He chose a table for two, and held a chair for her. "Shall I get you some more champagne?" he asked.

Charlotte's smile was pure mischief. "I'm not sure I should," she said. "It might make me reckless."

Hector returned the smile. "In that case," he said, "I'll bring the bottle."

Edward Cole was smiling broadly as he tucked into crusty fresh bread, baked ham with spiced apple chutney, and crisp salad greens—all washed down with more of McGill's excellent champagne. "This is marvellous food," he said to Ericsson. "But I must remember to leave room for dessert—Mrs McGill has hinted she has something special in store for us today."

"I thought I'd try the lobster," Ericsson said, settling into his chair. "I'm rather partial to seafood. And I find I have quite an appetite now that the morning's work is done."

"Capital idea," Cole said genially. "I see Mrs McGill's cook has provided an excellent lemon sauce to accompany the seafood."

But Ericsson had barely begun to eat before Buchanan tackled him about the consortium's project.

"Forgive me, Captain Ericsson," Buchanan said, "but I still cannot quite understand how you can imagine that such a tiny engine could hope to run a factory, much less an entire city."

Ericsson looked puzzled. "I am proposing no such thing," he said.

"But all that talk about dishes and cylinders indicated you prefer the smallest of engines," McGill said.

Ericsson shook his head. "The Sun Engine you saw today is merely a demonstration of the principles involved," he said. "It is not, as Ferguson supposed, a scale model: it will work perfectly well just as it is for small applications—say for farm use, or to pump out a flooded room. Its portability makes it ideal for such things. But a series of these small collectors can easily be linked for larger applications, to provide any capacity you require. Did Mr Cole not explain?"

"Alas, no," Buchanan said.

"I'm so sorry, Alec," Cole said. "I've corresponded with Ericsson so often on this matter I clean forgot to tell you that he was demonstrating just one component of his system."

"Then I apologise for the misunderstanding, Sir Alec," Ericsson said. "Of course one horsepower is useless for industrial applications—but imagine what you could do with ten, twenty, a hundred thousand horsepower..."

"Can you really achieve that?" McGill asked.

"In theory, yes," Ericsson replied. "I have successfully linked several collectors, but I haven't tried a really huge array as yet. There will be practical difficulties, of course—there always are. But I am certain we can overcome them. Mr Ellett has already suggested several very promising lines of development to improve the system for concentrating heat."

"I see," Buchanan said, his expression still dubious. "My major concern is, you will understand, the question of finance for such a huge undertaking. The solar city project will be the largest investment we have ever seen in Victoria."

"If we are talking finance, I'll just get Mr Pitman to join us," Cole said. "He is most well informed about the costs." Cole gestured to another table, where Pitman was deep in conversation with Ferguson and Ellett. "I'm sure Ellett can spare him for a while."

"Certainly, if you wish," McGill replied. "I'll have someone bring an extra chair."

Across the room, in an alcove perfumed by potted tiger lilies, Morag and Lola were eating oysters with lemon and chatting about the problem of the depleted fishpond when Ferguson and Ellett moved to join them.

"I must say I like your flexible table arrangements, Morag," Ferguson said, settling into a chair. "Your husband has deprived us of Jacob Pitman in the middle of a very political discussion, so I've persuaded Ellett here that we should take the opportunity to dine instead in your charming company." He grinned as a maid placed his heaped plate on the table before him. "Excellent luncheon, by the way."

"I do hope we are not intruding, Mrs McGill," Ellett said.

"Not at all, Mr Ellett," Morag replied. "Madame Montez and I were just talking about the garden—and the muddy mess that pump has made of my lawns. I must say, I had not expected that."

"I'm sure Wilson has it under control," Ferguson said airily. "Wilson is a most necessary man."

"Quite so," said Lola. She took another sip of champagne. "And I suppose you gentlemen were discussing next week's Independence vote in the Upper House?"

"You have us there," Ferguson said. "We are all on tenterhooks until the matter is decided."

"Mr Pitman is of the opinion that the issues are the same as the ones that provoked the Eureka uprising," Ellett said.

"Gold, and power," Morag said. "Yes, Mr Ellett, the issues are the same."

"I don't really know much about Eureka," Ellett said. "Was it so very important?"

"Oh, yes," Ferguson said softly. "It was. I fought at the stockade. Mrs McGill's first husband—Hector's father—died there. The uprising was a strike for liberty. The battle was lost, but the struggle continues."

"It's always about control," Lola said. "And it's plain for all to see that the British officials who put down the uprising are still in control. You can see it at every turn: the pompous Mayor who tried to close down my supper club actually banned Mr Cole from using the Town Hall for an Independence meeting." She took a breath, warming to her theme. "Why, just before you arrived here, Mr Ellett, I was in court when Judge Barry—the same man who tried the Eureka miners—attempted to convict Mr Cole of sedition just for publishing the Independence Petition. Nothing has changed."

"And William Mitchell, who was Chief Commissioner of Police at the time of Eureka, is now the President of the Legislative Council," Ferguson added. "These officials—beholden to their British overlords to a man—have been very busy in the last few years. They have gathered more and more power into their own hands. It's easy to see why we are worried that the Independence vote might fail, despite the overwhelming support for it in the Lower House."

"Is it true that the consortium will be unable to proceed with the plans for the solar city if the vote *does* fail?" Morag asked.

"Too true, alas," Ferguson replied.

Ellett looked puzzled. "May I ask why?" he said.

"Gold and power, in a nutshell," Ferguson said. "Without Independence, Victoria's gold will go to prop up Britain—so our banks will no longer be able to guarantee the necessary funds."

"And power?" Lola prompted.

Ferguson shook his head. "No Colonial government would dare to approve a project on this scale," he said. "And even if they tried, Westminster would veto it."

"I understand," said Ellett. "It seems that all our fates are entwined."

"You could say that," said Ferguson.

Lola looked suddenly pensive. "The whole situation certainly makes one think, doesn't it?" she said. "Surely something can be done."

Ferguson caught her mood. "One hopes so, my dear," he said. "One certainly hopes so."

Jacob Pitman smiled as he was ushered to McGill's table, trailed by a maid carrying his food.

A waiter followed, and swiftly topped up champagne for all the men.

"I'm delighted to join you, Sir Alec, and Consul McGill," Pitman said, settling in. He raised his glass. "My congratulations, Captain Ericsson."

Ericsson just nodded.

"Mr Cole tells me you are interested in hearing my cost estimates," Pitman continued.

"We all are," McGill said. "The question of finance weighs heavily upon the whole consortium."

"Well," said Pitman, "I have been corresponding with Mr Cole, and have based my preliminary estimates upon the information he has sent me." He glanced quickly at Ericsson. "I'm sure I shall need to update my figures, now that you are here, sir," he added.

"Then you will be pleased to learn that Mr Ellett and I have already been discussing improvements to increase efficiency: Ellett has suggested encasing the black-painted water pipe in a glass box, so that the trapped air will retain and concentrate the heat, thus raising the operating temperature. I can foresee considerable gain, especially if the glass is doubled, effectively reducing any heat loss to the surrounding air."

"Fascinating," said Pitman. "That would significantly alter my calculations."

Ericsson shrugged. "I will be most interested to hear your current estimates," he said. "Do continue." He returned his attention to his plate, and to doing justice to his luncheon.

"The big question," Pitman said, "is whether the construction of the solar city is economically viable, given the relative costs of developing solar steam power against using established coal technology."

"Quite so," said Buchanan.

Pitman sipped a little of his champagne, wetting his lips before he launched into what he knew would be a long explanation. "Solar powered machinery is currently expensive to set up," he said. "There are—begging your pardon, Captain Ericsson—a great many unknown cost factors as yet."

"We will need development money, of course," Ericsson said equably. "But once we get past the set-up stage, solar steam engines will be much cheaper to run than coal."

"My thought exactly," said Pitman. He turned back to Buchanan. "By my calculations," he said, "building an industrial-scale solar powered plant will not cost very much more than building an equivalent coal-fired plant: once we begin mass manufacture, the unit costs will come down, so the solar plant may even prove to be cheaper. By my reckoning, wear and tear on the engine, and therefore repair and maintenance costs, will be approximately one tenth of those associated with a coal-fired plant. I also estimate that staffing costs will be approximately one tenth the costs for a coal plant."

"That's sounding good," McGill said cautiously.

"The biggest cost differential," Pitman continued, "is that in the case of the Sun Engine, the fuel is free. This eliminates the cost of mining and transporting coal—which will be another huge saving."

"What's the catch?" Buchanan asked. "I always say that if something sounds too good to be true, it probably is."

Pitman smiled. "A wise precaution," he said. "In this case, the drawback is that the solar powered plant can only run for approximately eight hours a day out of twenty-four—even somewhere like central Australia, where the sunlight is intense. Whereas coal-fired plants can be kept operating through the night."

"I'm working on overcoming that," Ericsson said. "I have already been discussing improvements to increase efficiency with Mr Ellett."

"Naturally," said Cole. "I must say, given the other savings, Pitman's calculations show that solar power is a viable investment. I have no doubt that Ericsson here, and Ellett, will find solutions to the current difficulties."

"Then let me ask you about patents, Captain Ericsson," Buchanan said. "I assume you have taken out the appropriate patents to ensure that returns on our investment are properly protected?"

"As a matter of fact, no," Ericsson replied. "I have avoided patenting this invention. My previous experience has taught me that protecting the original concept in that way merely encourages men who specialise in patenting minor modifications, hoping thereby to profit from future development. Such men are leeches on the body of invention! Their interference actively discourages improvement."

Buchanan frowned. "Then how are we to protect our investment?" he asked. "Without legal patents, anyone can simply copy your work."

"But such men will always lag behind," Ericsson said. "We protect your investment by always staying ahead of the game."

"I'm not sure I'm convinced," Buchanan said. "Without patents, we will have nothing to sell if the project fails."

"If it fails," Ericsson countered, "the patents will be worthless anyway."

"I'm afraid that is not entirely encouraging," McGill said. "We have our investors to consider."

Ericsson bridled. "Then I suggest you leave me to take care of the science," he said.

Morag, ever the attentive hostess, realised at once that the conversation between Buchanan and Ericsson was not proceeding as smoothly as it might. She turned to her companions. "If you'll excuse me for a moment," she said, "I'll just have a word to my staff about serving dessert."

"Of course," Ferguson said. "I'm looking forward to that—your cook has a deft touch when it comes to pastries."

Morag laughed. "Then I'll be sure to tell her you said so."

"She doesn't miss a thing, does she?" Lola remarked, watching as Morag threaded her way across the room, pausing at McGill's table to speak to her guests, ready to smooth any ruffled feathers.

"No more than do you," Ferguson replied.

Lola smiled. She gestured to the small table where Hector and Charlotte were deeply absorbed in their own conversation. "I wonder what Morag makes of that?"

"I imagine she'd be pleased at the match," Ferguson said. "Now that Hector has a partnership in the Consortium, he's well placed to make Charlotte an offer of marriage."

"I know," said Lola.

"But Clara won't be best pleased," Ferguson added.

"Perhaps not," Lola agreed. "But Clara is a practical woman. I'm sure she'll see the sense of it, in time."

"If we're waiting for Clara to see reason, we could be in for a very long wait," Ferguson replied.

Lola patted his hand. "Never mind, Charles," she said. "These things have a way of working themselves out."

"Then let's hope they work out for the best," said Ferguson. "I'm very fond of Hector, and Charlotte too—they both deserve a little happiness."

At a word from Morag, McGill rose from his seat. He tapped his champagne glass with his fork, calling for attention.

"I have good news, my friends," he said. "Dessert and coffee are now being served. I understand that Cook has excelled herself today: she has created a new summer pudding for your delight. Please do help yourselves."

A smattering of polite applause greeted this announcement.

Cole squeezed Morag's arm. "Capital, my dear," he said. He lowered his voice. "And thank you for rescuing our conversation just now," he added.

"My pleasure, Edward," Morag murmured. "Do come and have some pudding."

McGill moved to his wife's side. "Nicely done, my dear," he said.

"Not at all," she replied. "I just hope all these scientists can work together. We need goodwill all around, and we need to get safely past the vote next week. Then we shall be well on our way to Independence, and to building the new city."

"Amen to that," said McGill.

Chapter 108

That same evening, Bishop O'Hanlon stalked into the bar of The Black Nag, one of the less fashionable hotels that lined the lower section of Little Collins Street. The room stank of smoke and beer slops, and the sticky sawdust on the floor was filthy.

O'Hanlon ignored the smell. "I have an invitation," he said curtly. He waved a buff envelope under the barman's nose.

"You'll be wanting the private dining room, sir," the man replied. "Your party is waiting for you." He gestured to an unpainted door at the back of the room. "It's through there, sir."

"I'll take a whiskey," O'Hanlon said. "Irish. Make it a double."

The barman poured impassively. "That'll be…"

O'Hanlon cut him off. "Put it on the bill," he said. He downed the whiskey, coughing as he put the glass back on the bar. "That's rough," he said. "But I suppose it will have to do. You can bring me another, later."

The barman just nodded.

O'Hanlon wiped his watering eyes with his sleeve as he strode towards the dining room, his clerical robes flapping against his long, thin legs. The door stuck, but he wrenched it open. He was halfway across the dimly lit room before he realised that he was alone with the room's single occupant—a businessman in a dark suit.

The man was seated at an oak dining table, sipping from a cut-glass tumbler. Before him was a decanter, and another glass. He did not rise to greet his guest.

"Where is everybody?" O'Hanlon asked. "I was invited to a meeting." He brandished the envelope he was still holding. "This is the Mayor's stationery. I was expecting him to be here."

"But you find yourself meeting me instead," the businessman said equably.

"And you are?"

"You may call me Mr Xu. I am, as you see, a heathen Chinese businessman."

459

O'Hanlon turned to go. "I don't meet with the likes of you," he said. "This is a Christian colony. You don't belong here."

For answer, the man poured a generous measure from the decanter into the second glass. "Won't you at least hear me out?" he said. "This is a private Scottish blend: you'll find it superior to the rotgut they serve in the public bar."

O'Hanlon eyed the decanter greedily. "Perhaps just the one drink, since I'm here," he said.

"Do take a seat."

O'Hanlon edged into a chair opposite Xu and accepted the proffered glass. He sipped appreciatively. "Excellent," he said. He drank quickly and pushed the empty glass towards his host.

Silently, Xu poured a second shot.

O'Hanlon drank again. "Why invite me here?" he asked. "What's all this about?"

"It's about Independence," Xu said. "Your carping in the press is interfering with the process, and with the business plans of my community. I hope to persuade you to stop."

O'Hanlon shrugged his bony shoulders. "You're wasting your time, and mine. And you needn't bother planning for Independence in Victoria," he said. "It will never happen."

"The Lower House has passed the legislation," Xu said mildly.

"But the Upper House will never ratify it." O'Hanlon's thin smile was smug. "And when the fuss dies down, Victoria *will* enact anti-Chinese legislation, just as the Americans have done. Your *business*, whatever it is, will be finished here."

"I think not."

O'Hanlon felt suddenly tired. He decided to leave. "We really have nothing further to discuss, Xu," he said. "I'll bid you good night." He tried to stand, but found that he could not. His legs would not move. He stared at his empty glass. "What have you done?" he asked, his voice beginning to slur.

Xu smiled. "I have taken certain precautions," he said.

"You can't do this," O'Hanlon managed.

"I can, and I have," Xu replied equably. "Now, Bishop, let me make myself plain: my associates will be much obliged if you will refrain, in future, from attacking us in the press."

O'Hanlon shook his head.

"And to ensure your co-operation," Xu continued, "I have arranged a little treat for you. Tomorrow morning, you will wake up in one of my brothels in the arms of a certain notorious lady of the night. A photographer will be present. Both have been well paid. I shall keep the photographs as an insurance policy—I have no doubt that the newspapers will take great delight in publishing them, should it become necessary. Your career in the church will be ruined. Do I make my meaning clear? Do I have your word that you will co-operate?"

O'Hanlon shook his head again. His tongue felt thick. He could hardly get the words out now. He tried again. "I have friends..." The rest of the words would not come. He slumped forward onto the table, resting his head in his arms.

"Ah, yes, your *friends*," Xu replied. "I'm afraid you have no friends to help you here tonight. I ask you again: will you co-operate?"

O'Hanlon made a last desperate attempt to defend himself. He tried to slip his stiletto from his sleeve into his hand. The blade clattered onto the table, in full view.

Xu pounced on it. "And you won't be using this," he said. He walked around the table and yanked O'Hanlon's head up by the hair. "Look at me," he said. He pressed the stiletto just above O'Hanlon's right eye. A drop of blood formed on the eyelid.

O'Hanlon didn't dare blink.

"You think you're so far above us, don't you?" Xu hissed. "I wouldn't have hurt you, but now you've pulled a knife." He pressed harder. "I know that there are men in the business community who feel that your miserable skin has value. But nothing has been said about the condition in which that skin should be preserved. You need a lesson in manners." He paused for a moment, considering. "Well, Bishop," he said coldly, "you will remember me." He leant harder on the knife, and flicked his wrist.

O'Hanlon screamed.

Two burly men stepped forward from the shadows.

"Take him away," Xu said. "And pay the girl extra to clean up the blood."

Chapter 109

The appointed day arrived, but the reception of the Independence Bill in the Upper House was far from enthusiastic. Already at loggerheads with the Lower House over issues of reform, a great many of the members were disinclined to discuss the issue at all. But the Bill had been passed by the Lower House: the members of the Legislative Council found themselves under intense pressure from their constituents to give it due consideration.

"Let's just get it out of the way," one of the squatters remarked, heading for the chamber. "We can't have the *hoi polloi* interfering with policy. It isn't done."

"I agree. We're fine as we are, Sir John," his colleague replied. "Market crashes don't bother my sheep, I'd have to say."

When order was called and the President of the Legislative Council rose to speak, few in the chamber doubted that William Mitchell, Chief Commissioner of Police at the time of Eureka and staunch supporter of British rule, would oppose the legislation. Nevertheless, correct protocol was followed: the Bill was tabled.

The debate split the House: members with financial interests in the market urged Independence as a matter of economic survival; members whose wealth was based in property saw no reason to change the status quo. The arguments were going nowhere when the speaker called a halt for lunch and the members spilled out gratefully into the parliamentary dining room and the restaurants of Bourke and Spring Streets.

When Mitchell returned from a rather good lunch of roast beef washed down by a glass of quite respectable claret, he paused on his way back to the chamber to check his mail. His pigeon-hole contained the usual pile of official correspondence, topped by a small, square, lilac envelope, bearing nothing but his name written in a delicate copperplate script: clearly, the envelope had been delivered by hand during the luncheon break. As he opened it, the perfume of rose and musk filled the air. The single lavender-toned sheet of writing paper was embossed with the gold letterhead of The Bohemian Supper Club. The leader's smile of anticipation dropped away as he read the handwritten note:

> *Dear Mr. Mitchell,*
>
> *I do sincerely hope that you have given your worthy support to the proposed Legislation for Independence currently before you in the House.*
>
> *I'm sure you understand that there would be such a dreadful scandal if it failed to be passed.*
>
> *My compliments to your lady wife,*
> *Lola, Countess of Landsfeld.*

Mitchell crumpled the letter and stuffed it into his trouser pocket. The threat was scarcely veiled. He stood for a moment longer in the lobby, angrily considering his options: he was in no doubt that such a scandal would cost him his promised knighthood—he was calculating the odds that he might also lose his position as President of the Legislative Council. He looked about, and realised, at that moment, that a great many of the pigeonholes arrayed before him also contained similar lilac envelopes. *So that's the way the land lies*, he thought. *It seems that there are Supper Club dues to be paid after all.*

The public gallery was packed: Independence supporters from all walks of life had crowded into the tight space to see the fate of their fledgling colony decided. The constables on duty had confiscated placards from the observers, but many men were still wearing lapel badges bearing the letters FK —*Finders Keepers*. Clara was there, sitting happily in the front row with reporters from *The Age* and *The Argus*, busily jotting notes for her readers. The artist, S.T. Gill, had squeezed in beside Clara and was deftly sketching the scene. The atmosphere was hushed, heavily expectant.

Mitchell did his best to ignore the crowded gallery as the gentlemen members of the Legislative Council filed back into the chamber. Stiff-backed, he performed his duties to the letter, but as the debate resumed it was soon clear that the mood had changed: many of the Members, the scent of roses and musk fresh on their fingertips, had had a change of heart.

By the end of the day, the Legislation had been passed by the Upper House of the Parliament of Victoria.

The crowd in the gallery erupted into wild applause, cheering their political representatives, as they never had before. Hats were thrown into the air, strangers embraced, and then there was an undignified stampede for the doors as the onlookers rushed to be first to announce the news.

Victoria now lacked only the signature of the Governor for its Independence.

Chapter 110

Next morning, the Melbourne papers were jubilant, the front pages of *The Age* and *The Argus* splashed with lively accounts of the passage of the legislation. Much was made of the question of economic necessity, and even Mitchell was quoted as having expressed a view that his duty to protect the financial welfare of Victoria's citizens had, in the end, outweighed his duty to support the interests of England.

In her sunny breakfast room, Clara was sipping her tea and putting the finishing touches to her own editorial: *The New Day* was due to go to press this very afternoon, now emblazoned with the headline: *Finders Keepers— Our Five Star Republic*. Always a fervent supporter of political freedom, Clara had written:

> *It was the great privilege of this writer to be present at yesterday's historic vote in the Legislative Council of Victoria, the vote that affirmed our political Independence from the political masters who have been bleeding us dry for so many years. On a day when the financial news from England was all of more bank collapses and financial ruin, our Leaders finally had the good sense to vote to maintain the Gold Reserves that guarantee our own Banks: as the slogan has it, Finders Keepers.*
>
> *Ladies, to all of you who were brave enough to sign the Petition for Independence that instigated this change, to all of you who have supported the Independence movement at public meetings, to those of you who have given financial support to it, I offer my heartfelt thanks. The newly Independent State of Victoria owes you its thanks. Future generations owe you their thanks. Without you, we would all still be under the oppressor's yoke. For those of you who remember the miners' uprising at the Eureka Stockade, for those of you who keep green the memory of the men who fought and died*

there, the significance of this moment is great indeed: the fire that burned so bright at Eureka has never died in the hearts of those of us who believe in the ideal of freedom. And now our time has come: together, we shall build a new nation here in Victoria, under the five stars of the Southern Cross.

But Ladies, we have won a battle, not the war. There are a great many challenges before us, and the greatest of these will be our determination to win back our Right to Vote. We own property, we pay our taxes, and yet we are denied a say in how those taxes are to be spent. Like many of you, I voted in 1864: and our political leaders responded by changing the definition of entitlement to exclude women once more. It is fervently to be hoped that the leaders of our new Five Star Republic will think beyond the bounds of mere banking, and prove to be more reasonable than their predecessors on the question of universal suffrage: it is the view of this writer that each and every citizen of our new Republic should be entitled to vote upon attaining majority—regardless of sex or ethnicity—for only then, Ladies, will our nation truly prosper. We have already achieved one impossible thing—we have our Independence. Why should we not achieve a second, and win the Right to Vote? We deserve it, Ladies, and with your help, we shall have it.

Charlotte put down the book she was reading and moved to stand behind Clara.

"I've also arranged to telegraph an article to the British newspapers," Clara said. "And Mr Train has kindly agreed to distribute it to the American Press."

"Bravo," said Charlotte. She bent forward, swiftly scanning the text.

"Pushing for women's rights again already, Mother?" she said. "Don't you think one victory is enough for today?"

"Strike while the iron's hot, I always say," Clara responded happily. "Everything is in play at the moment, and I intend to push very hard for Women's Rights whenever I have the chance. And that chance is now."

Later that morning, when Premier James Francis called personally upon the Governor to present the Independence Legislation for signature, Sir Alec Buchanan went with him.

"Well, Sir George, we come to it at last," Francis said. "The Legislation is here. Sign it, and you become the first Governor of Independent Victoria."

"And if I refuse, Mr Premier?" Bowen asked.

"Parliament will abolish your post. You'll be free to go."

"And return to England as a failure: my career would be over."

"As you say," Premier Francis replied. "The choice is yours." He shrugged. "The Colony is already lost: you have only to decide whether to lead it or leave it."

Bowen favoured Premier Francis with a long, hard look. But then he dipped the gold-nibbed pen into the waiting onyx inkwell, and signed his name with a flourish. "Just don't forget that I give the orders," he said.

The Premier merely shrugged, relieved to have the matter concluded.

It was Buchanan who replied. "Of course not, Sir George," he said, coating the threat in honey as he added: "but I trust you'll remember who your real friends are."

Chapter 111

At midnight on December 2nd, Victoria became an Independent State. On the morning of December 3rd, the anniversary of the Eureka Stockade, the Southern Cross flag flew proudly over Parliament House, five white stars on a white cross against a dark blue ground, shining in the brilliant summer sunlight. The Colony of Victoria was free.

At eleven o'clock the formal ceremony took place in the ballroom at Government House: Sir George Bowen accepted his new role with grace and dignity, his aristocratic wife watching proudly. Seated among the leading Ambassadors and Consuls, McGill could hardly contain his delight as the transition was completed smoothly: it was an elegant affair, after the rough and tumble of the petition and the dramatic passage of the legislation through the Upper House.

Later, the ballroom filled with dignitaries as Melbourne society embraced the inevitable. Among them, Mayor Smith and Judge Barry stood chatting amiably with William Mitchell. Most of the members of Lola's supper club were there, sipping champagne and making polite small talk.

Lola glanced at Mitchell. "I don't imagine any of them will introduce me to their wives," she whispered to Buchanan.

"Hush," he replied. "A lot of them are surprised enough to find you here at all."

"Not Mr Woo, though," Lola said, acknowledging his gracious bow. "It seems the leading Chinese bankers are all here for the occasion."

"It may prove to be a momentous day for them," Buchanan replied softly. "The Chinese have not been treated well by the British Empire, or indeed the United States—they are hoping to fare better in an Independent Victoria. They are certainly ready to finance new developments now that Victorian gold guarantees the safety of our banks."

"And will they finance our plans for the solar city?"

"Indeed yes," said Buchanan. "Woo is, after all, a valued member of our consortium." He smiled. "I'll admit I took some convincing, but I've looked over the cost estimates again," he said. "I'm happy to go ahead with the project, now that our Independence is assured."

"Then it's a good result all round," McGill commented.

"And who let *him* in?" said Lola, pointing with her fan at the scarecrow figure of Bishop O'Hanlon, making his unwelcome way deliberately among the guests.

"He's a bad penny—he always turns up," McGill replied. "That black eye patch is new. I wonder what happened to him?"

"I heard a whisper that he fell foul of certain Chinese business interests," Buchanan said.

"Unfortunate," said McGill.

"Indeed," Buchanan replied. "O'Hanlon is a storm crow: his presence here is a reminder that we will still face opposition in the years to come."

"Inevitably," said McGill.

"Well, I don't care if O'Hanlon *is* a Bishop," said Morag. "I don't want anything to do with the man—not after the shameful way he's treated Lola, and Clara."

McGill patted Morag's arm. "Don't worry, my dear," he said: "I'll make sure you don't have to speak to him."

"Thank you," Morag said, accepting a glass of champagne from her husband. "I'd appreciate that." She turned to her friend. "I for one am glad you are here, Lola," she added. "And I do wish Celeste could also have been here with us to witness this momentous occasion. The new French Consul is perfectly charming, but I miss the Comte de Chabrillan: Lionel was so gallant, and such a strong supporter of liberty. He would have enjoyed today. I must write to Celeste, to tell her the news."

"And I really must write to George Train," Buchanan remarked to McGill. "After the failure of the Eureka Stockade, he accused us of settling for a few crumbs of independence: now I shall be able to tell him we have the whole cake."

McGill laughed. "Train will enjoy hearing that," he said. "He was all in favour of Independence for the Colony of Victoria, as long as someone else paid for it. I couldn't convince him to give up his stock of pistols at the time."

"Ah well," Buchanan replied. "Business is business. And now we have our Independence. It's true it has been a little delayed, but here it is. You've worked hard for this moment, McGill. You never gave up on us, did you, not even after the defeat at the stockade."

"I guess not," McGill replied. "But it's your country now, Buchanan. I just help where I can."

"I couldn't help overhearing that," Edward Cole said, joining the group.

He favoured McGill with a shrewd glance. "I must add my own thanks for your tireless support, *Consul* McGill." He grinned. "But I will just say that from the first moment I met you at Buchanan's dinner, I knew you would liven things up here. And you have. We would not have come so far so quickly without America's guarantees to reassure our citizenry that Independence is in our best economic interests."

"Thank you, Edward," McGill replied. "And yes, of course, it will be financially advantageous for both nations."

"Which brings us back to George Train." Buchanan laughed. "He was most emphatic that Independence should be achieved by economic means."

"Indeed," said Cole. "And Train did come through for us when we needed him."

"True," said McGill, "though I must admit that in my less charitable moments I wonder how much Train would have done for us if Hector had not been there at the time."

"But Hector *was* there," said Cole. "And that's what counts. And George Train is certainly willing to involve himself in our current enterprises—he is very enthusiastic about our new City. He's already signing up new investors."

"Which is all to the good," said McGill.

Cole smiled. "Train was very impressed by Hector's performance in handling the share market crisis. And I've always said that Hector has a significant future ahead of him," he added. "Buchanan and I have been discussing appointing him as the first manager for the City of the Sun when it is properly underway: he's been involved with it from the beginning."

"That's an excellent idea—he's ideally suited for the job," McGill said. "Hector has acquired your business acumen, Buchanan, as well as Ferguson's fighting skills. It's an enviable combination."

"And he'll need all of it out there to control the City," Cole said. "It will be a frontier town for quite some time. But he's just the man to make something of it—ever since he returned from Bath he's been talking about building a better future. I must say I approve the sentiment. This will be his chance to put his ideas to the test." He glanced across the room to where Hector and Charlotte stood talking together. "Will Hector marry soon, do you think? The new post would suit a married man," he added.

"Hector and Charlotte only have eyes for each other," Morag said softly, following his gaze. "But Clara won't hear of it."

"At least she's still speaking to Ferguson," McGill said. "I saw them together earlier. Let's just hope she doesn't find herself in conversation with O'Hanlon!"

"I'm sure Ferguson would prevent that," Cole said, laughing. "I'd like to see the fireworks, of course, but now is not the time."

"Indeed it is not," Buchanan remarked.

"But Clara is still deliberately ignoring me," Morag said. "And she barely tolerates poor Hector. It's too bad. She knows we all still care for her."

"She'll come around," said McGill.

"She may have to," Lola remarked, smiling enigmatically.

Before Cole could ask her what she meant, Governor Bowen stepped up onto the flag-draped dais at the end of the ballroom, and his aide called for quiet.

A decorous silence descended upon the room as the Governor spoke. "Ladies and Gentlemen, the toast is: *Independent Victoria*," he said, raising his champagne in salute.

"*Independent Victoria*," his guests echoed. Consul McGill raised his glass, saluting Buchanan.

Buchanan and Cole exchanged a meaningful look. "To our Independence," Buchanan said.

"To Independence," Cole responded, happily sipping his champagne. "And here's to building our new city: to *Helios, the City of the Sun*."

The Governor's aide called for silence once more. "It's time for the Governor to take the salute," he said. "Those of you who wish to observe it are welcome to make use of the balconies."

"Capital," Cole said. "If you'll excuse me: I have already set up my camera equipment to one side of the main balcony—one of the aides has agreed to assist me, and the guards are keeping the area clear for me. Mine is to be the official photograph to record the event."

"That was well thought of," McGill said. "I'm sure you've chosen an excellent vantage point. Morag and I will come with you, if we may."

"Of course," Cole replied. "Follow me. Will you come too, Buchanan?"

"I've been invited to stand with the Governor's party," Buchanan said. "I'll re-join you all shortly."

"As you wish," said Cole. "We must make haste: I'm sure I can hear hoof beats approaching."

"We'd better hurry, then," said McGill, putting his glass down on the nearest tray and steering Morag through the milling crowd as they followed Cole out of the room. The skirl of the bagpipes at the head of the procession could already be heard through the open windows.

A few minutes later Cole was ready: he slipped under the black velvet camera drape, preparing to record the parade for posterity.

McGill took Morag's hand. "This is a great moment in history," he said, looking down at the approaching troops. "I'm glad we are here together to witness it."

"So am I," Morag replied, smiling up at him.

The bagpipes grew louder as the infantry marched into view, with the mounted cavalry riding behind them, led proudly by a small band of Aboriginal troopers, their banners fluttering in the slight breeze that stirred the morning air.

Morag caught her breath: bright sunshine glittered on red and gold ceremonial uniforms, polished leather and gleaming brass. The high-stepping horses had been groomed till their lustrous coats shone, and the crowds that lined the roadway were cheering and waving. "It's amazing," she said, as the infantry marched by, saluting.

"Quite the spectacle," McGill replied. "Ah—here's the moment we've all been waiting for."

As he spoke the leader of the cavalry shouted his command: "*Eyes Right!*" He dipped his sword in formal salute: the colours were lowered, and every rider lowered his sword, saluting the Governor and the new Flag as the procession moved slowly past Government House.

"Bit of a change from Eureka," Ferguson said softly. "It seems our California Rangers have won through after all. It's taken a while."

"Charles!" said McGill. "We didn't hear you come up."

"You wouldn't, over all that noise," Ferguson replied. He grinned: "I never thought I'd live to see the troops saluting the Eureka flag," he said. "Last time I saw the Southern Cross, they were trying to rip it down."

"It's the same flag," Morag said. "It's been repaired."

Ferguson's grin widened. "That's marvellous," he said. "It gives me great hope for our new Victoria, our Five Star Republic."

"I know what you mean," McGill replied. "Just once in a very great while, it seems that history unfolds as we think it should."

CODA:
London,
December 6th, 1874

O n the other side of the world, when the news of the State of Victoria's Declaration of Independence finally reached Whitehall, the announcement was greeted with shock, consternation, and mounting anger.

The Earl of Carnarvon, Secretary of State for the Colonies, pushed past Disraeli's assistant and walked straight into the Prime Minister's cosy, oak-panelled office. His thin face was mottled red under his bushy whiskers and his precisely tailored jacket was slightly awry over his bulky frame.

"I came immediately, Prime Minister," he said, his deep voice gruff with suppressed fury. "You've seen this, I suppose?" The hand that clutched the offending telegraph slip was shaking with rage. "How could this have happened?"

Disraeli looked up from his paperwork. "Ah, Carnarvon," he said. "I was about to arrange a meeting with you to discuss this very issue. Do come in. Take a seat. May I offer you sherry?"

"Sherry be damned. We need to do something about this, before things get any further out of hand. We simply cannot have colonies becoming independent states at will—it's a threat to the whole empire!"

"Agreed," said Disraeli.

Lord Carnarvon was not to be mollified. "I thought William Mitchell was a sound man," he said. "My office has received reassurances from his office to the effect that this damnable Independence Bill from the Lower House would never be passed. He'll never get his knighthood now! Have you any idea what went wrong?"

"None at all," Disraeli replied. "It must have been a last-minute complication."

"Complication indeed!" Carnarvon was almost shouting now. "Well, Prime Minister, I intend to get to the bottom of it!"

"Calm down, Carnarvon." Disraeli noticed that the Colonial Secretary was twitching badly, his habitual nervous tic more pronounced than usual this

477

morning. "I agree that this should never have happened, but it has, and we need to consider our strategy."

"This defection *cannot* be permitted," Carnarvon said.

"It's already done."

"Then it must be undone!" Carnarvon straightened his jacket and checked the set of his trousers as he eased himself into one of Disraeli's leather armchairs beside the fire that burned brightly in the grate. Despite the national shortages, there were no fuel problems for Britain's politicians. Carnarvon took a deep breath. "Perhaps I'll have that sherry after all," he said.

Disraeli pushed his dark curls back from his high domed forehead and allowed himself a small smile. He poured two tiny glasses of the fine amber liquid and settled himself in the matching armchair, facing Carnarvon. "Perhaps we might just talk this through, my Lord?" he said, trying to appear calm. He certainly didn't feel calm, but today—of all days—he needed to maintain his authority. He knew that the London press were about to have a field day: the loss of a colony would soon be front page news in *The Times*, and then the contagion of condemnation for his government would spread across the whole Empire. It could hardly be otherwise.

"I don't see that there's much to talk about," Carnarvon said. "We simply can't allow these upstart colonials to secede like this! We can't allow such a precedent!"

"I agree it presents a difficulty," Disraeli said. "But I fear we must proceed with caution."

"Caution!" Carnarvon's temper flared again. "I propose we send in the troops. Impose martial law until we get this sorted out."

"And which troops would those be?"

"We have troops in New South Wales," Carnarvon replied. "New South Wales is still loyal. And Queensland! And South Australia! We can call on all of them!"

"And leave those colonies undefended?"

"I don't imagine it will take long to restore proper order," said Carnarvon.

"But I doubt it would be the wisest course," Disraeli countered. "I have it on good authority that right from the outset the push for Victorian Independence has been officially supported by the American government. The American Consul has, by all accounts, been one of the prime movers—and he has the full support of his President. If it comes to armed conflict, we have no reason to suppose that President Grant will not authorize his Pacific Fleet to support this new republic. Do you really want to start a war with the United States? It didn't end so well for us last time."

Carnarvon shrugged. "I imagine that America might still be upset that we tried to take California," he said.

"Possibly," said Disraeli. "It's more likely that they are interested in establishing a free port in Australia. It would be most advantageous for their Pacific trade."

"I've no doubt it would."

"I'm told," said Disraeli, "that there's been a huge amount of business activity going on behind the scenes in the run-up to the final Independence vote."

"And how, may I ask, do you come to know so much about it? I must say that *my* people have found the telegraph system most unreliable."

"True," said Disraeli. "The Telegraph has not been as much use as one would have hoped—messages have miscarried with alarming regularity. But still, I have my informants. Letters take longer, but they do afford significantly more detail." He looked down at his manicured fingernails, deciding how much he might safely divulge to the irascible Colonial Secretary. "And I've been corresponding regularly with the Victorian Governor's wife, Lady Bowen," he added, perhaps a little too casually.

Carnarvon scented intrigue. "Oh?" he said.

"Her Majesty was kind enough to make a personal introduction," Disraeli said. "Her Majesty felt that it would be a most useful connection."

Carnarvon frowned. Like many of his peers, he was uneasy about Disraeli's too-close friendship with Queen Victoria. "I see," was all he said.

Disraeli warmed to his theme. "And Her Majesty was right, as usual," he added. "Lady Bowen is a most generous correspondent. One should never underestimate the value of an intelligent woman—Lady Bowen is, perforce, present at all Sir George's official occasions, and she has been good enough to send me her impressions of people and events in Victoria."

"And how does this help us now?"

"As I was saying," Disraeli continued, "Lady Bowen reports that the impetus behind this unfortunate turn of events is purely financial. Without the certainty of Victoria's gold reserves, the leading colonists, and their American backers, fear that they will lose their investments in the current financial upheaval."

"They're right about that," said Carnarvon. "And I've no doubt they'll have your sympathy on that score. You lost your shirt in a ruinous stock market crash, as I recall."

Disraeli's dark eyes flashed with anger, but his demeanour was calm as he replied. "My past personal difficulties are a matter of public record, my Lord. And my political opponents have made free with them before today. But I can assure you that my personal experience will not sway my political judgement in matters of national importance."

Carnarvon smiled. He'd scored his point. "That's as may be," he said.

479

"But the fact remains: we in Britain need that Victorian gold more than the colonists do. It's their patriotic duty to support us in these difficult times."

Disraeli laughed mirthlessly. "Clearly, my Lord, they don't see it that way. Why should they? England has scarcely treated them well. And at the end of the day, the members of the Victorian Parliament have chosen wealth over loyalty."

"Ungrateful wretches," said Carnarvon.

"With respect, that's hardly fair coming from you, is it, my Lord?" Disraeli favoured the Earl with a very straight look—scoring his own political point, tit for tat. There was no love lost between these powerful men. "You're one of the richest men in England, are you not, my Lord? Your landholdings are certainly most substantial."

"My personal wealth is not relevant to issues of government."

"Isn't it?"

"You know it isn't." Carnarvon shrugged. "I'm a peer of the realm. And if we're talking finances, Prime Minister, you must see that England can't just let Victoria go. We can't afford to lose the gold. Australian gold is underwriting a lot of our loans."

"True," said Disraeli. "But we haven't lost all of it. Victoria is the smallest Australian colony."

"But the richest."

"That remains to be seen. New South Wales has gold. Queensland has gold—in fact, Queensland is still being explored. The gold reserves there may prove the richest yet." He paused, sipping his sherry. "I've been thinking this over," he said. "I'll own that my first response, like yours, was to reach out and crush these upstarts. But they are a very long way away, and sending in the available troops would prove to be a very costly process, and a dangerous one. We might provoke a civil war—or worse, we might provoke the other colonies into joining Victoria in its newfound independence. And, as I said before, we risk conflict with the United States. We stand to lose the whole Australian continent if we take that path."

"I doubt it would come to that," Carnarvon said tersely. "This isn't one of your fanciful novels, Disraeli. This is real world politics. I tell you, we need a military solution. It worked in Canada."

"And I tell you, my Lord," Disraeli retorted, "it won't work in Victoria. Not this time."

"So what exactly do you propose to do?"

"At the risk of repeating myself," Disraeli said, "this situation is more about business than politics. A business rebellion requires a business solution, and I propose to fight business with business. Great Britain will no longer trade with the colony of Victoria. I propose to bring financial pressure to bear, to cripple the new enterprises that are emerging there to the point at which they are no longer viable. And when that happens, their supporters will see that it is no longer worthwhile for that colony to stay independent. They'll come crawling back to us."

"And how do you propose to do that?"

"As you said yourself, my Lord, we still control the other Australian colonies. I shall instruct their governors to withdraw co-operation from Victoria."

Carnarvon was unconvinced. "But the colonies are largely independent, as far as I can tell," he said.

"They do trade," Disraeli said. "And we can make it our business to support their merchants against the Victorians."

"It won't be enough," Carnarvon said.

"No," Disraeli agreed. "But ever since we learned that there might be a problem, my office has been doing some checking into which Victorian businesses are pushing hardest for Independence. And it appears that, at the forefront, there is a major copper consortium emerging, backed heavily by American investors. So it will be in our best interests to scuttle it before it can develop further."

"It might be a start, I suppose, if it damages the men behind the Independence movement," Carnarvon said. "But how to go about it? If there are American investors, we can't simply block their funds."

Disraeli stroked his clean-shaven chin, thinking through his options. "No," he conceded, "but a run on their shares might be engineered. We can certainly damage their international stocks."

"We'd need an American insider for that," said Carnarvon.

"And I think I know just the man," Disraeli replied. "I was introduced earlier this year to an American businessman by the name of Rockefeller—and he has, by all accounts, been spectacularly successful in destroying his rivals."

"Oh?"

"I've heard," said Disraeli, "that he has just taken over the last of his competitors in the American oil business. It's been a brutal affair: a great many investors were ruined."

"And why would such a man be interested in helping us to bankrupt Victorian businesses?"

"I'm sure we can offer appealing inducements," Disraeli said. "Our remaining Australian colonies are rich in resources, and access to their seaports will be most advantageous to an expanding American enterprise." He shrugged. "We have plenty to offer."

"And our hands will be clean," said Carnarvon. "No one here at home can accuse us."

"Precisely," said Disraeli. "We have only to wait it out until the Victorian businesses fail." He paused for effect. "And then, my Lord," he said, "we may graciously allow the upstart colonists to creep back into the financial safety of the Empire—at a price. We'll have our gold back before the next election."

The Earl of Carnarvon raised his almost empty sherry glass. "Amen to that," he said.

END BOOK I

APPENDIX: THESE
THINGS ARE TRUE

The Five Star Republic has its foundations in real life. The choices characters face, the decisions they make—and the outcomes they achieve—are based very closely on real personalities, and what they might have encountered.

These are the true stories.

Sir Redmond Barry (1813-1880)

Redmond Barry was born into an Anglo-Irish family in County Cork. His father was a General, but as third son in a middle-class family of twelve children, Barry was expected to make his own way in the world. He went to Trinity College, Dublin, moved to New South Wales in 1837, and was admitted to the Bar there. In 1839 he moved again, to the newly established settlement of Melbourne, and opened his own law practice, operating initially from his rented lodging.

In 1841, Barry was defence counsel for two Aboriginal men accused of murder. As part of their defence, he questioned the right of the British authorities to try men who were not regarded as citizens. The defence failed, and the pair became the first to be hanged in the settlement.

In 1851 the Port Phillip District was separated from New South Wales, and Barry's decade of local experience (and his social background) made him an obvious candidate to become the first Solicitor-General of the colony of Victoria. The following year he was made a judge of the Supreme Court, and in 1855 he presided over the treason trials of the Eureka rebels. His emphatic summing up in favour of the Prosecution failed to sway the jury, and earned Barry notoriety as a leading figure of the now mistrusted establishment. That, and his 1880 sentence of death upon outlaw Ned Kelly, cemented Barry's standing as a seminal—and controversial—figure in these two key events in Victoria's history.

Barry's reputation as the nemesis of the fledgling independence movement is balanced by his major contributions to Victoria: he helped to found the

University of Melbourne, the State Library of Victoria, and the Royal Melbourne Hospital. He was knighted in 1860, and made Knight Commander in 1877.

Barry's private life was unconventional. He had numerous affairs, meticulously recording them in his journal, but only one long-term relationship — Louisa Barrow, with whom he had several children. When he died, he left his estate to Louisa; when she died, she was buried with him. They never married, and Barry never officially acknowledged the open secret of his family. It was more than 120 years before Louisa's name was added to their shared grave.

Edward William Cole (1832-1918)

E.W. Cole was a self-made man. He was born into an English labouring family and, like many youngsters of the time, sought his fortune overseas — first in South Africa and then on the Victorian goldfields. He quickly spotted that the reliable money was to be made, not in digging, but in supplying the diggers. Commodities of all kinds were in short supply, and commanded huge prices. Cole had no capital to invest, but solved the problem by making and selling lemonade. He made enough to invest in the first tranche of goldfield urban land sales — and quickly lost it all when property values crashed. His next venture was photography. He rowed two-and-a-half thousand kilometres down the River Murray, photographing settlers and landscapes as he went. Back in Melbourne, Cole sold pies in the Eastern Market, then opened a bookstall, and soon after took over management of the whole market. When he could not find a publisher for a book he had written, he self-published: it was the start of a highly successful publishing company. In 1874 he opened a "book arcade" near the market. Its lively window displays included automata — large mechanical toys — to attract the passer-by. The Arcade moved to new premises in 1883, becoming the biggest bookshop in the British Empire (visited by Rudyard Kipling and Mark Twain). Cole never forgot his impoverished childhood and limited education: the bookshop catered to every taste, and made no demand to buy. Customers could sit and read all day if they wished, listening to the shop's own string quartet.

Having consolidated his fortune, Cole pragmatically advertised for a wife. He married Eliza Jordan in 1875, and the marriage was, by all accounts, successful and affectionate on both sides.

Céleste (1824-1909) and Lionel (1818-58) de Chabrillan

Céleste Vénard was an illegitimate child, living rough on the streets of Paris in her early teens. At sixteen she became a registered prostitute — a step up in the social hierarchy — then reinvented herself as Céleste Mogador, a dancer and star horse-rider in the Hippodrome. This was where she met — and became the lover of—the resoundingly named Comte Gabriel-Paul-Josselin-Lionel de Moreton de Chabrillan (Lionel to his friends). Lionel caused a scandal by running through his inheritance and marrying the former courtesan. And to make matters worse, Céleste published her life story. In 1852, following a brief stint as a miner on the Victorian goldfields, Lionel had returned home and been offered the post of honorary French Consul in Melbourne. On his first leave, in 1853, he and Céleste were married, and in 1854 she joined him on the other side of the globe—a chance to start again. Unfortunately Céleste's memoir beat them to it—by the time she landed in Victoria, Céleste was already *persona non grata* with local society women. Her short stay in the colony was not easy, and she welcomed a return to France in 1856 to sort out their financial affairs. Lionel joined her on leave for a few months and then, back in Melbourne in 1858, he died, leaving Céleste heartbroken and alone. She never remarried. When the Franco-Prussian War broke out in 1870, she turned her home into a hospital and orphanage. And she continued to write— the two Alexandre Dumas, the famous French father-and-son novelists, became her firm friends and supporters, and Céleste wrote several works of fiction set in Australia.

John Ericsson (1803-1889)

John Ericsson was born in Sweden. His father lost money in market speculations, and took work as director of blasting for a new canal. John and his brother—not yet in their teens—started work in the drawing office. By fourteen John was an independent surveyor. At seventeen he became a lieutenant in the Swedish army, still surveying, and beginning a lifelong fascination with mechanical invention and development. He moved to England in 1826, and in 1829 his steam engine—the *Novelty*—was narrowly beaten by Robert Stephenson's *Rocket* in trials for the new railway. The *Novelty* was a more advanced design, but less reliable, and—in a sign of the kind of resistance to innovation that Ericsson would meet with throughout his career—the railway company refused to take up Ericsson's modified designs. Ericsson's steam condenser, that allowed ships at sea to produce fresh water for their boilers, opened the way for steam-powered trans-Atlantic vessels. Another design, twin screw propellers, was rejected in Britain, so in 1839 Ericsson moved to America, where he went into partnership with Robert Stockton to develop the fastest, most advanced warship ever built. Stockton manipulated his less worldly partner, taking credit for much of the design, and when Stockton's new gun exploded during trials, killing eight men, he shifted blame to Ericsson. Stockton's refusal to pay Ericsson, or to let the Navy pay either, left Ericsson with a lifelong suspicion of the military-political system. He did, however, continue to develop naval designs, including a proposal in 1853 to the French Emperor for the first ironclad warship with gun turrets. This was not taken up, but in the Civil War Ericsson modified the design to create the iron-hulled USS Monitor, with the world's first rotating gun turret. After the war he returned to his early work on steam engines, and in 1870 published his design for the Sun Engine, a solar-powered steam pump (though, after his experience with Stockton, he omitted crucial details from the publication). A working prototype was built and exhibited in New York.

Before he died, Ericsson burned most of his papers, including the details of his Sun Engine and the improvements he had been working on. A gas-powered version enjoyed some commercial success, and a large solar array based on a modified version of his design was opened in Egypt in 1913—the world's first power station driven by the sun.

Charles Ferguson (1832-1925)

Ferguson grew up on a homestead in the small community of Farmington, near Cleveland, Ohio, one of eleven children. When he was fifteen, gold was discovered in California. For an adventurous boy, the lure was irresistible. Despite his parents' best efforts, in March 1850, at the age of seventeen, Ferguson set out for California with three friends. It took only days to make the easy journey by paddle steamer down the Illinois River to St. Louis, and from there up the Missouri to St Joseph. At Lebanon—last outpost before the daunting trek west along the Oregon Trail—they joined a small wagon train, with about twenty others. It would be more than three months before Ferguson and a handful of survivors reached the goldfields. They encountered blizzards, hazardous river crossings, five days wandering lost in searing desert, and a devastating attack by a large group of Shoshone—Ferguson was shot in the back by an arrow as he fought his way out. Twenty-four men set off; eight reached the goldfields.

Ferguson stayed two years, living and working in the hills around the boom town of Nebraska City. California had only recently been annexed by the United States. There was no legal system, but very little major crime. And contrary to popular perception, there were very few classic gunfights. Ferguson noted two formal duels (conducted strictly according to the rules), only one resulting in a death. There were two defensive shootings (again, one death), and just one gunfight—between two local doctors at a bar. The first challenge emptied the place, but Ferguson, caught out, took shelter behind a beer barrel. The doctors fired five times at close range, and missed with every shot. Then they shook hands, had a drink and went home. Guns were used more frequently in encounters with local tribes—Ferguson was twice attacked while alone. He was, however, quick on the draw, and a deadly shot with his Colt revolver.

In 1852 there was news of a big gold strike in Australia. Ferguson and his two partners (old Ohio friends) decided to head for the new diggings. In San Francisco they boarded a leaky old sailing ship, hastily and cheaply refitted for the trip to Australia, after lying two years on the stocks—there had been little demand for outward passage since the discovery of gold. After a brief delay when the Captain was arrested for debt, and a twenty-two-year-old replacement found, they set out on the long and dangerous journey. At a stopover in Tahiti, recently annexed by France, Ferguson was caught up in a police raid (almost certainly on a brothel, though he discreetly fails to specify). He escaped, trouserless and helpless with laughter.

In Australia, Ferguson headed for the Victorian goldfields. At the end of 1854 he was digging at Ballarat when miners' unrest over licence fees turned to open rebellion. Ferguson opposed James McGill's call for active American involvement, but he felt a duty to defend the miners if they were attacked. Ironically it was Ferguson, with a handful of other Californians, who found himself battling British troops in fierce hand-to-hand fighting when McGill and most of the Rangers were away.

After Eureka, Ferguson bought the Adelphi Hotel (the large tent in which the American miners had met to form the California Rangers), and sold it again at a profit. Each time he made money, he invested in another business venture—some he won, some he lost. He may have abhorred gambling, but Ferguson loved taking a chance. When he was flush, he spent money freely. He clearly loved women, and they loved him. Pressing his suit with an attractive young married woman in Melbourne, Ferguson found himself the subject of a neat sting by husband and wife, who tricked him into buying the woman new clothes for a ball. Ferguson was so embarrassed at being conned he paid the tailor £5 to keep the matter quiet.

He drove coaches, and cattle. He became a renowned horse whisperer. He dug for gold in southern New South Wales, then joined the ill-fated Burke and Wills expedition of 1860. Ferguson took charge of an extensive animal train, including twenty-six camels. But Burke argued with many of the men. A majority—including Ferguson—were dismissed. Never one to take things lying down, Ferguson successfully sued the Exploration Committee. Burke died in the outback.

For another twenty years Ferguson wandered between Victoria and New Zealand, digging, investing, taking odd jobs. Eventually he settled on the Victorian coast, at Bairnsdale in Gippsland, a small community that reminded him of Ohio. He fully expected to live out his life there. Since 1862 he had had no reply to letters sent to his family in America. But in 1881 a letter from his sister, sent initially to New Zealand, finally caught up with him. Then a nephew, unborn when Ferguson left home, came to Melbourne to visit. It was enough—in 1883, homesick, missing family, Ferguson headed back to America. From San Francisco he took the transcontinental railroad, and found himself speeding past the same stretch of desert where he had nearly died of thirst.

He returned to Farmington, but could not settle. Finally, in his mid-fifties and (he thought) getting old, he moved to Ogalalla, a small Nebraskan town that now stood where he had battled for three days to cross the freezing waters of the South Platte River. Here, in 1887, he wrote the account of his travels, *The Experiences of a Forty-Niner During Thirty-Four Years' residence in California and Australia*. And here he thought he would stay. But Ferguson was the original rolling stone, with a lot of life still to live. He was ninety-four when he died, back once more in California, not far from the diggings where it all began. True to the spirit of his life, which he lived to the full without concern for tomorrow, Ferguson died intestate. He left $221.55—just enough to cover administration costs, and pay for a funeral.

Chang Woo Gow (mid 1840s-1893)

Chang was born in Foochow (Fuzhou), China. His family was well-to-do, but his extraordinary height made life difficult for him—by the time he reached adulthood he was reputedly some eight feet tall. He found a solution by catering to the nineteenth century Western fascination for "freaks" of every kind. He went on exhibition, first in Hong Kong, then London and Paris (where, like Céleste de Chabrillan, he appeared at the Hippodrome). In 1869 Chang travelled to America, touring with his Chinese wife, Kin Foo. She died in 1871. In Australia in 1872 Chang married an Englishwoman, Kitty Santley. Their two children were born on tour—one in Shanghai, one in Paris. Chang spent a number of years in America, touring with "General" Tom Thumb in P.T. Barnum's circus. He finally retired to Bournemouth, a fashionable resort town on the South coast of England, and opened a tea shop.

Sir Charles Hotham (1806-1855)

Hotham came from a comfortable middle-class family (his father was a clergyman). He joined the Royal Navy at the age of twelve—not unusual at the time—and served almost thirty years. He retired with the rank of commodore, and was knighted, following which he became the kind of useful diplomatic functionary who kept the wheels of empire turning—competent, experienced, socially acceptable. He was a protégé of the Duke of Newcastle, who arranged the post of lieutenant-governor of Victoria for him. When Hotham arrived in the colony, in June 1854, he was apparently well-received by the miners, but he began a shake-up of the colony's finances that focused on raising licence money from the booming goldfields. The subsequent breakdown in trust between miners and colonial authorities was largely blamed on Hotham (and Commissioner Rede, as the governor's man on the spot). When Hotham refused to meet a deputation of miners to discuss their grievances, even the London-based industry publication, the *Mining Journal*, which kept a close eye on overseas events that might affect London investors, was heavily critical of his mishandling of the crisis. The editors also roundly condemned Hotham's proposal to auction off the goldfields to squatters as both unfair to the miners on whose labour the colony's wealth was being built, and bad for business.

The fears of the *Mining Journal* that the miners would face summary military justice were not borne out. Major General Nickle imposed martial law only long enough to ensure a restoration of order. And despite his certainty that the Americans were behind the uprising, Hotham seems to have worked with the US Consul to write them out of the picture after Eureka. Even Charles Ferguson, who had fought hand-to-hand against British forces, was freed by the examining magistrate, after covert intervention by Tarleton and British officials (and despite an awkward last-minute identification of him by a British soldier at whom he had fired).

Hotham was made full governor early in 1855. He offered his resignation towards the end of the year, when a government was first formed under the new constitution, but was still serving in December when he fell ill, and died on the last day of the year.

James McGill (1831-1883)

James McGill did not leave a personal memoir of his experiences, and much of what has been written about him relies on later accounts, often constructed from second-hand sources. There are, however, eye-witness accounts, official dispatches, and contemporary news reports of Eureka, and some reliable documentation for his life before and after the battle, and these dots can be joined. He was born James Herbert McGillicuddy, in the small town of Killorglin, County Kerry, on the west coast of Ireland. Some time in the 1840s, during the Irish Potato Famine, he emigrated with the rest of his family to Boston in the United States. From there he moved to California, to seek his fortune on the goldfields. He seems to have done well—well enough to reinvent himself as James McGill, an American gentleman of means, when he moved on to Victoria in 1854. McGill's claim to have been at West Point military academy in the US is not borne out by the evidence (he does not appear in any of their records), but he obviously had the charisma of a leader, and sufficient basic arms training to be given the task of drilling the miners.

McGill's role in the lead-up to the battle is covered in Rafaello Carboni's eyewitness account, *The Eureka Stockade*, published in 1855 and, from an

American perspective, by Charles Ferguson's memoir, *The Experiences of a Forty-Niner During Thirty-Four Years' Residence in California and Australia* (1888). Sarah Hanmer, then owner of the Adelphi Theatre at Ballarat, claims to have given McGill the sword (a family heirloom) with which he led the California Rangers into the Stockade on the afternoon of Saturday December 2nd 1854. Goldfields Commissioner Rede was in little doubt about McGill's pivotal role in the rising, and judging by Governor Hotham's official replies to Rede, and other documents, it was a view shared by the Administration. And businessman George Train wrote in some detail about his meeting with McGill in the days following Eureka, when the Californians might still have attempted a coup against the colonial government. Train claims (probably correctly) that he helped disguise McGill and get him out of Melbourne until the heat was off. He also says (incorrectly) that McGill returned to the US. In fact, once the treason trials had ended in the acquittal of all concerned and it was clear that no further action would be taken against the leaders, McGill went back to Ballarat. Unlike some of the other key figures, however, he did not enter local politics. In the aftermath of Eureka, the absence of the Rangers from the Stockade at the time of the British attack was interpreted by some as cowardice, and Hotham's decision not to prosecute McGill put down to special treatment of the Americans (given that the Crimean War had caused an immense drain on British military resources, and America had shown itself quite bullish in pursuit of expansionist ambitions, it is entirely possible that Hotham was eager to avoid any obvious confrontation—the only American to face trial was a black former slave). Carboni never condemned McGill, but there was enough ongoing resentment for obituaries of McGill's son, almost ninety years after Eureka, to record in detail the family's version of events, in an effort to "set the record straight". In 1857 McGill married Rosa Watt, and for some years he was a steady figure in the Ballarat business scene, and a member of the Stock Exchange. But his fortunes seem to have declined over time, and he died in 1883 of tuberculosis—according to some accounts, exacerbated by heavy drinking. A romantic interpretation might suggest that McGill was never able to recapture the excitement of his youth—the moment when he came close to reliving the American Revolution.

Lola Montez (1821-1861)

Lola claimed to have been born in Ireland in 1824. Her gravestone said 1818, her baptismal certificate 1821. But then, as she said in her *Autobiography*, "Lola Montez has had a more difficult time to get born than even that, for she has had to be born over and over again of the separate brain of every man who has attempted to write her history."

Lola was under no illusions. She was an object of erotic fascination for men, a threat to "polite" women, and for seventeen years the subject of scandal, rumour and public attack. As an independent, high-profile woman in a male-dominated world, she made herself a target. She broke just about every unwritten social rule of her time, and delighted in using her good looks and intelligence to manipulate powerful men. She also enjoyed the fictions of her life—she was, after all, quite literally a self-made woman, an invention of her own imagining.

Maria Dolores Eliza Rosanna Gilbert came from an Irish establishment family. Her father—a British army officer—died shortly after being posted to India, and Eliza's mother remarried, to another officer. The young Eliza's intelligence, independence and fiery temper were seen as major social handicaps, and at the age of six she was shipped back to Britain to be tamed. She was shunted around various relatives and schools, eventually settling in Regency Bath. When Eliza turned sixteen her mother returned to England with arrangements in train to marry off her daughter to a much older but well-connected man. Eliza promptly eloped with the army officer who accompanied her mother—a man she later described as a brainless shell. They returned to India together, but separated when Eliza was twenty-one.

In 1843, back in London, Eliza reinvented herself completely, as Lola Montez, the Spanish dancer. But "Mrs James" was recognised, and London society was scandalised by a woman of her social status appearing on stage. Lola headed to Europe, and was an immediate hit in Dresden, Berlin and Warsaw. In Paris, she became part of the literary scene. She had affairs with several high-profile men, including the composer Franz Liszt and the novelist Alexandre Dumas (who would later befriend Céleste de Chabrillan), and became the lover of a radical journalist, embracing his enthusiasm for political change. When he was killed in a duel in 1846, Lola moved to Munich, where she became the mistress of King Ludwig II of Bavaria, and was named Countess von Landsfeld. She used her influence with the king to bring liberal political reform to a system dominated by aristocratic influence and privilege. But as a foreigner—and especially as a woman—her influence was not popular. In 1848 an Austrian-backed coup brought down the new ministry. Ludwig abdicated, and Lola fled.

In London again, Lola married another young army officer. Her previous divorce, though, carried a proviso that neither spouse should remarry, and Lola returned to Europe with her new husband to avoid a bigamy action. As before, the marriage did not last. In 1851 Lola abandoned her husband and moved her career to America. In 1853 she settled in California, where she married—and separated—yet again. This husband later died in mysterious circumstances, but with no suggestion that Lola was involved.

In 1855-6 Lola toured Australia with her "spider dance", a sensual version of the Tarantella. In Europe and America the dance was seen as perfectly acceptable entertainment, but in Australia there was an echo of the establishment disapproval that had caused her to leave London ten years earlier. Among critics of Lola (though not for her dance) was the equally short-tempered editor of *The Ballarat Times*, Henry Seekamp, who published a no-holds-barred critique. Lola responded by hunting him down with a horsewhip, and the pair set about each other in the street.

Back in America, Lola retired from dancing, and went on the lecture circuit. She moved to New York, and settled into a quieter social life, but in 1860 she suffered a stroke. She died of pneumonia about six months later, shortly before her fortieth birthday. On her gravestone is the name: 'Mrs Eliza Gilbert'.

Major-General Sir Robert Nickle (1786-1855)

Nickle represents the most obvious voice of the British imperial establishment. His career spanned the whole trajectory of rebellions in other British colonies that were inspired by the success of the American Revolution. In every case Nickle was part of the British military response which prevented independence. His first action was as a junior ensign, in Ireland in 1798, helping to suppress a French-aided rebellion. In 1806 he was severely wounded, fighting with the British force that briefly occupied Buenos Aires (the British hoped to take advantage of Spain's alignment with Napoleonic France to seize key trading posts in South America). He then fought in Spain and, in 1814, at the end of the Peninsular War, he joined British forces fighting in America. After a period in military and colonial administration in the West Indies, in 1838 Nickle was sent to Canada, to help put down rebellions there. He was knighted for his service. And in 1853 Nickle was made commander-in-chief of British forces in Australia. He moved his headquarters from Sydney to Melbourne in 1854, in response to growing unrest among the miners. He was on his way to Ballarat with the artillery and reinforcements that the California Rangers hoped to intercept, when Commissioner Rede ordered the attack on the Eureka Stockade. In the immediate aftermath it was Nickle—not Rede—who defused the situation, and helped prevent a general rising. The Canadian experience had taught him the value of concession. But he paid a high price for campaigning in his late sixties in the summer heat and primitive conditions of the goldfields. He died just six months after Eureka.

Jacob (1810-1890) and Sir Isaac (1813-1897) Pitman

Jacob and Isaac grew up in an English market town. Their father was a cloth merchant, and Isaac started work as a clerk in a local cloth factory. Jacob was apprenticed to a builder. Both had some further education in London—Isaac at the British and Foreign School Society College, Jacob at the training school of the British and Foreign Bible Society. Both taught for a time, Isaac eventually founding his own school in the city of Bath. In 1837 Jacob moved his young family to the infant settlement of Adelaide — the planned capital of Australia's first free colony. So confident were the city's founders about the calibre of settler they would attract that no gaol was included in the city's plan. Apart from the lure of this utopian vision there was also a promise of civil liberty, and freedom from religious persecution. As a follower of the marginalised religious teachings of Emmanuel Swedenborg, Jacob would have valued this promise very highly (in England, his brother Isaac would be dismissed from his teaching post when he joined the Swedenborgian Church, in 1839). And Jacob was a builder and architect — skills in prime demand for a brand-new city. He did very well at first, and invested heavily in land, only to go bankrupt in 1843, after a sharp downturn in the local economy. In 1837, shortly before Jacob left for Australia, Isaac developed a shorthand system — Pitman's — which would eventually become the world standard. When Jacob sailed, he took with him a hundred copies of Isaac's book, and in 1846 he began teaching Pitman's shorthand throughout the Australian colonies. He also founded a branch of the Swedenborgian Church, and acted as minister for fifteen years. In 1870 he became Superintendent of Public Works at the South Australian town of Mount Gambier. Back in England, Isaac continued to vigorously promote his shorthand system, and the reform of English spelling. He established his own publishing company, becoming wealthy enough to take a house on the magnificent Royal Crescent in Bath. He was knighted in 1894.

Robert Rede (1815-1904)

Rede came from a well-to-do English family — part of the untitled but socially respected landed gentry. He was privately educated, and for a while studied medicine, joining the exclusive Royal College of Surgeons in London. He did not, however, settle to the conventional career path that might have been expected. He abandoned the comfortable security of upper-middle-class English life, moved to Paris, and travelled widely in Europe. When gold was discovered in Australia, he headed out to the diggings, working for a while as a miner. In 1852 he got a job with the Goldfields Commission. His family background gave him a guaranteed head start, and in May 1854 he was appointed Commissioner at Ballarat. Having been a digger himself, Rede initially had some sympathy for the miners' cause. His poor handling of the situation, though, was a major factor in turning civil disobedience to open resistance. Nothing in his experience had equipped him to deal with this kind of situation. As unrest deepened, his own attitude hardened, and he met each escalation with an increasing determination to enforce the letter of the law. When the miners openly burnt their licences on November 29th, Rede responded by ordering an immediate licence hunt, leading to the building of the Stockade, and the miners' organisation of military-style defence. With McGill in charge of drilling, and the US Consul on the spot, Rede suspected that unrest was about to be turned to open rebellion by an American-led rising. He called for reinforcements, which Governor Hotham immediately despatched. When the California Rangers left the Stockade to intercept Nickle's force, Rede saw a chance to redeem himself before the arrival of the experienced old campaigner. He ordered an immediate attack, and succeeded in taking the Stockade. But when Nickle arrived, martial law was declared, and Rede was sidelined anyway. A commission of enquiry set up in 1855 criticised many aspects of the handling of the miners' complaints. Rede fared less badly than many officials in the commission's report, but he had become a liability. The government applied the traditional method of dealing with its embarrassments—Rede was promoted, to prestigious but largely ceremonial duties as deputy-sheriff of Geelong and commandant of the Volunteer Rifles. He settled into his new role with some grace, becoming at last what he was born to be: a respected and unexceptional member of the British establishment.

Clara (1819-1908) and Henry (1829-1864) Seekamp

Clara Lodge, an Irish actress, married George William Du Val. In 1847 they moved to Victoria, where Clara started a theatre company catering to the entertainment-hungry young colony. There she met Henry Seekamp, a young digger with radical views, a fiery temper and a taste for drink. In 1854, following Du Val's death, Clara and Henry became a couple and, with Clara's money, opened Ballarat's first newspaper, *The Ballarat Times*. Henry was its editor. *The Times* became a passionate voice for political reform, and hailed the miners' Reform League declaration as the beginning of Australian independence. The day after the battle at the Stockade, authorities raided the newspaper offices, confiscated all copies of the paper, and arrested Henry on charges of seditious libel. He was taken to the government compound and chained to Charles Ferguson. In the end, only Henry Seekamp served time as a result of Eureka— in January 1855 he was sentenced to six months imprisonment. Clara took over as editor, and—in a clear declaration of her intentions—renamed the paper *The Ballarat Times and Southern Cross*, in tribute to the flag the miners had died under. Henry and Clara dissolved their personal and business partnership in 1856. They sold the paper, and Henry headed north. His drinking grew worse, and—still digging for gold and for news—he died at the age of thirty-five, in Queensland. Clara moved to Melbourne and, despite a government grant of £500 in 1861, struggled to support her three children. In 1868 her eighteen-year-old daughter died, and her older son was gaoled for stealing to buy food. He, too, died young, in 1884. Though Clara never again took part in public life, her death drew obituaries that recalled her championship of reform, and praised her for her strength of character and intellect.

James Tarleton (1808-1880)

In 1836 the US Department of State appointed its first (unpaid) consul to the Australian colonies, based in Sydney. The consulate opened in 1839. But with Melbourne several sailing days away, there was no effective US consular assistance there. At first this was unimportant—very few Americans made their way to the far-flung British outpost. But the discovery of gold changed everything. Americans in their thousands flocked to the Victorian diggings. And some were targeted by corrupt police. Police Sergeant-Major Milne—eventually dismissed—made two attempts to extort protection money from an American storekeeper on the Ballarat diggings. When his victim refused, Milne had him prosecuted and jailed on trumped-up charges. In 1853, with their many complaints largely ignored by colonial administration, miners in Victoria became more aggressive in demands for reform. Britain responded by sending out its military enforcer, Major-General Nickle. America sent Tarleton.

Tarleton came from a well-to-do Southern family, but was looking to restore his fortunes after bankruptcy. In 1853 Franklin Pierce became US President. He and Tarleton had been boyhood friends, and Tarleton lobbied for a consular post. Melbourne was a remote and demanding position, but it offered huge opportunities to an astute businessman. But Tarleton was no George Train. He carried out his consular duties efficiently enough, but never managed to turn his official position to financial advantage.

On arrival in Melbourne, Tarleton and his wife, Sarah, lodged for some time with the radical democrat George Train (a vocal advocate for the spread of the American political system), and established a close relationship that would prove particularly important in subsequent events.

The US Department of State was still emerging from a long period of neglect. Consuls, once appointed, were largely on their own, and Tarleton's actions before and after Eureka went beyond mere representation. On November 28th 1854, Tarleton was guest of honour at a dinner given by the American miners in Ballarat, also attended by McGill and Dr. Kenworthy. Tarleton urged peaceful adherence to the law, but Rede, in his report to Governor Hotham, was not at all convinced. And the next morning the miners met to burn their licences, triggering the rapid escalation of hostilities.

Tarleton attempted to deny any American participation at the Stockade, but McGill's role was too prominent, and the Consul's bland denial was dismissed by Hotham. Both Rede and Hotham saw the Americans as instigators of a planned revolution, and Rede at least suspected the Consul's direct involvement. But British officials worked closely with Tarleton to secure the early release of Charles Ferguson and most other Americans.

Tellingly, despite his close involvement in Eureka, Tarleton made no mention of the affair or its aftermath in his reports to the State Department in Washington. Indeed, following his report on the burning of Bentley's Eureka Hotel at the end of November, Tarleton sent no report of any kind for four months. When the State Department queried his silence, he responded (eventually) with a bland account of shipping movements and consular assistance. Of his own role in the events of Eureka and its aftermath, and the role of Americans at the stockade, he made no mention at all.

When, in 1857, Franklin Pierce was replaced as US President by James Buchanan, Tarleton's position was part of the political spoils. Despite lobbying from members of the American community in Melbourne, his tenure was at an end. He returned to the US, to Mobile in Alabama, where he became—for a while—postmaster.

The Southern gentleman had never really developed either the business acumen or the political skills needed to foster his career. As Tarleton's fortunes declined, he lost his last official post, and split from his wife (they remained friends until his death, and from time to time she sent him money). By 1880 he was living in a single room above a shop in an unfashionable part of Washington. He remained, according to an acquaintance, the perfect gentleman, always neatly dressed, but his days were spent on the street and in the parks. And when the winter of 1880 turned to the coldest on record, the former consul became another unnoticed victim. He developed hypothermia, and never recovered, dying on Christmas Eve.

George Train (1829-1904)

Train was a larger-than-life character, a businessman with a keen mind and persuasive manner who loved the thrill of turning world-changing ideas into money-making reality. But for him, unlike many of the nineteenth century's super-rich, neither money nor power was an end in itself. These were simply the means by which the world could be improved.

Train's earliest memories were of a cholera epidemic that swept New Orleans in 1833. In a memoir written as an old man, he recalled with terrible clarity seeing the body of his little sister nailed into a coarse pine box, then listening for the awful cry, "bring out your dead". He watched three more times as his mother and other sisters were taken away to the family vault. Finally his desperate father tied an address label to the boy and sent him alone to his grandparents' farm in Massachusetts. With no other family left in New Orleans, Train's father vanished without trace in some anonymous mass grave.

Train rejected religion, but his Methodist family background was reflected in a lifelong belief in hard work, abstinence, and equality of opportunity. His grandfather's near self-destructive belief in Christian poverty had a different, opposing effect, making Train a firm believer in the virtues of wealth. He started paid work at fourteen. At sixteen he claimed family connection, and camped out in his cousin's shipping office until he was given a job. At seventeen he made his first successful independent business venture—smuggling opium into China. At nineteen Train commissioned the largest clipper ship in the world. At twenty-one he was managing the company's business in Liverpool, England (and doing so well that he returned briefly to America to get married). He demanded a larger share in the American end of the firm and, when his cousin refused, went to establish a new branch—in Melbourne, Australia.

Train whole-heartedly embraced his adopted country. Within months of his arrival, he was sole owner of the new branch, and one of the wealthiest businessmen in the booming colony. He was young, energetic, full of ideas, and not afraid to harass businessmen, politicians and administrators when he saw the need for reform. Per head of the population, Americans punched far above their weight in Victoria, and Train was one of the hardest hitters. He helped give much-needed focus to the development of new infrastructure, at a time when the colonial administration floundered in the face of rapid change. It was natural that the American miners looked to him for support—Train was a fervent believer in spreading American-style democracy. But he was first and foremost a businessman, averse to wild schemes that might disrupt trade. He wrote passionately in favour of Australian independence, but believed it would happen within a few years by constitutional means. He helped McGill escape after Eureka, but would not directly support the miners' armed republican cause.

A year after Eureka, Train left Victoria for a much-needed holiday, fully expecting to return. He never did, and the rapid Americanization of the colony, about which he had written in 1853, quietly faded away. In truth, Victoria was probably always going to be too small a stage for Train. He loved new technology—in England and Europe he developed street tramways on the US model, battling uphill against vested business and aristocratic interests to provide a public transport system that undercut the bus companies. In the USA he brokered major railroad development, starting with the Atlantic and Great Western Railway. In typical Train fashion, the complicated deal was stitched together between investors in Spain, Britain and America, using promissory notes from one country to leverage debt in another.

During the American Civil War, Train wrote and lectured passionately in defence of the North. He was not an avid supporter of Lincoln's policy of slave emancipation, but he did believe that the war was a largely pointless battle between very different economic systems—a battle that the South's slave-based economy was bound to lose against the North's industrial might.

As before, in Australia, Train had a Darwinian view of economic and political evolution, and thought the deaths of countless young Americans on the battlefield far too high a price to pay for hastening or delaying the inevitable.

During the war, Train used his railroad expertise to drive the early development of the transcontinental line. When the war ended, and investors were slow to come forward, he bought out a minor Pennsylvanian finance company which was used as a vehicle to circumvent some of the Federal Government's restrictions on investment. Renamed Crédit Mobilier of America, the company made a number of its backers very wealthy men before, in 1872, its operations were revealed as, in effect, a scam. A Congressional enquiry made adverse findings against about thirty leading politicians, accused of accepting shares as sweeteners. Two of Train's business partners were revealed as main instigators, but Train was not named. The scandal did, however, seriously weaken the Union Pacific Railroad, which went bankrupt a few years later. It also shook public confidence in booming railroad investment, and contributed to the stock market panic of 1873, which brought down hundreds of companies.

Beginning with his time in Australia, Train wrote regularly for American newspapers. In his columns, his books, and his public speeches, he was a passionate supporter of republican democracy. On his first return to America, Train was approached to stand for public office, but he refused. Then in 1868 he was asked to be number two on the Democratic Party presidential ticket. This offer got him thinking, and he decided instead to stand as a candidate in his own right. He began campaigning in 1869, giving his first speeches from the back of the train which made the first transcontinental journey by the new railroad. Then in August 1870, with his business interests doing well and a mansion under construction at Newport, Train took a break and set off on a trip around the world in eighty days (the basis for Jules Verne's novel, first serialised just twelve months after Train's return).

This was the year that France and Prussia went to war. The French Emperor Napoleon was defeated and captured at Sedan. The French Assembly voted for a new republic. Later in the year a Russian anarcho-syndicalist revolutionary, Mikhail Bakunin, tried to provoke a popular rising in Lyons. He failed and fled to Marseilles, just as Train arrived in late October. As he left the boat, Train found himself in the middle of a power struggle between the rival republican factions. He threw in his lot with the Bakunin-inspired Communards. For a day or so, it looked as though this time Train would be part of a successful revolution. But the military quickly regained control. Train narrowly avoided being shot, was arrested, spent a fortnight in a Lyons prison, and finally was deported.

Back in America, Train re-entered the presidential campaign—in 1871 he toured the country, giving 800 speeches. It was the high-water mark of his business and public life. At the 1872 Liberal Republican Party convention, Train was soundly defeated for the nomination by Horace Greeley (who, ironically, died just before the election).

A short time later, Train was embroiled in another controversy. Two women—Victoria Woodhull and Tennessee Claflin—had been charged with sending obscene materials by post, an offence in a number of US states. The material in question included biblical quotations which particularly offended the narrow sensibilities of Anthony Comstock, a New York postal inspector. Comstock was founder of the New York Society for the Suppression of Vice, self-appointed guardian of public morals, and a thoroughly unpleasant character, proud of the thousands of arrests and multiple suicides caused by his targeting techniques. Train, outraged, leapt to the women's defence by publishing still more 'obscene' Biblical quotations. Comstock took the bait, and had Train arrested.

It was, of course, never going to be possible to sustain a charge that relied on defining parts of the Bible as obscene. The women were soon released. Train, too, was given every opportunity to walk away and save all-round embarrassment. But this was not his style. He stood his ground, refusing to be released until he was tried. He was found Not Guilty, but on the ground of insanity.

This was a much easier position for the system to maintain. Despite numerous appeals, Train never succeeded in having the verdict overturned. He remained legally insane for the rest of his life—a convenient way to smother an inconvenient populist. He lost control of his businesses to court-appointed trustees. He was committed to an asylum, but never sent there. He was allowed to go free, and continued to travel, making two more trips around the world, which he paid for by lecturing.

Train ended his days in poverty, unable to access his fortune. He lived at a rooming house in New York built by one of his old business friends for down-on-their-luck gentlemen. The building closed by day, to encourage inmates to search for work, so Train—well past working age—passed his time on a bench in Central Park, communing with squirrels, birds and children.